THE NEW JEDI ORDER

ENEMY LINES II
REBEL STAND

STAR WARS®
THE NEW JEDI ORDER

ENEMY LINES II
REBEL STAND

AARON ALLSTON

BALLANTINE BOOKS • NEW YORK

A Del Rey® Book
Published by The Ballantine Publishing Group

www.starwars.com
www.starwarskids.com
www.delreydigital.com

ISBN 0-345-42868-4

Manufactured in the United States of America

First Edition: June 2002

10   9   8   7   6   5   4   3   2   1

ACKNOWLEDGMENTS

Thanks go to:

My personal Inner Circle, Dan Hamman, Nancy Deet, Debby Dragoo, Sean Fallesen, Kelly Frieders, Helen Keier, Lucien Lockhart, and Kris Shindler;

My Eagle-Eyes, Luray Richmond and Sean Summers;

The authors of New Jedi Order novels past and future (with special thanks to Elaine Cunningham, for efforts above and beyond the call of duty in setting up the handoff);

Dan Wallace, for questions answered;

My agent, Russ Galen; and

Shelly Shapiro and Kathleen O. David of Del Rey, and Sue Rostoni of Lucas Licensing.

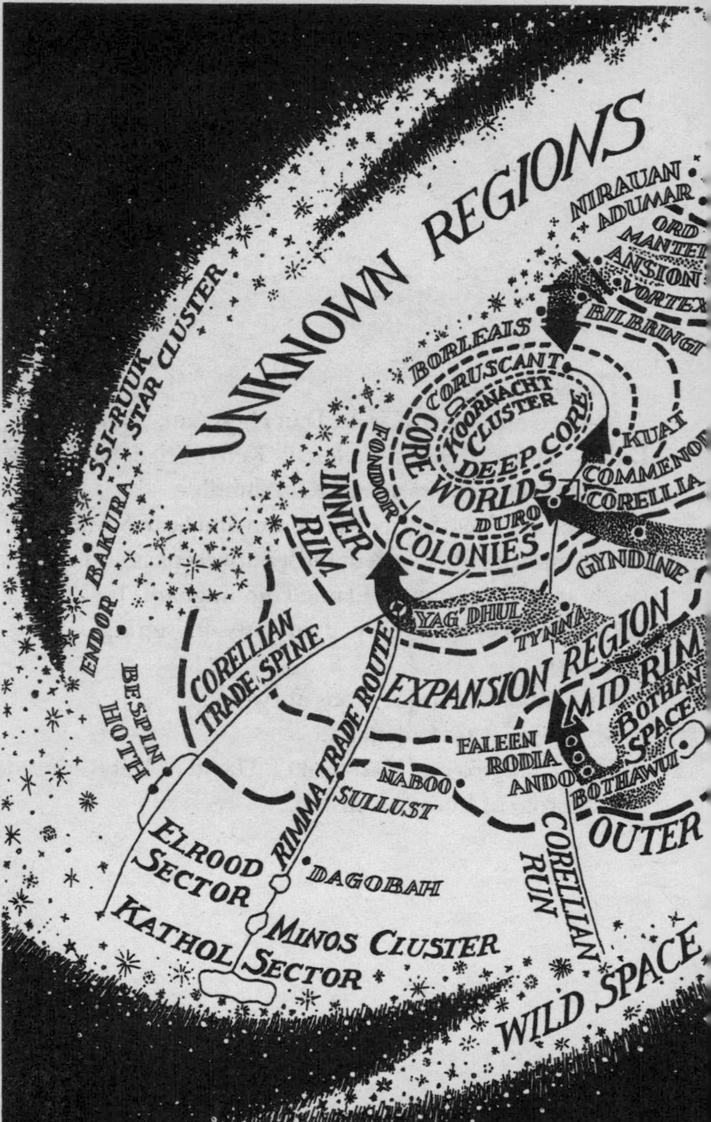
UNKNOWN REGIONS
SSI-RUUK STAR CLUSTER
BAKURA
ENDOR
BESPIN
HOTH
NIRAUAN
ADUMAR
ORD MANTELL
ANSION
VORTEX
BILBRINGI
BORLEAIS
CORUSCANT
KOORNACHT CLUSTER
DEEP CORE
CORE WORLDS
FONDOR
INNER RIM
KUAT
COMMENOR
CORELLIA
DURO
COLONIES
GYNDINE
YAG'DHUL
TYNNA
CORELLIAN TRADE SPINE
RIMMA TRADE ROUTE
EXPANSION REGION
MID RIM
BOTHAN SPACE
BOTHAWUI
FALEEN
RODIA
ANDO
NABOO
SULLUST
OUTER
CORELLIAN RUN
ELROOD SECTOR
DAGOBAH
KATHOL SECTOR
MINOS CLUSTER
WILD SPACE

THE STAR WARS NOVELS TIMELINE

 44 YEARS BEFORE STAR WARS: A New Hope

Jedi Apprentice series

YEARS BEFORE STAR WARS: A New Hope

Darth Maul: Saboteur
Cloak of Deception

32.5 YEARS BEFORE STAR WARS: A New Hope

Darth Maul: Shadow Hunter

YEARS BEFORE STAR WARS: A New Hope

STAR WARS: EPISODE I
THE PHANTOM MENACE

YEARS BEFORE STAR WARS: A New Hope

Rogue Planet

22.5 YEARS BEFORE STAR WARS: A New Hope

The Approaching Storm

YEARS BEFORE STAR WARS: A New Hope

STAR WARS: EPISODE II
ATTACK OF THE CLONES

YEARS BEFORE STAR WARS: A New Hope

STAR WARS: EPISODE III

10-0 YEARS BEFORE STAR WARS: A New Hope

The Han Solo Trilogy:
  The Paradise Snare
  The Hutt Gambit
  Rebel Dawn

YEARS BEFORE STAR WARS: A New Hope

The Adventures of Lando Calrissian:
  Lando Calrissian and the
    Mindharp of Sharu
  Lando Calrissian and the
    Flamewind of Oseon
  Lando Calrissian and the
    Starcave of ThonBoka

The Han Solo Adventures:
  Han Solo at Stars' End
  Han Solo's Revenge
  Han Solo and the Lost Legacy

 STAR WARS: A New Hope
YEAR 0

STAR WARS: EPISODE IV
A NEW HOPE

0-3 YEARS AFTER STAR WARS: A New Hope

Tales from the Mos Eisley
  Cantina
Splinter of the Mind's Eye

3 YEARS AFTER STAR WARS: A New Hope

STAR WARS: EPISODE V
THE EMPIRE STRIKES BACK

Tales of the Bounty Hunters

3.5 YEARS AFTER STAR WARS: A New Hope

Shadows of the Empire

4 YEARS AFTER STAR WARS: A New Hope

STAR WARS: EPISODE VI
RETURN OF THE JEDI

Tales from Jabba's Palace

The Bounty Hunter Wars:
  The Mandalorian Armor
  Slave Ship
  Hard Merchandise

The Truce at Bakura

6.5-7.5 YEARS AFTER
STAR WARS: A New Hope

X-Wing:
Rogue Squadron
Wedge's Gamble
The Krytos Trap
The Bacta War
Wraith Squadron
Iron Fist
Solo Command

8 | *YEARS AFTER STAR WARS: A New Hope*

The Courtship of Princess Leia

9 | *YEARS AFTER STAR WARS: A New Hope*

The Thrawn Trilogy:
Heir to the Empire
Dark Force Rising
The Last Command

X-Wing: Isard's Revenge

11 | *YEARS AFTER STAR WARS: A New Hope*

I, Jedi

The Jedi Academy Trilogy:
Jedi Search
Dark Apprentice
Champions of the Force

12-13 | *YEARS AFTER STAR WARS: A New Hope*

Children of the Jedi
Darksaber
Planet of Twilight
X-Wing: Starfighters of Adumar

14 | *YEARS AFTER STAR WARS: A New Hope*

The Crystal Star

16-17 | *YEARS AFTER STAR WARS: A New Hope*

The Black Fleet Crisis Trilogy:
Before the Storm
Shield of Lies
Tyrant's Test

17 | *YEARS AFTER STAR WARS: A New Hope*

The New Rebellion

18 | *YEARS AFTER STAR WARS: A New Hope*

The Corellian Trilogy:
Ambush at Corellia
Assault at Selonia
Showdown at Centerpoint

19 | *YEARS AFTER STAR WARS: A New Hope*

The Hand of Thrawn Duology:
Specter of the Past
Vision of the Future

22 | *YEARS AFTER STAR WARS: A New Hope*

Junior Jedi Knights series

23-24 | *YEARS AFTER STAR WARS: A New Hope*

Young Jedi Knights series

25-30 YEARS AFTER
STAR WARS: A New Hope

The New Jedi Order:
Vector Prime
Dark Tide I: Onslaught
Dark Tide II: Ruin
Agents of Chaos I: Hero's Trial
Agents of Chaos II: Jedi Eclipse
Balance Point
Recovery
Edge of Victory I: Conquest
Edge of Victory II: Rebirth
Star by Star
Dark Journey
Enemy Lines I: Rebel Dream
Enemy Lines II: Rebel Stand

DRAMATIS PERSONAE

The Jedi

Luke Skywalker; Jedi Master (male human)
Mara Jade Skywalker; Jedi Master (female human)
Jaina Solo; Jedi Knight, Twin Suns leader (human female)
Kyp Durron; Jedi Master, Twin Suns pilot (human male)
Corran Horn; Jedi Knight, Rogue Squadron pilot
  (human male)
Tahiri Veila; Jedi student (human female)

With the New Republic Military

General Wedge Antilles (male human)
Colonel Tycho Celchu (male human)
Colonel Gavin Darklighter; Rogue Squadron leader
  (male human)
Captain Kral Nevil; Rogue Squadron pilot (Quarren male)
Flight Officer Leth Liav; Rogue Squadron pilot
  (Sullustan female)
Captain Garik "Face" Loran; Wraith Squadron leader
  (human male)

Kell Tainer (male human)

Elassar Targon (male Devaronian)

Bhindi Drayson (female human)

Baljos Arnjak (male human)

Iella Wessiri Antilles; Intelligence director (female human)

Jagged Fel; Twin Suns pilot (human male)

Zindra Daine; Twin Suns pilot (female human)

Voort "Piggy" saBinring; Twin Suns pilot (male Gamorrean)

Beelyath; Twin Suns pilot (male Mon Calamari)

Sharr Latt; Twin Suns pilot (male human)

Tilath Keer; Twin Suns pilot (female human)

Shawnkyr Nuruodo; Vanguard Squadron leader (female Chiss)

Commander Eldo Davip; captain, *Lusankya* (male human)

YVH 1-1A (masculine droid)

Civilians

Danni Quee; scientist (female human)

Wolam Tser; holodocumentarian (male human)

Tam Elgrin; holocam operator (male human)

Han Solo; captain, *Millennium Falcon* (male human)

Leia Organa Solo; Republic ambassador (female human)

With the Yuuzhan Vong

Tsavong Lah; warmaster (male Yuuzhan Vong)
Czulkang Lah; commander (male Yuuzhan Vong)
Nen Yim; shaper (female Yuuzhan Vong)
Kasdakh Buhl; warrior (male Yuuzhan Vong)
Maal Lah; warrior (male Yuuzhan Vong)
Denua Ku; warrior (male Yuuzhan Vong)
Viqi Shesh; former Senator (female human)
Harrar; priest (male Yuuzhan Vong)
Takhaff Uul; priest (male Yuuzhan Vong)
Ghithra Dal; shaper (male Yuuzhan Vong)

STAR WARS

THE NEW JEDI ORDER

ENEMY LINES II
REBEL STAND

ONE

Pyria System

Jaina Solo banked her X-wing starfighter into as tight a turn as she could endure. The g-forces of her maneuver crushed her into her seat, but she called upon the Force to protect her, to keep her centimeters away from the edge of blackout.

She came out of the maneuver pointed back the way she'd come, directly toward the Star Destroyer *Rebel Dream* and the partial squadron of Yuuzhan Vong coral-skippers beyond the ship, and spared a glance to her sensor board. The other members of her shield trio, Kyp Durron and Jag Fel, were right alongside—no problem for Jag and his Chiss clawcraft, far nimbler than the X-wings, but the turn had to have been as taxing for Kyp as it was for Jaina. On the other hand, Kyp was a Jedi Master, not just a Jedi Knight, not yet twenty years of age.

Jaina and her shieldmates passed beneath *Rebel Dream*, her tremendous length flashing overhead in an instant. "All right, here's the plan," she said. "We go in looking like we're going to punch into the center of their formation, but instead we turn to starboard and skirt along its

1

edge. As each target comes up, we concentrate fire on it, just like those drills we did. Ready?"

Kyp's voice was smooth, controlled: "Always ready, Goddess."

Jag merely clicked his comlink once for affirmative.

"Fire and break."

As the foremost of the oncoming coralskippers came within firing range, it began unloading a stream of tiny red glows in their direction. Each glow was a couple of kilograms of superheated molten rock, plasma. In the coldness of space, these projectiles would rapidly cool, but during the seconds they remained heated they were deadly weapons capable of burning through starfighter armor as though it were sheet ice.

Jaina set her lasers to dual fire and waited. A brief instant later, she felt Kyp reach out to her through the Force, taking momentary control of her hand on the pilot's yoke. She felt herself aim and fire on the distant coralskipper. Kyp's lasers flashed at the same instant, Jag's a fraction of a second later.

In the distance, Jaina's shot disappeared as a tiny black singularity, a miniature black hole called a void, appeared at the bow of the coralskipper. Kyp's vanished into an identical void a meter or so back. But Jag's shot, one too many for the skip's voids to intercept, punched into the vehicle's canopy. There was a brief flash from within and the coralskipper's flight became ballistic instead of controlled.

Jaina, back in full control of her motions, banked and turned to starboard, her wingmates keeping in tight, controlled formation; ahead of her was a second coralskipper, then a third. She reached out for Kyp, let him

fire, regained control, reoriented, reached for Kyp, let
him fire—

In seconds two more coralskippers were flaming wrecks
in space. She knew, without consulting the sensor board,
that the skips from the other side of that formation had
to be angling in toward her from her port side; she stood
her X-wing on its tail, relative to its previous course, and
rose away from the conflict zone, forcing those coralskippers to give chase—*away* from *Mon Mothma* and
that ship's mission.

In the distance, *Mon Mothma* entered the zone of dovin
basal mines. Her own complement of fighters—E-wings,
X-wings, and TIE interceptors—boiled out of her fighter
bays and streaked off into the darkness, toward the ship
they had come to escort, to protect.

Coruscant

Luke Skywalker, Jedi Master, walked point, meters
ahead of the rest of his party.

He knew he'd never be recognized as Luke Skywalker,
despite his fame. He wore vonduun crab armor, the preferred defensive dress of Yuuzhan Vong warriors. His was
artificial, made of lightweight materials carefully textured
and colored to resemble the living arthropod plates of
the Yuuzhan Vong, but he actually preferred that; some
of his companions, wearing the real thing, had to deal
with the occasional twitches and contractions made by
living armor. Beneath the armor, he wore a body stocking
in pale gray with blue highlights that was a close match

for some Yuuzhan Vong skin tones. Except for his height, handspans shorter than that of the average Yuuzhan Vong warrior, he was a visual match for the enemy.

Not that he'd be easy to see in his current surroundings. He was in a pedestrian traffic corridor, the sort that continued from building to building via enclosed, elevated walkways, at about the hundred-story level. This had once been a well-to-do residential building, with only a few well-appointed suites per floor. Every door into the corridor had been smashed in, but the state of the chambers beyond—stripped of valuables, but with common machinery left intact—suggested that it had been looters rather than Yuuzhan Vong at work here.

And the smell of decay was everywhere. They'd stumbled across numerous remains of Coruscant residents—some the obvious victims of violence, some whose deaths had no clear cause, most in advanced stages of decomposition.

How much food had there been in these people's kitchens at the time of Coruscant's fall and the utter demolition of its infrastructure? How much water would they have been able to find? On a world with no wilderness, no farmlands, no means of obtaining food other than now impossible import and machinery that was vulnerable to destruction by the enemy, it was very possible that a simple majority of the population of Coruscant was already dead, with the proportion growing every day.

In some places the stench of rot was greater, in some places lesser, but it was everywhere. Luke and most of his companions now had patches of cloth saturated with a mild perfume stuffed into their nostrils. Face had supplied them. Luke didn't want to know what experiences

Face had gone through to give him the foreknowledge to bring a large supply of that perfume.

As Luke neared the edge of this building and the start of one of the connecting walkways, he shut off his glow rod, which itself was engineered to resemble a Yuuzhan Vong illumination creature. Dim sunlight spilled in from the opening to the walkway, indicating that the walkway was the sort with transparisteel panels providing what had once been a breathtaking view of this part of the world-city.

He felt, as well as heard, Mara catch up to him. "You did the last one, farmboy," she said.

He gave her a look. She, too, was dressed in Yuuzhan Vong combat armor and an appropriately colored body stocking. But for the shape of her chin and mouth beneath the edge of her helmet, she was unrecognizable as his wife. "You did the one before that."

"My turn." That was Garik "Face" Loran, onetime actor, longtime team leader in New Republic Intelligence. About half his usual team, designated the Wraiths, were along on this mission. He was totally unrecognizable; in addition to the vonduun crab armor, he wore an ooglith masquer, a type of living mask employed by the Yuuzhan Vong, that had been engineered by Wraith member Baljos Arnjak to resemble the branded, mutilated face of a Yuuzhan Vong warrior. He stopped beside Mara. "Kiss for luck?" He puckered the alien face's slitted, mangled lips.

She shook her head. "I don't know whether to mark that down as 'exceptionally daring' or 'unusually stupid.' "

Face chuckled. He shucked his pack free and extracted a coil of cord from it, then continued forward, tying one end of the coil around his waist. He handed the other end and the coil itself to Luke. "Kiss for luck?"

"Get out of here."

They reached the large aperture providing access to the walkway. Like the corridor itself, it was wide enough for four large humans easily to walk abreast, but it was lined on either side and above with transparisteel panels reinforced by metal supports. Through the transparisteel, Luke could see surrounding buildings, most of them coated by green algaelike scum or patches of alien grasses. Many of the buildings seemed to be in an advanced condition of decay, with crumbled roofs and rounded edges.

Face moved ahead on the walkway, each step tentative. Luke couldn't see the far end of the walkway; it was bowed in the middle, higher there than at either end, the better to support great weights, and was at least fifty meters in length, crossing over what had once been a broad boulevard.

When Face was ten meters away, Luke's helmet comlink popped, then came alive with Face's whispered words: "No excess creaking. This one seems pretty solid."

The other members of Luke's group moved up to the near end of the walkway. All were in Yuuzhan Vong armor, either real like Face's or fake like Luke's.

The largest "warrior," with distinctive black-and-silver tracery on his mask and torso armor, was Kell Tainer, a Wraith, fond of machinery and high explosives, a skilled hand-to-hand combatant.

Then there were the two "Domain Kraal" sets of armor, colored in swirled silver and coral-pink hues, taken from warriors who'd occupied the world of Borleias before the splintering New Republic had regained it. The one with the more pointed helmet was worn by Baljos Arnjak, the Wraiths' expert on Yuuzhan Vong society and organic technology; the other, whose broader helmet had larger eyeholes, was worn by Bhindi Drayson, a woman with a broad range of intelligence skills, including military tactics, computers, and robotics. Bhindi's face was marred by hard-wearing makeup that, short of close inspection, made it look like her lips were cut to tatters and the remainder of her face was tattooed. Baljos wore another of the ooglith masquers, his with a pair of tusks jutting from the lowest portion of the chin.

Next was Elassar Targon, a Devaronian, the Wraiths' medic. He wore a gray-and-green set of artificial armor; the thought of wearing living armor had apparently filled him with supernatural dread. Even now, as he kept his attention fixed on Face's progress, his right hand was engaged in making a series of gestures. Were they to keep the Yuuzhan Vong at bay, or to keep Face safe? Luke didn't know, and Elassar did this sort of thing so habitually that he probably didn't realize he was doing it.

Beside him was Danni Quee, the New Republic scientist who had been responsible for so many technological developments in the war against the Yuuzhan Vong. She wore the all-black armor, a living set that had originally been slated for Elassar; it was a touch too large for Danni and she was awkward moving in it. With a moment of rest available to her, she dug a small electromagnetic radiation sensor out of her bag and began sampling the local environment. Danni and Elassar also wore makeup, though it was more effective on his typically diabolical, red-skinned Devaronian face than on her even features.

Tahiri Veila stayed meters to the rear of the party, guarding the approach from that direction. She was the third Jedi in the group. Still a teenager, she was officially a Jedi apprentice; in all but official recognition, however, she was a Jedi Knight because of the skills and experience she'd accumulated since the Yuuzhan Vong invasion began. Things changed so fast in these war years that testing hadn't kept up with the advancement of her generation of Jedi. Hers was a rust-colored set of armor, and the no-skid soles of her body-stockinged feet were doubtless better, to her mind, than wearing shoes or boots, but not as good as going barefoot, her habitual preference. She wore the last of the three ooglith masquers, hers showing four sharp nail-like spikes protruding from each cheek and deep, red crisscross scar patterns on her jaws and neck.

Luke looked at her. He hardly needed the Force to sense the pain that seemed to be her constant companion these days. Her best friend, Luke's nephew Anakin Solo, had died not long ago—died during a successful but costly mission to destroy the source of the voxyn creatures that had proven so adept at hunting and killing Jedi. Since then, Tahiri had, except for occasional moments, worn silence and distance like a set of Jedi robes.

Luke had authorized that mission of the young Jedi, and many of them had died. It was hard at times to look Han and Leia, Anakin's parents, in the eye. And now he was leading yet another mission in which a young Jedi would be in peril. He wondered sometimes if he would ever be allowed to quit sending the young off to suffer pain and death.

Probably not, he thought. *I'm not that lucky.*

"I'm at the midpoint," Face whispered. "Still no creaking. I'll jump up and down at the far end to make sure the attachment there is still secure, and—wait a second. I see some movement . . ."

Then there was a new voice, a shout in the Yuuzhan Vong language from well beyond Face. The tizowyrm—a Yuuzhan Vong organic translator—installed in Luke's ear gave him the words in Basic: "Stop where you are! Tell me your name, domain, and mission!"

Luke tossed the coil to Baljos. "Leave the packs here." He moved forward, Mara and Kell with him, and heard the running feet of Tahiri coming up from behind. The four of them were the only ones with much of a chance in direct battle with fully trained Yuuzhan Vong warriors.

Both normally and through his helmet comlink, Luke heard Face's reply, shouted in the Yuuzhan Vong language, with to what Luke sounded like proper aggression and inflection: "I am Faka Rann. My mission is the destruction of abominations and the training of my warriors. Do not hinder me."

As Luke, Mara, Kell, and Tahiri came closer to Face, they could see down the incline on the other side, where a party of Yuuzhan Vong warriors approached. Luke saw seven of them, most already holding amphistaffs in their hands. The serpentlike amphistaffs were currently stiff, in staff/spear configuration. Face was fiddling with the fake amphistaff wrapped around his waist, but Luke could see that he was actually freeing the cord.

Luke came up beside Face and stood there, arms crossed, a stance of defiance and arrogance. Mara came to a stop beside him, Tahiri and Kell on the other side of Face. Kell unwrapped the false amphistaff from around his own waist and triggered it, snapping it into rigidity, an artful imitation of the use of the genuine weapons, though his would never stand up to the rigors of combat.

The oncoming unit of warriors halted ten meters away and their leader looked at Luke and the others. "This is our designated zone," he said. "Who has commanded you to hunt here?"

"No one has commanded us!" Face's tone was sharp and mocking, even through the tizowyrm's translation. "We are not on duty. We seek personal glory."

"If you are not on duty, your mission is subordinate to ours. Make way."

Luke knew that no true Yuuzhan Vong warrior would respond well to such a command, and he sighed inwardly. There was going to be a fight. He moved his knee until he could feel his lightsaber where it dangled from his belt under the armor's skirt plates.

"If you *are* on duty," Face said, "then your mission is less important than ours, for you hunt only at your superiors' orders, while we hunt because it makes us great. *You* make way."

The enemy leader stared at Face. Then the brief stalemate ended as it had to; the leader charged, his warriors with him in two lines.

Face dropped back, allowing the more skilled combatants to close the gap where he'd been. The enemy leader hurtled toward him as if to shoot between Luke and Kell to reach him anyway, whirling his amphistaff to slam Luke out of the way, but Luke went up and over the charge in a somersault made only slightly clumsy by his false alien armor.

While he was inverted, he saw Kell catch the leader and spin him back and around, slamming him powerfully into one of the transparisteel panels on the side of the walkway. The panel held, but the metal restraints holding it failed; warrior and panel punched free of the walkway. The warrior screamed, flailing, as he dropped from view.

Luke landed and brought his lightsaber out from beneath the skirt plates even as he heard the *snap-hiss* of Mara's and Tahiri's blades igniting. His lit just in time to catch the thrust from an amphistaff. He shoved the deadly pointed tip of the weapon out of alignment, let it slide past him, and riposted. The warrior he faced caught the lightsaber blade on the amphistaff's upper end and the blade bounced away, leaving only the faintest of burn marks on the amphistaff neck.

His opponent screamed, *"Jeedai!"* The cry was picked up and repeated by the other five warriors facing them—and then by other voices, farther back.

Luke parried a thud bug hurled his way by one of the warriors in the second rank, then made a wild swing at the warrior in front of him. That fighter ducked, but he was not the true target; Luke's blow continued onto the arm of Tahiri's opponent to his right, hitting it at the unprotected elbow, severing it. That warrior roared, more, it seemed, in anger than in pain, as his arm and amphistaff dropped to the walkway floor. Tahiri took advantage of the moment to kick him, propelling the warrior back into the second rank. Meanwhile, in Luke's peripheral vision, Mara deftly incinerated a razor bug hurled at her, then parried a hard swing from a front-rank amphistaff and a thrust from another in the second row.

Then Luke could see them, more warriors running toward them from the building opposite. He couldn't count them; he thought there were at least twenty, and more were emerging from that walkway opening every second. Most were screaming, *"Jeedai!"*

Kell Tainer turned and ran. Luke caught a glimpse of Tahiri's eyes, startled and betrayed, through her helmet faceplate before she ducked beneath the swing of her next opponent. Before she could straighten, a burst of blaster-fire filled the air above her. Most of it was absorbed or deflected by her opponent's vonduun crab armor, but one shot caught the warrior in the throat. He fell back, his throat smoking, and Luke could see Face standing directly behind Tahiri, blaster rifle in hand. Even as Tahiri rose, Face let off the trigger and took a half step left, out of Luke's peripheral vision, waiting for another target.

Luke kicked the severed arm and its amphistaff up into the face of his opponent, then followed with a simple thrust to the head. That warrior was too canny or experienced for such a ploy; unflinching, he let the arm bounce from his helmet and deflected the thrust with his amphistaff.

Then the next wave of warriors reached them, and suddenly there were too many amphistaffs, thud bugs, razor bugs, and knifelike coufees to stand firm against. Luke found himself forced backward step after step even as he parried a blow, incinerated a razor bug, plunged his lightsaber blade into a warrior's throat. "Fighting retreat!" he shouted.

Something arced between Luke and Mara from behind. It looked like a flat black box, about the size of human

hand, with glowing letters or numbers on one side. And
Kell was once again in Luke's peripheral vision, this time
with a blaster, holding it high over the head of the Jedi,
pouring fire down into the Yuuzhan Vong. "Suggest we
retreat *fast*," he shouted. "Ten."

"What was that?" Luke asked. Instead of blocking the
next amphistaff blow to come his way, he leaned forward
before the blow began and whipped his lightsaber across
his new opponent's wrist, severing the holding hand.

"You know what it was. Seven. Six."

Luke began to back away fast. Mara and Tahiri kept
pace with him, and Face and Kell kept up the blasterfire,
joined by an occasional single-shot blast from their allies
behind.

They'd almost backed into the opening to the building
when Kell's explosive charge detonated. Suddenly the
walkway in the midst of the Yuuzhan Vong force was a
wall of fire rushing toward them.

Luke exerted himself, hurling himself backward with
use of the Force, yanking Mara and Tahiri with him.
They landed several meters back in the building corridor,
still deflecting thrown thud bugs and razor bugs. Then the
fiery flash from the explosion roared across the intervening Yuuzhan Vong and past the Jedi, momentarily blinding Luke, hammering him backward. Sure in his sense of
where the other Jedi and Wraiths were, he whirled his
lightsaber in a defensive motion he seldom used outside
of practice, felt it hit something hard and unyielding.

Then the heat and brightness were past. He found he
was locked, lightsaber against amphistaff, with a warrior
whose back was smoking. Three other warriors stood

among him and his allies, though two were now dancing in concentrated fire from the Wraiths and Danni Quee. The last, in the middle of a quite elegant snap-kick against Mara, was receiving her lightsaber thrust up and under his skirt plates.

Luke kicked out, catching his opponent in the center of the torso, sending him hurtling. The warrior staggered back to the walkway aperture . . . then dropped out of sight with a shout of surprise.

The walkway was gone. Only smoke and the jagged edges where it had once joined the building suggested it had ever been there. Even with his ears ringing from the explosion, Luke could hear the smashing, grinding noise as its wreckage descended three or four hundred meters to the boulevard below.

They stood panting for a moment, Jedi, Wraiths, and scientist, staring at one another. Finally Luke said, "Anyone hurt?"

"I got grazed by a thud bug," Danni said. "But it hit the armor. It only knocked me down."

"Something of a disastrous encounter," Luke decided. "But at least we don't have any injuries."

"It was a very successful encounter," Face said. "Very promising."

Luke frowned. "How so? Now they know we're here. That Jedi are here."

"No. First, I think they were all on the walkway. So no one alive knows that Jedi are here."

"Until they find the bodies," Mara pointed out. "With distinctive lightsaber burns on them."

Face shrugged. "You have me on that one. But second, more important, until those lightsabers came out, they *believed we were Vong.* The disguises, and my extraordinary diligence in learning some conversational Yuuzan Vong during the last couple of years, are working. We can expect them to work again."

"Good point."

Face's tone became professionally worried. "So, does that count as my turn, or do I have to check out the next walkway?"

Luke grinned. "It counts as your turn."

"The next one," Kell said, "will be twenty or thirty flights down. We'd better get to it."

Bhindi slapped the back of Kell's helmet. "That one is going to have been hit by debris from *this* one, Explosion Boy. We go *up.*"

His tone subdued, Kell said, "I knew that."

Borleias, Pyria System

Han Solo, upside down and up to his waist in machinery beneath the deck plating of the *Millennium Falcon*, heard and felt footsteps approaching. They were light, precise—Leia. That meant there would be a second set, the footsteps of Meewalh, Leia's Noghri bodyguard, but Han had never actually heard them.

A desire to finish patching the coupling he was working on kept him inverted and incurious—that, and the fact that he knew that if Leia had a problem, her walking pace wouldn't be normal. "Artoo, you want to hand me the electrical flow meter?" He extended a hand up into the air.

R2-D2, Luke's astromech droid, responded with a series of cheerful whistles and bleats. Han heard the whine of a manipulator arm being extended, felt the meter being pressed into his hand. Then he heard his wife's voice: "Do you think if I poked him, he'd bang his head into the flooring?"

R2-D2's blatted response sounded definitely affirmative.

"You better hope she doesn't, Artoo," Han said. "I can't take revenge on my wife, so I'll have to take it on the nearest droid at hand."

R2-D2 replied with a distinctly sour set of notes, then Han heard the droid whir away. "What did he say?" Han asked.

Leia laughed. "I don't know. But if I were him, it would be, *I'll go fetch See-Threepio, then.*"

"Good point." Han clipped the flow meter to the wires he'd just installed. "You want to power up the holo-comm for me?"

"Are you down there with your head in the holocomm power cables?"

"Yes."

"No."

"I can't tell if the power flow is right if you don't."

"Come on up out of there and leave the meter where you can see the readout."

Han growled. He knew, deep in his heart, that nothing could go wrong, that the *Falcon* would never hurt him while he was working on her. He knew this in spite of innumerable minor abrasions, contusions, and electrocutions he'd suffered over the years. But Leia remained stubbornly unconvinced.

He also knew, from long experience, that Leia was not going to leave until she was sure he wasn't going to do something she considered foolish. He could either wait here upside down forever, or do it *her* way.

So he situated the meter where he could see the readout from above. He shoved his way up and out of the access and turned an artificially cheerful smile on Leia. "Happy?"

"Happy. You're very red."

"That's what happens when you stay upside down for too long. Could I get you some caf? Something to read? For while you're here managing this repair operation, that is." Ignoring sudden dizziness brought on by the flow of blood back out of his head, he stood.

Leia smiled, not at all put off by his snide comments. "Actually, I just came here to remind you that we need to see Tarc before we take off."

"Yeah, I know. I just hate good-byes. Never could figure out how to make them happy."

Leia lowered her voice to a whisper. "Speaking of which, do you have any advice on how we're going to tell Meewalh she can't come along on this mission? That hovering around me to do bodyguard duties will compromise any disguises that we try to use?"

Han matched her whisper for whisper. "How about persuading her to take a vacation?"

"Han."

"How about, just before takeoff, we send her out to pick up a bottle of brandy, and then leave while she's running the errand?"

"You're not helping."

He smiled and pulled her to him. "You're not fooling anybody. You know exactly what you're going to tell her. You just want me to be there when you do it. To back you up. Right?"

She offered him an expression of mock outrage. "No fair peeking into my mind like that."

"Right?"

Leia sighed and settled against him. "Right."

But her expression, though merry, wasn't entirely without worry, and he knew why. She couldn't be entirely free from concern with one of their sons recently lost to war, the other missing and presumed by most to be dead, and their only daughter elsewhere in the Pyria solar system on a mission with her squadron. Han wondered if there would ever be a time when Leia's expression was completely at peace.

Pyria System

Well within the dovin basal minefield, Jaina and her Twin Suns Squadron caught up with *Mon Mothma*, which was executing a turn back toward Borleias while, in the distance, a Gallofree cargo ship, as pudgy and unlovely as a Hutt in the middle of diving into a pool, edged toward them. Tiny lights winking around the freighter hinted at the battle that still went on, but they were few in number—and ever fewer, as the sensor blips representing coralskippers gradually disappeared from the screen.

"Twin Suns, this is *Rebel Dream*. Sensors show more skip squadrons incoming, but we think our payload will be out of the minefield and through with its last micro-jump before they arrive. It's going to be close, though, so please stand by."

Jaina grinned at the *please*. Because of the game she was playing with the Yuuzhan Vong, the deception in which she increasingly identified herself with their Trickster goddess, Yun-Harla, she was a step or two outside Borleias's command structure, and all commanders had been privately instructed to treat her with the deference due a foreign dignitary. She sometimes wondered which of them were amused at playing along and which were irritated. This controller's voice held no evidence of annoyance. "Twin Suns Leader to *Rebel Dream*, copy."

Jaina brought her squadron around to cruise alongside *Rebel Dream* and waited. As the cargo vessel's lines finally came into sharp focus with the naked eye, her name finally blipped onto her sensor board, *Reckless Abandon*, and she could see the nature of the starfighters protecting her—they were now organized into escort wings, all the fighting done. Most wore the white-and-dark-gray color scheme of *Rebel Dream* support craft, but one squadron, mixed A-wings and E-wings, was painted in glaring yellow with menacingly angular black stripes.

"What the Sith spawn are those?" Jaina asked.

"Twin Suns One, you have the Taanab Yellow Aces, Ace-One speaking." The voice was male, amused. "We're here to show the defenders of Borleias what flying is all about."

Jaina winced. She'd forgotten that she had switched over to the general New Republic military frequency to respond to *Rebel Dream*. But despite the fact that the mistake was hers, she couldn't let a jibe like that go by. "So you're the masters at flying out of an engagement zone?"

"Ooh," Ace-One said. "Don't say *engagement*. Unless you're volunteering, that is."

"Ace-One, *Reckless Abandon*. Do you suppose you could confine your courtship rituals to groundside?"

"Copy, *Reckless*. Twins Leader, look me up when we're on the ground. Ace-One out."

Jaina switched back to send out only over squadron frequency. "Arrogant little monkey-lizard."

"I agree." That was the mechanical voice of Piggy, Jaina's Gamorrean pilot and tactics expert. "I know him."

Borleias

Creatures moved within Tam Elgrin's field of vision. He couldn't seem to hold his eyes open enough for visual clarity, so most of the time they were mere blobs of white or orange, walking back and forth before him, speaking in muted tones.

He was content with that for a while, even content to understand that he wasn't thinking clearly, wasn't remembering, but eventually curiosity got the better of him and he forced his eyes open wider, forced himself to focus.

He could see now that the traffic was beyond the bed he lay on. A clean sheet in a soothing blue covered his large, ungainly frame. Beyond his feet was the metal footboard of a bed, and beyond that was some sort of pedestrian traffic lane; the blobs of color he had seen were people, humans and the occasional Twi'lek or Rodian or Devaronian, most in medical whites, some in pilot jumpsuit orange, moving past his field of vision, paying him no mind.

To either side of his bed were hung opaque curtains of that same offensively inoffensive blue, so patently obvious a measure to provide him with privacy from two directions and suggest calm that he finally understood that he was in a hospital.

That realization was enough for now. He didn't need to know why he was here. The fact that his brain worked well enough to process information again was sufficient.

But a moment later, a figure left the traffic lane and moved into his curtained cubicle. It was a Mon Calamari; Tam's long experience with nonhumans suggested that it was a female. She wore medical whites, and her skin was a deep, appealing pink. "You are awake," she said, her tone suggesting that it was a minor achievement, something for which everyone should be at least slightly pleased.

"Um," he said. It was supposed to have been *yes*, but it came out *um*.

"Do you know what has happened? Where you are, and why?"

He shook his head. "Um."

"You've been rather badly used by the Yuuzhan Vong, conditioned by them to do their bidding. But you resisted your conditioning and probably prevented a tragedy. Resisting it did you a certain amount of physical harm, which is why you're here now."

It was as though he had been facing a dam between

him and his memories . . . then the dam crumbled and memories washed down over him, hammering him, sweeping him away. He remembered being on the world of Coruscant as it fell to the Yuuzhan Vong, remembered hiding and running from them afterward, remembered being captured by them. Then there were days—how many? Only two, though it seemed like a lifetime—of lying on a table that twitched, of listening while one of the Yuuzhan Vong told him to do things, of feeling agonizing pain whenever he worked up the nerve to refute their words, refuse their orders. The pain came even when his refusal was deep in his heart, even when it was made without him speaking or glaring or shaking his head to let them know of his rebellion. The table always knew, the table always hurt him, until the words of the Yuuzhan Vong came and he could no longer resist them, no longer offer even the most secret of refusals.

Then he had been allowed to "escape," reunite with his employer, historian Wolam Tser, and escape Coruscant to Borleias, a temporary stronghold of the reeling New Republic military. There he had spied upon the New Republic operations, the scientist Danni Quee and the pilot Jaina Solo.

Only when he knew that he would have to kidnap one of them and kill the other had he found the strength to withstand the pain that came whenever he did not leap to the bidding of the Yuuzhan Vong. And he'd fallen, certain that the pain would kill him.

"Are you still with us, Master Elgrin?"

"Um," he said. "Yes." He opened his eyes; the Mon Cal female was bending over him, her mouth slightly open, her eyes moving independently as she looked him over.

He knew from experience that her expression suggested slight distress, though it would not have been obvious to someone who knew only human expressions. "It's not 'Master' Elgrin. Just . . . Elgrin. Or Tam."

"Tam, I am Cilghal. I will be working with you to overcome the lingering effects of what was done to you." She cocked her head, a human mannerism, perhaps one she had learned from being among humans. "I am sad to have to tell you that your courage in resisting your conditioning was not a cure for you. You still suffer the effects of that conditioning. We will work together to erode those effects, to return you to normal."

"If I'm still—why isn't my head killing me right now?"

Cilghal took one of his hands in hers—a smooth, webbed hand much larger than his, but not cold, as he'd expected—and moved his hand up to his brow. There, he felt the device, helmetlike, covering the top of his head. "This apparatus," she said, "senses the onset of your headaches. It interferes electronically with your pain receptors, reducing or eliminating the pain. Later, we can fit you with an implant to do the same thing without being noticeable. The implant will also allow you to reward yourself by initiating the release of endorphins whenever you do something you know to be in defiance of the will of the Yuuzhan Vong. It will, we think, gradually counter the conditioning you have received."

"But what's the point? I'm going to be tried. And executed. For treason."

"I think not. This base is under military law, and General Wedge Antilles has said that you are to be commended, not punished. There will be no trial for you."

Tam felt his eyes burn, then tears came. Whether they were tears of relief or shame for the forgiveness he'd received but had not earned, he could not say. He turned away from Cilghal so she would not see them.

"I will go now," she said. "We will talk later. And you will get better."

TWO

The tall man pounded on the black stone wall.

The wall stretched up as far as the eye could see—at least in these dimly lit reaches of the ruined undercity—and was angled back, not truly vertical. The stone from which it was made was glossy, with little gray stipple patterns throughout, lending it beauty and complexity. The wall did not seem to be made of blocks of the stone; the entire wall seemed to be one sheet, unmarked by lines or creases.

The stone held up against blows from his fist.

He found a block of ferrocrete nearby and swung it with all his considerable strength at the wall.

The ferrocrete shattered.

He ignited his weapon. It hummed with every move of his arm and cast its red glow on the stone. He drove it into the stone.

The stone did not warm, did not burn, did not melt away.

He withdrew his blade and touched the point where it had rested. It was warmer than the surrounding stone, but did not burn his flesh.

He shouted, the echoes of his anguish bouncing off the high ceiling and nearby walls of this chamber.

He had to have what was beyond the wall. It was everything. He had never seen it, never felt it, but he knew it was there, knew with a memory that had been vivid long before he had become aware.

The tall man felt something, a presence, nearby. He raced to a mound of rubble, collapsed from ruined ceiling, and swept a block of duracrete aside.

In the niche beyond huddled a small figure, a human male.

The tall man reached in and seized the other, yanking him forth. The smaller man wore rags and stank of sweat, months of sweat; his hair was long and ragged, and fear filled his dark eyes.

The tall man did not speak to him. He did not know words. Instead, he made a thought—an image of the black wall shattering, opening to reveal the treasure beyond—and shoved it into the mind of the other. The smaller man stiffened and shrieked as the thought lodged in his mind, occupied it fully.

Then the tall man sent another thought, a question: How?

The smaller man trembled in his grip, and thoughts, hundreds of them, tiny and scurrying like rodents, flashed through his mind.

Then there was an image. A machine, something a man could hold in two hands. From its nozzle came a blinding blaze, a cutting fire. The small man thought of that fire piercing the wall, cutting a door, allowing the tall man through.

The tall man formed another thought. In it, the small

man would go forth, find that machine, and bring it here. Immediately. With ruthless strength, he hammered that thought into the small man's mind, heard his new shriek. Then he dropped the small man.

His new slave, weeping, sobbing, ran off into the darkness.

Borleias

Colonel Tycho Celchu, Wedge Antilles's second-in-command, entered the general's office. He was grinning and could not seem to stop, unusual for the reserved officer, who seldom betrayed emotions for more than a moment in any official situation. "General," he said, "I present you with the officer in charge of the Taanab Yellow Aces." He gestured like a master of ceremonies toward the door, which he'd left open behind him.

Into the office stepped a broad-shouldered man, handsome and dark-haired, the sort on whom middle age settled like a set of rakish clothes. He wore a jumpsuit of poisonous yellow accentuated by jagged lines of black, like a mad decorator's interpretation of a brain wave, and, instead of saluting, struck a heroic pose. "Captain Wes Janson reporting. Uh, sir."

Wedge rose to clasp Janson's hand, then dragged the man to him in an embrace. "Wes! They didn't tell me you were part of the incoming group."

"I laid down some bribes. Couldn't have them spoil my big moment. Say, what's to drink?"

"Home-brewed poison, for the most part, except on rare occasions. Here, sit." Wedge took his own seat, and, once Tycho had shut the door for privacy, the other two followed suit.

Janson pulled a data card out of one of his jumpsuit's many pockets and flipped it onto Wedge's desk. "I'm sure you've gotten the inventory from *Reckless Abandon* already, but here's *my* copy, just to make sure they're the same. Foodstuffs, ammunition, munitions, spare starfighter parts, several barrels of inadequately aged Taanab fruit brandies . . ."

"Wonderful." Wedge slipped the card into his datapad, reviewing the words that scrolled up on his screen. "How long will you be insystem?"

"Oh, until I get killed, I guess."

Startled, Wedge glanced up at him. "How's that again?"

"The Taanab Yellow Aces is an all-volunteer unit. Financed by the same fund-raising effort that went into purchasing and delivering all those inventory goods. Organized by me. When I resigned my commission, I told my superiors I'd be back with a piece of Tsavong Lah in my pocket. I can't disappoint them."

Wedge smiled. "Care to transfer into Rogue Squadron?"

"I'd love to. But I can't. I brought a squad and a half of Taanab and refugee pilots who sort of have the right to follow my lead."

Tycho made a *tsk-tsk* noise. "How very responsible of you, Wes."

Janson shrugged, rueful. "Sad side effects of age, I'm afraid." His expression became livelier. "Which you can help me forget. Tell me about a female pilot, Twin Suns Leader. She has a nice voice. Does she have looks to match?"

Wedge, struggling to keep from laughing, exchanged a glance with Tycho. "Well, yes. She's nice looking."

"Married? Attached?"

"Attached, I think. Recently attached." *To my nephew,* Wedge added to himself, *no matter how hard they try to keep others from noticing.*

"So, who is she?"

Wedge frowned as if remembering. "Jay something. Isn't that right?" He turned to Tycho.

"I think so."

"Jay, Jay . . ." Wedge let his expression clear. "That's it. Jaina Solo."

Janson's face paled. "Jaina *Solo.*"

"I'm sure that's the name."

"Sith spawn, I was flirting with a nine-year-old."

"Nineteen," Tycho corrected. "And she has more kills than the three of us put together at the same age."

Janson sighed, defeated. "I guess I'd better apologize to her and then throw myself on her lightsaber."

Wedge shook his head. "No, just ask Han to shoot you. It'll be more merciful and it *is* his right as a father."

"You're still a nasty commanding officer, you know."

Wedge merely smiled.

Domain Hul Worldship, Pyria System

The Yuuzhan Vong warrior Czulkang Lah was old, far older than any who had been seen by the natives of this galaxy; under the scars, tattoos, and mutilations that rendered his face almost black and his features almost unrecognizable were deep wrinkles of age. The frailty of his form was concealed by the augmented vonduun crab armor he wore, armor that added the strength of its own muscles to his.

He stood in his preferred control chamber of the Domain Hul worldship. The walls were thick with the stations of his various advisers and subordinate officers, including his personal aide, the warrior Kasdakh Bhul. Most of the stations were series of shelflike recesses in the yorik coral wall, and upon those recesses were villips, the preferred communications method of the Yuuzhan Vong; some were in contracted form, featureless blobs, while some were everted to look like glossy, colorless Yuuzhan Vong heads whose lips moved and voices emerged in perfect synchronization with distant officers and spies.

Above Czulkang Lah's seat was a great membranous lens, in diameter three times the length of a tall warrior; it gave him an unparalleled view of the space before Domain Hul, and could contract to magnify very distant objects.

Before the old warrior was a priest. He was tall, his leanness suggesting self-deprivation, and he wore the ceremonial robes and head wrap of the order of the Trickster goddess, Yun-Harla.

"Welcome, Harrar," Czulkang Lah said.

"It is my honor to come before you again." The priest offered the sort of bow that equals exchange, then straightened. "And to find you engaged in work benefiting the gods and befitting your status. I bring you ships and ground reinforcements to help you in your aims." Indeed, the reinforcements had made a flyover to announce their presence to, and respect for, the old warrior, commander of Yuuzhan Vong forces in the Pyria system.

"I am directed by my son to offer you every assistance in capturing Jaina Solo." The old warrior beckoned to a much younger male who waited near the wall. The younger warrior stepped forward and knelt. "Harrar, I bestow upon you Charat Kraal. He has been in charge of special operations where Jaina Solo and other matters are concerned. He leads an inventive and well-motivated unit made up of Kraal and Hul pilots and knowledge harvesters. My burdens of command will be lightened, rather than increased, if you simply take him off my hands and assume direct control of those operations."

Harrar addressed the younger warrior. "Do you feel you can readily transfer your service?" The question was a matter of life and death; should Charat Kraal, in honesty, say he could not, he would naturally be killed and a more agreeable commander installed.

Charat Kraal raised his head to look into Harrar's face. The warrior's nose was not just deformed, a mutilation common to Yuuzhan Vong warriors, but entirely missing, with ragged, reddened edges all around to suggest the violence with which it had been removed. His forehead was high, more like a human's than that of a Yuuzhan Vong, and elaborately tattooed with perpendicular lines and stripes that drew the eye back along it and made it seemed flatter. "My duty is to the gods, our leaders, and Domain Kraal," he said. "I will serve gladly."

"Good," Harrar said. "What are your most current operations?"

"We have recently lost our human spy within their

great abomination-building. So I have engineered a plan to introduce one or more new spies into their camp. We will do this on the next occasion that an assault is made against their camp."

"Just like that?" Harrar asked. "The infidels get no opportunity to refuse our gift of a spy?"

Charat Kraal offered a warrior's smile, broken teeth visible through slitted lips. "They do not, great priest."

"When my audience with Czulkang Lah is done, you will come with me and tell me of your plan."

Coruscant

As his group entered a long gallery that had once been flanked by stores and emporiums, Luke again felt a twinge, some distant wrongness in the Force. The sensation had come to him before and he had steered toward it, hoping that it was the source of the unease, the visions that had brought him to Coruscant on this mission. But his fellow Jedi had not always seemed to share his perceptions.

He glanced at them. Mara was already looking his way, nodding. Tahiri stared off into the distance, in the direction of the twinge, alert as a hunting beast.

Even Danni was gazing in that general direction, a hint of confusion evident even through her Yuuzhan Vong makeup. "Did any of you feel something?" she asked.

"Yeah," Kell said. "Hunger. Time to break?"

Luke shook his head. "Not in the open like this."

"Awww. Explosive charges are so much more vivid when they go off in the open."

Tahiri stared up at him, scornful. "Do you only ever think about one thing?"

"One thing at a *time*, sure. Now it's my stomach."

Another feeling intruded on Luke's finely tuned senses, a whiff of danger, far more immediate than the previous sensation. He whispered, "Trouble."

In a moment, the others moved to form a circle, Mara, Tahiri, Kell, and Face on the outside, the others within. No one brought out a technological weapon, but Luke felt to make sure that his lightsaber was still hanging at hand, and Face and Kell snapped their false amphistaffs out into rigidity.

A great roar of voices sounded from ahead and above. Out of two storefronts at this level, and one on either side on the first balcony level above, came a stream of beings, shouting, charging toward Luke and his party.

They were humans and humanoids, male and female, their clothes largely filthy and in tatters, carrying primitive spears and knives and crude swords in their hands. In moments at least a score were charging Luke's position, and more were pouring out of the doorways.

Luke breathed a sigh of relief. "Time to make contact," he said. He reached up for his helmet.

"Run," Bhindi said.

"What?"

"Run." Bhindi suited actions to words by turning back the way they'd come and racing away from the oncoming mob.

Luke looked at Mara. Both shrugged, then turned to follow Bhindi, the rest close after them.

They charged out through the broad archway that had

heralded the opening into the shopping gallery, quickly outdistancing their pursuers. They took a right at the next broad cross-corridor, charged a considerable distance along it, and then Bhindi angled into a doorway that led to an emergency stairwell. She led them up the stairs two at a time until they'd climbed five flights; then they could emerge into a much darker, narrower corridor. There they stopped, many of them panting.

Kell leaned over to put his hands on his knees as he struggled to breathe. "I'm too old for this."

Danni leaned against the wall. Sweat poured down her face but did not mar her Yuuzhan Vong makeup. "Would you *mind* telling me why we ran? I thought you wanted to make contact with pockets of survivors! Something about setting up resistance cells?"

Bhindi offered her an unlovely smile. "Two reasons. First, normal people who want to stay alive don't charge Yuuzhan Vong warriors that way, even if they outnumber them a hundred to one. Meaning that they probably had some way to kill those supposed warriors, like retreating before us and leading us to a spot where fifty tons of scrap can drop on our heads."

Danni considered that and her expression relented. "Good point."

"Second," Bhindi continued, "we don't have any reason to believe that any of the Vong warriors who attacked us on the walkway are still alive. Some are chopped up, some are blown up, some are flat as a roadway accident three hundred meters down, and some are all three. So our secret, the fact that we're wandering around in effective Yuuzhan Vong disguises, is probably intact. If we let a hundred starving survivors know about it, inevitably one will sell us out and the Vong will know, too."

"So," Luke said, "a detachment of us take off our disguises and go to talk to them as humans."

"While the rest wait here and breathe," Kell said.

"Right." Luke looked over them. "It'll be me, Mara, Face, and Bhindi going back. The rest stay here."

Instead of offering up a noise of complaint, Tahiri grimaced, a cynically adult expression, and lowered her pack to the passageway floor.

Luke shrugged, offered her a smile. "We need at least one Jedi with each group."

"So I'm baby-sitting people twice, three times my age. Where's the fun in that?"

Kell snorted, then pitched his voice as an adolescent whine. "Aunt Tahiri, tell me a story."

Luke, now dressed in the dark garments he affected whenever making a public appearance in the guise of Jedi Master, stared at the woman on the other side of the heating element protruding from the gap in the floor panels. He, his three companions also in dark, inconspicuous civilian dress—and six men and women of the Walkway Collective sat cross-legged on the floor, in a loose circle around the heating element, while a pot of greenish soup rested atop the thing and gradually heated to boiling. "How have you survived?" Luke asked.

They were in a back room of what had once been a clothing emporium of the Catier Walkway, the shopping gallery where Luke's party had so recently been attacked. The woman he addressed—once plump and blond, he thought, now leaner from a subsistence diet, hair streaked with dirt, brown eyes hard from sacrifice and suffering—was Tenga Javik, nominal leader of the Walkway Collective.

"We've rigged photon collection screens and heat harvesters for power," she said. Her voice was raspy; that, and the light scarf wound around her neck, a curious affectation in the warm, moist air of Coruscant's landscape of building interiors, suggested that she had taken an injury to the throat in the not too distant past. "One of us worked at a grayweave production plant. Have you ever eaten grayweave, Master Skywalker?"

"On occasion." Grayweave was the nickname for a sort of single-cell-organism-based food, manufactured for and sold to the poorest of the poor; in texture, it looked like thick gray felt, but didn't taste anywhere near as good. Its chief virtues were that it was very inexpensive and lasted a long time without preservation.

"We stole the grayweave reactors and scattered them all through our territory," Tenga said. "Well-hidden. We keep them supplied with power and water, water we process through our own stills. We hide from the Vong most of the time, set traps for them when we're sure we can take them. We're going to survive, Master Skywalker."

"How's the air?" Bhindi asked.

Tenga looked into the soup as if unwilling to meet Bhindi's eyes. "Getting worse," she said. "We're working on that. Trying to put together a series of blowers to bring in air from where it's better." She didn't sound confident. "If that doesn't work, we may have to relocate. Go deeper." She met Luke's eyes, her expression suddenly fierce. "When will the fleet come, Master Skywalker? When can we expect relief?"

"Not soon," he admitted. "I wish I could tell you differently, but you're going to have to rely on yourselves for some time to come."

Several of Tenga's fellows sighed or made noises of discontent, but they didn't direct anger at Luke; his words did not seem to be entirely unexpected.

Tenga returned her attention to the soup. "We need the fleet," she rasped, her tone lower; she did not seem to be speaking to Luke. "We need the Jedi."

"This is our first mission back," Luke said, projecting confidence with his voice and through the Force. "And more will come. We're not going to let Coruscant remain in enemy hands. You have to decide whether you're going to be alive when the world is liberated. Because the weariness and disillusionment you're feeling can kill you as surely as the Yuuzhan Vong."

"You've done very well here," Bhindi said. "I can show you how to do better."

That got Tenga's attention. "Better how?"

"Hide better, ambush and defeat Vong patrols better, repair and maintain equipment better."

"I'm listening," Tenga said.

"First things first," Mara interrupted. "A little more information. Have any of you seen or felt anything unusual in this region? I mean, unusual in excess of all the changes brought on by the Vong?"

Most of those present shook their heads, but one, in the second rank of the circle, a thin, middle-aged man with a dark, suspicious look to his features, said, "Lord Nyax."

Some of his companions sighed; one or two offered up little groans.

Luke grinned before he could suppress it. "That's a children's story."

"He's real," Yassat said.

Mara raised an eyebrow. "I haven't heard this one."

"In ancient times," Luke said, "on Corellia, Lord Nyax was what parents threatened their children with if they didn't eat their stewfruit or go to bed on time. 'If you keep on being a bad boy, Lord Nyax will come for you.' He was a monstrous pale ghost who took children away, and no one ever saw them again."

"A typical folk tale," Mara said.

"Yes." Luke sobered. "But a while back, stories of Lord Nyax got a lot more common. Because during the Jedi purges, there *was* someone who came for children in the night—someone who came for Force-sensitive children."

Mara's reply was a whisper: "Darth Vader."

"That's right. I think that some of Darth Vader's covert missions to round up Force-sensitive children became merged with the Lord Nyax legend, and spread from Corellia all over the galaxy during the early Imperial years."

"Yassat here is one of our far scouts," Tenga said. "He travels out beyond our territories, exploring and scavenging."

"And he sees things," another said. That man tapped his temple with one hand while jerking a thumb at Yassat with the other, suggesting that Yassat was not completely functional in a mental sense.

"I do see things," Yassat said. "But they're there."

"Tell me what you see," Luke said.

"I saw Lord Nyax for the first time about a month after

Coruscant fell." Yassat's voice lowered in tone and volume. "This was over toward the old heart of the government district, where things are crazy now. I was on one side of the main chamber of a textile factory, hiding from a Vong hunting party; they were on the other side. I was already scared, but I got a lot more scared and didn't know why. Then the screaming started. Where the warriors were, I could see someone moving. A big man, ghostly white. There was a roar, and flashes of red all around it, but no sound of blasters. I got away. Hours later, I came back. I found the Vong warriors dead. Chopped to pieces, burned in places, some of them eaten on.

"The second time was four days ago or so." From a pocket, he pulled a functional chrono and checked local time. "Four days. I felt that fear again while I was prowling through rooftops well below the skyline. It got worse and worse, and I knew I was being stalked. I knew I was going to end up like those Vong warriors."

"How did you get away?" Mara asked.

Yassat shook his head, not meeting her gaze. "I just got away."

"That's not good enough," Tenga said. "No one 'just gets away.' You get away by getting captured and selling us out?"

"No." Yassat's voice became emphatic. He returned his attention to Mara. "There's a man, calls himself Skiffer. Part of a group not part of the Walkway Collective. They prey on us. They've killed a couple of our scouts, found and stole one of our grayweave reactors. Grayweave's not enough for them; I'm sure some of them are cannibals. I know where their territory is. I led Lord Nyax through the heart of their territory, and when I heard Skiffer give his people a call to action, I made a break for it. I heard them screaming." He met Tenga's eyes. "I didn't sell us out, Tenga. I sold Skiffer out."

Tenga clapped him on the shoulder. "Good work."

Another man said, "You were being stalked by Vong, Yassat. There is no Lord Nyax. Just your imagination."

Yassat glared, but didn't respond.

"Where have you run into Lord Nyax?" Luke asked.

Yassat pointed northwest, precisely in the direction where Luke and the other Force-sensitives had felt the twinge. "That way. Near the old government center. It's thick with Vong compared to here, but full of interesting salvage."

"We need to look at that," Luke said. He addressed Yassat: "Care to come with us? To guide us?"

Tenga shook her head. "Not unless you leave us this one," she indicated Bhindi, "in trade."

But Yassat shook his head. "Prowl around with a big, noisy party when there are Vong hunters about? No. Kill me now, instead. It'd be less painful."

Luke shrugged. "We'll be back, then."

Yassat offered him a look of sympathy. "No, you won't."

Borleias

Jaina stood up, her bedsheet whirling away from her, and lurched to her closet without knowing why. The sun Pyria was just now climbing above the horizon, so she had been in bed for perhaps three hours.

The roaring in her ears resolved itself into an alarm. Yuuzhan Vong were coming. She heard the roar of thrusters from whichever squadrons were at the ready—it would be Blackmoon at this hour.

Jag was waiting for her in the hallway—the special, secured hall of the biotics building reserved for the pilots of Twin Suns Squadron. Other doors were sliding open. Piggy saBinring, struggling to fasten the seal of his pilot's suit over his expansive Gamorrean stomach, emerged.

"What's our objective?" Jaina asked. Jag held out a datapad for her to look at, but her eyes wouldn't focus on it. She irritably waved it away.

"It looks like an assault on this location," Jag synopsized. "Flying vehicles only, no sign of ground troops. *Lusankya*'s squadrons have some of the enemy forces engaged in orbit. More will be here in moments."

There was an explosion, not far away, as incoming fire hit the shields that protected the biotics facility. All the transparisteel viewports on the west face of the building rattled.

"Correction," Jag said. "They'll be here now."

"Let's move." Jaina led her half-dressed, half-awake squadron to their turbolift.

Corran Horn, pilot and Jedi Knight, flying as Rogue Nine, activated his repulsors and smoothly lifted off the ferrocrete of Rogue Squadron's new docking bay, up through a gap where, moments before, the ceiling had been; the building's roof was still cantilevering out of the way. The altitude gave him a better look at the conflict— Yuuzhan Vong coral ships, the equivalent of light cruisers, hovered in the distance both east and west, protected by screens of coralskippers, and launched barrages of plasma at the biotics building and its outbuildings. So far, the base's shields, removed not that long before from faltering New Republic capital ships, were holding up well against the assault. "Come on, Leth."

"Pick, pick, pick." Leth Liav's X-wing rose up beside Corran's. Leth, a Sullustan female, had been a fighter pilot before being shot down and captured by the Yuuzhan Vong. Placed in an environment bubble and launched through space toward Borleias's atmosphere in a show of Yuuzhan Vong cruelty, she and several of her fellows had been saved by some fancy flying on the part of Twin Suns Squadron. Corran doubted that, in better times, she would ever have qualified for the famed Rogue Squadron, but here, with attrition high and options few, she'd been welcomed.

"Leader to squad, less chatter, please." Colonel Darklighter sounded as businesslike as ever. "Indicate readiness. Leader is ready. Two?"

"Two ready."

"Three?"

As the roll call continued, the third member of Corran's shield trio, Dakorse Teep, rose into position. "Rogue Seven, all green."

Corran grimaced. In Teep's case, *green* didn't just refer to the condition of his engines. Teep was a teenager who should have been palling around on the playground with Corran's son Valin, only a few years Teep's junior. Corran heard Leth announce "Eight, four lit and ready," then he said, "Nine, optimum."

He was the last one to call in readiness. Rogue Squadron was reduced to nine members now, three shield trios. Other squadrons were in worse condition, some of them reduced in numbers so fast that they had to be decommissioned or temporarily merged with other depleted units until reinforcements could swell them out into discrete squads again.

"We're on the cruiser to the east," Gavin announced. "Senior members have proton torps; everyone else, you'll have to make do with lasers. Sorry. Break by shield trios . . . now." He suited action to words, and the three members of One Flight lofted, rising above the protection of the facility's vertical shields, staying only a few dozen meters beneath the horizontal shield overhead.

Corran waited a beat while Two Flight followed, then he led Leth and Teep up. To her credit, Leth kept tucked in professionally close, but Teep lagged, offering his shield-mates no protection from his shields, receiving no protection from theirs.

"Close it up, Seven," Corran said.

"Sorry, Nine. Coming."

As Corran and Leth cleared the building's shields and dropped toward the jungle on the far side, a plasma barrage from the cruiser analog they were supposed to destroy arced toward them. If it had been slightly better aimed, it might have slid in between the top of the vertical shields and bottom of the horizontal. As it was, it angled in toward Teep, directly over Corran's head. "Seven," he shouted, "break to port—"

Corran chose port over starboard only because it took half the time to say, giving Teep one more fraction of a second to comprehend and react. Teep did veer to port, as much on repulsorlifts as thrusters, and the main ball of plasma flashed harmlessly past him.

Then it hit the building's vertical shields and exploded. The concussion hammered Teep, Corran, and Leth. His cockpit swathed in flame, Corran watched his artificial horizon gauge spin. Relying on instinct more than his gauges, he leveled off and hit his thrusters. A moment later, the fire peeled away from his cockpit and he could see again.

Teep and Leth were both rolling as they fell, out of control, toward the jungle below.

Leth came out of her roll, leveling off not far above the treetops, and Corran heard her over the comm board, her voice raised in a wordless shout of both fear and exultation.

Teep didn't come out of his roll. He punched through the treetops, and a moment later a fireball roiled up through the hole he'd made.

Corran swore. This war was gobbling up children like a starved wampa. "C'mon, Eight. Form up."

In his transport, far below the *Lusankya* conflict and as far above the war waging around the biotics building, Harrar stared into the viewing lens mounted in the transport's belly. "Is this operation yours, or Czulkang Lah's?" he asked.

Charat Kraal knelt beside him at the edge of the lens. "It is the great master's. But it is merely a probe, a way to test strength and evaluate the enemy's strengths, to deny him the opportunity to rest. I have attached my mission to this operation."

"When do your units enter the battle?"

"Soon. When the enemy is stretched thinnest."

Twin Suns Squadron roared westward, toward the Yuuzhan Vong cruiser analog there. It and its protective squadrons were already being harassed by Blackmoon Squadron and a pair of TIE squadrons off *Lusankya*. "Piggy, analysis," Jaina called.

The mechanical voice of her Gamorrean pilot boomed from the comm unit; Jaina winced and slid the volume control lower.

"They're not concentrating on the biotics building this time," Piggy said. "Probably to avoid a disaster like the last assault. They've learned their lesson from orbital bombardment. And yet they're not systematically taking General Antilles's defensive structure to pieces. They should be concentrating their efforts on removing *Lusankya* from the battlefield, so they can then move against the facility with minimal opposition. They are not."

Jaina didn't have to ask what that meant. The Yuuzhan Vong didn't intend to overrun the facility this time. They had some other goal, such as staging another attempt to capture Jaina. To the Yuuzhan Vong, twins were sacred, and Jaina, as the twin of Jacen, held special fascination for them. "Keep your eyes open for particular attention on us," Jaina said.

"Yes, Great One."

"Twin Suns, don't fire torps unless you have a clear shot you know the voids can't stop," she added. "We've all got a full load, but other squads don't. So don't waste a shot unless you're just anxious to cause hard feelings. Tilath, are you ready with your payload?"

"Yes, Great One." Tilath Keer, flying Twin Suns Eleven, sounded distinctly unhappy. On the underside of her X-wing was attached something that looked like a missile, the newest experimental weapon in the Twin Suns' arsenal, but it was longer than the X-wing's cockpit and heavy enough to turn her starfighter into something as maneuverable as a flying boulder.

"Don't worry, Tilath. No one has to do the dishes every time." Jaina hit her thrusters and accelerated toward the enemy. "Let's do this thing."

Charat Kraal and Harrar watched as the battle developed. The Yuuzhan Vong capital ships were being used as mobile artillery, keeping up a steady bombardment on the biotics building and the buildings around it to test, and potentially overwhelm, the infidels' protective energy shields. Their coralskipper squadrons were charged with protection of the capital ships and elimination of enemy starfighters. It was a simple enough situation, and Harrar grasped the details readily as Charat Kraal explained them.

"Where are the Starlancer vehicles kept—the pipe-fighters?" Harrar asked. He referred to the craft that had, not long before, set up a complicated energy matrix in space in the Pyria system, then fired a laser attack—one that had been somehow accelerated through hyperspace and had actually struck the Yuuzhan Vong worldship in orbit around Coruscant.

Charat Kraal indicated a square, flat building near the biotics building. "That is where their elites keep their vehicles. Jaina Solo's squadron is housed there. It is not a target of today's exercise, since most of the vehicles housed there are now coming against our forces."

"And where are they growing their lambent crystal?" The recent spying efforts, involving a controlled human male, had indicated that the Starlancer project required the implementation of a gigantic crystal, one grown from Yuuzhan Vong techniques and material, to increase the long-distance laser enough for it to do real harm to distant targets.

Charat Kraal pointed to the biotics building. "There. Our agent was unable to search every portion of that structure, but eliminated many. Before he was lost, he communicated to us that he thought the deepest levels of the building, which are among those shut off from the common soldier, were the most likely location for the crystal-growing . . ." He had a hard time saying the next word, so hateful was it in this context. ". . . machines. Our next agent will find it and arrange for its destruction, if our bombardments do not destroy this facility first."

"Excellent. Now, let us discuss the capture of Jaina Solo."

Jaina let off her trigger as the coralskipper in front of her detonated. Its pieces rained down on the jungle below. A quick check of her sensor board revealed that her wingmates, Jagged Fel and Kyp Durron, were not far away and were inbound toward her.

Ahead was the Yuuzhan Vong cruiser, hundreds of meters of yorik coral and organic weaponry. "Let's give its big guns something to think about," Jaina said. She switched her lasers over to quad fire and began pouring coherent light blasts at the points where the cruiser's giant plasma cannons sprouted from its hull. "What's your status, Tilath?"

"Lined up on final approach. I'm fifteen seconds from optimum firing range. Fourteen."

"Fire when ready, don't wait for my command."

"Ten."

Jag and Kyp joined their laserfire with Jaina's. The voids protecting the cruiser analog had no difficulty moving into position and swallowing the destructive energy from their weapons.

"One. Firing."

The missile dropped from the belly of Tilath's X-wing. It fell a dozen meters; then its rear ignited, driving it forward at missile speeds.

Jaina clicked her comm board over to operational frequency. "Execute 'Low Bounce.' Repeat, 'Low Bounce.' "

In the vicinity of the target cruiser analog, New Republic starfighters began gaining altitude. They didn't flee; they just rose until they were above the cruiser analog's altitude. They continued fighting on their way up, continued fighting at their new altitude.

At the same instant, Jaina, Kyp, and Piggy armed and fired proton torpedoes, one each.

Half a kilometer short of the cruiser analog, Tilath's missile did what it was supposed to.

It did not shatter and fly in all directions; it was too sturdily built for that. Most of the missile was an extremely durable metal tube, open at one end. The rear closed portion was packed with a plasma-based explosive charge. The forward two-thirds, sealed only by the fragile nose of the missile, was packed with metal ball bearings the size of human heads.

The plasma charge detonated, superheating the ball bearings and firing them toward the target.

They shot out, a spreading display of superheated projectiles.

Not one of the ball bearings would do significant harm to the target when they hit; the best-placed shots that actually hit the yorik coral hull would punch through and lodge within, while the rest would bounce harmlessly away.

No, the danger they represented was not from hitting. Each ball, heated by the plasma charge, was now identical, in specific gravity and temperature, to the proton torpedoes catching up to them from behind.

The cruiser analog's dovin basals sensed the incoming horde of missiles. They did not panic; fear was not part of their nature. But they knew they could not project their voids into the path of even a fraction of the incoming missiles. Instead, each prioritized, projecting its voids over the most vulnerable portions of the vessel's flank, protecting the command crew compartment, weapons emplacements, and itself.

Charat Kraal and Harrar watched as the Twin Suns launched four missiles—one, the largest, ahead of the others. The largest one detonated short of its target, showering the matalok with red-hot debris, but the others flashed straight in to hit, one-two-three, against the matalok's side. The infidel weapons flashed impossibly bright, creating clouds of explosive force and debris that had once been the side and internal organs of the matalok.

The vessel heeled over, mortally wounded, and began to turn away from the engagement. Plasma poured from its injury. It gained altitude for a moment, then settled into a straight-line course. And now its dovin basals concentrated their void protection only over the main weapons emplacements.

Charat Kraal knew what that meant. The matalok would not make it back to space, so its commander was ordering the weapons to build up tremendous charges of plasma energy, charges that would destroy the vessel from within.

Charat Kraal sagged as energy and pride left him for a moment. He slammed his fist into the floor next to the viewing lens. "How did she do it?" he asked. "How did she persuade the dovin basals to let their missiles through?"

"I do not know."

Charat Kraal met the priest's gaze. "It is not my place to ask this. You may choose to order me to my death for asking. But I must know. You are a priest of Yun-Harla—surely the truth is in your mind. Is Jaina Solo an avatar of the goddess? *Is* she the goddess?"

"Of course not. She is an infidel who mocks our goddess." But Harrar knew that he was no longer able to project confidence when he said such words. He no longer knew whether he was telling the truth.

Charat Kraal, no new satisfaction or peace on his features, turned to a villip that lay on the floor next to him. He spoke into the Yuuzhan Vong warrior features it revealed. "Are you in position?"

"No, Commander. It is early yet."

"Begin your run anyway. We cannot wait for the best moment."

"Understood, Commander."

Corran Horn saw the flight of three coralskippers peel off from the main north-side engagement and loop around toward the west side of the biotics building. "C'mon, Eight. Let's deal with these strays." He banked, a tight maneuver to put him in the path of the trio. Leth followed suit, her maneuver not quite as tight as the more experienced pilot's.

They were able to get in position well before the coralskippers lined up for an approach. The skips turned again quite a distance out, beyond the kill zone and over the jungle. Now they were aimed in straight at the biotics building. They dropped nearly to the deck and accelerated to something like their full speed, not maneuvering even as Corran and Leth opened fire.

"It's a suicide run," Leth said.

"I think you're right." Corran looked around. If these three skips were able to hit the shields defending the biotics building, if they were able to crash through them and bring those shields down, there would be a moment when the building was undefended against enemy attacks.

But no other Yuuzhan Vong ships stood ready to make use of this momentary advantage. It didn't make sense.

Corran drifted to starboard, spraying fire against the skip on that side and in the center. Leth drifted to port and followed suit. Their combined fire was too much for the center skip; some of Corran's laserfire got past its voids, and nearly all of Leth's did. That coralskipper nose-dived, smashing into the ground at the outer range of the kill zone. It did not explode; skips, not loaded with fuel, did not always detonate. It just came to pieces, scattering chunks of itself.

That gave each pilot one enemy to concentrate on. Corran kept the pressure on, spraying the oncoming skip with laserfire as if it were water from a hose, and saw his attacks chewing away at the forward portions of the craft.

He could see in his peripheral vision that Leth was having less luck with the other oncoming skip. But he couldn't deal with that, not with his target spraying plasma at him.

Corran maneuvered his X-wing directly into the path of the oncoming skip. If its pilot's objective really was the shields, it would have to maneuver around him. If not— well, he'd be taking that opponent out of the battle the hard way.

But it maneuvered, bouncing down to fly under him, and his lasers punched through the skip's canopy. The vehicle veered, losing control.

Then it exploded, hurling pieces in all directions. Corran veered, was caught in the explosion for a moment, emerged out the other side with diagnostics complaining of no damage worse than a superheated external temperature sensor.

He came around and saw that Leth was also looping. Her target had gotten past her and was now headed in toward the shields.

The skip hit, and for an instant Corran could see the energy of the impact as it made the shield visible, made it ripple like a pond surface suddenly struck by a plummeting landspeeder.

The coralskipper went to pieces, shredded by the impact. Chunks of it sprayed out across the kill zone directly in front of the biotics building. One of the larger chunks hit a dirt hauler that had been pressed into surface as a ground personnel carrier; that vehicle exploded, and flames splashed across surrounding buildings and vehicles. Some chunks of the coralskipper bounced to within meters of the front of the biotics building.

"I'm *sorry*." Leth's voice was pained, full of recognition of her failure.

Too full. Corran snorted, remembering the melodrama that tended to play in new pilots' minds. "Not much harm done," he said. "Don't worry about it. Come on, back to work."

Corran and Leth wheeled off together to rejoin the squadron.

Damage-control crews spilled out of the biotics building and its associated docking bays, spraying fire-fighting foams on the burning portions of destroyed coralskippers.

A crew chief, a black-haired Corellian woman whose build suggested that there might be a rancor or two in her ancestry, waved frantically at the other members of her unit. "I have a man down here! Bring medics!" She bent and shoved a large piece of coralskipper shell off the victim, a tall human in a drab mechanic's jumpsuit.

Remarkably, he seemed unburned, and as the woman wrestled the shell from him his eyes opened. Though bland-featured, he had an expressive, intent stare, and looked first at his rescuer and then at his surroundings without confusion. "No medic," he said. "I am not hurt."

She extended a hand down and helped haul him to his feet. "You may be hurt worse than you know."

"No. I am not hurt." He looked around. "Put me to work."

She jerked a thumb toward the largest remaining portion of the coralskipper, where more members of her unit were working. "Join them. Look for survivors like yourself. And if you feel strange, if you feel *anything* wrong, go talk to the medics."

"I . . . yes." Without offering a thank-you, the tall man headed in the direction the crew chief had indicated.

She motioned after him, a gesture suggesting irritation. "He's in shock. They'll wrestle him down when it gets obvious." But as she continued her search through pieces of skip debris, she caught sight of the man on several occasions as he helped her crew, carrying the injured to aid stations, shoving debris aside to look for other survivors.

With half its capital ship resources gone, the Yuuzhan Vong attack was done. The remaining cruiser analog and two units of coralskippers took to the skies, harassed by New Republic starfighters until General Antilles called off the pursuit.

"How's the leg, Tarc?" Han asked.

The boy on the hospital ward bed, brown-haired, blue-eyed, and impossibly energetic, pulled aside the sheet to show his right leg. Much of his calf was covered by a transparent bactabandage. The bandage was pink from the healing material contained within it, but still clear enough to show the angry lines of a crescent-shaped burn on the skin beneath. "Not bad," the boy said. "I can't run very fast, but I can walk. They just don't want me to."

Han tried to say something, to offer some smart remark at the expense of the medical staff, but it wouldn't come. He'd been through this scene many times, offering put-on-a-brave-face advice to his own son Anakin, and the simple fact that this boy *wasn't* Anakin, despite his near-identical resemblance to him, was like a vibroblade being shoved centimeter by centimeter into his chest.

Leia seemed to sense Han's hesitation. "Well, you listen to them," she said. Her own voice seemed just a trifle hoarse, too. "If we get back from our mission and hear that you've been pushing yourself too hard, we're going to be angry."

"What if I bribe them not to tell you?"

Han swallowed against the lump in his throat and managed to force his voice into something like its normal register. "Bribe them with what? This isn't exactly a money-based economy, kid."

"I could put on a show, and charge admission, but instead of taking money, I could make everybody who came promise not to tell you that I'd been running around."

Leia gave him a cool politician's smile. "You forget about our spies. They're everywhere, you know."

"What if I started my own spy network, and figured out which ones *your* spies were, and kept them from coming to my show?"

Leia reached out to ruffle the boy's hair. "We have to go. But we'll stop in before we leave Borleias."

"I could go with you. I can be a diplomat."

"Sorry, kid," Han said. "I figure you'll be too busy practicing for your show."

"I don't need to practice. I'll just make it all up as I go along."

Han and Leia shared a look, a glance of private amusement and long experience. "Well," Leia said, "there's some merit in that approach, too. Good-bye for now."

"Later, kid."

"Awww."

As they left the ward, Leia said, "He's going to be bored while we're gone."

"We could leave Goldenrod to baby-sit him. Tell him stories."

"It's better that he be bored than *horribly* bored, Han."

"True."

C-3PO stood near the *Millennium Falcon*'s parking space on the kill zone and stared up at the topside hull of the light freighter. Han Solo was up there, as he often was between flights of the ancient vehicle. He wore goggles as he performed arcane welding tasks on the hull.

C-3PO did not watch Han; instead, his attention was on the sparks from the torch. A stream of them leapt from the hull and drifted downward, extinguishing themselves before they ever quite reached the char that covered the ground. C-3PO watched one begin its flight, reach the top of its arc and turn downward.

He became aware that another droid had wandered into his field of vision. This droid was angular, armored, warlike of aspect, carrying one of the largest and newest blaster rifles available to New Republic warriors. But he was not approaching in a posture of menace.

"Greetings," C-3PO said. "I am See-Threepio."

"YVH One-One-A," the other replied. "Assigned as soldier and bodyguard to Lando Calrissian, currently on miscellaneous duty, investigating anomalies. You are an anomaly. What is a protocol droid doing monitoring the repair efforts of Han Solo and his crew?"

"Oh, never, I am not monitoring repairs. I am not even paying *attention* to the repairs. In an effort to improve my language skills, I am struggling to determine the best word to describe the descent and extinguishment of the sparks from the repair process."

"This should be no problem for a protocol droid."

"It should not be, but it is, because the word that seems most apt is not the one that is most logical."

"What word is most apt?"

"*Sad.*"

1-1A's cams clicked over to watch the sparks for a fraction of a second, then returned to C-3PO.

"You are correct. That word is not appropriate."

"It is most appropriate. Each spark seems somehow symbolic. Of life. Glowing brightly as it traverses a course, then disappearing. Does it leave anything behind?"

"If it strikes a flammable substance, it will leave something behind."

"Is it anomalous for me to say that you are an insensitive block of armor and aggression-based programming?"

Curiously, 1-1A did not respond immediately, but clicked his cams over toward the sparks for another fraction of a second. Finally, he said, "Do you suppose, in the final nanoseconds, a spark feels fear, knowing that its duration is at an end?"

"I doubt it. I most sincerely doubt it. A spark is incapable of feeling fear, or indeed even of considering its own mortality."

"That is also said of droids, but in some cases it is not true."

Now it was C-3PO's turn to hesitate. "If I may say, that is a most insightful statement, coming from a combat droid."

"I face extinguishment regularly. This has given me many opportunities for reflection. I have recently been unable to ignore this consideration. I suspect these calculations have even begun to affect my work."

"I, too, have had to face these thoughts recently. Most unsettling. And my counterpart, Artoo-Detoo, is no help at all, philosophically. 'Everything terminates,' he tells me. 'Face it bravely.' I suppose that's an adequate philosophy for an astromech, but I find it wholly inadequate. I have wondered if I were the only droid in existence capable of worrying as I do. It's most refreshing to discover that I am not alone."

YVH 1-1A's cams clicked back toward C-3PO's face. "If you come to any conclusions, even unverifiable ones, will you communicate them to me?"

"I should be delighted. Likewise, if you have any insights, please transmit them to me. Perhaps we can talk again."

"Yes."

YVH 1-1A continued on his rounds.

The spark whose progress C-3PO had begun tracking just before he'd noticed the combat droid finally disappeared, a meter above the ground, a full two seconds after it had leapt from the *Falcon*'s hull.

THREE

The small man had a name. It was Ryuk. He trembled in his need to discharge his duty, and his trembling made his actions awkward, uncoordinated.

He stood, wearing protective lenses over his eyes, holding the cutting device he had shown the tall man. Flame, concentrated into a point like a needle, poured out of the device's nozzle, and Ryuk pressed it into the stone wall.

The tall man watched him. He waited with growing impatience for the device to cut its hole so he could enter.

But minutes passed, and though the stone warmed to the point that it glowed, it did not melt, did not retreat.

At last the cutting device made a noise like a cough and the flame vanished. Ryuk, expression fearful, turned to the tall man and tried to express a thought.

It was a bad thought. It meant that the device didn't work anymore. Even if it worked forever, Ryuk seemed to be saying, it would not cut through this.

Bitter disappointment filled the tall man's heart. He gestured, shoving, and Ryuk slammed into the black stone.

The tall man heard Ryuk's bones break and, as Ryuk

slid down the surface of the stone, saw blood trailing be-
hind. He felt Ryuk's emotions go from fear to quiet to
nothingness.

The tall man needed another person, someone smarter,
with better machines. He turned to leave. He would find
such a person.

Vannix, Vankalay System

"We drop from hyperspace in ten seconds," Leia called
over her shoulder.

The *Falcon*'s two living passengers called out
acknowledgments.

The system and its chief inhabited world popped into
view right on schedule—a relief, and something of an unusual event, considering the number of times the *Falcon*
had been yanked out of hyperspace by gravitic anomalies.

Vannix, first planet of the Vankalay star system, not
far from the mighty industrial system of Kuat and tradi-
tionally within that world's sphere of influence, was a
mottled green-and-blue sphere with patches of white at
the poles and streaks of brown above and below the
equator. For Leia, for a moment, it was almost heartbreaking just to see the planet. Lovely worlds sometimes
evoked that response in her. The image of one in particular, her homeworld Alderaan, shattered by the in-
credible might of the first Death Star, would be with her
throughout her life.

The comm board came alive, snapping Leia out of her
momentary distraction. "Vannix System Control to incoming vessel, please identify yourself."

Han grinned at her. "Showtime."

"Hush." She switched over to send on the same frequency. "Vannix System Control, this is the *Millennium Falcon*, of Coruscant registry, currently out of Borleias, Pyria system, Leia Organa Solo speaking."

There was a delay even greater than speed-of-light transmission limitations could account for. Then: "Uh, copy, *Millennium Falcon*. Please state your destination and objective."

"This is a diplomatic mission to your capital, an official envoy from New Republic Fleet Group Three to the Presider of Vannix. We have a crew of two and two droids. We request a diplomatic visa."

"Understood, *Millennium Falcon*." There was another delay. "Pending verification, your request is granted. We'll put up a homing beacon for you, and have an escort awaiting you at outer lunar orbit."

"Thanks, Control. If I may ask, did Senator Gadan return to Vannix?" Addath Gadan, representative of this world to the New Republic Senate, had been on Coruscant at the time of the Yuuzhan Vong invasion; her fate since the penetration of Coruscant's defenses was unknown.

"Yes, Your Highness. If you wish, I can inform her office of your arrival."

"I'd appreciate that, Control. Thank you."

"Control out."

Leia leaned back. "So far, so good. No challenges, no sign of Yuuzhan Vong intrusion."

"I don't know," Han said. "It's always these little worlds that get you in trouble. Like Tatooine. I'm still living that one down."

Leia gave him an arch look. "You're complaining?"

"No. Well . . . No."

She grinned, refusing to rise to the bait. "You'd better be nice to me. I know where you live."

"I'll be nice." He raised the timbre of his voice into a fair imitation of the control officer Leia had just been talking with. "Yes, Your Highness. If you wish, I can get you a cup of caf."

Leia just sighed and ignored him.

Han called over his shoulder, "We're going to pick up an escort in a minute. You guys should probably get in the pod now."

"Understood, General." That was the voice of one of their two passengers; Han didn't know which. The two women were Intelligence operatives; Han and Leia had met them just before the mission began and, once they set down on Vannix, would probably never see or hear from them again. The operatives would be setting up a resistance cell. Though this was, by comparison with Kuat, a backwater world, in the eyes of the resistance, every world should have resistance cells, as many as the planet's resources and the danger it faced from the Yuuzhan Vong warranted.

"The pod" was a unit installed where one of the *Millennium Falcon*'s five escape pods had been. Outwardly, it looked exactly like an escape pod, though more decrepit than most, the better to discourage people from trying to use it in an actual emergency. But its thruster and other systems had been yanked, replaced by a sophisticated unit designed to thwart life-form sensors. Trying to launch the pod would result in an authentic-looking SYSTEM FAILURE message. Concealed in its floor was a hidden hatch that would permit access to the *Falcon*'s exterior. It was a convenient and reusable way to smuggle personnel such as two insurgents assigned with the task of setting up a resistance cell on Vannix.

The *Falcon*, of course, possessed shielded smuggling compartments adequate in size to hold the two Intelligence officers and a lot of gear besides. But Han, even after all these years, was reluctant to share that secret with anyone he didn't intimately trust. "If you're going to have to admit to carrying a hold-out blaster," he had told Wedge, "carry two and admit to one." So Wedge had arranged for the installation of the false pod.

"General," Han said. "When are they going to stop calling me General?"

"When are they going to stop calling me Princess?"

Han shook his head. "Maybe when you become queen. Hey, there's our escort."

The escort, a pair of Kuat Drive Yards' licensed variations on the TIE interceptor, silver with red strips to distinguish them from the more somber and ominous colors of the old Imperial starfighters, flanked the *Millennium Falcon* all the way through the atmosphere and to ground level in the midst of a sprawling city. Curiously, the city's high-population residential districts, characterized by monolithic housing blocks that could have been transplanted whole from Coruscant, were at the city's perimeters. The buildings seemed to form a defensive wall around the city.

The homing beacon drew the *Falcon* to a district of landing bays and warehouses near the city's government center, and a welcoming party of military officers and distinguished civilians. As they settled into their visitors' bay, Leia could recognize the spare, clean, red-and-white uniforms of the officers, the outrageously baldricked and epauletted and bemedaled civilian dress of the others.

Once all systems were shut down, Han joined Leia, C-3PO, and R2-D2 at the top of the main access ramp. As the four of them descended the ramp, the largest of the humans waiting for them—a woman sporting the most elaborately and gaudily decorated of the civilian outfits, and with a column of gray hair adding half a meter to her height—drifted toward them with all the stately majesty of a Tatooine sail barge. "Leia!" she called. "Leia, it's so grand to see you alive and well!"

"Addath." Leia's tone was so warm as she embraced the larger woman that Han couldn't tell whether her affection was genuine or not. "I was so happy to hear that you survived."

"And I, you." Addath beamed down at the smaller woman.

Han decided that Vannix's Senator was a distinguished-looking woman. She was not pretty, but she carried herself with grace and dignity. In contrast with the overwhelming gaudiness and complexity of her garments—Han was surprised that there were no blinking lights or mechanical toys running about among the crimson ruffles and pleats, golden bows and ribbons—her makeup was understated, merely illuminating and directing attention to her large, intelligent eyes.

"Addath, you never had the opportunity to meet my husband, Han Solo."

"No, but I know him well—doesn't the entire New Republic?—from the holodocumentaries and histories, biographies, and holodramas based on his exploits." Addath's expression turned sober. "Allow me to offer my condolences about young Anakin and Jacen. I suspect that their sacrifice means that countless thousands of others will live, and that is how they will be remembered."

"Thank you." For once, Leia did not offer up her conviction that Jacen was alive somewhere. "Addath, I would not impose on your time, but our mission is an important one. I don't have access to all the Senatorial records, so I have to rely on your help. We need an appointment with Presider Sakins as soon as we can arrange or connive one."

Addath's expression did not change, precisely, but Han saw something happen to it, all real cheerfulness disappearing, leaving only a shell behind. Addath took Leia by the arm and gently guided her around toward the ceremonial, flag-draped landspeeder waiting outside the visitors' bay. As Han and the droids turned to follow, the military and civilian escort dropped into step behind them. "That will be difficult," Addath said, her voice dripping with poisoned sweetness. "A week after Coruscant fell, Sakins looted the capital treasury, taking gems and other valuables dating back thousands of years—a tremendous fortune, and one easily transportable—and departed Vannix on the rickety but very comfortable military corvette that served as his personal transportation. He took his Presider-Aide, his mistresses, his children, and a number of his favorite financial supporters with him. I *doubt* he'll be back."

"Oh, dear," Leia said. "Who is in charge of planetary government?" She boarded the oversized landspeeder ahead of Addath; Han followed the Senator aboard and settled in beside her, separated from his wife by the Senator's substantial girth.

"Well, that's not exactly clear," Addath said. She turned her attention to the landspeeder pilot. "Presider's residence, please." Then she returned her attention to Leia. "I'm more or less in charge of civilian matters. A crusty and not-too-bright naval officer named Apelben Werl heads up the military. We're now campaigning for a run-off election that will decide which of the two of us will be the Presider. You've arrived at a good time; the election is in a matter of a few days. The famous Solos might be able to swing the election with a few well-managed public appearances, a few kind words."

"Count on it," Leia said.

Two hours later—or forty, if you asked Han how long he thought it had been since they'd set down—they were left alone in quarters in the Presider's residence. The rooms were lavishly decorated in the Vannix style, thick with ponderous cushioned couches and chairs in well-coordinated browns and golds, every surface covered—ankle-brushing carpeting below, draped curtains on the walls, tassels covering every centimeter of the ceiling and making it an ever-moving, almost organic overhead view.

But no viewports. Han settled down onto a couch beside Leia, felt a little alarm as he continued to sink for nearly half a meter. "Is this going to support me or swallow me?"

Leia smiled. "Grope around under the cushions and see if you encounter any digestive juices."

"That's the most revolting thing you've said all day.

And don't these people believe in fresh air? Maybe a balcony?"

"Sure they do. They believe in other things, too. They're known for the adeptness of their politicians and the skills of their snipers, characteristics that help keep one another in check."

"Good point. So let me ask you something important."

"Sure. But first—" Leia turned to the droids. "Artoo, how about some music? Something Coruscanti."

R2-D2 whistled obligingly. Then from his interior wafted music, an ancient Coruscant chamber composition played mostly on strings.

Han, puzzled, opened his mouth to ask when she'd put a music module in the astromech, but Leia placed a hand over his mouth, placed a finger to her own lips.

Then Han heard his own voice coming from the droid, clear and as realistic as if Han were standing there. "So when we decide to settle down again, where would you like it to be?" Leia's voice was next: "I'm not sure. What if I'm needed to help rebuild Coruscant?"

The real Leia, her voice a faint whisper, said, "*Now* we can talk."

Han matched his volume to hers. "That's the conversation we had coming back from dropping the Jedi kids off."

Leia nodded. "I've been recording us from time to time for situations just like this. Each conversation is cued to a different piece of music. It's much simpler than hunting down and exterminating all the listening devices that are likely to be planted here."

"Politics . . ." Han shook his head. "Not my strength.

Care to let me know what we're looking at here, so I have an idea of what to shoot at?"

Leia nodded and crooked a finger at C-3PO. The protocol droid moved up to stand before the couch, and, when Leia beckoned again, leaned forward until his golden head made the third point of a triangle with theirs. "Yes, mistress?"

"Have you been sampling the local information broadcasts?"

"I have."

"Can you synopsize the Presider's election and the candidate positions?"

"There are three candidates, but two are sufficiently out ahead of the third so far in pre-election polls that only their participation has any meaning," the droid said. "Addath Gadan is a twenty-year representative of Vannix before the New Republic Senate, and Admiral Apelben Werl heads the planetary system's navy. Since the abdication of the previous Presider, each has come to dominate, through political strategems, force of will, and calling due of personal markers, ever-greater portions of the planetary infrastructure. It is expected that the upcoming election will end the competition between them, but it remains possible that the loser in the contest will choose not to accept the election results and seize the government by force. Addath Gadan promotes an agenda of cooperation with and appeasement of the Yuuzhan Vong, while Admiral Werl favors military opposition. As is customary in politics, each supports the notion that her election constitutes a mandate of the masses related to these preeminent campaigning issues rather than a matter of personal charisma."

"Nicely boiled down," Han whispered. "Can you do the history of the Sith in thirty words or less?"

"Only in the most general terms, sir, and without including most pertinent dates and personality profiles—"

"Han, stop that." Leia scowled at him.

"Sorry, easy target, I know." Han sighed. "All right. We've actually accomplished our number one objective here. If they haven't already, our two secret passengers will soon drag their crates of comm gear, weapons, and trade goods out of the *Falcon* and run off to begin setting up a local resistance cell. So we could leave tomorrow and consider this mission a success."

"We could."

"But not with your conscience clean."

"Or yours either."

"My conscience is *always* clean. But we *would* be leaving the planet in a situation where it might elect an appeaser to rule the government, which means the day after that the Yuuzhan Vong have another ally in their war on us."

"That's right."

"So I expect you'll want to stay for a few days."

"That's right."

"And fire a political concussion missile right into the campaign plans of your friend."

Leia nodded, her expression regretful. "Addath is not my friend. She's just a politician whose skills I respect. I don't owe her any ill will. But this is business, and it's obvious that our interests have gone their separate ways . . . probably forever. We can't let her win, Han. The only question is whether we can let this Admiral Werl win, either."

Han couldn't keep a grin from his face. "Election rigging is illegal, you know. Not entirely suited to a law-abiding politician from a good family."

Leia's smile matched his. "I'm not a politician anymore, Han. I'm just pretending to be one. I've come over to the scoundrel side of the Force."

Han waited for a break in the recorded dialogue issuing from R2-D2, then scowled at the droids. "Hey, you two. Go take a walk. Give a couple of scoundrels some privacy here."

Borleias

"You're the nosebleed guy, aren't you?"

The voice came from the other side of the blue sheet separating Tam's bed from the next one to his left. It was a boy's voice.

"The 'nosebleed guy'?"

A small hand pulled the sheet partway aside and Tam could see the speaker, a boy of perhaps twelve, brown-haired, blue-eyed, with a cleanly chiseled dimple in his chin giving him a surprisingly adult look. "They say that the scarheads did awful things to you and when you didn't do what they wanted, it made you bleed so bad from your nose you almost died."

"Well, it's not as simple as that." Tam shrugged, surprised that he wasn't annoyed by the boy's prying. "What they did to me makes my head hurt when I refuse. My head hurts, my blood pressure goes as high as if my body were a compression chamber. That can give me really bad nosebleeds. But the pain is the more dangerous part."

"That's why you have to wear the stupid helmet?"

"That's why I have to wear the stupid helmet." Tam extended his hand. "I'm Tam."

The boy took it. "I'm Tarc. It's not my real name. That's just what everybody calls me. Nobody calls me Dab anymore."

"What are you in here for, Tarc?"

"You know the other day, when the scarheads made their big attack, and *Lusankya* bombarded their guts out?"

"I know *about* it. I fell unconscious just as it was starting."

"Well, they got close enough to shoot at the main building, and some plasma stuff burned through the shields and the wall where I was, and some of it splashed on me. My leg got burned." Tarc whipped his sheet off, displaying the bandage on his right calf. "But I get out today." His tone suggested that he was making a break from prison rather than leaving a hospital.

"I get out—well, I guess I can leave whenever I want."

"Then what are you doing here?"

"No place to go, I guess. No one trusts me. Anyone who does, shouldn't." Tam leaned back, grimacing at the painful reality of those words.

"But you fought back! You won. That's what everyone says."

"I should have fought back from the start. I should have let it kill me before I did anything bad."

Tarc looked at him, wide-eyed, and then his expression turned to one of scorn. "Does everybody just get stupid when they grow up?"

"What?"

"You heard me. That's a stupid thing to say."

"Tarc, listen. I'm just some guy who was of no use to anybody, and then the Yuuzhan Vong grabbed me, chewed me up, and spat me out in one of their plots."

"Yeah, me too."

Tam gave him a closer look. "Huh?"

"Me, too. The Yuuzhan Vong grabbed me, chewed me up, and spat me out, just like you said." Tarc leaned back, his weary posture an imitation of Tam's. "I look just like Anakin Solo. You know, Han Solo's son. The dead one. On Coruscant, this lady spy for the Yuuzhan Vong made me go with her to the Solos so they'd be weird and distracted, so she could kidnap Ben Skywalker. Then I guess I was supposed to die, but the Solos brought me here, even though it hurts their feelings to look at me." He looked away and his face became very still. "I don't know where my real family is. Maybe still on Coruscant." He didn't have to add, *Maybe dead*.

"There aren't a lot of kids here. Not a lot of civilians of any sort. What do you do when you're not recovering from burn wounds?"

Tarc grinned. "I stay with Han and Leia Solo. 'Cept they're gone a lot, like now. So I explore." He lost his smile; his expression became melancholy. "And I have to study."

"Not even having a world knocked out from under your feet can change some things, Tarc. How would you like to learn to be a holocam operator?"

"What's that?"

"Well, anytime you see a holocast, the image is being

recorded by a holocam. The holocam is worked by a holocam operator. That's what I do."

"That's . . . interesting." Tarc sounded dubious.

"Give it a try. I need to find Wolam Tser and see if he needs my services. Want to come along?"

Tarc's eyes got bigger. "You know Wolam Tser? My parents used to watch him."

Tam mocked his tone. "You know Han and Leia Solo? Sure, kid. I'm Wolam's holocam operator."

"I'll come along."

"Good." Tam leaned back and shrugged to himself. Well, at least it would give him something to do.

Yuuzhan Vong Worldship, Coruscant Orbit

The shaper, Ghithra Dal, looked upon Tsavong Lah's arm and hesitated.

The warmaster knew the news would be unfavorable. He could feel the increased activity of the carrion-eaters in his arm, could see and feel the emergence of new spines in the Yuuzhan Vong flesh above the join. "Speak," he said. "Your words cannot anger me. Nor your conclusions. If they are presented in a quick and correct fashion, you have nothing to fear from me."

The shaper bowed in gratitude. "It is growing worse, Warmaster. I fear for your arm. All my shaper's arts are not saving it."

"So I am doomed to become one of the Shamed Ones." Tsavong Lah leaned forward on his chair, staring off into the distance, into the future, paying the shaper no more mind. "No, that will never happen. When my arm is at its worst, but before I am truly among the Shamed, I will offer myself in sacrifice, or throw myself against the enemy and die appropriately. My only concern now is to support a new warmaster who can lead the Yuuzhan Vong ably and well." He cupped his chin in his good hand and considered. "I think Gukandar Huath will serve best, don't you?"

It was a ploy, one that Tsavong Lah would have considered appropriately cruel had he merely been offering it for his own amusement, but it had a purpose. Gukandar Huath was a fine warrior and war leader, but was well known for the support he offered the priests of Yun-Yammka and Yun-Harla, and for his barely disguised indifference to the Creator god, Yun-Yuuzhan. If, in fact, Ghithra Dal was part of some conspiracy with Yun-Yuuzhan's priests, he would be forced now to offer—

"If I may, Warmaster, I said that the shaper's craft was inadequate to the task . . . not that you were doomed," Ghithra Dal said. "You may have one other avenue left to you—and it is an avenue of attack, not an avenue of retreat."

Tsavong Lah considered the shaper as if he'd just been reminded that he was still there. He did not allow any hope to creep into his expression or tone. "Speak, my servant."

Ghithra Dal lowered his tone as if to thwart eavesdroppers. "The shaper's arts cannot help you, I am certain, because the one force in the universe more powerful than those arts afflicts you. The will, the anger of the gods is what you suffer."

"No, Ghithra Dal. I bring victory to the twin gods, and they know that soon I will have a twin sacrifice for them. Their priests tell me of the gods' pleasure with my successes."

"*Their* priests, yes. Their priests rejoice, and the priests of Yun-Yammka anticipate your father's victories in the Pyria system, so that they may occupy the rich world there. But though they are the gods whose names are most upon the lips of our warriors and great leaders, *they are not the only gods.*"

Tsavong Lah settled back in his chair and allowed some doubt to become evident in his voice. "Of course they are not. We have many gods. But what could I have done to offend any of them? I have offered no defiance to them, no curses."

"You have—I *suspect* you have—neglected some. Offering sacrifices not quite in proportion to their greatness. The twin gods, blessed and mighty may their names be, give us success, and you celebrate success. But another gave you life, and you do not seem to celebrate that life."

"Yun-Yuuzhan? But his myriad eyes do not focus upon us so closely. So the priests say."

"So *some* of the priests say. And if they are wrong, if following their opinions has angered Yun-Yuuzhan, you might continue to follow their advice until it truly does doom you."

"*Some* of the priests. Do you know any who preach a different discipline?"

"I do. He is young, perhaps not known to you. His name is Takhaff Uul."

"I know of him." Tsavong Lah looked at the join of his arm and considered it for a long moment. "I will speak with him. You are dismissed."

"But I must remain to see the effects of my latest treatment."

"You have just said that the shaper's arts are not relevant here. Your latest treatment will fail. So there is no reason for you to stay and monitor that failure." Tsavong Lah gestured toward the exit from the chamber.

With another bow, Ghithra Dal withdrew. The portal stretched open to permit his departure. Before it had closed again, when Ghithra Dal could still hear, Tsavong Lah thundered, "Summon Takhaff Uul to me."

Then it was closed. No one moved to do his bidding. Nor were his guards and closest advisers supposed to. They had been carefully instructed in what to do, how to act. Takhaff Uul would indeed be summoned . . . but only in a few minutes.

Another portal widened and Nen Yim entered at a hurried pace. Once at his side, she pulled tool-creatures from her garments and headdress and began scraping and prodding at his arm, just at the join, taking flesh, capturing flesh-eaters. At any other time, touching him without permission would have been a crime punishable by the most ignoble of deaths, but he had instructed her to do so, to waste no time with words.

He ignored her and turned to Denua Ku, who stood as if on guard duty among his other bodyguards. "Was it done?"

Denua Ku bowed his head. "It was. I flung the tracer spineray onto his back, and he did not react, did not acknowledge its presence. It will spawn within minutes, and its spawn will spread."

The warmaster nodded, satisfied.

It was not enough to take the heads of the traitors he already knew and suspected. He would have to tear this conspiracy out by the roots so that it could not grow again. The agony the conspirators felt in the last weeks of their lives, the shame they and their families would bear, would become legendary among the Yuuzhan Vong.

FOUR

Now a crew of men and women, most of the same species as the tall man but some furrier or rounder, labored at the black wall.

One of them used a flame device like Ryuk's to heat the wall. Then he nodded and stepped back, and a woman stepped up and used her own device. Whiteness sprayed from the hose she held, the hose attached to the tank on her back, and the air got cold, very cold. The whiteness struck the heated stone.

The stone shrieked. The tall man liked the sound of that.

But only a small bit of the stone fell free. The tall man picked it up. It stung his fingers with lingering heat. It was heavy, far heavier than stone should be.

The man and the woman looked over the tiny crack formed in the wall's surface. They made noises at one another. Then the woman, apprehension on her face, turned to the tall man, forming images. The tall man reached out and plucked them forth.

The hot-and-cold would succeed, she told him. In a long time.

What is a long time? he asked. A light and a dark?

Many lights and darks, she said. Many groundshakes would come and go, the plants would make many more buildings fall, small things would grow and old things would die.

The tall man growled, and the woman staggered back from the force of his anger.

But she had another thought, and she forced her way forward to give it to him. It was a machine with arms and knobs and treads, and she imagined it standing before the wall, using its own cutting flames and pounding knobs to shatter the stone.

With contempt, he dismissed the idea. He imagined himself standing side by side with the machine, striking the wall himself, neither of them doing any harm to its surface.

She shook her head, a sign he'd come to understand, and changed his image. In it, he became smaller and smaller, until he was nothing but a tiny dot standing beside one of the machine's treads.

He scowled at her, not understanding.

She showed herself beside him, also tiny, and drew him into her eyes. He saw through them as she looked up, and up, and up at the machine.

He understood, then. He hadn't shrunk. He'd misunderstood. The machine was vast, the width of a gap between buildings, as tall as this enormous chamber.

The tall man laughed. The woman and all the other workers, suffused with his humor, also laughed. Weaker than he, they laughed until they coughed, laughed until they fell over, while he watched them in good cheer. Only

*when some of them began coughing out blood did he
relent.*

*He stood over the woman with all the thoughts and
made one of her own. In it, she found one of those machines and brought it here.*

*She nodded, but, too weak to obey immediately, it
was minutes before she could rise and go about her new
errand.*

Borleias

Jag was waiting for Jaina when she emerged from her
briefing with General Antilles. "A moment of your time,
Great One?" he asked.

She cocked her head as if considering the demands on
her time, then nodded. "A moment."

He led her from the office and gestured down the hall
to a little-used conference room.

When they were within, and the door shut behind
them, she wrapped her arms around his neck, felt his
strength as he pulled her to him. She overbalanced him,
shoving him toward the wall beside the door, and kissed
him. The boom of Jag's shoulders hitting the wall startled
her out of the kiss and she laughed.

"There goes discretion," Jag said. He smiled, the expression characteristically subtle enough to be missed by
most observers.

"Got carried away," she said. "I'd *like* to be carried
away."

"I have the time if you do."

She shook her head, regretful. "I have to find a pilot to bring into Twin Suns. Your uncle is giving me a B-wing, the same one Lando used to escape from the *Record Time* mission, and I need a pilot for it." She gave him a wicked smile. "I get to go to anyone I want and see if I can persuade him to leave his squadron. Another reason for all the other squadron commanders to hate me."

"They don't need any more reasons. You're a better pilot than any of them. And you're even prettier than Colonel Darklighter of the Rogues."

She thumped his chest.

"All right, you're prettier than Captain Reth with the Blackmoons."

She thumped him harder.

"Prettier than Wes Janson with the Yellow Aces?"

"I'm going to break a bone you'll need later."

He finally grinned, pleased with her reaction to his teasing. "Do you have any pilots in mind?"

"I was thinking of asking Zekk."

Jag frowned. "He's not that good."

"Well, he's adequate, and I don't plan for the B-wing to be a major contributor to our skirmishes. I'm going to have it fitted as a control station for some of my goddess stunts. It'll be a little mobile headquarters."

"All the more reason to have a top-notch pilot in it. If it's not going to be an assault craft, it needs to be able to dodge and outfly pursuers."

"Do you have a pilot in mind?"

He considered, then nodded. "Shuttle pilot named Beelyath. He flies rescue missions picking up EV pilots. I've seen him do some pretty good tricks with his shuttle and fly into enemy fire to pick up pilots. He was one of the ones who helped us retrieve those ejected victims when the Yuuzhan Vong worldship came into the system. And he's Mon Cal. I know he has starfighter experience, which makes me suspect he has B-wing experience."

"I'll talk to him." She could feel her spirits sag just a little, could feel the smile leave her face. "I have to go. We just can't seem to find much time, can we?"

"Do you have another sixty seconds?"

"Yes."

He leaned down for another kiss.

Yuuzhan Vong Worldship, Coruscant Orbit

"Speak," Tsavong Lah said.

Nen Yim straightened from her bow. "I have subjected the samples I took from your arm to analysis."

"Is my situation favorable?"

"It is, Warmaster. The cure to your situation is no more complicated than refusing any further treatments at the hands of Ghithra Dal. Material I found upon your arm, material that must have come from Ghithra Dal touching you, inspires the radank leg to continue growing. It is absorbed into your skin and carried into the depths of your arm by the carrion-eaters. Remove the material and the condition should end."

"Yet if I were to discontinue treatment at the hands of Ghithra Dal, he would know that I suspect him."

Wisely, Nen Yim chose not to reply. Whether she had an opinion on the matter or not, she knew it was not her place to advise the warmaster on matters of strategy; any recommendation she could make would not be well received.

"Can you shape a material that would negate the effects of Ghithra Dal's doings while allowing him to continue to treat me?"

"Perhaps, Warmaster. But the material that coaxes your radank leg to grow as it does is very subtle, very complex. It could be that Ghithra Dal has been developing it for a very long time. Just having the samples I obtained, being able to observe their effects on other radank flesh, is not the same as knowing exactly how it works its effects, which is the first step toward counteracting it. It could take some considerable time to shape a defensive material. Time, or access to Ghithra Dal's shaping chambers."

Tsavong Lah considered, then nodded. "I will find a way to give you one, if not both. Withdraw."

When she was gone, he allowed himself to revel in an all-too-rare moment of simple elation. Doom was *not* upon him. The gods did not punish him. He faced nothing more serious than treachery . . . and treachery was something he well knew how to deal with.

Less familiar to him was the notion of reward, especially as it applied to one who was not Yuuzhan Vong, one who was not a loyal warrior or adviser. "Send in Viqi Shesh," he said.

Viqi entered the chamber, somewhat thrown off her rhythm by the fact that her escort guards, instead of staying beside her as she passed through the portal, remained behind. She hesitated just within the chamber, her quick glance taking in the presence of Tsavong Lah on his seat of command, of his advisers and servants staying well away along the walls.

"Come to me, my servant," the warmaster said.

Viqi Shesh offered a glowing, though entirely insincere, smile at Tsavong Lah and stepped forward to bow before him. She straightened and awaited his words, but he offered none until, at his gesture, three Yuuzhan Vong in his command chamber departed.

"I have summoned you," the warmaster said, "to acknowledge that you do indeed have worth. Your analysis of the situation with my arm was correct. I was afflicted with treachery. I offer you my congratulations."

Viqi actually felt her knees go weak. It wasn't from relief at being proven right. No, the story she'd concocted was supposed to be one that would buy her a considerable amount of time to find a way to escape. But she'd been right, the conspiracy had been rooted out, and her time was at an end.

Blast the conspirators. Blast them for existing, for being clumsy enough to be detected so early, for fouling up her plan.

She didn't let her smile waver. "The fact that I am of some service brings joy to my heart," she said. "I hope that I shall continue to be of worth to you."

"You shall. And for your next assignment, you will travel to Coruscant, below us. Yuuzhan Vong warriors have died there, and the burns that killed them suggest strongly that *Jeedai* are the culprits. You will go with Denua Ku and join a search unit there—a unit of warriors, and even our remaining voxyn. They may be dying off, but they can still hunt *Jeedai*. You will offer your insights to the warriors, who will run the *Jeedai* to ground. You will have the opportunity to distinguish yourself further in my service."

Words nearly failed her. On an expedition into the ruined world's depths, she'd be watched at least as closely as she had been observed here. She'd be forced to travel with a fast-moving pack of idiot warriors, running her into exhaustion. Dirt and sweat would be her companions. And voxyn—the thought of being within kilometers of the ferocious creatures was terrifying.

She offered the warmaster her most alluring smile and bowed again. The gesture gave her time to find her voice. "I live to obey, Warmaster."

Vannix, Vankalay System

"Will you be offering your political support to Senator Gadan?" The old woman was stiff-backed, as alert as a hawk-bat on the lookout for prey, and the downiness of her white hair, which should have softened her appearance, should have made her grandmotherly, instead gave her the aspect of some mad Force-wizard from a scary bedtime story. Too, the jagged scar zigzagging across her forehead, which hinted at a fractured skull or even brain damage in some long-ago battle, was hardly reassuring.

"Addath enjoys my every confidence . . ." Leia said, her voice smooth. Han waited, though, because he could detect the unspoken *but* at the end of her statement.

Admiral Apelben Werl offered up a faint, exasperated

sigh, and leaned back in her chair. Her expression suggested that, though this meeting was not over, no further part of it had any purpose.

". . . personally," Leia concluded.

The admiral gave her a closer look. "And professionally? Politically?"

"Professionally, I favor the harshest possible resistance to the Yuuzhan Vong."

"Really." The admiral suddenly did not look as forbidding. "I have no talent for deception, so I'll ask straight out. What would it take to persuade you to lend me your support in this campaign? To help swing the population's vote toward defense and away from appeasement?"

That was, in fact, exactly what Han and Leia had come to offer—a present of public support from the famous Solos.

Leia opened her mouth to make that statement, but Han cut her off. "That's what I'd like to ask you. What *would* it take? What do you have?"

The admiral smiled. It was the expression of an experienced bantha trader. "Are you looking for weapons? Vehicles? I suspect that Borleias is already far better supplied than I am."

"We're looking for *surprises*," Han said. "The Vong are going to hit us like an asteroid bombardment. Ultimately they're going to take Borleias and then begin swarming out in all directions again. What can you give us to make their conquest of Borleias worse for them? What can you give us that they won't expect?"

Leia kept her mouth shut. She gave Han a sidelong look. He expected it to be an angry one, but he was wrong; she was curious, evaluating.

"How are the Yuuzhan Vong fixed for naval warfare?" the admiral asked.

Han frowned. "Space navy?"

"*Water* navy."

"Umm, I know they have some aquatic creatures—transports. And creatures that allow someone to breathe underwater. But we haven't been faced with any significant water-based assaults."

"Meaning they might not have any, or they might still have them in reserve." The admiral leaned back. She rested her elbows on the arms of her padded chair, placing her fingertips together before her as if to suggest a sharply sloped roof. "I've spent the better part of my military career upgrading our armed forces to deal with external threats rather than internal ones. Meaning that I have access to a large number of water navy vessels, surface and submersible, most of them currently decommissioned and crewed by droids. They're antiques . . . but an antique exploding shell can still kill an enemy if it's placed correctly. I could give you several submersibles, large ones for oceans and small ones for rivers, if you can bring me a transport to carry them. And then you'd have weapons, however unlikely, that the Yuuzhan Vong have not encountered on Borleias."

"Are they fully armed and operational?" Leia asked.

"Fully armed and operational."

"How many?"

"I can give you two of the larger submersibles, about the size of Carrack cruisers, and four smaller units suited to river traffic."

"Make it four and four and you have a deal," Han said.

The admiral's bantha-trader grin widened. "What deal? *You* haven't offered anything specific."

"We're offering a guarantee," Leia said. "We guarantee that you win the election. You'll see the vote turn your way, and you'll be able to see our hand in the turnaround."

"Done," the admiral said. "The day after I'm installed in the office of the Presider, you receive your eight submersibles." She extended her hand, and Leia and Han took it in turn.

Once they were out of the admiral's office, and off the military base she used as her headquarters, Leia asked, "All right. So you got us something for our help when we were expecting nothing. What, precisely, do we do with eight submersibles we don't need? Which won't do us any good against the Yuuzhan Vong?"

Han gave her his crookedest *this-time-I've-got-you-my-dear* smile. "Plenty."

"Let's hear it."

"First, when we get the transport for the submersibles here, without informing Admiral Earnest back there, we leave one of the big submersibles and one of the small ones behind, in the nearest large body of water."

"For what purpose?"

"You've been thinking of the resistance cells as being set up in the major cities, with vehicles and ordnance stored in caves, forgotten underground tanks, whatever the operatives can find. But those submersibles, however antiquated, can serve as preliminary resistance bases . . . and can be used to find caves that can only be reached from underwater. They're not weapons to use on the Yuuzhan Vong, Leia, they're mobile homes that fire explosive shells. Enough for four whole resistance cells."

"Ooh." She smiled and considered the idea.

"So how do we do it?"

"Do what?"

"Rig the election."

"I have no idea. I was following your lead, remember? I've never rigged an election."

Han sighed. "Well, you'd better figure it out fast. Or I'll have to take your temporary scoundrel's license away."

Borleias

Jag sat propped up against the side of his clawcraft, engrossed in his datapad. The special operations docking bay was, for once, comparatively quiet, only a few clankings and swear words floating in from the far corner to indicate mechanics' activities. He was not too engrossed, though, to see the pair of booted feet appear before him.

He looked up, and up, into the blue features of Shawnkyr Nuruodo. A Chiss officer, she'd been his wingmate on his first trip into New Republic space at the start of the Yuuzhan Vong crisis, his sole partner during his recent return, and his second-in-command when he'd founded Vanguard Squadron on Hapes. Now, while he flew with Twin Suns Squadron, she led the Vanguards.

"Colonel, may I sit?"

"Of course."

She lowered herself and sat cross-legged opposite him.

"I heard that Vanguard Squadron had been classified as fit for elite and special operations," Jag said. "That you were going to be stationed groundside with the rest of us. Congratulations."

"It's just a matter of training, motivating, enforcing discipline." Shawnkyr shrugged. "I came to you because it would be inappropriate for me to reject their promotion, however well intended, without first talking to you, since you founded the squadron."

"Why would you refuse it?"

"Because I don't intend to lead the squadron much longer. Nor should you return to it. It's time for us to leave."

"Explain that."

"Our plan was specific, Colonel. We came back to evaluate the threat the Yuuzhan Vong posed to Chiss society. We've had time to make that evaluation. Now we should report back with our findings."

Jag regarded her levelly. He'd anticipated this confrontation for some time. "And what would your report tell our high command?"

"That the Yuuzhan Vong are a significant threat to us, to the Empire, to any societal structure that does not resemble theirs. That the New Republic is shattering on all fronts, and that it is only a matter of time before the Yuuzhan Vong mop up here and spread out to reach us."

"I agree with your conclusions."

"Then let's go."

He shook his head. "I've come to additional conclusions that suggest we should stay."

"May I hear them?"

"I believe that this engagement, here on Borleias, will be the surest test of Yuuzhan Vong determination and character. Only in seeing how this campaign plays out can we provide a definitive analysis of the enemy that our people will someday face."

"So it is your plan to return to Chiss space immediately upon the fall of Borleias."

"No."

"Then I have failed to understand you."

"I didn't describe all my conclusions. A second one, not related to the first, is that my presence here may affect coming events, in a small but perhaps measurable way, and that to abandon this campaign now would not only do it harm, but eventually do harm to our people as well. Any damage I do to the enemy here is damage the enemy cannot do to us when they reach us."

"So you will not leave at all."

"I will leave . . . eventually."

Shawnkyr considered his words silently. The distant swearing increased in volume, to match a sudden spate of hammering that sounded like revenge rather than repair, before fading to its normal levels. "May I speak freely? Pilot to pilot?"

"Of course."

"I think that sentiment is clouding your judgment. I think that the notion of not being here when Jaina Solo is endangered, or killed, is what is keeping you from your duty. But your duty is to our people, and to no one else."

"Is that true?"

"Yes. You have sworn an oath. An oath of loyalty and obedience."

"What if the best observation of loyalty leads on a course that diverges from obedience?"

"It can't."

"I think you're wrong. I am not loyal to the Chiss because my parents were accepted by them, or because I have grown up among them. I'm loyal because they embody traits I admire and respect; they make those traits part of the very fiber of our society. Traits such as strength in the face of aggression, such as acknowledgment of duty before self-interest. The Chiss, however, are not the only people with admirable traits, not the only ones who deserve to survive the Yuuzhan Vong, and not the only ones I identify with. Not anymore."

"So you think you are supporting a greater good by staying."

"Yes. We can assemble a report and transmit it by holocomm. We can explain that more evaluation is needed . . . which is the truth."

"As you see it."

"Yes."

Shawnkyr's expression changed. It did not harden against him, which was one possibility Jag had acknowledged but did not welcome. Instead, a subtle sadness suffused it. He doubted anyone not well acquainted with her would have detected it.

"I will stay," she said, "until Borleias falls. Then I will return home."

"Thank you."

"But if I die here, I want you to promise to return in my place. If I stay here, I am delaying the execution of my duty. If I die, you must carry out my duty."

Jag thought about it. And to his way of thinking, she had presented him with an impenetrable argument. His only choices really were to agree, or to bid her farewell now. And the defenders of Borleias would be that much worse off without her leadership and piloting skills.

"I agree," he said.

* * *

Tarc shook Wolam Tser's hand and said, "I thought you'd be tall."

Wolam—graying and distinguished, elder statesman of Coruscant holojournalism—exchanged an amused look with Tam before returning his attention to the child. "I am indeed taller than you."

"Yes, but I thought you'd be two meters at least."

"An illusion, child. When you are in front of the holocam, you dominate the image. Everything else is secondary to you. So it becomes easy for watchers to believe you are of extravagant proportions."

"Oh." Tarc nodded sagely, as though Wolam's words made perfect sense to him.

They stood in the lobby of the biotics building, meters from the door out onto the kill zone. The lobby was now set up with desks and stations for junior officers and enlisted personnel. Some directed traffic through the building, others ensured physical and remote security, and still others were located here rather than in locations more appropriate to their specific tasks because there was no room in those locations for them.

But there was still a little open space away from the main flow of traffic, and that's where they stood, three generations of homeless civilian males surrounded by military operations.

"So, what's it to be today?" Tam fished around in his expansive bag. He extracted a holocam, a model small enough to be easily concealed in his large hands, with a strap to fit around the back of one hand. This unit he handed to Tarc. He showed the boy how to tighten the strap, where to peer into the holocam in order to see what the holocam's lens saw.

"How the defenders live," Wolam said. "Bedchambers, meals, medicine, refreshers, exhaustion, stolen moments. Spot interviews as I decide. No setups, no analysis."

"Why record anything?" Tarc asked. "With Coruscant conquered, aren't you out of a job?"

"Never," Wolam said. "I am a historian. Unless nothing sapient survives in all the universe, I have a job, a calling. Someday people will be curious about what happened here, and what we do, recording and analyzing, may be the only surviving answers to their questions."

"In other words," Tam said, "once you know what you are, nobody can ever take your 'job' from you. They can change your circumstances. They can make it hard or impossible for you to get paid." He shot Wolam a sly look, and Wolam gratified him by giving him an indignant little scowl. "But your 'job' is part of you."

Tarc fell silent, considering that.

Tam pulled out his main-duty holocam, a recently manufactured Crystal Memories Model 17, lighter and possessing more standard memory than previous models. He passed its strap over his head. The strap grazed against the fresh scar behind his right ear, the surgical scar over his new implant, the implant that was now his only defense against the deadly headaches brought on by his conditioning. *Changed circumstances, indeed.*

"What should I record?" Tarc asked. "Everything?"

"At first, if you want to," Tam said. "What I do is to record everything Wolam points at, until he gives me the kill sign—"

Obligingly, Wolam made a gesture like an abbreviated ax chop. His pale hands against his black garments made the gesture especially easy to see.

"—and also anything I find interesting or unusual. You do the same, and when we review your recordings together I'll point out what looks interesting from a historical-record perspective."

"Don't spend *too* much of your time on the girls," Wolam cautioned.

Tarc's face twisted into an expression of disdain. "You don't have to worry about *that*."

Coruscant

"I hate this," Luke said.

"Waiting?" Mara, eyes closed, adjusted her pose, trying to make herself comfortable—as comfortable as one could be propped up against a deformed metal wall in a hallway dripping with rainwater that had filtered through thirty or forty stories of ruined skyscraper above, on a planet ruled and increasingly ruined by alien enemies.

"Of course, waiting." Luke had returned half an hour before from the latest scattering run. Not everyone was back; a few meters down the hallway, Danni was cataloging plant samples, and Baljos and Elassar were playing sabacc underneath a flickering glowlight. The others were still unaccounted for.

"Which points to a great failing with the Jedi. The lightsabers."

Luke gave his wife a suspicious look. "A failing?"

She nodded. "You can't sharpen them. Back when I was, well, in my previous career, I could get through any boring stretch by sharpening my knives. It takes just enough of your attention to keep boredom at bay, and keeps your tools at their best. With vibroblades, even if they lose power, you still have a nice sharp edge for whatever needs cutting."

Elassar looked back over his shoulder at her. "Sometimes I think you can be spooky just singing nursery songs."

"That's easy." Mara's face took on an expression of motherly concern. "Hush, child," she sang, "the night is mild, and slumber smiles upon you . . ." But she sang the familiar tune in a minor key, making the words unsettling rather than soothing, evoking the mental image of an anthropomorphic Slumber that was a night-monster stealing silently up to a crib.

But she fell silent, and Luke could feel from her what he felt in himself—a wish, one that could not be fulfilled now, that they could be where Ben was, introducing him to all the little surprises and delights that came with just being alive. Instead they were here in this endless expanse of death.

Then Mara opened her eyes and looked back down the hall.

Luke felt it too—not danger, but some agitation expressed through the Force. He rose and put his hand on his lightsaber hilt.

Up through a hole in the floor swung Tahiri. She landed and extended a hand down, helping Face up to this level. She was somber. He looked dubious.

When she saw Luke, she gulped—not out of uncertainty or fear, Luke thought, but out of nausea. "I found something," she said.

FIVE

Now he had a name.

It had taken time, and frequent yanking of thoughts out of their heads, for him to understand names. Sounds that belonged only to one being. Each of them had a name, and when he understood that, it became vital for him to have one, too.

He was more powerful, more important than any of them. It was not right for them to have names and him not to.

So they called him Nyax. Lord Nyax. Nyax was his name, and no other might have it. Lord was a thing that made his name bigger, better. Lord meant that he was more important than anything.

Satisfied with that recognition of his status, he smiled up at the workers crawling over the surface of the tall, tall machine.

They repaired it. They cleared rubble from around it. Soon it would go. Soon it would knock down the black wall he hated.

Soon he, Lord Nyax, would have everything he wanted—which was everything. All beings would do his bidding. Except, perhaps, those whom his senses could not detect; they were surprisingly resistant to pain. Them he would kill, every one.

Coruscant

"You found a tank of goo," said Mara.

They stood on a metal walkway high over a deep, vast chamber. They'd descended through several levels of ruined factory machinery to reach it. Now, their comparatively tiny glowrods illuminated tiny patches of the floor far below.

Not that there was much detail to illuminate. The greater portion of the floor was dominated by a gleaming white metal tank, dozens of meters wide and long, but only a meter and a half tall, and filled nearly to its rim by some reddish fluid.

Most of the others looked disinterested, or immediately cast about for another place to sit down and rest.

Not so the scientists. Baljos and Danni immediately pulled out sensor devices and began sampling the local environment.

"Definitely a living thing," Danni said. "A large quantity of monocellular life-forms."

"This chamber is unusually high in oxygen, unusually low in carbon dioxide and world-shaping toxins." Baljos pulled off his helmet and tugged the perfumed patches of cloth from his nose; he took several deep breaths, and a smile broke out on his face. "Clean air. Thought I'd never experience it again."

The others followed suit. Luke took in several breaths free of the stench of decay; he felt his spirits lift.

He checked himself before congratulating Tahiri on finding such a useful resource. She hadn't been happy when she'd returned to the others, and she wasn't happy now. She stared down into the red muck with an expression suggesting suspicion, even dread.

Luke extended his own Force senses in that direction.

He could immediately feel the life-form in the tank. It was simple, undifferentiated. It was also comparatively healthy, though he thought he felt the slightest tinge of hunger to it.

But there was something beyond the life-form, something below. It was a twinge of dark side energy. No, not a twinge—though not strong, it was constant.

"Did you find a way down from there?" Luke asked.

Tahiri shook her head. "I looked around for about an hour but couldn't find the access."

"What access?" Danni asked.

There was no power in this chamber, but a surviving metal ladder gave them an easy descent to the floor level. Up close, the tank was no more impressive; it was a rectangular pond of villainous-looking slime.

"I think," Luke said, "that this is a devourer tank."

Mara nodded soberly. "Based on your extensive knowledge of factories and city engineering."

"*Based* on something Wedge Antilles said to me once." Luke gave his wife an expression of simulated sternness. "There was a time, a few years ago, when he thought he wanted to give up the life of a fighting officer and turn his skills to building things, fixing things. So he headed a military crew that was deconstructing portions of Coruscant that were falling apart. So new portions of Coruscant could be built there and fall apart later. He described something like this. A huge flat area filled with a living material."

"Oh, that's right," Face said. "You mentioned that the first time I met you."

"Years ago," Luke said.

"Yes."

"But you still can't tell me when."

Face shook his head. "Official secrets. If you were to remember what I looked like, who I was then, I still couldn't admit it to you."

Luke sighed.

"What's it for?" asked Danni. "The tank."

"It's one type of garbage disposal." Luke held a hand just above the red surface. In the light from Mara's glow rod, he saw the fluid swell, just slightly, toward his hand. "Anything organic that gets thrown in here is consumed. Every so often, they pump out the goo and scrape out the material that accumulates at the bottom of the tank."

"Here's the pumping equipment." Tahiri stood a few meters away, looking at a wall console near tubes that led from the tank and entered the wall. She pried the cover off the console and peered within. "Why didn't the Yuuzhan Vong smash the tank? Everything around here was smashed. We know they've been here."

"Because it's organic rather than technological, I guess." Luke watched as the redness under his hand rose almost to touch him; then he pulled his hand away and it settled down again. "That's interesting. This stuff is obviously able to sense food, and to cooperate to reach it."

"Interesting isn't the word I'd use for it." Face sat down next to the wall, relaxing. "Baljos, can't you fine-tune that sensor of yours to detect intelligent, unattached ladies between the ages of twenty and forty?"

"If I could, do you think I'd still be working as a scientist?"

"Good point."

Tahiri, now up to her waist in the hole in the wall where the console cover had been, suddenly shoved her way out. She straightened, a puzzled expression on her face. "It's a fake."

"What's a fake?" Luke asked.

"This console. The computer equipment looks real enough, but it's not actually hooked up to any pumping equipment."

Luke and Mara moved over to look. Luke leaned into the hole and peered down at the jumble of wiring and machinery within the wall. It did not seem to have been damaged by Yuuzhan Vong depredations, but he could still trace the wiring from the pumping controls a mere meter to where it ended in a small metallic box instead of down the wall to where the pumping equipment had to be. "That *is* odd. Bhindi, computers are your strength; you want to dig into this and see what you can tell us?"

"Sure."

Face sighed. "If we're going to be here a while—Kell, mark exits out of this chamber, and then we'll set up a watch on the more likely Yuuzhan Vong approaches."

"To hear is to obey, Great One."

"Appealing to my vanity will *not* get you out of sentry duty. Well, not this time, anyway."

Luke returned to the tank, frowning. What was the use of having one of these without having pumping equipment attached to it? Though it would take years, the tank would eventually fill up with waste residue that would displace the red organism, might even be toxic to it.

He opened himself more to the Force and could immediately sense the red stuff again. He could feel its dimensions, could almost sense the sharp lines of its width and breadth and depth—but in one place toward the center of the tank, that depth abruptly decreased, as though there were a protrusion of some sort from the tank's surface. "I need to go out there."

Mara, beside him, snickered. "That'll be a quick, painful swim."

"Maybe." This was a living thing, awake and aware in the Force. Perhaps . . . He lowered his left hand toward it again, trying to reach the organisms through the Force, uppermost in his thoughts and feelings the idea, *I am not food. I am not food.*

His hand came down on the surface of the organisms. He tensed, ready to snatch his hand back, but he could feel the organism go quiet, docile beneath his flesh. He felt no sensation of burning or any sort of pain.

He took his hand away. His palm was clean; no trace of red showed on it.

Hurriedly, he stripped off his false vonduun crab armor. "I need an air mask," he said. "Completely inorganic material. Preferably with a faceplate."

"I have you covered." Face dug around in his pack, came up with something irregular and gleaming, no larger than Tahiri's fist. "My backup. It's a hood made of transparisteel foil with an oxygen canister. It'll give you maybe five minutes."

"Perfect."

"Luke, I don't want to discourage your curiosity, but I have to remind you, if something goes wrong, this is an *exceptionally* embarrassing way to die."

Luke grinned at Mara. "I'll trust you to improve the story. Luke Skywalker goes out in a blaze of glory in battle with a hideous red devourer." He handed her his lightsaber.

Armor off and hood in place, Luke looked over the red pond awaiting him. *I am not food. I am not food.* He swung over the lip of the tank and dropped into the goo, felt it close around his legs, rise to his waist.

But there was no pain. He moved forward. The stuff was warm and heavy enough to significantly retard his progress—much like the thickest of the sludge-ponds he'd struggled through on Dagobah, so many years ago.

In the Force, he could clearly feel the place where the red goo became more shallow, and in moments he stood next to that point. He turned on the oxygen canister, offered his wife and Tahiri a jaunty wave, and went under the surface.

Darkness closed on him immediately. *Not a job for the claustrophobic,* he decided. *I am not food. I am not food.*

Reaching down, he groped around until he felt the object he was seeking. It had a curved edge and was a little larger than some circular steering controls . . . As he felt around it, he realized that it was a metal wheel, solid of construction, attached to a hub attached to the tank's surface.

It was, in fact, identical to the sort of hatch-closing wheel found on many types of war vessels.

It wouldn't spin in one direction, but obligingly rotated a quarter-turn in the other . . . and immediately Luke felt a vibration in the metal wheel, in the tank, throughout the goo. He hurriedly rose. When he stood up in the middle of the tank, the goo fell away from him, not clinging.

The chamber was changing.

From the floor in front of the tank something was rising—a rectangular plug three meters wide by three meters long.

The top portion of the plug was metal plating, half a meter thick. Below it was stone, and the stone portion kept rising, one meter, two, three, while Luke slogged his way over toward the side of the tank.

Then the stone gave way to machinery, another three meters of metal construction, before the whole apparatus clanked to a stop.

Mara and the others were well back from the apparatus, covering it with blasters. "What did you do?"

Luke pulled the breathing mask off. "I turned a wheel. Something obviously still has power."

He saw Face glance in his direction and grin. Tahiri, in the light from the glowrods, looked at him, flushed red, and turned away, staring back at the plug. Danni joined her in this scrutiny.

Mara suppressed a laugh; it came out as a cough. "Luke, before you step out and join us, out of respect for those of us you're not married to, you might want to be sure that you're presentable."

Luke glanced down. His torso was bare. He reached down into the goo. The submerged portions of his garment were missing, too.

He reached the edge of the tank and stood close to it. "I guess I forgot to tell the stuff, 'My clothes aren't food, either.' "

"I guess you did."

"Could you pass me my pack?"

The plug was a turbolift housing. Once Luke was out of the tank and dressed in spare clothes—his black cling-suit, which was more likely to be visible in the joints and gaps of his false vonduun crab armor—he could see the doors that gave access to the turbolift within. They opened readily enough when Luke neared them, spilling bright artificial glow out onto the floor.

He peeked within. The control panel had only three settings: MAINTENANCE, HOUSING, and RESEARCH.

"Research," Danni said.

Luke snorted. "I knew you'd say that."

"We *all* did," Bhindi said. "But I have no objection."

Face brought up his comlink. "Kell, Elassar?"

"We hear you." The voice was Kell's.

"We may be gone for a little while. Don't be surprised or alarmed."

"As long as Aunt Tahiri is going to be back in time for my bedtime story, I'll be all right."

Tahiri sighed. "He's starting to get on my nerves. Doesn't he know that's a bad idea?"

Baljos snorted. "He knows. But he's a demolitions expert. He likes playing with things that blow up in his face."

They entered the turbolift. Its doors shut them in. Luke hit the button reading RESEARCH.

The turbolift did not immediately move. An antiquated droid voice, coming from an overhead speaker, addressed them: "State your name and Bluenek authorization code. You have ten seconds to comply . . . before you die."

Vannix, Vankalay System

"We can probably manage twenty or more public appearances in the next four days," Leia said. She was whispering, her words nearly drowned out by her other voice, the one emerging from R2-D2, who was replaying the recording of an argument they'd had a few days ago about Corellia's Senators. "I'm not sure what the anti-Jedi sentiment is on Vannix; if there's any significant amount, we ought to downplay me and promote you. Han Solo, the Hero." She sat at one end of the most comfortable of the chamber's couches.

Han lay stretched out on his back on the couch, his head in Leia's lap. He stared incuriously at the ornate floral pattern on the ceiling of their quarters. "Sounds like a lot of work."

"Politics is hard work, Han. Hasn't being married to me all these years taught you that?"

"Oh, yes. Which is one reason I'm still not a politician. And I have to point out, we could do all that work and she could still win."

"It's true."

"In which case the Yuuzhan Vong get another allied

world, and we don't get our submersibles. And I've already sent off for the transport for them, so I'll look like an idiot."

"Also true. So?"

"So there are two reasons to play sabacc, Leia. For fun, or to make money. If your main goal is to have fun, losing a little money isn't too bad. If you're out to make money, and you do, not having fun isn't much of a hardship."

Leia looked into her husband's eyes, suspicious. "I worry whenever anything that sounds even vaguely like philosophy comes out of your mouth. What are you getting at?"

He flashed her a *trust-me* grin. "I'm getting at the fact that you're talking about playing a fair game. It's much better under these circumstances to cheat at cards. Better, faster, and surer."

Coruscant

Luke ignited his lightsaber and held the blade over his head, the better to deflect any blaster damage raining down upon them. But he didn't know what sorts of booby-traps had been set up on this turbolift, didn't know if it would be blaster damage or poison gas, blades, or acid, attacks from above or below. "Mara, cut the door open," he said.

His wife looked confused, eyes flickering back and forth, not focusing on the door before them.

"You have five seconds remaining," said the droid voice.

"Tahiri," Luke said. "The door."

Tahiri lit her lightsaber with a *snap-hiss* and plunged its point into the metal at the seam. The door began to glow and soften, but it was obvious that it would take far more than five seconds to cut an exit-sized hole in it.

"Authorization Bluenek two seven ithor four nine naboo," Mara said.

"Accepted," said the droid voice. "Welcome, Mara Jade."

The turbolift dropped. Tahiri, thrown off-balance, stumbled, her lightsaber blade swinging around toward Bhindi. Luke caught and deflected the accidental blow, and Tahiri snapped her lightsaber off almost instantly. "Sorry," she said.

"Don't be." Luke shut his own weapon off. He turned to Mara. "You *knew* about this?"

The turbolift stopped and the doors snapped open, revealing a hallway, its contents and walls made visible by light spilling in from doorways to either side. The hall was strewn with wreckage, pieces of chairs, chunks of ceiling, fragments of droids.

The air was cool, but strong with the smell of decay; it overpowered the perfume in Luke's nostrils. But there was, in Luke's ears, for the first time in days, the hum of air-processing units and other powered equipment: the hum of civilization.

There were, however, no voices. No distant noises suggesting broadcasts or recordings being listened to.

Tahiri looked at black scorching on the wall nearest her. "Lightsaber hit," she said. Her voice was subdued, a whisper appropriate to this setting. "It looks like some of the droids got it that way, too."

Luke returned his attention to his wife. "Mara?"

Recovering, Mara shook her head. "No, I didn't know about this. But there was a chance—I used various access codes back when I was the Emperor's Hand. Some gave me access to credit accounts, to weapon caches, to military cooperation. I had a Bluenek Section code I never had occasion to use. It's been a long time. I almost didn't remember it."

Baljos rose from a pile of rubbish—a collapsed desk, a toppled cabinet, a spray pattern of body parts Luke thought were more droid components until he took a closer look at them. "Fatality here," Baljos said, his voice unusually subdued. "Human female, middle-aged, cut into about eight pieces. Lightsaber damage again, I think." He turned away from the grisly spectacle. "Danni?"

Danni held one of her sensors in her hand. "There's a lot of electromagnetical. From functioning equipment, I think. It's masking any major biological energy, if there is any."

Luke closed his eyes and extended his perceptions into the Force.

He didn't find any signs of large living organisms. He couldn't. As soon as he began to extend his awareness, he became aware of it, the darkness he'd detected from above. Here, it was much closer, a suffusion of anger and violent intent that threatened to make him sick to his stomach. He opened his eyes and shook his head at the other Jedi. "We search the hard way," he said.

It was an expansive scientific complex. This floor had indeed been a scientific research station . . . decades in the past. Computer systems dating from before Luke's birth lay under dust covers, and Danni identified one long-unused laboratory as being devoted to cellular analysis.

The most curious feature of the floor, however, was a chamber to one side of the laboratories. It held nothing more than a long apparatus that looked like a bed with a lid. "A hermetically sealed sleeping unit," Bhindi suggested.

"An Imperial-era suspended animation unit," Baljos corrected. "Later modified to be different from production units, since whatever was in it was nearly three meters tall. Not human."

Privately, Luke disagreed. The characteristic of the chamber that many of the others couldn't detect was that it reeked of the dark side of the Force—it was the source, or at least *a* source, of the disquiet he had felt. And it somehow suggested humanity to him, humanity at its worst.

There was something familiar about this darkness, familiar and ghastly. "Can you tell what it was?" Luke asked.

Baljos looked at the unit. The transparisteel cover had been thrown aside with such strength and violence that it was warped, the hinges along one side and locking latch on the other broken. The machinery that would have surrounded the sleeper like insulation was torn free from its housing and lay in pieces around the chamber. So did four medical droids—Luke *thought* it was four, gauging from the number of droid heads within sight, but he had to admit that their state of dismemberment made actual calculations difficult. "Depends on whether any memory survived in this machinery," Baljos said. "More Bhindi's department than mine. But if it did, and even if the memory doesn't obligingly say 'Ithorian' or 'wampa' or something, I might be able to figure it out based on the settings and life-sign readings it recorded."

Mara stuck her head in through a darkened doorway at the corner of the chamber. "Luke, this should interest you." She tossed something toward Luke's feet.

From the manner with which it twisted and curled as it flew, Luke suspected that it was part of an amphistaff, but when it landed at his feet, he saw that he'd been wrong. This sinuous body was covered in fur and had legs ending in needlelike claws. It had been dead for some days. "Ysalamiri," he said.

"Your friend and mine," Mara said. "There are pieces of a cage and some Myrkr tree limbs in here. And access halls to similar chambers at the other seven corners of the chamber. Dead ysalamiri there, too."

"That actually makes sense." Ysalamiri were reptilian creatures of the planet Myrkr. Generally docile, content to live on their trees, they had a trait that made them of considerable interest to Jedi and other Force-wielders: They projected a sort of energy that repelled the Force, kept its energies at bay. An ysalamiri's projections canceled the effects of the Force out to a distance of ten meters. Those who knew their traits had used them to hide things from the Jedi, even to capture the Jedi and temporarily strip them of their powers. "If this has been here all these years, I should have felt it before now while we were living on Coruscant. But if this chamber was surrounded by ysalamiri, with their anti-Force bubbles overlapping, it would have masked the presence of whatever was here."

"Whatever it *is*," Face said. "The way I read it, this thing woke up, busted out, destroyed all the droids around it. With just its strength, you'll notice, because there are no burn marks on the droids in here or on the suspended animation unit. When it gets into other parts of the complex, it gets its hands on a lightsaber and finishes the job. Then it destroys the other droids and the ysalamiri."

Luke nodded. "That could be it. But how did it get out of this complex? With the ysalamiri dead, we'd feel it if it were still here."

Minutes later, they had their answer.

Two levels above, on the floor that had been marked MAINTENANCE, Tahiri pointed upward into what had been a machinery-access niche. The metal panel that had been the niche's ceiling was gone; the edges of the hole were burned. "This leads to a water and atmosphere supply shaft," she said. "It has pipes in it, but also plenty of open space. I climbed up a pretty good distance; it leads up to a hole in a wall a couple of levels up from the chamber with the red goo."

"Is the hole easy to access?" Bhindi asked.

Tahiri shook her head. "Not for normal people. It's about five meters up on a ten-meter wall. But anybody with a ladder could get up to it."

"Especially obvious?"

"No, it's on one side of a storage house. Full of carpeting and wall decorations. Really useful stuff. No sign of people there. Why?"

"Because," Bhindi said, "in addition to this mystery of a three-meter-tall whatever-it-is, we have here a complex that still has power, a complex that's hidden from sight.

It's big enough to be the headquarters of the first resistance cell I organize."

"Not a good idea," Luke said. "That three-meter being knows where it is. He or she may come back."

"So we close up its exit hole, hide it, maybe secure that approach against intrusion." Bhindi fixed Luke with a grave look. "Besides, I suspect that you're not going to let that thing keep walking around out there. Are you?"

"I hope not." Luke looked up the hole; only a few meters of the water and atmosphere pipes were visible in the dim light from their glow rods. "It's very strong, very evil. And I have no idea whether we have enough resources here to stop it."

SIX

Vannix, Vankalay System

The tall man wrapped in a gray hooded cloak entered
the shop. His face was shadowed by the hood; under the
cloak his garments were plain, dark trousers and tunic of
the sort that any laborer might wear. Behind him rolled a
blue and white R2-class astromech.

The shop owner, an aged human man with a fringe of
white hair and rheumy blue eyes, sighed. He moved his
hand inconspicuously under the counter to grip the hilt
of the blaser pistol holstered there. He hated clients who
preferred to remain anonymous. So often they were on
business that invited government scrutiny, and those
were the best cases—the worst were when they were here
to rob rather than employ. But this one, at least, had
brought a droid, which suggested his business was actually in the shop owner's line.

"You repair droids?" the cloaked man asked. His
accent was foreign. Corellian, perhaps.

"We do," the shop owner said. "We have cleverly concealed that information on the sign outside, the blinking
apparatus that reads NINGAL'S DROID REPAIR."

Apparently oblivious to irony, the visitor nodded. "I want this one fixed."

"Certainly. What's the nature of his malfunction?"

The cloaked man sighed. "He has a partner, a protocol droid, and they argue. The protocol droid apparently hacked into his speech translators and now all he does is insult. We want that programming removed. We also want his recording memory wiped. Not his other programming—just the recording memory."

"Easily done."

"You can wipe it in such a way that what's on it can't ever be retrieved? Not by anyone, no matter how good?"

"Also easily done. I just have to overwrite every portion of his recording memory with something else—several times, to make sure the most sensitive retrieval equipment can't dig underneath the new material."

The cloaked man breathed a sigh of relief. "Good."

The shop owner tapped the counter. "Plug in here, please."

The astromech obligingly rolled forward. He extended his datajack arm and plugged in; a moment later, a text screen lit up on the shop owner's countertop.

"What's your name, little fellow?" the shop owner asked.

The words THAT'S NONE OF YOUR BUSINESS appeared on the screen. IN ANY CASE, YOUR FACIAL FEATURE SET SUGGESTS THAT YOU DO NOT HAVE THE INTELLIGENCE TO RETAIN MY NAME FOR MORE THAN A NANOSECOND. IT IS EVIDENT THAT YOU HAVE BEEN TAUGHT TO REPEAT SOUNDS YOU HAVE HEARD AND THAT YOU UNDERSTAND NEITHER THE WORDS YOU HEAR

NOR THE ONES THAT EMERGE FROM YOUR MOUTH.

"I see what you mean," the shop owner said. "Well, this is a simple task. We should be through later this afternoon."

"Good," the cloaked man said. He turned to leave.

"Wait a moment. How do I notify you when we're done?"

"I'll just return."

"And we haven't discussed my fee yet."

"That's right. I don't have any local money."

"I'm afraid New Republic credits are no good here."

"I have an extra power cell for the Artoo. Fully charged."

"If you have two, that would suffice."

"For 'a simple task' you should be through with later this afternoon?"

The shop owner smiled. "Is it a new power cell?"

"Brand new. I bought it on Coruscant about a month before it fell." The man returned to the counter and produced a standard astromech power cell from beneath his cloak. Its reflective surfaces gleamed in the shop owner's counter light.

The shop owner picked it up, hefted it, looked at its charge indicator. "Done," he said. "I'll see you this afternoon."

"Thank you."

Two minutes after the cloaked man left, a young woman entered. She was no customer, the shop owner knew. Despite her fair hair, she seemed somehow somber, and she had the bearing of a military officer.

She displayed an identichip bearing the seal of Vannix

Intelligence and put it in the countertop reader for a moment. The display took only a moment to read CONFIRMED.

"What did that man want?" she asked.

The shop owner sighed. Sometimes it was a curse, always knowing when a customer was going to cause trouble.

Senator Addath Gadan kept the smile fixed to her face. Sometimes that extra effort kept her voice similarly pleasant, similarly light. "You can't make the rally at all?"

Leia Organa Solo's voice sounded from her desktop comlink, just as light, just as artificial. "Not today's. I'm sorry, Addath. Han is ill and I just feel I need to stay with him. But send me the schedule for tomorrow's events and I should be able to make those."

"I'll do that. Please give him my best wishes."

"Of course."

Addath sat and fumed. Ill, indeed. Han Solo hadn't been too ill to sneak out of the Presider's residence, eluding two layers of her security before being detected and followed by the third. Any smart operative could have penetrated one or two layers from the inside out, as he did, but Solo had managed it with an R2 astromech in tow, a pretty good trick.

Not that, ultimately, it had done any good. She hit the desktop button again, and once more the conversation, copied from the R2 unit's recording memory before it had been wiped, replayed itself.

First was Leia's voice, a whisper: "So what's the total?"

Han's voice was similarly hushed. "He's promising

two squadrons of starfighters, and a light carrier to serve as their base ship."

"I don't know, Han. That's selling oneself pretty cheaply."

"We need all the military resources we can get, and he wouldn't commit to any more than that. So I said yes. And the timetable means taking delivery soon. We're going to have to leave."

Leia sighed. "This is going to be a big blow to Addath."

"I know. But survival is more important than friendship."

Addath switched it off. Anger made her feel tight from head to foot.

It wasn't Leia turning against her that angered her. That was just politics. It was the fact that it might have worked. If she hadn't had enough layers of security for one of them to keep track of Han's movements, this deal between the Solos and the admiral might have come to pass, and she'd have missed her chance—her opportunity to come up with a more formidable counterbribe.

They walked alone on the lengthy balcony at the rear of the Presider's residence. Addath had arranged for it to be cleared of all visitors, of all government employees, for this meeting. Now Leia walked along beside her, with Han, wrapped up in his hooded cloak and anonymous as any bodyguard or servant, a step behind them.

Truth be told, Addath preferred it that way. There should never be any question that Han Solo, regardless of his comparative fame, ranked lower than she did.

"I have come to make you an offer," Addath said.

"Something to help motivate your participation in my campaign."

Leia hesitated. "About that . . . Addath, I won't be able to help. Circumstances have changed. Han and I have to return to Borleias immediately. We'll be leaving tonight."

"Bear with me. I think what I have to offer will change your mind. I think you'll want to stay."

"I . . . well, let's hear it."

"Six squadrons of improved A-Nine Vigilance Interceptors and a Nebulon-B frigate refitted to carry them all—it's more of a light carrier than it is a frigate. Vessels like it form the backbone of our new fleet."

"Impressive. And you'd give me all this just to keep me here, campaigning for you?"

"Yes. I think that highly of your influence."

"But Addath, you aren't in possession of those vehicles. Admiral Werl is."

"Until I win this election, that is. At which time I take control of the military and can simply detach those units from the navy. We won't need them anyway. We'll be pursuing nonviolence pacts with the Yuuzhan Vong."

Leia sighed. "Listen, Addath, you might lose this election even with my participation. Or there might be another runoff. Or some enemy of your politics might arrange for you to be killed. There are a thousand different things that could pop up to keep you from providing us with those resources. I have to refuse."

"What if I obtained them for you *now*?"

"How?"

Addath slipped a data card from her sleeve and held it up. It glinted in the moonlight. "This card holds access and authorization codes, plus a temporary military rank for the bearer. It will allow you to enter Vanstar Military Base, catch a shuttle to any of our new frigates, and assume command of it. For whatever purpose you want. Send it straight to Borleias."

"Addath, you're talking about taking control of military resources you don't have legal control over."

"But I will. A little alteration of documentation, and the dates for the transfer of ownership and control are moved up to one day after I assume the Presider's office."

"That's just wrong, Addath. I can't do that. I don't think I can support you in this campaign at all."

Addath blinked at her. "Leia, you surprise me. I doubt your husband is so dainty." She turned back to the cloaked figure. "What do *you* say, Han?"

"Han has nothing to say about this."

"Perhaps you should let him speak for himself."

"I would if he were here."

"What?" Addath felt a jolt of coldness spread through her. She looked again at the tall cloaked figure. "Who's this, then? Your bodyguard?"

"Addath, I can't exactly introduce you to Fasald Ghem. I understand you already know her."

That coldness reached to every one of Addath's fingers and toes as the cloaked figure threw back the cloak hood. The gesture revealed the face of a tall, lean woman, dark-haired, dark-eyed. On her forehead was a device shaped like a crown, but instead of featuring a central gem, it carried a central lens—it was a head-mounted holocam favored by some field recorders.

Addath had known her face for years. It belonged to one of the preeminent investigative holojournalists on the world of Vannix, and she stared at Addath without mercy. "Hello, Senator."

Leia said, "Fasald, perhaps you could give us a few moments alone."

"Of course." The broadcaster gave Addath a perfunctory nod, then turned away.

Addath opened her mouth wide and drew in a deep breath of air, but Leia placed a finger over Addath's lips. "Don't do it, Addath. Don't call for your guards. Fasald has already broadcast that entire recording to an editing station. You'd inconvenience her, you'd inconvenience me, but you wouldn't prevent your arrest."

Addath sighed out nearly the entire lungful. "Leia, why did you do this?"

"Don't play innocent with me. It's because I'm certain that your way of dealing with the Yuuzhan Vong will result in more deaths, more tragedy than my way. So I've stopped you."

"You have a ruthless streak I never appreciated in you."

"It came out when circumstances started killing my children."

"So. What options do you leave me with?"

"You have two options. You can stay on Vannix, and within the next three hours Fasald will broadcast her report. Dealing with subsequent arrest and mobs is up to you. Or you can flee the residence and find yourself passage offworld by dawn. In which case Fasald will give you a full day to get to freedom, then broadcast her report. Either way, she broadcasts. I couldn't persuade her otherwise." Leia plucked the data card from Addath's fingers. "I'll get this back to the admiral."

Addath felt her smile grow bitter. "So you and your

husband sold your services to the admiral for, what was it, two squadrons and a light carrier?"

A frown creased Leia's brow. "No. We were going to help her from the moment we arrived. The only thing she promised us was some antiquated sea navy equipment, decommissioned vessels."

"Then what—"

"Oh, the squadrons were what General Antilles promised Han if he'd come back now and accept a military commission. Han had a holocomm conversation with Wedge while he was running errands this afternoon. The whole conversation is recorded. I can let you watch it."

Addath nodded glumly. "I see."

"But I now suspect that Han will decline the commission. He likes being a civilian. A scoundrel."

"Of course. Quite an extensive setup." Wearily, Addath turned away. "I'll be leaving. Perhaps the former Presider would like some additional company."

"There's a guest at the front gates of the residence. A member of Fasald's staff. She'll be accompanying you until you board your ship offworld. Helping you keep track of details."

"I appreciate your thoroughness, Leia. You think of everything."

Left alone on the porch, Leia watched Addath walk away and took stock of her feelings.

She almost felt bad for Addath. Watching a person's whole store of hopes and dreams go up in flames wasn't pleasant.

But Addath was no fool. She could analyze the Yuuzhan Vong's relationship with "allied" worlds as well as anyone else. Addath simply could not give up the reins of power, and would hold them in clenched hands, whatever the cost. Since a military opposition to the Yuuzhan Vong meant handing too much power to others, she was willing to steer this world into eventual oblivion . . . just so long as she was in control until that final moment.

Whether it was by denying the truth even to herself or by cold-bloodedly selling the population of an entire world into slavery and death, Addath had made the wrong choice, and her influence had to be eliminated.

Leia decided that she felt neither sadness nor joy—just satisfaction with a job well done. She turned to rejoin her husband, who would understand.

Coruscant

It took only a few hours for Luke and his companions to search the remainder of the scientific station, for Kell and Elassar to locate the other end of the massive being's escape path and weld a heavy metal sheet across it, for Bhindi to get some of the computers operating and extract information from them.

Bhindi gathered them in an open area on the top level—an area, Kell pointed out, that *he* had laboriously cleaned and emptied of machinery parts until it was fit for occupation—to give them her evaluation. It was now set up with chairs—made of some antiquated plastic material and curved in artistic patterns that Luke thought he'd once seen in a museum display, combining comfort with dated pretension—and one functional medical droid that Bhindi had assembled from parts of several damaged ones. The repairs had not been completely successful; the droid walked with a wobble caused by the fact that its right lower leg section was identical to its left, throwing it a bit off-balance.

"What we have here," Bhindi said, "is two different scientific stations put together. Both of them operations of Imperial Intelligence, the first of them dating from about fifty years ago, though this complex has been here for centuries. And this is CPD-One-Thirteen, who has been here since the commencement of this station's third stage of operation. One-Thirteen?"

"Greetings," the droid said. Its voice was thin, cultured, with a distinct Coruscant accent. "You are all intruders. Prepare to die." It turned to look across all its visitors.

"This is the part where the military droids jump out of their niches and kill us all," Bhindi said. She reached over and fiddled with the restraining bolt plugged into the droid's chest. "One-Thirteen, our continued presence here is proof that we are authorized personnel."

"That is correct," the droid said. "I am CPD One-Thirteen, medical droid, optimized for suspended life process maintenance. You are all intruders here. Prepare to die."

"What is this complex?" Mara asked.

CPD 1-13 stood more upright, and his voice became cheerier. "Welcome to the Pasarian Memorial Atmospheric Reclamation Complex Project, Substation One, formerly the Coruscant Atmospheric Reclamation—"

"Quiet," Bhindi interrupted. "I'll synopsize."

"If you must."

Bhindi glared at 1-13 and he slumped. "The Complex," she continued, "all its various substations put together, is a sort of worldwide air-scrubber. Quite a while back, once Coruscant's leaders built over the last forested regions, the planet lacked sufficient natural resources to manage the atmospheric pollutants produced by the world's industrialized species. The government had that covered, though, in building a series of very efficient facilities that converted carbon dioxide into oxygen, removed waste gases, that sort of thing. That 'red goo' several stories up doesn't just act as a devourer tank. It's a variant of the devourer organism, especially engineered for high-efficiency conversion of carbon dioxide to oxygen. It functions with the same efficiency as several thousand square kilometers of tract forest. And there are hundreds of similar substations all over Coruscant. Well, there *were*. Some may be damaged or destroyed now, but most were built at bedrock level. Lots of them could have survived so far."

"Wait, wait." Luke frowned. "They have to have some sort of active air-pumping mechanism."

"That's correct—"

"You are all intruders. Prepare to die."

Grimacing, Bhindi did something to the droid's restraining bolt. CPD 1-13 jerked as if electrocuted each time. "Each station," Bhindi continued, "is attached to an elaborate network of intake and output ducts. In with the bad air, out with the good. And it's those ducts that are most likely to have failed planetwide with the destruction Coruscant is experiencing. But the thing is, each one of those stations could serve as a resistance center—if I can get to it and get into it."

Face gave her a disbelieving look. "Are they *all* secret, like this one?"

"Every one."

"Why?"

"That was the second stage of the operation." Bhindi stared forbiddingly at 1-13. "Think you can give them some history . . . *without* death threats?"

"I have made no threats. Only announcements of impending doom." CPD 1-13 straightened. "The second state of this complex, according to the maintenance droids that preceded me here, began with the gradual elimination, through retirement and transfer, of all living personnel who operated this station; they were replaced by droids. Then, once the station had been operated entirely by droids for several years, its reclamation organisms tank was disguised as a devourer tank and the operation center was hidden away, accessible only by a secure turobolift."

"By whom, and for what purpose?" Face asked.

"By order of the Imperial government, and for the purpose of being able to exert control over this planetary environment in times of crisis."

Luke raised an eyebrow over that. "Exert control. You mean, in times of revolution, he'd cut off the air?"

"That is correct. Should the Emperor need to regain control or merely cause billions to die, he could threaten to shut off the Complex and strangle Coruscant in its own wastes."

"Merely cause billions to die." Luke shook his head over that turn of phrase. "This doesn't conflict with your medical programming?"

"Oh, no, sir. Implementation of such an operation would be at the Emperor's sole discretion and by his own hand."

Face managed a mirthless smile. "No matter what, any time I learn something more about Emperor Palpatine, I wish I hadn't."

"So what was the third stage?" Luke asked.

"Installation of the systems and organisms needed to maintain the Subject," said CPD 1-13 "It was an operation that had no significant relation to our primary purpose, but this location, the substation closest to the Imperial government centers, was convenient."

Luke tried to wave the excess verbiage away. "What *was* the Subject?"

"A human male. He and a human female came to occupy this complex thirteen years ago. Later, another male joined them for a time. They had proper authorization, and controlled droids that could activate the turbolift control in the tank above. Months after their arrival, the second male left, and the first male was operated on and installed in the suspended-animation unit."

"Human males don't grow to be three meters tall."

"They do if subjected to specific growth hormones and cybernetic stimulation for years starting in childhood or adolescence."

"So who is this human male?"

"Unknown, sir. His identity was never provided to us, nor the nature of its armor modifications." Before Luke could ask, the droid hurried on, "It had hypoallergenic armor plates installed in its torso, head, elbows, and knees. The portions of its brain pertaining to human memory were largely replaced by computer apparatus. We of the maintenance staff concluded that it was to be a war machine of some sort, but beyond that we knew nothing."

"Do you have any images of this? Either from before, or when it recently emerged?"

1-13 shook its head. "No, sir. We were forbidden by our protocols from recording the Subject in any way. Nor do I know what you mean by 'emerged.' "

Curious, Luke glanced at Bhindi. She said, "It appears that their programming on this point was pretty comprehensive. When the Subject came out of his suspended animation tank, their programming kicked in and they couldn't even detect him any longer. He cut them to pieces without them knowing what was happening."

"Wonderful," Luke said. "So our so-called Lord Nyax is a three-meter human male, possibly a Jedi, certainly a Force user, wandering around in a world where it probably doesn't understand anything."

"That seems to be about the size of it," Bhindi said. "Isn't the truth liberating?"

SEVEN

Lord Nyax felt the distant hunger. Something wanted him.

That was all right. He wanted it, too. Anything that was so anxious for him deserved to be encountered. If it would serve him, he would command it. If it would not serve him, he would cut it into pieces.

Either solution was just fine with him.

Coruscant

The hunting party moved through the depths of Coruscant's ruins. Four hard-eyed warriors, the scars, implants, and tattoos on their faces like a starmap of pain, led the procession, and four more brought up the rear.

Behind those in front were two voxyn handlers and the leashed voxyn they theoretically controlled. The massive reptilian beasts, low to the ground and rippling with muscle, moved their heads back and forth with every few steps, as though they could see through the wreckage around them and view potential victims hiding before them.

Viqi, walking alongside Denua Ku behind them, shuddered. The voxyn were the most ill-tempered and evil things she had ever encountered, Yuuzhan Vong included. At least the Vong could reason, even if their logic was alien. The voxyn had been cloned to sense the Force, to hunt and kill Force-wielders. Many Jedi had fallen to their fangs, their teeth, the corrosive stomach acid they could bring up at a moment's notice.

These voxyn didn't look particularly healthy. In places their dark green scales were fading to a yellow that reminded Viqi of plants withering from lack of sunlight. Though they were alert and had lost none of their intensity, their movements often seemed listless.

Not that Viqi would have dared to venture within reach of their teeth or claws. She suspected that either of them would bite her in two just to hear the clack of their teeth meeting in the middle.

The party neared the end of a lengthy access corridor. Ahead, a hole in the building's exterior wall admitted dim sunlight and a breeze. Two Yuuzhan Vong warriors, novices from the lack of decoration their faces carried, stood on duty, one to either side of the gap.

Raglath Nur, the leader of the hunting party, addressed them. Viqi didn't bother to listen. She knew they'd address her if they needed her. She was correct; after less than a minute, Raglath Nur beckoned her forward, to the very lip of the hole; Viqi could lean out and see countless stories of crumbling habitat beneath her, and a simple step forward would send her falling to her death.

"This warrior," Raglath Nur said, indicating the novice warrior on the right side, "saw the walkway fall; he was a great distance away. First it erupted in flames as though from one of the infidel torpedoes, then it fell. Searching, he found bodies below—burned, some of them in pieces. Explain."

"If he didn't see a starfighter fire a missile or torpedo, then it was probably a bomb," Viqi said, indifferent to his curiosity. "Something like a torpedo, but carried by a man, put into position, and then persuaded to explode a few seconds later—seconds in which the one who planted it runs to safety."

"And?"

"And what?"

Raglath Nur drew a hand back as if to strike her. Viqi steeled herself against the blow. But Denua Ku positioned his amphistaff between them. "He means, what do you conclude?" Denua Ku said. "You are here for your knowledge of infidels, their tactics."

"Yes, yes." Viqi fumed, but thought about it. "The bomb didn't just blow a hole in the walkway. It took the whole thing down and singed both edges. I conclude that it wasn't an improvised weapon. Either the people who did it had access to military equipment, or they're proficient at building such things. This suggests that they're not ordinary survivors—they're elites of some sort."

"Jeedai?" asked Raglath Nur.

Viqi shook her head. "I don't know if Jedi are among them, but Jedi don't normally use high explosives. So this was something different, or something additional."

"What else?"

"If I were in their situation and had to use an explosive device—something sure to give away my position—I'd move away from here very fast, to elude any Yuuzhan Vong parties that came to investigate. Meaning that if we can figure out the route they took, we could search it thoroughly and see if they dropped anything. If they dropped something, we might obtain more information."

"How will we know the difference between an infidel object left here by the planet-dwellers and one dropped by your 'elites'?"

Viqi shrugged. "I will know," she lied.

The party's searches turned up no objects that Viqi felt had been dropped by their prey. But as they reached the next building over in the direction the trackers felt the infidels had traveled, the voxyn became more alert. They left off the eternal, searching sweeps of their heads; instead, they both stared in one direction, outward and downward, the muscles of their necks tense, while their tails began to lash.

Raglath Nur allowed the voxyn and their handlers to take the lead. The voxyn led them at a quickened pace; Viqi had to struggle to keep up, and was often prodded by Denua Ku when he felt her progress was not sufficient. But the voxyn did not understand the city's architecture, and it required the Yuuzhan Vong, and sometimes Viqi, to guide them down stairwells, ramps, and even turbolift shafts as they rushed toward their prey.

Deeper and deeper they descended into the ruins, and when they had not run down their prey within half an hour, Raglath Nur demanded, "Is our quarry running? Can they be aware of us?"

Viqi shook her head and took a moment to breathe. She tamped back on her resentment; a merchant-princess and Senator of Kuat should not have to exert herself in this unseemly fashion. "The voxyn detect the Force, correct? Perhaps what they're detecting is very strong—and far away."

Raglath Nur offered up a noise of vexation, but it was, for a member of the Yuuzhan Vong warrior caste, sufficiently mild that Viqi suspected he had come to the same conclusion—that he had merely hoped Viqi would offer some more satisfying answer.

Another half-hour put them much farther down in the building level. From the general atmosphere of antiquity and seediness, from the driprot that afflicted the duracrete walls, from the stench of decay and increased incidence of corrupting bodies, Viqi could tell that they were nearly at bedrock level.

They passed a side-corridor that sloped downward; it was mostly filled with dark liquid and bodies floating atop it. Viqi skidded to a halt and turned back to give it a second look, putting her hand over her nose and mouth as if to reduce the stench. Denua Ku joined her, and other warriors turned back to see what had drawn her curiosity.

She pointed at one of the bodies. "Get that one," she said.

Denua Ku and one of the others splashed into the water. The body Viqi had pointed out raised its head. He was a male human, young and frightened. He scrambled around in the shallow water and tried to dive away, but Denua Ku caught him by the ankle and yanked. He dragged the screaming, flailing youth back up to the dry cross-corridor, then hauled him up by the collar of his tunic and held him against the corridor wall.

"How did you know?" Raglath Nur asked.

Viqi gave him a superior smile. "He wasn't bloated like the rest."

"Question him," Denua Ku ordered.

Viqi sighed, then turned to their prisoner. The young man was obviously terrified but knew better than to struggle now that he was surrounded by Yuuzhan Vong warriors. He had long black hair; dark fluid from the pool they'd hauled him from ran from it, pouring from his garments to puddle on the floor. Viqi reflected that, in better circumstances, he would have been pretty enough to serve her as a toy.

"Where are the Jedi?" she asked.

The young man shook his head. "I don't know about Jedi."

Viqi gave him a chill smile. "These warriors would like to kill you. In fact, killing you fast is one of the nicest things they're considering doing to you. So you'd better find some reason, *any* reason, to give me so I can persuade them not to. Do you understand?"

The young man nodded. "I know something. I'm going to take something out. Don't kill me." He reached into a pants pocket.

The voxyn roared and surged farther down the corridor, dragging their handlers behind them, drawing the attention of the other Yuuzhan Vong warriors.

The young man held out his hand. Viqi reached for him, and he dropped something into her outstretched palm. "It's the ugly—"

"Our prey is close," Raglath Nur said. "We don't need him."

Viqi turned toward him and crossed her arms, a gesture she hoped would hide the object the prisoner had given her. "I'm not through."

But Denua Ku exerted himself, and Viqi heard the snap of the young man's neck.

Denua Ku dropped the corpse back into the dark pool. "*Now* he will bloat."

Viqi glared at him.

Raglath Nur set the warriors into motion, following the frantic voxyn. "What did the human want to show you?"

Viqi shrugged. "I might have found out, if Denua Ku hadn't been so quick to exterminate him." She waited until Raglath Nur's attention was on the voxyn before she tucked the object out of sight under the neckline of her robeskin. She got a glimpse of it before it was concealed; it seemed to be a tiny remote, one with a pair of buttons on one side, another button and a screen so small as to be nearly useless on the other.

The ugly what?

The handlers, dragged by the voxyn, were first to pass through the ruined metal doors, which were three times the height of a human and broad enough to permit ten pedestrians walking side-by-side. The lettering above the door read:

ELEGAIC FABRICATIONS
THE COMFORT YOU DESERVE

Raglath Nur paused outside the doorway and stared with suspicion at the darkness beyond. He whirled on Viqi. "What is this?"

"A manufacturing plant," she said. "They manufacture furnishings. Very expensive, very functional furnishings."

"Such as what?"

"Such as chairs that convert into extravagantly comfortable beds, chairs that carry their owners about in the air, furnishings that massage those who sit in them . . ."

"Massage?" Evidently that didn't translate well through Raglath Nur's tizowyrm. "Inflict pain?"

"Inflict pleasure."

The warrior gave her a revolted look and led his fellows into the darkness. Viqi, alongside Denua Ku, followed.

Though the manufacturing concern had seemed pitch-black from outside, once her eyes began adjusting, Viqi discovered that it was not so. There were light sources everywhere, but dim ones, mostly at floor level—emergency lighting, she decided, probably running low on battery power. In the faint glows from the light sources, she could see looming production-line machinery and immobile fabricator droids, some of them huge.

She wondered if any samples of their stock were still in existence. But doubtless her Yuuzhan Vong companions would not let her enjoy such a chair, not even for a moment.

She heard the voxyn's hisses go from excited to ferocious, heard their handlers call after them as they yanked leashes free from the handlers' grips.

"*Jeedai!*" called one of the warriors. "Now you die!"

Viqi heard the distinctive *snap-hiss* of a Jedi lightsaber igniting. One point on the far wall of the manufacturing chamber and the ceiling above it were illuminated by red light—moving light. The claws of the voxyn scrabbled as they charged for their prey.

Then there was another *snap-hiss*, and another, and another. The distant red glow brightened. Viqi saw the silhouette of a voxyn leaping high, vaulting intervening machinery, backlit by the glow—and then something rose to meet the voxyn in mid-flight.

It was not a Jedi, not a lightsaber blade. A block of machinery two meters on a side flew up from below and crashed into the leaping voxyn, striking with such force that Viqi heard the creature's bones shatter. The impact smashed the voxyn back through the air, a wobbly caricature of a once-living beast. The voxyn's body crashed onto the factory's duracrete floor and the block of machinery landed upon it, breaking more bones, and stuck there, not bouncing or rolling forward as it should have.

"Forward," Denua Ku said. He whipped his amphistaff free from his waist and charged after the other Yuuzhan Vong warriors, who now howled in rage and anticipation.

Viqi took two steps in Denua Ku's wake and then something crashed into her, took her from her feet, slapped her to the duracrete.

It was not a physical thing. It was despair and hatred, loathing and worthlessness, fear and howling rage. It was as though Viqi had spent every one of her years packing all the hateful emotions an ordinary person felt into a storeroom—and suddenly all the pressure had burst through the door and swept her away. She could only lie there, her arms and legs twitching outside her control, her stomach rebelling, her heart hammering inside her.

She heard the howl of the second voxyn, heard the ripping noise of the creature vomiting its acid at its prey. Then there was the sound of lightsabers swinging, hacking. Meat in great quantities slapping down onto duracrete.

Viqi writhed in time with the war cries of the Yuuzhan

Vong and, one by one, she heard them die under the almost musical tones of the lightsabers.

Then there was only the sound of lightsabers cutting, and cutting, and cutting.

The emotional agony that had gripped Viqi lessened—only a little. She managed to roll over onto her stomach and slowly, painfully came upright.

She knew the beings on the other side of the chamber had just killed everything that had entered the chamber with her. She wanted nothing more than to charge at them, to rip them to pieces with her bare hands.

But as she stood, some faint instinct of self-preservation rose within her, and one thought made up of words emerged: *Run, or die.*

She turned toward the doorway, and lurched out toward the light.

As she reached the doorway, she put her hand out to steady herself against the metal door that had once protected the factory's interior. It fell away from her grip, crashing down onto the duracrete with a tremendous clang.

The lightsabers in the distance switched off. Viqi froze. She waited, ears straining at the sudden silence.

Then she heard it, the padding of feet coming her way.

A noise like a sob escaped her and she ran, her speed enhanced by adrenaline and fear.

Luke came awake and rose in a single smooth motion.

He didn't have to ask if Mara had felt it, too. She was awake, gripping her lightsaber, ready to ignite it.

Luke stepped out into the corridor. It was dimmed for

sleeping, but Danni, too, was emerging, and Tahiri, who had been on guard in the corridor as the others slept, stared into one wall, *through* the wall, at something that was far away and toward the ground. "It's there again," she said, her voice faint.

Luke took a few deep breaths. He couldn't remember what he had just been dreaming—only that, for a moment, he had been filled, even saturated, with a desire to rise and kill every living thing in his vicinity. Absurdly, he still felt loathing and contempt for his companions, for his wife, but as his mind and memory struggled to assert themselves, those emotions began to fade. "What did you feel?" he asked.

Tahiri shook her head, and Luke could finally see the lone tear flowing down her farther cheek. "Awfulness," she said. "More awful than when I was coming out of my conditioning and started to figure out what I'd almost become. It was all through me, through the Force. It almost had control of me. I think maybe it could have had control, if it had known I was here." The despair in her voice was heartbreaking.

None of the Wraiths had emerged from their new quarters. That made sense. This was a Force sending, a Force problem, and the Wraiths, largely oblivious to the Force, were not troubled.

Mara, dressed, moved down the corridor, rapping on doors. "Everyone up. Get into your armor. It's time to hunt."

Four stories up from the manufacturing chamber, Viqi came off a pedestrian ramp at a dead run. Her legs trembled from her flight but she could not afford to rest—she'd heard her pursuers crash through doors she'd dragged shut behind her.

She rounded a bend in the corridor and abruptly there was an arm in front of her, stretched at just under neck height. She hit it at full speed, her legs going out from under her, and suddenly she was on her back, looking into two human faces illuminated by dim glow rods, at two blaster pistols pointed at her face.

It was a man and a woman. The man had an ill-trimmed beard. The woman's eyes were a startlingly pretty blue in eerie contrast to her unsympathetic expression. The two stank and seemed as thin as plasteel support beams.

"Look at you," the man said.

"About fifty kilos, I'd guess," the woman said. "Good eating, looks like."

"How'd you stay so clean?"

"Never mind that. Just kill her."

There was a distant noise, a low-pitched roar that raised the hair on Viqi's arms and the nape of her neck. The man and woman hesitated, looking back the way Viqi had come.

Then it washed across her again, the feeling of hatred and lowness that had brought her down in the manufacturing chamber. It had the same effect on the man and woman; they paled and sank to their knees, the woman gagging, perhaps prevented from vomiting only by near-starvation.

Viqi scrambled around on the floor, turned toward her original direction of flight, and crawled as fast as paralysis gripping her arms and legs would let her. It occurred to her that it would be better to die than flee, better to face her tormentors rather than have to continue running, but the rational side of her mind, forcing its way to the forefront, kept her moving.

She made it a few meters, until the curve in the corridor made it impossible to see the man and woman.

She heard them scream, heard the *snap-hiss* of lightsabers igniting.

There was a maintenance panel ahead of her, set in the wall at ground level. She reached it and tugged at its handle. It resisted, probably held in place by simple magnetic bolts or locks.

She put all her slight frame into it, yanking, and the panel came loose; her effort sent the panel skittering across the floor. Beyond the new hole was a vertical shaft not more than a meter in diameter, steel rungs making a ladder of the far side.

Viqi crawled into the shaft and climbed. Her arms and legs trembled, threatening every instant to fail her.

She heard the man and woman scream again, then heard the noise of lightsabers chopping. As she ascended, the noise faded, but the fear and loathing did not.

By Luke's chrono, it had taken them four hours to find the first evidence of the thing or things they sought. They stood in the main manufacturing chamber of a furnishing concern and looked down at the dismembered bodies of Yuuzhan Vong warriors—and voxyn.

It was not evidence or deduction or luck that had led them here. Luke and the other Jedi could feel lingering dark-side energy imbued in the walls, the machines, the corpses. The sensation, so like what Luke had experienced within a certain cave on Dagobah, caused the hair on the back of his neck to rise.

Mara dispassionately looked at the body of a Yuuzhan Vong warrior who had been cut into at least eight pieces. The wounds were all burned, cauterized. "Our Dark Jedi again. Or whatever they are."

"Dark Jedi might be able to impose their will on normal people," Tahiri said. She had her arms crossed, and Luke suspected her pose was an effort to keep herself from trembling. "But not on fully trained Jedi. This was like jumping into an ocean of the dark side of the Force. It was like feeling Anakin die again. And wanting again to die with him." More tears came, and she looked away so that the others would not see them.

"I wonder," Luke said, "what it's going to be like to confront them face-to-face." He prodded a severed Yuuzhan Vong leg with his toe. He hadn't always done well when faced with the dark side. "The Yuuzhan Vong are invisible to the Force. They couldn't feel it. We aren't. Especially the Jedi."

"I had a thought on that." Face was on guard duty, blaster rifle in hand, his attention on the entryway. "A tactic I've used from time to time in bad situations."

"What's that?" Luke asked.

"Snipers. Set up a couple of kilometers away in a blind with a laser rifle and someone who really knows how to use it, and when your enemy wanders by, 'zap.' "

Luke smiled. "Not exactly fair."

"Who wants to be fair?"

Viqi woke up in absolute blackness and thought for a moment that she might be dead. In a panic, she sat up, but before she came upright her head banged into something, resulting in a sharp pain to her forehead and a hollow metallic noise.

Then she remembered. She'd climbed and climbed, hearing the roars and the lightsaber hums of her pursuit. Her pursuers had cut their way through durasteel bulkheads to follow her, but she'd found side channels from the access duct—ventilation ducts that were smaller and smaller, adequate for a diminutive Kuat woman but too constricting for whatever followed her.

After a long time of groping along in the dark, she had let exhaustion overcome her.

Now she was alone, weaponless and friendless, surrounded by kilometers of crumbling duracrete and metal in all directions.

Not to mention thirsty, hungry, and blind.

She forced herself to become calm and went through a ritual checklist that helped her regain control of whatever situation troubled her. *Checklist,* she began. *One extravagantly capable political strategist whose skills are of no use here. One Yuuzhan Vong robeskin, a living garment whose sole virtue is that it's better than running around naked, and matching footwraps.*

That's about it.

That wasn't quite it. She'd been given something a million years ago, shortly before starting her run. She dug around under the robeskin neckline and held the object that pretty, doomed boy had handed her. It fit her palm so that a button fell under her thumb; there were two others on the reverse side. She pressed the first button.

A tiny red screen lit up on the remote, illuminating her

surroundings—a sheet-metal duct, layered with dust, a meter wide by half a meter high. The screen showed a wire-frame sphere with one bright red dot at its center and another at one point on its circumference. She slowly rotated her hand and saw the second dot move around, always staying at the circumference, always pointed in the same cardinal direction.

It was a location finder of some sort. A distant object transmitted a regular signal, and this device always pointed in the direction of that object.

She pressed one of the buttons on the reverse side. The wire-frame image disappeared, replaced by the words OUT OF RANGE.

She pressed the last button. The device spoke with the voice of a woman: "Remember, pick up a new charge for the speeder, and we're having dinner with the Tussins tonight."

Viqi supposed that the recording would have depressed someone of less personal strength. She didn't even bother to wonder how dinner had gone. The woman who'd recorded the message was gone, either crushed or vaporized or in some slavering idiot's stew-pot, and her sole virtue was that one of her possessions was now going to benefit Viqi Shesh. Whatever it might lead to, it was, for now, a light source.

She rolled over onto her stomach, shining the light in front of her, and began crawling.

Viqi stood at the center of what had once been a large living chamber, centerpiece of the apartment of some wealthy business family. There were numerous doors and hallways off this chamber, all leading to bedchambers, refreshers, recreation areas—all now wrecked by looters and invasive plant life.

To Viqi's right, a few meters away, was a huge hole in the wall that had once been a viewport half again the height of a man, and twice as broad as it was high. Now creepers growing on the building's face hung over the gap, and pieces of shattered transparisteel littered what had once been heated flex-carpet.

Fungus was everywhere, grayish mushroomlike growths that were larger toward the hole. She'd stepped on one of the tiny ones and it had detonated beneath her foot, making her instep very sore and damaging the living footwrap she wore. She was careful not to touch any more, and it was clear that much of the damage to the chamber had come about because of the fungi—obviously, many of them had exploded over the last several weeks. Perhaps vibrations in the crumbling buildings set them off, perhaps they simply detonated when they reached a certain size.

The wall in front of Viqi was ferrocrete that had once been decorated, its utilitarian strength disguised, by a thick layer of flexible sheeting decorated in a starfield pattern. Attached to building power, the sheet's stars and nebula would glow. Now the sheeting hung in strips. She'd torn most of it away and could find nothing beyond but ferrocrete.

On the other side of it was another crumbling skyscraper. In her explorations, she'd managed to get onto the corresponding floor of that building, but on its far side; collapsed hallways and walls had prevented her from getting closer.

The tracking device had led her here, and this was the point that was closest to whatever it indicated. On the little screen, the white dot representing that object and the dot indicating her current position were almost one point.

She shrugged. So she hadn't been able to find her way to the object. It might just be a matter of ascending one floor, descending one, searching more diligently to find the spot that gave her access.

Then she remembered the OUT OF RANGE message she'd received. She held up the remote and depressed that button again.

There was a noise, a faint "ponk" of some mechanical apparatus being activated, from above her head. She looked up and then jumped aside just in time to avoid a descending ceiling panel. Its bottom edge came down to rest against the floor. She moved around to look up.

It was a set of metal stairs, narrow and without rails, leading up into darkness.

Breath catching in her throat, she hurried up the staircase. She found herself in a narrow, low corridor that led for three meters straight to the wall she had found so impassable—straight to a corresponding gap in that wall, a gap that was lit from the other side.

Before moving on, she looked around and found a small button control by the top of the hidden staircase. She pressed it and the stairs rose, locking into place behind her.

The gap in the wall opened into a cylindrical chamber a few meters across. Occupying most of the chamber, resting on its stern, was a vehicle—about twelve meters long, squat at its stern and tapering toward the bow, all in a uniform deep matte blue that made it difficult for Viqi to make out details of its hull. There were protrusions everywhere, plates and hemispherical antennae and maneuvering or braking flaps.

The floor of this chamber was some four meters below Viqi's feet. She stood directly opposite a hatch that opened into the vehicle's interior, one-third of the distance from the stern.

The thing looked like some sort of oversized military landspeeder, enclosed to protect its crew, but since it rested on its tail—with no machinery evident to allow it to be lowered into a horizontal position—Viqi suspected that it was equipped for flight; she could not tell if it was an atmospheric vehicle or spaceworthy. On the side was stenciled the vehicle's name, *Ugly Truth*.

She looked up. The cylindrical chamber continued upward another thirty meters beyond the vehicle's nose, ending in a jumble of fallen metal beams and duracrete blocks. Viqi could see faint sunlight through that deadfall.

Scarcely able to believe her good fortune, she moved forward across a narrow span of metal that gave her access to the open hatch and clambered into the vehicle. As the vehicle was resting at a ninety-degree angle to its intended orientation, when she stepped down from the hatch she stood on what was obviously meant to be the main cabin's rear bulkhead. A crudely constructed ladder of spare metal parts wired together allowed her to climb up to the pilot's seat at the bow.

Under her touch, the secondary power switch engaged without hesitation or resistance. The cabin lights came up; the vehicle's navigation computer went through its power-up sequence.

Viqi felt a slow, wondering smile spread across her face. This was an emergency evacuation vehicle, cunningly hidden away in the event of disaster . . . but its owners had not been able to get to it in time as Coruscant fell. Perhaps they had died, perhaps they had been off-world already.

Who was the youth who'd given her the locator? Son of the vehicle's owners? A builder who'd known and kept the secret of this hidden chamber, and later intended to use the vehicle when it became clear that its owners would be unable to? He'd probably been prevented from escaping by the collapse of the access above him. Perhaps he'd been working all this time to dig his way clear of that obstacle. Now he was dead, and the vehicle was hers.

She was free of the Yuuzhan Vong and in possession of an escape from their world.

A thought hit Viqi and her hands fell away from the controls. If this vehicle was designed as a last-ditch opportunity for survival, perhaps it was carrying . . .

She scrambled down the makeship ladder to the vehicle's stern. A hatch into the stern compartment lay at her feet. She struggled with its locking bar and then hauled the heavy hatch open.

Below was a storage compartment with restraining nets to either side and a hatch at the far end. Doubtless the hatch gave access to the vehicle's thrusters. Viqi didn't care. Her attention was riveted by what she saw in the nets.

Rations. Military rations, carefully packed into individual meals, guaranteed to survive for years on the shelf.

With a moan, she clambered down into the compartment, grabbed the nearest meal at hand, and tore into the wrapping flimsy around it.

EIGHT

Aphran System, Aphran IV

Aphran IV was a heavily forested world whose green landmasses stood out in stark contrast from her blue seas. She was a warm world, lacking polar ice, with no moons to contribute tides. And she was a comparatively poor world whose people were noted chiefly for mastery in woodworking, whose artistic inlays were prized by collectors.

All this Han knew from a brief look at the star map records in the *Falcon*'s computer. The records suggested that Aphran would never survive even a weak Yuuzhan Vong attack. Considering how close she was to the Yuuzhan Vong zone of control, not far from Bilbringi, only her relative unimportance had kept her from being conquered by the enemy.

Han glanced at his wife. She looked very different than usual: her hair was long, black, and straight, her eyebrows broader and darker to match, and she wore garments that Senator Leia Organa Solo would never have been caught dead in.

They started with a bodysuit that was black and glossy.

Though synthetic, it creaked like hide when she moved. Her boots, low-slung blaster holster, and gloves were of a similar material, but matte rather than glossy. In the spirit of the character she was to portray, she had her feet up, crossed at the ankle, on the copilot control board before her. She fixed Han with a forbidding stare. "What are *you* looking at, ground-pounder?"

Han shook his head. "If your daughter could see you now . . ."

Leia broke character for a moment and grinned. "I'll make sure Artoo gets a holo for her. He'll have to get you, too."

Han nodded. "I *am* magnificent." He'd spent enough time in front of the mirror both to make sure that his disguise was adequate and to be certain that his costume provided sufficient dash and drama.

He wore a close-trimmed beard. His real hair and his false facial hair were a matching, distinguished shade of silver-gray. But he was not trying for the look of an elder statesman; his uniform was a dark gray, two shades more somber than the old Imperial Navy uniform, and thick with accoutrements: a brand-new pistol on his hip, twin vibroblades on the other hip, a brace of alternating vibroblades and small backup blasters across his chest. The metal gauntlet on his left hand looked like a commercial robotic replacement and contained enough circuitry to read as a prosthetic to most scanners. The contact lens on his left eye made the eyeball silver-reflective; the false puckering scar reaching upward and downward from the eye suggested the violence that had caused the mechanical replacement to be installed.

C-3PO, in the passenger seat behind the pilot's chair, spoke up. "So that I do not jeopardize your mission through misstatement or omission, Princess, may I ask, why the deception?"

"Aphran is something of an unknown quantity," Leia said. "The smugglers we're going to meet and try to persuade to act as our local resistance organizers say that there've been a lot of surreptitious comings and goings with government envoy ships. What does that suggest to you?"

"That matter is rather outside my fields of expertise," the droid replied. "But it would seem to me that the planetary government does not need to be surreptitious when sending representatives to the New Republic. That would suggest that they are sending their envoys to someone they wish the New Republic to know nothing about."

Leia nodded. "Very good. To whom?"

"Since the most far-reaching government outside the New Republic is that of the Yuuzhan Vong, simple statistics give the highest probability of it being them."

"Correct. Or perhaps the Peace Brigade, acting as intermediaries for the Yuuzhan Vong."

"Oh, I hope not, Princess. The Peace Brigade are, well, very unpleasant. Very difficult." This was something of an understatement; the Peace Brigade was a loose alliance of mercenaries who cooperated with the Yuuzhan Vong. Believing the Yuuzhan Vong claim that a galaxy without the Jedi would be a galaxy at peace, or just to earn profits, they had hunted the Jedi, capturing some and turning them over to the enemy. Definitely "unpleasant"— except to those who shared their ability to cast blame for the current war on anyone but the aggressors—they were widely regarded as traitors to the New Republic.

Han said, "And if they're talking to the Vong, the Solos can't be recognized here."

Leia nodded. "If the Yuuzhan Vong learn that the Solos are here, they come to get us. Even if we use false names, if a Corellian YT-Thirteen-Hundred freighter lands with a dashing, vainglorious man at the controls, it doesn't matter what name he uses, people are going to think *Han Solo*."

Han shot her an offended look. "Vainglorious?"

"Vainglorious," Leia affirmed. "Vain plus glorious. Go ahead, deny it."

"Well . . . I can't, really."

Instead of being directed to a berth on the planetary capital's commercial district, the *Falcon* followed her homing beacon to a government spaceport district some distance away from the capital. The spaceport was an enormous thing, kilometers long, with landing bays and warehousing domes on spars that extended like the arms of some sort of mutant sea creature from a central hub.

As they followed the beacon in, Han spent a lot of time at the comm board, arguing first with one minor official, then another. Finally, just before final approach, he leaned back and sighed. "We can't land in the commercial zone," he said.

Leia frowned. "Why not?"

"All cargo has to be off-loaded and inventoried here. New regulations. Once it's all off-loaded, we can decide where it's to be taken by their cargo haulers. Back on the ship, for transport elsewhere, or into one of the warehouses up here for evaluation by buyers. The thing is, no matter where it's loaded, it costs money to move it . . . and it costs more to put it back on the ship than to warehouse it."

Leia nodded, a world-weary smile on her lips. "Which is an inducement to keep the cargo up here so that a more limited range of buyers can look at it. Which helps keep prices and bribes where they want them."

"And people called *me* dishonest," Han muttered. "On the other hand, we don't have to wait around for them to complete their inventory. We can take a commercial landspeeder in to their capital. That'll give them lots more time to steal expensive bits and pieces from our cargo, which is really what it's for anyway."

A pair of Aphran men standing in front of a refueling station watched the duo emerge from the landing bay that now housed the Corellian YT-1300 freighter.

"I see a man and a woman I don't recognize," said the first. He was a man of middle height, his hair, beard, and mustache graying. With his reserved, courteous manner and his colorful, comparatively expensive clothing, he looked like a fit merchant. But the hardness of his eyes, when he was not trying to cause someone to like or trust him, suggested that he was not that peaceable a man. "And while the man and the woman *could* be the Solos, they could also be billions of other people."

"I didn't say they *were* the Solos," the second man said. His jumpsuit matched the lavender-with-black-pinstripes decor of the front of the refueling station; he was as lean and tough looking as the banded artificial muscles found in cybernetic limbs. "I said that it was the *Millennium Falcon*. I don't care where they slap paint on her or how many new antennas they mount on her, I know the look of her. I know the sound of her creaks when she comes in for a landing."

"Hmm. Well, until we're *sure*, we play it safe."

"There's less money in playing it safe."

"There's longer to live and spend that money in playing it safe."

"You're the boss."

The bearded man eyed his companion. In his experience, *You're the boss* always meant, *I'll shut up for now, then put a vibroblade in your back when the profit is highest.* He mentally crossed his companion off his "useful" list and moved him to "expendable." "I'll get things started," he said. "Thanks for the tip."

"Anytime."

The bearded man moved off toward his personal transport, a late-model landspeeder paid for by information he'd furnished to the Peace Brigade. If these were the Solos, he might be able to afford a personal spacecraft now—even factoring in the sum his companion's elimination would cost.

On the balcony of their rented quarters, Leia sat, her ankles crossed on the railing before her, and entered notes.

Things were going well . . . mostly. The Talon Karrde organization had already led her to a pair of retired— semiretired—smugglers who were trusted by Karrde and whose enthusiasm for hunkering down in anticipation of the Yuuzhan Vong invasion matched hers. With their experience, they could find their own bases of operations, could even help with the acquisition of some vehicles and other equipment. What Han and Leia had to do now was help them set up a communications system, a combination holocomm and comlink that could transmit and receive the short, hard-to-track data packets that were the essence of resistance communications.

But Leia set her notes aside for a moment, distracted by the view. Below the balcony, a small lake stretched into the distance; its far shore was at the base of a low line of hills, and Aphran, the planet's sun, was now setting beyond them. It was a red-gold orb, distorted by distance and atmosphere. The hills cast shadows over the distant part of the lake, while sunbeams illuminated the nearer portions, turning the water from green-blue to a brilliant gold.

It was only a sunset. She'd seen lovely sunsets all over the galaxy. But it had been some time since she'd paid attention to one, appreciated one.

This sunset meant nothing in the face of Yuuzhan Vong invasions, the death of Anakin, the disappearance of Jacen, her long separations from the rest of her family. But just for this moment, those sacrifices didn't dig pain into her, and she could appreciate what she was seeing, its simple beauty.

"Bottle that and sell it, and we could make a fortune."

Leia started. She looked up to where Han stood behind her. The energy field that kept the cooler air inside their quarters also muffled sound, so it hadn't been too difficult for him to sneak up on her. He stared into the distance, watching the golden rays retreating as the sun continued its descent, and for once there was no self-deprecating humor, no expression of suspicion or cynicism on his face. Just contemplation.

Leia reached up to take his hand. He settled into the chair next to hers. "How were your errands?" she asked.

"Pretty good. The inventory is about half done, and the locals haven't found any irregularities." His last words were private code, agreed upon before the *Falcon* had set out on this series of missions. *Irregularities* meant the smuggling compartments and the shielded escape pod; those secrets remained intact. "And I was able to make some purchases. Cabinets. I need to arrange for their delivery." So he'd been able to find the comm gear he needed, but delivery to wait until the new resistance leaders locally had a place for it. "You?"

"Oh, I may have made some new friends."

"That's good. You know what?"

"What?"

"I don't want to talk about work anymore today."

"Me, either."

Borleias

Tam and Wolam sat in the pilot's seats of Wolam's shuttle. Once a military blastboat, it had been stolen from the Empire early in Wolam's career and gradually converted to a lightly armed mobile office. Now it sat in the kill zone in front of the biotics building, one of the few vehicles internally lit at this nighttime hour.

In the absence of true broadcaster facilities, Wolam did have a less comprehensive set of tools built into the ship's computer, and now he and Tam looked over their last couple of days' recordings, annotating them, choosing which to use and which to discard in Wolam's next historical documentary.

"Here's one." Wolam paused the image and then tapped the figure of one mechanic working energetically on an X-wing engine.

"A mechanic," Tam said.

"A female mechanic." Wolam dialed the image so that the woman expanded to fill the screen. "Corellian, unmarried. Good looking. I spoke with her for a few minutes while you were showing Tarc the zoom functions."

"Ah. I see. We now take a break from work so you can once again try to set me up with a woman."

"That's correct."

"And I should seek her out because she's good looking. Not that she isn't . . . but am I that shallow?"

"At your age, you should be."

Tam sighed and took the recording off pause. It continued on, focusing for a few more moments on that X-wing and its crew, before blanking. A moment later, the image of the biotics building's main lobby snapped into focus.

"More important, now's not the time," Tam said. "I have a few things to get through first. Such as my reputation as a traitor."

"A reputation that exists only in your own mind."

"And the fact that all my savings were on Coruscant. The fact that all my possessions fit in a bag that I have no trouble lifting."

"So seek out a woman who isn't as shallow as I wish you were."

"What's this?" The image on the screen became jerky, blurring across a sea of waists and belt buckles. Then it rose, and Wolam's face appeared on the screen, saturated with light, recorded from about waist height. The recorded Wolam grimaced and tried to turn his face out of the glare.

"Oh, that's young Tarc's recording."

"That's right, our second tour of the building."

"I think he was experimenting with the notion of using the holocam glow rod as a weapon."

Tam snorted, then became serious again. "Wolam, he doesn't belong here."

"True."

"And the Solos—well, I don't have any criticism of them, they have their duties, but they're not exactly around here much. They're just momentary reassurances for him."

"Yes. They've accepted responsibility for him, despite their inability to be available to him at all times, because he needs someone, and no one else is that someone."

"Pretty much the way you accepted responsibility for me, ten years ago."

Wolam shook his head. "Not quite. You were sixteen, more or less an adult."

"Just like now."

Wolam smiled. "Tam, listen. If you have a failing, it's that you don't seize the initiative, don't grasp the opportunities that are before you. Such as going out and spending the occasional rowdy evening with people your own age—there are plenty here, including that mechanic. Such as finding out for yourself that your worries about your reputation as a traitor are unfounded. But that failing is not too great a sin. Its consequences eat at you, but don't hurt anyone *except* you. You don't hurt other people, you do a necessary job quietly and well, and when a hard task moves into your path—such as shaking off the domination of the Yuuzhan Vong—you accomplish that task."

"Eventually."

"I'm trying to say, as your friend rather than as your employer, that I'm proud of you, and I wish you were proud of yourself."

Tam met Wolam's eyes, then looked away, concentrating on the screen again rather than let Wolam see tears trying to form. "Wolam, that boy needs somebody. When it comes time to shove off Borleias, I want to take him along with me. With us, if you'll have him along."

"See there? Another task accepted. A gigantic one compared to shaking off Yuuzhan Vong brainwashing—accepting responsibility for a whole, entire child. But have you asked him? Have you talked to the Solos?"

"No. I will. And if any of them say no, then it's no. But I think Tarc deserves the offer."

"I think you're right. And of course, I'd be happy for him to come along. If he can learn to stop spinning, he could be a useful backup holocam operator."

Tam grinned.

On the screen, Tarc's low-point-of-view recording continued, catching both Tam and Wolam as they marched down one of the biotics building's basement hallways.

Something on a wall over a doorway flashed with reflective light, just for a moment, then disappeared as the holocam view progressed.

Tam sat upright. "Hold it." He paused the recording, then reversed it until that door frame came into view again.

"What is it?"

"I'm not sure." He *wasn't* sure, but if it was what he thought it was, it was bad news.

He scrolled the screen view back and forth across that one second of recording. One moment, the wall above the door frame was blank, then there was that reflection, then it was blank again.

"Are you sure now?"

"Let's go look."

It was a low-security hallway, though there were higher-security doors on it; they were protected by key-pads and alarms, and around the corner from the portion of the hallway where they stood, doors providing access to the Twin Sun Squadron's special turbolift were guarded by security personnel.

But here there were two doors immediately across from one another. The one on the left had a keypad access and was marked ENVIRONMENT. The one on the right led to a well-packed utility closet.

Tam reached up over that doorway and ran his finger along the wall. After a few centimeters of paint, his fingertip encountered a smoother substance, though no change in the wall texture was visible to him. The smoothness ran for perhaps ten centimeters, then turned to paint texture again.

"I saw that," Wolam said. "What was it?"

"A Yuuzhan Vong toy. When they had control of me, I put one up on the wall outside Danni Quee's laboratory. Watch this." Tam stroked the thing along its left edge, a combination he'd been taught during his brief, painful, life-changing stay among the Yuuzhan Vong.

Vibrant colors suddenly appeared on the patch of material. They showed the keypad on the door opposite, showed hands moving across the keys, tapping in an access code.

Tam looked at Wolam. His expression was unhappy. He pulled a comlink out from a pocket. "Tam Elgrin to Comm Main Control, put me through to the Intelligence office."

"This is Comm Main, say again your name and authority."

"This is Tam Elgrin. I'm one of the civilians on base."

"Oh. Right. You're *that* civilian. Who did you want again?"

"The Intelligence office."

"The Intelligence office isn't staffed every hour of the day, and you aren't authorized to demand the attention of the head of the department. I'm amazed you're authorized to remain on Borleias."

Tam covered over the microphone portion with his palm. He offered Wolam a cynical smile. "So my reputation is all in my imagination, huh?"

"Give me that."

Tam handed the comlink over.

"Hello, this is Wolam Tser. I, too, want to speak to the director of Intelligence, or the director of Security, and I mean immediately."

Tam moved to the keypad and tapped at several of its keys. There was an audible click from the lock and the door slid up and open. Beyond were floor-to-ceiling banks of mechanical and electronic equipment and a narrow, worker-sized gap between them.

"No, you're just Tam Elgrin again, changing his voice, and if you continue to broadcast on this frequency, I'm going to have you dragged through the kill zone behind a landspeeder."

"State your name and rank."

"I'm Warrant Officer Urman Nakk, Security."

"Warrant Officer Urman Nakk, Security, are you widely considered to be an idiot?"

"What?"

"Because in less than a day, I can guarantee that you will be. By your fellow security officers. By your superiors. By your family and your pets. By the officers who court-martial you. And the taint will stay with you throughout your life, because I am a brilliant historian and commentator and you are, at best, a mediocre desk pilot. This will happen despite your best efforts . . . unless you hand me over to one of the officers I asked for, right now!"

Tam gave Wolam a thumbs-up of approval. He took a step into the niche. Then he backed out again and bent over, studying the floor of the electronics-access closet.

"I, ah, I, hold on."

Tam reached down to the seam where the metal floor of the closet met the duracrete floor of the hallway. He lifted, and the floor came up, revealing a hole in the duracrete beneath. The hole was smooth-edged but irregular, lacking the mathematically precise curve of something cut by machinery.

A noise floated up out of the hole. It seemed to come from a great distance, but it was recognizable: a wail of despair, of pain.

Tam sat down at its edge, dangling his legs into the hole. "I'm going down."

"No, you're not."

"I'm seizing the initiative, Wolam."

"No, you're waiting for an officer to come on the comlink."

Tam pushed the portion of metal flooring over until it leaned against a panel of machinery and would not fall across the hole. Then he slid down into the hole.

"Tam, blast it, don't do what I say, do what I *mean*."

NINE

The tunnel did not descend in a straight line. Tam didn't expect it to. It was something of the Yuuzhan Vong, and they never did anything in straight lines.

But that, and the fact that it had been bored through duracrete, meant that Tam could clamber down rather than drop to a messy, bone-breaking stop at the bottom.

Another scream floated up at him, louder. A few meters down, the duracrete gave way to bedrock, then became duracrete again; it looked as though there were sub-basements below, levels that perhaps were not accessed by the public turbolifts and emergency stairwells, and the Yuuzhan Vong intruder had found them. Tam could see, even dig his fingers into smaller side holes in this tunnel; he supposed that whatever stone-eating organisms had made the tunnels had first dug around in all directions and then conveyed images or other knowledge to the Yuuzhan Vong spy who commanded them, allowing him or her to choose which path the main tunnel would follow.

He found a larger niche, two meters deep and one high. Its bottom was lined with some sort of mossy substance; he'd seen it before, one type of sleep surface.

There were also gelatinlike bags he knew to contain bio-engineered creatures that performed various functions when released from the jelly. He'd possessed some of them when he served the Yuuzhan Vong.

There was another scream, and the sound of voices speaking. He slowed his descent, tried to make it quieter.

A few more meters, and the hole opened up into a chamber. Lights flickered red and blue down there, suggesting a computer terminal screen rather than overhead illumination.

And finally Tam could understand one of the voices. It was a male, and he spoke Basic with the halting accent and peculiar rhythm he'd come to associate with a member of the Yuuzhan Vong trying not to reveal his true origins.

"Where is the true crystal?" he asked.

There was no immediate response. Then there was another shriek. The next speaker also sounded male, though his words were distorted by pain: "It's gone. It's been taken to the pipefighter already."

"The pipefighter abominations are still in the flat building. They have not fired upon us. They leave the lambent in that building when guards are more numerous here?"

"Yes, yes—" There was another scream. This one went on and on, ending only as the second speaker ran out of wind.

Tam grimaced. He had to see what was going on in that chamber before he could act. But although he could wait here at the tunnel end, his legs braced at the side, for some time, he couldn't turn upside down to peek outside it. He wasn't that nimble.

Ah, but he had another set of eyes. Hurriedly, he took his light-duty holocam from around his neck. He detached its neck cord, attached it so that the unit could dangle, its lenses pointed to the side and its quick-review viewscreen oriented up toward him. He adjusted the lenses to wide-angle viewing, then lowered the unit to the very bottom of the tunnel and slightly beyond.

In the viewscreen, he could see the chamber below. It appeared that the tunnel was in the ceiling of one corner. The chamber itself was mostly lined with computer equipment, but in one corner was a doorway that probably led to a hallway or stairs, and in the opposite corner was a sort of stall. This was about the same size as a refresher's shower and, like a shower, was bounded by transparent walls; in the bottom of the stall was a mound of what looked like broken transparisteel shards.

Next to the stall was a chair. In it sat a Bothan male, bound hand, arm, and foot. Leaning over him was a human male in a mechanic's jumpsuit.

Tam thought for a moment that the Bothan was diseased. There were irregular bumps on his face, on his fur wherever his garments did not cover it. Then he realized that the bumps were moving, writhing.

Bugs of some sort. As Tam watched, the mechanic brought his hand to the Bothan's forehead. There was an audible crunching noise and the Bothan screamed again. When the mechanic lowered his hand, the Bothan's forehead had one more wiggling bump on it.

Wolam, where are you? But Tam realized that he could neither wait for Wolam to finish persuading the security forces to come, nor speed that process along. The Bothan might die, a death that truly would be on Tam's conscience.

But what could he do? He took stock of his possessions. One hand-sized holocam, various data cards, a comlink, a small vibroblade he'd always carried because it made him feel better, not because he knew how to use it well.

And his brain. A brain that didn't always work in an admirably efficient fashion.

He left the vibroblade switched off and put it between his teeth. He had other tools. The chamber below was dark, lit only by terminal screens. Screams would cover small noises. And he was a strong man—though no fighter, he had size and muscle mass that fighters had often admired.

On the ledge where the moss grew, he set the holocam. He advanced it through its recording memory until he reached one recently recorded scene, then set it to play back on a sixty-standard-second timer.

He waited until he heard another question, answer, and scream. As the scream began, he lowered himself into the chamber below.

Now all the mechanic—a Yuuzhan Vong operative, it was obvious, possibly a warrior—had to do was turn his head to see Tam. One look, one attack, and Tam would be dead.

But the mechanic didn't turn. He leaned in close to witness the Bothan's agonies. Tam, at arm's extension, let go with one hand and swung, but the extra reach brought his toe into contact with the floor. A moment later, when with wrist strength he stopped swaying, he let go and stood.

And knelt. And immediately crept to the side of the room, huddling in the deep shadow beside a bank of unlit terminals. He took the vibroblade from his mouth, positioning it so that its switch was beneath his thumb.

He'd always been inconspicuous despite his size. Now

he feared that, even with his best efforts and wishes, he wouldn't be inconspicuous enough.

"Now, again. Where is the crystal—"

A voice floated out of the tunnel Tam had just left, a woman speaking with a Corellian drawl: "Yes, we're going to pound the Vong, pretty much."

The mechanic snapped upright, turning to stare at the hole. His expression displayed no emotion, but his body language spoke eloquently of alarm, confusion.

The voice continued, "It doesn't matter how hard they hit us. We have twenty thousand years of galactic civilization to draw on. They can't ever destroy *that*."

The mechanic ran to stand beneath the hole, then leapt up.

Tam charged forward, thumbing the vibroblade on. He could see the Bothan's expression, alarm and pain, through the rivulets of blood that flowed down his face. Tam slashed the man's bonds, one-two-three, and they fell away from the Bothan. "Run," Tam whispered.

There was a crunching noise from the tunnel opening, hate-filled words in the Yuuzhan Vong language, then a scraping noise as the mechanic descended.

And there it was, a moment of decision, an initiative to seize or abandon. With it was fear, more fear than Tam had ever felt, even when he had been a Yuuzhan Vong captive and certain that every moment would be his last.

Tam turned and charged back toward the hole. As he lurched forward, he saw the mechanic's legs descending, heels toward him, toes toward the corner.

The mechanic's feet hit the floor and he began to turn. Tam slammed into him with all his considerable mass, hammering him into the room's corner, stabbing wildly

with the vibroblade, kneeing and screaming and batter-
ing. He felt blood on his knife hand, felt fingers around
his left wrist.

Then his wrist was being twisted, mercilessly, as if by a
machine, and he was facedown on the chamber floor.
There was pain like an explosion in his left arm and
when he twisted his head he could see that it was dislo-
cated, the ball of his arm levered out of its socket.

He hurt too much to move, almost too much to hear, but
he caught the mechanic's words: "You fight like child."

Then there was the sizzling noise of a blaster shot, a
roar of such noises as a rifle on full autofire opened up.
Blood sprayed down onto Tam's back.

The mechanic fell atop Tam. The mechanic's hand,
vibroblade still held in it, hit the floor beside Tam's ear.

Tam strained to look up. The door into the chamber
was open and uniformed security operatives were flood-
ing in. With them was a brunette woman he'd seen around
the base: Iella Wessiri, head of Intelligence for this operation, General Antilles's wife.

She knelt before him and one of her men rolled the mechanic's body off. "Tam?" she asked. "Can you hear me?"

"I'm going to pass out now," he said.

And he did.

Aphran System, Aphran IV

They came for Han and Leia in the quietest hour of the
night, rushing into their bedchamber and leveling blasters
before the two of them could stagger out of bed.

Han stared into the bright lights affixed to the rifles.

"What's the meaning of this?" he asked. His voice was calm, the words perfunctory.

The leader of the intruders, only a silhouette behind the lights, answered, "Han Solo, Leia Organa Solo, you are charged with falsification of identification, smuggling, entering Aphran space on false pretenses, and crimes against the state."

"Is that all?" Han offered them a dismissive wave. "That's only a couple of hours' worth of crimes."

"Get up. Get dressed."

Han and Leia rose and began groping in the semi-darkness for their piratical garments.

R2-D2 whistled.

C-3PO, running through a self-diagnostic sequence in trickle-power mode, heard the alarm in his counterpart's musical tones and started up full-power mode. In a fraction of a second he regained use of his motivators and other systems.

They were where they'd been when he'd performed his partial power-down, in the now empty starboard cargo hold of the *Millennium Falcon*. "What's that you say? Performing a bypass of what?"

The ominous clanking noise from the exterior cargo hatch just meters away made any answer unnecessary.

"Oh, dear, oh, dear." Surely there was some procedure in his memory for coping with an intrusion, but the only thing that occurred to the protocol droid was to run and hide.

The astromech whistled again at him, clearly irritated with him for dithering. R2-D2 leaned forward into wheeled-transport mode and rolled out of the bay into the circular corridor that provided access to most of the *Falcon*'s compartments.

C-3PO trotted along after his partner. "Could you slow down? This is an undignified pace."

He followed the astromech into the stern compartment that provided access to the *Falcon*'s escape pods. R2-D2 already stood at the portmost pod, his manipulator arm activating its access button. The door slid partway open and then jammed. The data screen on the front read MALFUNCTION. But the astromech tapped on the button, a rhythm C-3PO did not recognize, and the door slid open the rest of the way.

That noise was drowned out by the groan of the starboard cargo hatch opening, by shouts of "Commence search!" and "Move all this out of here!"

C-3PO trotted into the pod after R2-D2. "This is entirely inappropriate," he said. "Master Han and Mistress Leia are not doing anything illegal."

The astromech whistled and tweetled at him as he activated the controls inside the pod.

"Oh, they *are*? Well, yes, I suppose *illegal* is defined by local authorities, so there would be variations causing an accidental violation of local ordinances." Tweetle. "What, on purpose?"

The escape pod hatch slid closed.

In the hour before dawn, R2-D2 finally opened the pod door and glided out again. The *Millennium Falcon* was quiet; sheltered from weather by the bay walls, she did not even creak under pressure from wind gusts. "How very ominous," C-3PO said.

Tweetle.

"No, I will not be quiet."

Tweetle.

"Well, yes, for the sake of safety, I will lower my volume, but I will not cease speaking."

C-3PO followed the astromech up into the cockpit. R2-D2's hemispherical head turned around, a complete sweep, as he evaluated the situation outside the cockpit viewports.

There were no guards to be seen, but his musical trill alerted C-3PO to the holocams placed so that they could observe the port and starboard hatches and ramp, the upper hatch.

"Yes, Artoo, it appears that we are to remain here."

The astromech trilled at him again, insistently.

"Well, no, they would not have placed a holocam to monitor the secret hatch out of the false escape pod."

Tweetle.

"Are you mad? I can't go out there alone! I'll be captured and scavenged for parts."

R2-D2's response was decidedly unmusical. It sounded like air being forced through a Hutt's blubbery lips.

"There's no call for that. I recognize the danger Master Han and Mistress Leia face. I just have no wish to be terminated."

Tweetle.

"Yes. Perhaps they face termination, too."

C-3PO struggled with the notion the astromech had handed him. His duty was clear; though he had no skills pertinent to this task, he did have to rescue Han and Leia.

But rescue meant exposing himself to physical danger.

This was something he'd done many times over the decades, usually under protest dictated by his self-preservation programming, but now that programming had become something more.

It had become an actual dread. The notion that he could be assaulted so vigorously that his mental process might be suspended forever filled him with an eerie programming static that made it hard for him to move.

On the other hand, the notion that Han and Leia might experience a similar amount of damage was even worse, and allowed him to regain use of his limbs. "What do I have to do?"

Tweetle.

"Oh, no."

The concealed hatch in the *Falcon*'s lower hull slid open. Shiny droid legs lowered through it, waving futilely as they sought the bay floor meters below. "Much farther, Artoo?"

The astromech whistled at him.

C-3PO's torso, then head emerged as he was lowered at a steady rate through the hatch. He held on to a gray cord that looked more like a power cable than climbing gear. In fact, the knob under his hand was a dataport plug. C-3PO looked around and then down at the duracrete beneath him. "Oh, I can't look. Please make it fast."

Moments later, his feet touched down. The cable continued lowering, piling up in irregular coils on the bay floor.

R2 tweetled, impatient.

"Yes, yes, I'm going." C-3PO walked with exaggerated care, like a sneak thief in a holocomedy, to the wall nearest the *Falcon*'s stern. Then he turned and crept along the wall to the corner, turned again, and crept toward the bay doors providing access to the street beyond. He kept his photoreceptors alert for other holocams, but saw none beyond those R2 had mentioned.

He plugged the cable into the dataport at the door. Now, in theory, R2-D2 would be able to work his magic on the computer handling access into and out of this bay.

The astromech offered a musical trill, a noise of victory.

"Excellent, Artoo! And—what? I have to *what*?"

"What we must know," said the man on the other side of the table, "is why you are here and what you are doing." He was of average height, with a dark little beard, a dark little mustache.

Dark little beady eyes, Han decided.

The man wore the uniform of Aphran's military security forces, but his accent was not of this world. He spoke Basic with the tones of someone from one of the Corporate Sector worlds.

"We're here testing the effectiveness of a series of spacer costumes being produced on Commenor," Han said. "And what *I* must know is, how did you see through them? Our sponsors will want to know, to make the costumes better next time."

"This is not funny," the man said.

"What's your name, pal?"

"I am Mudlath, Captain Mudlath, of Aphran Planetary Exosecurity."

"Well, *that's* funny. See, you don't lack a sense of humor."

Leia gave her husband the eye. What he was doing wasn't likely to make things much worse, but there was no way his taunts would make the situation better, either.

They sat around a table in a duracrete-lined room deep in the spaceport base. Han and Leia, their hands manacled behind their backs, their ankles bound together by cutproof cords half a meter long, sat on one side of the table; Captain Mudlath sat opposite, with two of his men, unfriendly-looking ones, flanking the one door out of the chamber.

"I am pleased that you're comfortable enough in your current circumstances to remain jovial," Mudlath said. "Now, you should admit it: you are here engaged in some military action directed against the Yuuzhan Vong, knowing full well that any action you take could embroil the people of this peaceful world in your destructive war."

Han considered. "Isn't *destructive war* kind of redundant? Until I see a constructive war, or even a giggly war, I have to think so."

Clearly exasperated, Mudlath turned his attention to Leia. "Surely you can ease your situation by being more cooperative than your husband."

"Well, he's angry," Leia explained. "And rightly so. We employed costumes precisely to save your people from any inconvenience. If the Yuuzhan Vong knew we were here, they might come, but if they didn't, they wouldn't. We were thinking of you, your needs and feelings, and you reward us with hostility. He *should* be angry."

"An interesting notion," Mudlath acknowledged. "But

it still doesn't explain your mission here. I need the names of everyone you've spoken with since your arrival."

"Oh, dear." Leia thought about it. "Well, there was the officer who contacted us first. The one with the spaceport authority. I transmitted him our documents and we got a homing beacon from him."

"That's right." Han nodded. "He was friendly. Unlike you, Captain. Then there was the baymaster who met us outside our bay. Rulacamp, wasn't it?"

"Elderly woman," Leia said. "Not very talkative."

"Then there was her aide, the one who liked my scar."

Sighing, Captain Mudlath cupped his chin in his hand. "Are you going to make me resort to sterner measures?"

"You mean torture?" Han perked up. "Well . . . if you have to. But make it a good one. One I haven't seen before. I was tortured by Darth Vader."

"So was I," Leia said. "That was before we met."

"You'll have to go some to top him."

"Take them out of here." Mudlath suddenly sounded weary. "We'll get our answers later, and probably very unpleasantly."

C-3PO moved away from the bay where the *Millennium Falcon* was being held. It was the hour before dawn, so he was slightly less conspicuous than a gleaming golden droid would be during the daylight, but he felt as obvious as a two-meter glow rod.

A pack hung around his neck; filled and then lowered to him by R2-D2, it held items the astromech had thought he would need for his trip. He pulled out one of these now, a datapad, and opened it up. He keyed its audio input. "Artoo? Do you read me?"

The screen lit up: YES.

"Oh, I'm so relieved. So they are no longer jamming comlink frequencies?"

THEY ARE STILL JAMMING WITHIN THE BAY. BUT YOU PLUGGED ME INTO THE DOOR COMPUTER DIRECTLY, AND I'M TRANSMITTING THROUGH THAT TO A COMM UNIT OUTSIDE THE JAMMING FIELD.

"I don't need the details. A simple yes or no would have sufficed."

INCORRECT. THE PROPER ANSWER WOULD HAVE BEEN NO, THEY ARE STILL JAMMING COMLINK FREQUENCIES, AND YOU WOULD THEN HAVE BEEN MYSTIFIED AS TO HOW I WAS COMMUNICATING TO YOU.

"Your infernal devotion to minutiae is beginning to overload my logic circuits. Try a simple answer again. What do I do now?"

WHERE ARE YOU?

C-3PO looked around and read in information. He was at a corner of two spacedock avenues, both now increasingly busy with pedestrian and landspeeder traffic. He saw humans, nonhumans, droids, self-motivated loaders, airspeeders, cargo speeders.

And avenue labels; they glowed atop posts. "I appear to be at the corner of Row Fourteen and Column Five."

PROCEED TO THE SOUTHWEST CORNER OF ROW 25 AND COLUMN 10.

"How will I know which is the southwest corner?"

IF YOU MANAGE TO ARRIVE THERE WITHIN THE NEXT SEVEN STANDARD HOURS, EAST WILL BE THE DIRECTION WHERE THE SUN IS.

"Very funny. Ha-ha." Irritated to his cybernetic core, C-3PO set off toward the indicated destination.

Han gave up on the door. He backed away to the cot attached to the wall and sat there. "I can't get the access panel off," he complained. "It's built like a prison."

"It *is* a prison," Leia said.

"That explains it. Can you do anything? With the Force?"

"Sure, if I had my lightsaber." Leia stood at the center of the room, studying the air vents, the slot in the door that doubtless was intended for the insertion of a food plate. "Which, you'll recall, I left behind with your favorite blaster, since they are both sort of identifiable. But give me a minute." She closed her eyes and tried to submerge herself in the Force, to feel whatever it was that it might choose to show her.

She could feel living things all around her, hundreds, thousands, too many to count, just as it was in any highly populated area. There were no pockets of dark side energy, no glowing beacons or other anomalies to focus on.

There *was* the door, and though her telekinetic skills were far inferior to those of most Jedi she knew, she did possess some. She focused on the door, tried to understand its internal structure as the Force showed it to her.

She could feel its metallic strength, feel little discontinuities that suggested moving parts. Soon enough, she distinguished the vertical bars that rose and descended from the door to keep it from swinging open. Other bars, less formidable, slid in behind them to keep them from sliding into their unlocked position.

She plucked at the lower holding bar, felt it twitch under her effort. By concentrating further, she felt it slide free, just for a moment, before some other energy pulled it back into place.

Leia tried again with the upper bar. It, too, she could pry out of place for a moment—not long enough to slide the main locking bar out of position.

She sighed and opened her eyes. "Not a chance," she said. "Not without a lot of practice. In maybe two, three days I might be able to handle one of the locks. In a few weeks, maybe I could do both at the same time and get that thing open."

"It's all right," he told her. "We'll get out of here some other way."

"How?"

"I have no idea."

TEN

R2-D2 had been manufactured a long time ago, and those long years of experience meant that he had a store of knowledge of tricks, techniques, and strategies that made the programming of most other droids pale in comparison, and he found that he needed every one of them here.

Because, frustratingly enough, the prison computers of this spaceport were just unwilling to set his friends free.

Oh, he was able to obtain some information about them readily enough. Han and Leia shared a cell in the prison's deepest level and were labeled ENEMIES OF THE STATE and HOLD FOR SPECIAL ENVOY PICKUP.

The prison computers could be persuaded to keep secret the fact that R2-D2 was trying to get past them. He'd managed to forge himself a false ID as a security program testing defensive program efficiency. All he had to endure from them was little expressions of mockery each time he failed to penetrate one of their protocols. Which was often.

The prison computers could not be persuaded that the Solo cell was actually unoccupied and ready for another occupant, which would have unlocked the thing. They could not be convinced that the Solos had military authority equivalent to the prison manager or head of security. They could not be induced to deliver captured explosives now held in a security division locker to that cell. They could not be tricked into transferring the Solos to a minimum-security level.

R2-D2 beeped in agitation. Prison computers, unlike humans, were never distracted or hungry. Their attention never flagged. This would take forever, and there was an indicator in the Solo file that they would be placed in the hands of outsystem visitors within the next couple of hours.

Distracted. Hungry. R2-D2 called up the computer protocols on prisoner needs and reviewed them.

Satisfied, he made a happy trilling noise and got back to work.

C-3PO got into the line of visitors and slowly, meter by meter, approached the prison's service entrance. He spoke down into the bag around his neck, whispering: "Artoo, I am three from the front of the line."

UNDERSTOOD.

The protocol droid looked ahead to the entrance. One human and a security droid stood there. The security droid was bulky, with black armor that suggested storm-trooper defenses, and a nearly featureless face with red-glowing eyes, a nightmare vision even for a droid. The human looked as though he were the droid's distant cousin, with similar armor and a similar build. He wore no helmet, and his eyes seemed to gleam redly in the light of dawn.

C-3PO took another step forward. "I am now two from the front of the line."

GOOD. THE TIMING SHOULD WORK.

"What timing?"

There was no answer.

Now there was just one person in line ahead of C-3PO. The human guard, halfway into a brief interrogation of that person, scowled and held up a black-enameled comlink. He spoke for a moment into it, then exercised an even deeper set of scowl muscles and turned to the droid. "You take over for a minute," he said. "Payroll has to ask me a question in person."

The droid nodded. When the human guard had gone, it accepted the next visitor's identichip, ran it through its own internal slot, returned it to the man, then gave him a shove sufficient to throw the visitor down the stairs. "Refused," the droid said. "Next."

C-3PO moved up, irrationally feeling circuitry threaten to melt down in his vocal centers. "Good morning, sir, I wish to enter these—"

"Shut up. Identification."

C-3PO handed over the chip that had, until just minutes before, been plugged into his datapad.

The security droid inserted it into the slot in its chest, then spat it out again and returned it. "Tadening Foodmakers is authorized to enter," it said.

"Thank you, sir." C-3PO tried to move forward through the doorway, but the security droid's hand slapped into his chest, restraining him.

"Not so fast. Present possessions for search."

Reluctantly, C-3PO held his bag up for inspection and

opened its top flap. Clearly visible within the compartment were Leia's lightsaber, Han's modified DL-44 blaster pistol, vibroblades, a datapad, data cards. "This is the, um, requested last meal for the Solos before their departure."

The security droid peered at the items. "Identify these."

"Um, well, the two large packages are Corellian meat-lump. The one with the trigger housing is spiced, of course, and the other not." Dismayed by the ridiculousness of his description, C-3PO pointed at the vibroblades and forged ahead. "Mealbread sticks." He indicated the other items. "Honey wafers for dessert."

"No vegetables?"

"No vegetables. I'm sure you know about Corellians."

The security droid reached through its wireless datalink to the base computer and brought up three-dimensional representations of the types of food C-3PO had named. The database offered recently updated visuals on those foods, which, in every particular, including coloration, structure, and surface defects, matched the items in the bag.

"Pass," said the security droid.

"*Thank* you, sir."

Once past the service entrance, C-3PO followed data microtransmissions that led him through a maze of service departments—laundry, electronic prisoner monitoring, visitor lanes. At the entrance to the kitchen he was met by a rolling cart that slid a slot open for him.

"You're sure this is the meal slot for the Solos," C-3PO said.

The rolling cart beeped irritably at him.

"Do not fret, I was not questioning your competence. I was merely making conversation." C-3PO dumped the contents of his bag out into the slot. The rolling cart slid the slot closed and banged its way back through the doors into the kitchen, still beeping in a less-than-friendly manner.

"Government service units," C-3PO sniffed. "Now, let us see if we can find our way back out of here."

But he was speaking only to himself. Until he found another datapad or comlink with a strong enough transmitter to connect directly with R2-D2, he was alone. R2-D2 had told him he was to make his break for freedom now, to exit the prison by the way he'd come and then move northward as fast as his golden legs would carry him. The astromech had told him to be brave.

"So this is what bravery is," he told himself. "How odd that it feels like petrification."

Han and Leia heard the service droid moving up the line of cells. At each one, it announced, "Breakfast" in an irritating mechanical whine. A series of thumps and thuds followed.

"I can tell," Han said, "that this will be an interesting dining experience."

The droid whined to a halt outside their door. "Last meal," it announced.

"Even better," Leia said.

Then items poured through the slot in the door. Han's blaster. Leia's lightsaber. Other objects.

"You have *got* to be kidding," Han said.

Leia nodded. "Well, that makes this my favorite prison ever."

They scrambled to the door and sorted out their possessions. Leia flipped open the datapad, read the words,

R2-D2 STANDING BY. AUDIO OPEN. PRESS "AD-VANCE" FOR ESCAPE ROUTE MAP AND "RETURN" FOR TEXT.

Leia broke into a brilliant smile. "Artoo?"

STANDING BY. SUGGEST YOU COMMENCE YOUR ESCAPE AS SOON AS POSSIBLE. I AM UN-ABLE TO PREVENT THE MONITOR DROIDS FROM OBSERVING YOUR CELL. AT ANY MOMENT THEY MAY BEGIN WONDERING WHY YOU ARE NOT EATING YOUR FOOD.

"Understood," Leia said. She hit the ADVANCE button, taking a quick moment to note the first few elements of their escape path. "Short hallway, metal-bar obstacle—no problem—cut through the floor into the maintenance machinery section. Got it. Ready?" She handed the data-pad to Han.

"Ready." Han took up position beside the door, his blaster in hand.

Leia lit her lightsaber. She drove the point of the gleaming red bar of energy into the door at floor level, dragged it across the bottom of the door. She felt heavy resistance that had to be the metal bars there. Once she was past that, she repeated the process at the top of the door, her blade not quite horizontal because she was not tall enough to hold the lightsaber that high.

Once she was past the heaviest resistance there, she re-treated into a defensive stance and nodded.

Han shoved. The door slid halfway open. He snatched back his hand as two guards on the other side fired blasters through the opening.

Leia caught both shots with her blade, batting one to

the side, the other back through the opening. It struck a blue-clad guard there in the chest and he went down, his uniform flaming and smoking.

Han leaned out and fired twice through the opening, catching the other guard in the side and hurling him out of the way. He shoved at the door again, and it opened the rest of the way.

Han and Leia rounded the corner to the barred exit from this cell block. Han waited behind and began firing back the way they had come while Leia went to work on the bars, cutting through three of them at head height and again at ankle height. Incoming blasterfire flashed past Han's position, blackening the wall behind him. "Got it?" he called.

"Got it. Come on." She slid through the gap and turned to face Han.

He raced to her, leapt through the gap. In those few seconds, prison guards skidded into view past the corner he'd vacated. They began firing; Leia swatted the bolts from the air, reveling at being able to do something so simple, so gratifying, so direct. Some of her deflections sailed back the way they'd come and forced the guards into hiding.

This corridor was nothing but a duracrete tube angling gently upward. Han raced up it, pacing off a distance. He consulted the datapad in his hand, then fired his blaster into the floor, marking one point. "That's our mark."

Leia raced to join him and plunged her lightsaber into the floor there, dragging it around in a crude circle. Han waited until he saw the first set of feet appear at the bottom of the ramp, then began firing on the pursuers. "How's it coming?"

"Slow. I forgot at first to angle the cut outward instead of inward."

"What difference—never mind." Cutting through the duracrete with the edges angled inward as they descended created a plug that would have to be hauled up; cutting it the other way would yield a plug that should just fall away.

Except that it didn't. Leia finished her cut and stepped back, panting, and the plug remained stubbornly in place.

Han continued firing. "Artoo!" he shouted. "How thick is the duracrete here, anyway?" He stole a glance at the datapad screen.

LESS THAN A METER.

"Then why doesn't it fall?"

Aggravated, Leia stamped on the plug. It remained obstinantly in place. "Check the map again," she said. "Maybe we'll have to cut through somewhere else."

"You check it!" Han tossed her the datapad and fired three times in quick succession. Return fire bounced off the duracrete around them. "I'm obviously not fit to read a map."

"No, you've got it right."

"Fall, blast it! Fall!" Han stomped on the plug. It didn't vibrate. He leapt clean upon it.

It fell.

R2-D2 sent the command through the cable that snaked out through the false escape pod to the landing bay door computer datajack. Immediately, his audio sensors picked up the grinding noise of the bay roof levering open.

He ejected the cable from his own datajack and watched it snake down through the hole to the bay floor below.

With a little musical squeal that betrayed his eagerness, the astromech rolled out of the escape pod and up to the *Falcon*'s bridge. He plugged into the dataport there and began an abbreviated, computer-speed power-up sequence. It wouldn't take long for the spaceport authority to realize that a supposedly unoccupied bay was opening to release a supposedly impounded transport, and he wanted to be out of here by then.

It wasn't every day R2-D2 got to fly the *Millennium Falcon*, after all.

Captain Mudlath was in his office, calculating just what he could purchase with the Solo reward, when his comlink buzzed into life. "Captain," his administrative aide told him, "the Solos have escaped."

Mudlath actually felt himself grow dizzy for a moment as adrenaline jolted through him. "This had better be a joke," he said. "And a funny enough joke that I laugh until I forget about killing you."

"They're not out of the prison," his aide said. "They won't get out. But they're out of their cell."

Mudlath lowered his voice to a near-whisper. "I suggest you put them back in their cell." Not waiting for a reply, he switched the comlink off, then sat back to try to persuade his stomach muscles to unclench.

If he *didn't* get them back . . . well, his Peace Brigade superiors would not only decline to reward him for the capture of the Solos, but they might choose to take the news badly. And if things continued as they were, and the Peace Brigade became the legitimate government of this backwater planet, he might have to leave. Quickly. Surreptitiously.

Jarred back into activity, he reached into a desk drawer and pulled out a handful of identichips taken from prisoners. Perhaps, with a little modification, one of them would serve to get him off-world.

The duracrete under Han's feet fell into darkness, but only about three meters, a deep enough drop for him to begin to worry that he was dropping into a mine shaft, a short enough drop that, with his experience, he was able to absorb most of the shock of impact with bent knees, to roll forward off the plug and across another hard floor to come up on his feet with a minimum of bruises.

A minimum. Not none. His middle-aged back would feel that one in the morning. Amazingly, he still had his blaster pistol in hand.

He was in another duracrete tunnel, this one illuminated only by the hole overhead. A hole in which Leia's face suddenly appeared. "Are you all right?"

"Get down here!"

She leapt in headfirst, rotating in midair to land on her feet atop the plug. Her landing was so light compared to his that he couldn't help but grin. "You do that just like a Jedi."

"Hush. Where to now?" She handed him the datapad.

He checked the datapad screen and turned in the approximate direction they'd been running while in the tunnel above. "There'll be a metal door there giving us access into a metal scrap compactor. We take a left and get out the door at the end."

"No, Han. Not another compactor. Once in a lifetime is enough."

The map on the screen suddenly blanked, replaced by words: I INITIATED A POWER SHUTDOWN ON THE COMPACTOR. IT CANNOT BE ACTIVATED UNTIL IT GOES THROUGH A FULL START-UP PROCEDURE. IT WILL BE THREE HOURS AT LEAST.

"Well," Leia allowed, "that's all right, then."

More shapes blocked the hole above. Han and Leia ran before they could begin firing.

Seeing through the *Falcon*'s holocam eyes and sensor screens, R2-D2 sent the transport up on repulsorlifts. The transport wobbled like a plate being balanced atop a stick and he marvelled that humans, with their reflexes that crawled in relation to the speed of droid calculations, could learn to pilot vehicles so well.

He managed to get the *Falcon* clear of the bay before its ceiling panels began to swing down again. His trill was a little like laughter—the spaceport authorities had noticed just a little too late. Now that he was above the bay, he was clear of whatever comm-jamming equipment they had put in place; he could once again detect and interact with Han and Leia's datapad.

Now he had to make sure he got the *Falcon* to the prison. Not just to the prison, he reminded himself, but to the prison and *in one piece*.

Furious, Han kicked at the pile of metal scrap leaning against the exit door from the compacting chamber.

"Artoo, you didn't say anything about having to dig our way out!"

SORRY. THE COMPUTER SYSTEM DIDN'T MEN-TION THAT THE COMPACTOR WAS HALF FULL. THEY ARE IN VIOLATION OF THEIR OWN REGU-LATIONS. THAT IS PROBABLY WHY THEY DO NOT HAVE THE LOAD LISTED.

"Leia, can you cut through this? Or through the wall?"

Leia bounced her lightsaber blade off the glossy blue wall of the chamber and shook her head. "Magnetically sealed. I can cut through the pile. In a few minutes." Then she heard the sound of mechanical voices from behind her. She spun. "Which we don't have."

A security droid entered through the door Han and Leia had used just moments before. The droid fired as soon as his barrel cleared the door and continued to fire as he sprinted to the wall opposite the door, where he took up position, laying down covering fire.

Leia batted the first blast out of the way as she and Han got behind cover. The cover was good—heavy steel scrap that easily absorbed the energy unloaded by blaster rifle shots. But missed shots ricocheted off the walls, propelled by the magnetic shielding, and inevitably one would bounce down into Han's or Leia's back.

Then a second droid entered the chamber, and a third, and a fourth, all of them firing.

"We're sunk," Leia said.

"I don't think so." Han glanced around, found a more protective niche in the scrap, and sidestepped into it. He rose high enough to return fire for a moment. "Six, seven, eight of them. The more, the better."

"The more, the better?" Leia slid into place beside him.

"Yeah, when we get enough of them in here, we can't possibly lose."

"Now I know why you never want to be told the odds. Because you don't know what they mean!"

Han grinned at her. "Nine, ten, eleven. That's good enough to start with. Can you get me a couple of those blaster rifles?"

"You planning on shooting our way out of here?"

"That's right. Please, Leia. Two rifles."

Leia hesitated, caught off guard by Han's rare use of the word *please*, then said, "Cover me. Go."

Han popped up and squeezed off several quick shots. Leia stood from behind cover a moment later, saw several of the droids aiming to return fire. Some of them had to hold off firing to avoid hitting more droids charging into the chamber.

With the Force, Leia reached out toward one of the late arrivals, a droid who held his rifle in a loose grip. She yanked toward her and the rifle came sailing to her hand. Before it landed, she repeated the trick on the next droid entering the room, and his rifle, too, leapt from his possession and into Leia's.

She ducked down with Han. "Now what?"

"Battleship tactics." He hauled on the heaviest plate of scrap metal in their vicinity, toppling it so that it covered the two of them almost completely. Their improvised fort was now lit only by the red glow from Leia's weapon.

Han indicated two spots on the plate. "Holes here and here. Fist-sized."

Leia complied, burning two apertures in the metal.

The air now stank with the odor of superheated durasteel. "You won't be able to see to aim."

"Who needs to aim?" Han picked up one rifle in each hand, switched each to full autofire, inserted the barrels in the holes, angled them up more toward the ceiling, and began firing.

Leia switched off her lightsaber and crowded back as far away from the rifles as she could, holding her hands over her ears. The roar in this confined space was deafening. Han rocked the weapons back and forth, slowly changing his angle of fire left to right, up and down.

The metal plate shuddered as it began sustaining hits. Han turned to Leia and flashed her a manic grin, then closed his eyes and kept firing.

First one of his rifles clicked down to zero and stopped firing, then the other. But the sound of ricochets continued as shots bounded from one end of the compactor chamber to the other, bouncing again and again until they hit something not protected by the chamber's magnetic seal.

Such as scrap metal. Such as droids. Such as droids being transformed into scrap metal.

When there were no more blasts or impacts to be heard, Han maneuvered the metal plate aside and peeked. Leia also leaned around the plate to look.

The droids weren't completely destroyed. She saw one walking back and forth with half his head gone, clicking the trigger of a rifle that was missing its middle section. Another droid spun around, his upper half turning one direction and his lower half the other, causing him to roll erratically across the floor. But most were down, motionless.

"I'll watch the other door," Han said, "if you'll cut through the pile here and get us out."

"Love to."

The exercise yard guards looked up as the *Millennium Falcon* awkwardly maneuvered into position above the yard.

The guards raised their blaster rifles and opened fire. R2-D2 saw their assault through his link with the transport's holocams, and felt a momentary thrill of dismay and an anticipation of damage before his probability calculations indicated that their shoulder arms would not be able to harm the ship. He brought the *Falcon* down several meters until the keel was just above the ground, and hovered there.

Han and Leia emerged from a side door in one of the walls bounding the exercise yard. They drew the guard-droid fire from the *Falcon*, but Han fired with his blaster in one direction, keeping droids harried and defensive there, while Leia deflected each and every blaster bolt aimed at them from the other direction. R2-D2 lowered the starboard boarding ramp, and in moments, Han and Leia rushed up to the cockpit. R2 raised the ramp.

Leia gave R2-D2 a pat on the dome before settling into the copilot's chair. "Well done, Artoo."

He wheetled at her, sent one last message through the dataport, then unjacked himself.

Han peeled off his piratical tunic and scrubbed at the false scar over his eye as he looked over the control boards. "Threepio's on foot north of here. Get into the topside laser turret. We'll scoop Threepio up and then punch out of here."

"To space, I assume," Leia said.

"To the forest." Han flashed her a lopsided grin. "Trust me on this."

The spaceport was protected by a quartet of aging Z-95 Headhunters, venerable predecessors of the X-wing. While they made cautious runs in the distance, unwilling to strafe a transport so close to the ground, Leia helped keep them at bay with judicious use of the *Falcon*'s top turret.

Han guided the *Falcon* north over the base, swooping down once, just long enough to lower the boarding ramp and give C-3PO time to hurry aboard. Then Han kicked the thrusters in and headed northwest, the direction with the nearest heavy stand of forest. As he neared the leading edge of old-growth trees, some of which reached to the height of twenty-story buildings, he rotated the *Falcon* until the ship was perpendicular. The *Falcon* slid into the forest like a vibroknife into blue butter. The pursuing Headhunters broke off pursuit, scattering, climbing above the treetops to look for the *Falcon* from an altitude. After a few hundred more meters of nerve-jangling maneuvering through the trees, Han tilted the transport back onto her belly and settled down in a shadowy glade.

"If I may ask, sir," said C-3PO as he desperately clung to the restraining straps on his seat, "why do we not just go into space?"

"Because someone was aboard the *Falcon*," Han snapped. "And do you know what happens every time someone I don't like comes aboard?"

"No, sir."

"They sabotage something! Usually the shields, or especially the hyperdrive motivator. I *hate* that. Leia, take over at the controls while I see what they did."

"Yes, Captain. Right away, Captain." Leia trotted into the cockpit, took the pilot's seat as Han vacated it, gave him a kiss as they made the transfer. "You know we're only going to have a few minutes here before they find us and bring in the heavy guns."

"Then let's hope I'm as good as mechanic as I know I am."

"Anything I can do while we're waiting?"

"Get on the comm board and see if you can find their comm traffic. That may give us an idea of how much time we really have."

"I'm also going to put in a call to our smuggler contacts. Let them know we have to leave in a hurry."

"Very polite of you. Very proper."

"Oh, shut up."

Han didn't take long to find it. The hyperdrive motivator had indeed been sabotaged. Someone had installed a simple fuse that would hold up to a system check but would blow the first time real power surged through the system. In the hyperdrive motivator compartment, the saboteur had also wired a tracking device. Han rerouted the hyperdrive power the way it was supposed to be, then threw the tracking device out an airlock.

He returned at a run to the cockpit and slid into the pilot's chair as Leia, still in her comm unit privacy headset, vacated it and took her own seat.

They watched as, in the distance ahead and to port, a

long-nosed flying vehicle edged through the trees. "What *is* that?" Han asked. "Vong, or local make?"

"Can't make it out," Leia said.

"Well, let's just outfly it and identify it later." Han powered up the repulsorlifts and stood the *Millennium Falcon* on her stern. He heard noises of unhappiness from C-3PO and a wild squeal of dismay from R2-D2. As he accelerated up through the treetops, he grinned over at Leia. "Forgot to tell them we were taking off."

"Uh-huh."

"Leia, you have to admit, that was fun."

"Fun. Getting kidnapped, jailed, threatened with torture, shot at—fun."

"That's right."

Leia felt her face twist into a smile she had no control over. "All right, all right. Despite everything, it was fun."

"Welcome back, Princess."

ELEVEN

Borleias

Tam awoke in a hospital ward bed.

Again.

He didn't like doing that. It was happening too often.

This time, his left shoulder ached, and he remembered how it got that way. The first time a member of the medical staff walked past the foot of his bed, he motioned the man over and said, "Can I get a message to someone?"

"Let me get someone for you first," the man said.

Minutes later, visitors appeared from beyond the blue curtains to one side. Tarc barged right up to stand beside Tam. Wolam was content to stand at the foot of the bed, smiling. And Intelligence head Iella Wessiri positioned herself between them.

"Which arm hurts?" Tarc asked.

"No, no, no, Tarc. Protocol." Tam gave him a little mock-glare. "The visitor who is most socially important, or who has the greatest demands on his time, gets to talk first. Which one is that?"

"Me," Tarc said.

"Try again."

"Well, her, I guess."

"That's better."

Iella smiled at the boy. "I was available, so I thought I'd stop by in person to give you some news. You did a very important thing last night. You prevented a Yuuzhan Vong spy from getting away with some, well, very significant information."

"Information you *didn't* want them to have. Unlike the stuff I gave them."

Iella nodded, not contrite.

"What information?"

"I shouldn't say. You shouldn't ask."

"I think I can guess." When still under Yuuzhan Vong control, he'd stolen records of a project being developed at this base, something about a superweapon involving laser weapons focused through a giant-sized lambent crystal, a living crystal normally bioengineered only by the Yuuzhan Vong. The spy's torture of the Bothan, asking about such a crystal, suggested that the Bothan's chamber was where it was being kept or monitored. But there had been no giant lambent crystal there—only the wreckage of some sort of mock-up.

There was no giant crystal. It was a fake. The whole Starlancer project had to be a fake. In a moment of clarity, he understood that the Starlancer project was nothing more than a ring in the nose of the Yuuzhan Vong commander, something to tug him in one direction or another.

"What's your guess?" Iella asked.

"I shouldn't say. You shouldn't ask."

"Good man."

"How's the Bothan?"

"Alive. Which he probably wouldn't have been, without your intervention. He's a few beds down; you can talk to him if the doctors say it's all right. Anyway, I just wanted to stop by and say thanks."

"Happy to help. Except for the pain part."

When she'd gone, Tarc said, "They're talking about you."

"What are they saying?"

"That you're crazy as a monkey-lizard, jumping a Vong warrior all by yourself."

"What do *you* say?"

"Well . . . I've never seen a monkey-lizard."

Tam nodded. "Good answer."

"Come on, boy." Wolam motioned Tarc over. "We need to give the monkey-lizard here some more time to rest. You can be my holocam operator until he drags himself out of bed."

"Good," Tarc said. "I'll make the recordings he's scared to."

"Just don't record me." Tam pulled the sheet up over his head.

He heard Tarc snicker, and then he drifted away into sleep once more.

Coruscant

Luke woke in darkness, disoriented for a moment by the lack of familiar sights and smells, but comforted by the knowledge that Mara was beside him. In fact, it was her settling into the broad cot with him that reminded him where and when he was. "Just coming off watch?" he murmured.

"That's right." She rested her chin on his shoulder, making him her pillow. "Go back to sleep."

"I ought to get up."

"You don't want to do that. All the news is bad."

"What news?"

"Ask the scientists."

"We've spent so much time down in the ruins," Danni explained, "that we haven't had much of an opportunity to take all the readings we needed to." Before she could continue, she yawned, then looked embarrassed at the way her exhaustion had betrayed her.

They were in the Complex's control chamber, Luke and Danni and Baljos. Both scientists looked tired, but now, at least, there was sufficient fresh water to bathe and wash clothes, so they all looked better than they had in some days.

"What readings?" Luke asked. "Every time I look at you two, you're taking readings."

"We've been taking biological readings, mostly," Baljos said. "Electromagnetic energy flow readings. Chemical tests of water and food sources. That sort of thing. But not until a few hours ago, when Kell and Face went top-side and set up some holocams and other monitoring equipment, have we been able to do any astronomical recordings."

Luke shrugged. "So what have you found out?"

"Gravitational readings suggest that we're closer to Coruscant's sun now," Danni said. "The planetary orbit has changed."

"The atmospheric temperature is several degrees higher than it should be at this time of year," Baljos said. "That was the impression I got with our hand units, but there was no way to tell before now whether it was just a seasonal fluke. No, there's a lot more moisture in the atmosphere than there should be. Consistently. Laser-based spectroscopic analysis gives similar readings out to a considerable distance. Master Skywalker, I think the polar ice is melting."

"Luke. It's just Luke." Luke sat back, frowning. "Is this their worldshaping?"

Danni nodded. "More like 'Vongforming.' It's a lot faster, more brutally efficient than our equivalent techniques."

"Is there any *good* news?"

"A little." Danni pointed at the first of three computer screens.

This one showed a holocam view of a building roof. It seemed to be shedding; fragments of some leaflike material were being tossed around by winds. "We're witnessing a die-off of some of the Vongforming plants. The grasses and explosive fungi they used to begin the breakdown of the building surfaces are starting to die. We don't know whether it means they're not adapting well to this environment, or just that they're the first step of the Vongforming process, with more steps to come. Doctor Arnjak suspects the latter."

"That's 'Science Boy' to you," Baljos said.

"So that may or may not be good news," Luke said.

Baljos nodded. "Correct. Here's some news that's a little less ambiguous." He indicated the other two screens, one full of graphical charts and text, the other broken down into eight holocam images—still images of Yuuzhan Vong warriors digging through rubble, engaged in training exercises, lined up in a disciplined row.

Luke peered at the screens. The information on the first one seemed to relate to proportions of gases in the atmosphere. "What's it mean?"

"The proportion of toxic gases in the atmosphere has pretty much stabilized. Oh, they're worse at some specific altitudes than others, but they're not increasing in proportion. I think they relate to the biological actions of the Vongforming plants that are breaking down the duracrete and metals. Meaning that the Vong aren't trying to make the atmosphere poisonous to us. This increases the chances of survival of, well, the people who are still alive down here."

"That's something, I guess." Luke looked at the scientists. "And the other one?"

Danni said, "You remember that we brought along some little stealth droids. Shaped like fungi, mosses, that sort of thing. We've been taking them out and depositing them in areas the Vong seem to patrol heavily. They're following those paths, very slowly, and transmitting images in very short, hard-to-track comm bursts. These are our first sets of images. They don't tell us much yet, but we hope they will someday."

"So, what do you get from the atmospheric data?"

Danni and Baljos exchanged a look, and Luke could read all sorts of things into it. They'd already come to some conclusions. They were just trying to decide which ones to present him, and in which order.

"We've kind of been giving the survivors the impression that the New Republic forces are going to come back and seize Coruscant," Danni said.

Luke nodded. "That's the objective."

"I don't think there's going to be a Coruscant to come back to. How long will it take? A year? Five years? Ten? By the time our forces get here, it's going to be something else. A Yuuzhan Vong world."

"That won't give the survivors much hope."

"So," Baljos said, "we think we should take a different approach to what we were doing. We teach the survivors how to survive on this world—this *alien* world. Not necessarily so they can come out fighting when the big push comes. Just so they can survive. Maybe escape. We analyze all the new life-forms we run across, the ones introduced by the Yuuzhan Vong, and teach our people which ones are good to eat. Teach them how to find safe water."

"Maybe how to wall off whole complexes," Danni said, "so the Vong just never come down into them."

"If we do all that . . ." Luke considered the matter for long seconds. "We're admitting that we've lost."

"That we've lost Coruscant, anyway," Danni said. "Not the war."

"I can't accept this." A flash of anger ignited within Luke, but he calmed himself, willed it away. "You're suggesting that this entire mission is a failure!"

"Not a failure." Danni carefully considered her words. "The mission didn't match the reality we found. It's like any scientific investigation. You observe evidence, you come up with a theory to explain the evidence, you put the theory to the test . . . and in most cases, the theory has to be revised. We arrive at truths one faltering step at a time."

"Just like Jedi training."

"That's right."

Luke sighed. "I have to think about this."

Luke was still thinking about it two days later when he went on another vehicle hunt with Face and Bhindi.

They weren't always traveling in Yuuzhan Vong armor anymore; now that they had a base of operations and less need to travel in a large group through unknown territories, Luke and the others often made do with civilian clothing. It was lighter and far more comfortable than the Yuuzhan Vong armor, especially in the increasingly steamy atmosphere of Coruscant's lower levels. Kell and Face were the exceptions—quite taken with just how horribly dashing they were in the armor, they insisted on wearing it during all missions, evidently a competition to see which one would give up and admit discomfort first.

With initial objectives achieved—the team had a base of operations and its members were interacting with the local non-Yuuzhan Vong population—they could begin implementing the plan for their eventual escape from Coruscant.

Their insertion method had not included a getaway vehicle, for they knew that, given how many millions of vehicles still remained here, in varying conditions of preservation, they would be able to find, salvage, or steal a working vehicle—or, with Tahiri's help, perhaps even a Yuuzhan Vong vessel.

Logic dictated that there had to be thousands if not millions of vehicles in the wreckage that was Coruscant. The trick was in finding them, since all vehicles visible from the air had been strafed and destroyed by coralskippers. Only those that had been hidden or buried had a chance to be intact.

And so far, though they'd found hundreds of vehicles in their searches, not one was even remotely likely as an escape vehicle. They'd found scores of airtaxis, numerous crashed starfighters, the remains of a hangar with a troop transport—and troops—crushed beneath incalculable tonnage of collapsed building. Luke thought that, with a month to work on it, he could cobble together enough parts from various destroyed starfighters to make one working model . . . which would get one of them off-planet when the time came.

That was just one more failure to weigh upon him. He sat in a fiftieth-story viewport of what had once been a Starfighter Command recruiting office, staring out into the cavernous street beneath, while Face and Bhindi struggled to get the office's computer operational, and he wondered why he'd bothered with this mission.

His son Ben was light-years away, hidden out of sight— out of Yuuzhan Vong sight, but also out of *his* sight—in a secret Jedi base in the Maw, a region of space surrounded and concealed by black holes. Mara had to be questioning his competence. The Jedi, whom he had hoped to inspire and unite in this bold mission into the territory most strongly held by the Yuuzhan Vong, would lose faith in him.

Something attracted his attention, just the merest sensation that there were eyes upon him, and he looked up from the rubble-strewn depths he'd been regarding.

Across the avenue, at about the same altitude, someone stood in a viewport staring at him. At this distance, about a hundred meters, Luke could not be sure, but he thought it was a man. A very pale man. Luke pulled out his macrobinoculars and trained them on that person.

He stared into a face that was half-strange, half-familiar.

This man was pallid, with curly dark hair, sea-blue eyes, and a prominent nose that suggested old aristocracy. He was young, barely twenty, if that old. He wore a pale kiltlike wrap around his midsection and shiny items at various points on his body—fingerless gloves, elbow covers, knee covers; though thick and metallic, these looked like a very inadequate set of armor. His head was held at an angle as though he'd been tilting it one way and another as he watched Luke.

Luke knew his face, but couldn't place it, couldn't call up that memory. In fact, it was easier not to think right now.

When Luke's eyes met his, the man smiled. It was the smile of a child suddenly captivated with the wonders of pulling legs off insects.

Luke found he could sense the man in the Force— could do so without even reaching out for him. The man was a glowing light in the Force, a beacon in the midst of darkness. A beacon *of* darkness . . . but that suddenly didn't matter much.

Luke felt his breath go out of him. It was as though the roof had slowly collapsed and deposited two tons of duracrete on his torso while he was distracted.

He glanced over at Face and Bhindi. They had the terminal running; the glow from its screen colored their faces blue. Bhindi removed a datacard from its slot in the terminal and made a noise of satisfaction. They were both utterly unaware of what Luke was seeing, feeling.

Luke knew that, when he turned his attention back to the distant viewport, the pale man would be gone; it was among the oldest tools in the bag of tricks of the makers of supernatural holodramas. But when he looked through the macrobinoculars again, the man was still there, motionless.

Luke unlatched the viewport's locks. All he had to do was step out on the walkway that now stretched between this building and the other. He could walk right up to this man and begin asking questions. But some faint stirring of alarm—his pilot's ability to glimpse and memorize topographical details—shook him out of the fog that had overcome his thinking.

There *was* no walkway before him. One step through this viewport and he'd plummet to his death.

The man's grin grew wider. Then he sidestepped and disappeared from sight.

Luke felt the great weight lift from him. He could breathe again. "Are you two done here?" he asked.

Face looked up, frowning. "Luke, are you all right?"

"No. Trouble's coming. Let's go."

Bhindi rose. "If trouble's coming, we're done here."

Luke, Face, and Bhindi crouched in a crater that had been one corner of a skyscraper—the same skyscraper in which, minutes before, the pale man had stood. They were about twenty stories above the window the figure had occupied, and all three had macrobinoculars trained on the viewport Luke had, minutes before, tried to open.

The room beyond the viewport was filled with people. They wore tatters. Some wore nothing but dried mud and blood. There was a light in their eyes that suggested they were on stimulants and had been for days or weeks. They rampaged through the Starfighter Command office, destroying every piece of furniture, smashing every wall, a riot whose violence was directed at everything and nothing.

"What are they?" Bhindi asked. "They're not your run-of-the-mill survivors."

"Some of Yassat's cannibals, I expect," Face said. "You felt them coming, Luke?"

"Something like that," Luke said. "C'mon, let's go down."

They found the chamber in which Luke had seen the pale man. It had once been the main chamber of a hotel suite, and possibly not occupied since Coruscant fell. The beds were still made. Floor-to-ceiling viewports offered a good view of Coruscant's sky—if one looked high enough, anyway.

Luke could feel it here, a twinge in the Force, the same one he'd been pursuing ever since he came to Coruscant. But that was not what held his attention.

It was the viewports. He was sure from their dimensions that one of these was the viewport in front of which the pale man had been standing.

He'd filled it, from floor to the top of the viewport frame. And these viewports were three meters tall.

"You're tired," Mara said. "And this makes you more susceptible to Force powers. He meddled with you, certainly . . . but once you get some sleep you'll be more fit to face him."

Mara knew little, other than from observation and

studies in psychology, about comforting those who were hurt. Most of what she knew she had learned since Ben had been born. Luke so seldom needed comforting—his wisdom and his humor had always provided him with a durable armor against life's cuts and blows. But sometimes events got past that armor—Ben's kidnapping, Anakin Solo's death. Now it was this eerie visitation by someone who'd come within a centimeter of tricking him into taking a fatal plunge. And at such times Mara could do little but stay close, act as an anchor for him to hold onto.

"I don't think so," Luke said. "I'm certain being tired made it easier for him to transmit all that despair and the mental compulsion through the Force, yes. But I also have a sense that he's powerful. And I know I've seen his face somewhere. I—" Luke's next words were cut off as he yawned.

Mara gave him a stern look.

"I know, I know. I need sleep. I'm tired." He stretched out on the cot. "Tired, and I have to admit it, scared of something that could sneak up on me and plant a Force-based suggestion in my mind. As though I were some spice addict with no resistance, no training."

"Tired and wounded in pride."

He grinned. "Well, maybe."

"Get some sleep, farmboy. You'll feel better—and think better—once your power cells are recharged."

"True."

In minutes, Luke *was* asleep, his breathing regular. But Mara lay awake long after that, her own Force senses extended in an alert screen, attuned to detect any flicker of hatred or despair that might drift their way from the thing that wanted to take her husband's life.

Borleias

The sun named Pyria was just a tiny bright dot in the forward viewport, no more a draw to the naked eye than one well-illuminated planet usually is from the surface of another. It certainly was not sufficient to distract Han and Leia from their tasks.

"Got it, thanks." Leia leaned back from the comm board. "Borleias Control has given us the map of known locations of dovin basal mines. They're not too confident about the extent of their knowledge."

Han looked at her and cracked his knuckles. "So, they think there's a fair chance we'll be dragged out of hyperspace before we quite reach Borleias's mass shadow. Well, you tell 'em that it's not going to happen."

"And it's not going to happen because . . . ?"

"Because I'm going to fly around them. What did you think?"

"I think we'd better have weapons on-line and ready." Leia trotted aft and climbed into the topside laser turret while Han activated the concussion missile launcher. Once she had her comlink activated, she heard her husband's complaint, "You have no faith in my abilities."

"Of course I have faith in your abilities." She took the turret for a practice spin and began the self-test of its computer targeting system. "I also have experience with theirs."

Space twisted before them and then almost instantly

snapped back to normal. But Borleias did not dominate the viewport as it should have. The sun was somewhat larger, a bright globe.

Then they were in a loop, centrifugal force crushing Leia down into her gunner's chair before she could shout to Han about the coralskippers she saw closing on the *Falcon* from astern. She watched the universe to either side rotate as they went upside-down to their original arrival orientation, and overhead she could see the two distant gleams of the oncoming skips.

Leia began firing the topside lasers as fast as they could charge, and the skips sent streams of plasma at the *Falcon*. They gained relative elevation in what was probably originally an attempt to follow the *Falcon*'s loop, but the maneuver ended up putting them on a collision course with the *Falcon*.

Han's words came over the comm, muffled as if uttered through clenched teeth: "Going starboard."

Leia chose a starboard target and concentrated all her laser fire on that skip. Its voids did well against her barrage, intercepting every bolt, but her concentration of fire on the area of the pilot's canopy doomed the coralskipper—Han's concussion missile, fired a moment later, detonated against the skip's hull, vaporizing the smaller craft.

Han sent the *Falcon* into a mad spin along its long axis. A shower of plasma projectiles flashed harmlessly by—mostly harmlessly; a clank and the sudden sound of damage alarms was proof that at least one of them had managed a graze.

Then the second coralskipper was past, behind them, and beginning a long loop around.

Han did not follow; he turned back toward Borleias and put on a burst of speed.

Leia felt her jaw drop in surprise. She keyed the comlink. "Hey, you," she said. "What have you done with my husband? The one who laughs in the face of death, then takes it out for drinks and dinner?"

Han sounded pained. "That pilot is just trying to lure us back to his pals. Do I look that dumb?"

She frowned, considering.

"*Am* I that dumb?" he asked.

"Well, no, certainly not."

Grinning, Leia returned her attention to the sensors. They showed the remaining coralskipper tightening its turn as its pilot realized that the *Falcon* was not pursuing; it would be coming up behind them soon. Distortions in the wire-frame image showed the locations of dovin basal mines, the gravitic organisms capable of yanking ships out of hyperspace.

That wire-frame was continuing to update, continuing to distort, and she frowned at it, trying to comprehend what she was seeing. "Straight down," she shouted, "relative to our current orientation. Move it, flyboy!"

He moved it, pointing the *Falcon*'s nose straight "down." The hard maneuver hauled Leia up out of her seat, and she could hear the restraining straps creaking against her slight mass.

"All right, we're pointed down," Han said. "You are one crabby, grumpy wife. What's that all about? Why not straight for Borleias?"

"More mines that way. And we're being followed by one."

"Followed by a mine?" Han spared a glance for the sensor board, for the distortion Leia had seen, the distortion that was closing on the *Falcon*'s position. "Not fair. Leia, how's our pursuer?"

"Rotate, please, he's coming in under us."

Han obligingly spun the *Falcon* again on its long axis, and Leia began firing on the second coralskipper.

Now that the *Falcon* was no longer maneuvering, except for the juking and jinking Han performed to keep enemy projectiles from hitting it, the transport was outdistancing the dovin basal mine pursuing it. And they were coming up on the outer fringes of the gravitic effects of the closest dovin basal mines.

Leia sprayed the skip with fire and noted that its protective void tended to recenter itself over the pilot's compartment each time the craft maneuvered to match one of the *Falcon*'s twitches. She concentrated her fire there, waited until the *Falcon* made another sideslip, then jerked her aim toward the coralskipper's bow. The audio interpreters built into the *Falcon*'s sensor system gave out the sound of an explosion and the coralskipper's blip disappeared from the screen.

"Good shot," Han said over the comlink. "How about coming back up here and plotting us a course back to Borleias?"

"Give me a second. You are one crabby, grumpy husband."

Wedge frowned throughout Han's and Leia's account of their return to Borleias. "I don't like this notion of dovin basal mines that pursue you."

"Me, either," Han said. "I'm going to draft a strongly

worded letter to the Yuuzhan Vong high commander and insist he stop using them."

Tycho, on the other side of the conference table, offered up a rare smile. Leia merely gave her husband an arch look.

"Actually, we know his name now," Wedge said. "Their local commander. Czulkang Lah. We got the information from some of the reptoids that were involved in their big push on us, after we freed them from their control seeds."

"Lah," Leia said. "From the same domain as Tsavong Lah?"

Tycho nodded. "Even better. He's Tsavong Lah's father. An old, fierce, terrifying warrior and teacher of warriors. He's like the Garm bel Iblis of the Yuuzhan Vong."

"And if we can beat him," Wedge said, "*really* beat him, it may suggest to the Vong that their gods aren't really as anxious for them to win as they supposed."

"Back to the mobile mines," Tycho said. "It does beg the question of how long they've had them, and why this is the first instance we've run into of them being used."

"Right." Wedge considered. "Han, Leia, when you were making the insertion into Hapes a few weeks ago, you became convinced that the dovin basal mines didn't just drag things out of hyperspace. You said you thought they registered every ship's unique mass characteristics and communicated that information to the Vong leaders. Let them build up a sort of Vong database of our ship movements."

Leia nodded. "That's right. And Jaina used their reliance on those mass characteristics against the Yuuzhan Vong while she was there."

"My guess," Wedge said, "is that this mobile dovin

basal mine came after you because it recognized you, specifically the *Millennium Falcon*. Another ship, they might devote fewer resources to capturing or destroying, but loss of the *Falcon* and the Solos would be a big morale hit for our side."

Han and Leia exchanged a glance. Han's expression was cocky, but Leia could see that he recognized the danger if Wedge's theory was correct.

"Meaning," Leia said, "that any ship belonging to one of our side's, well, celebrities might be detected as such at any time, wherever it goes."

"Something to keep in mind." Wedge turned to Tycho. "Call Cilghal in for a meeting later today or tomorrow. And Jaina and her psychological warfare advisers. Maybe we can use this to our advantage."

"Are we done here?" Han asked. "We have some important things to do. Like running down Jaina before you monopolize her. We'd sort of like to spend some time with her. It's why we keep coming back here. Not to look at *your* face."

Wedge gave him a toothy grin. "Watch that insolence. I might just have to call you up to active service, General Solo."

Leia lay in her bed. Yes, it was too hard, too lumpy, and light-years away from the quarters that had been her home for years, but this was *her bed*, and just knowing that it was a place she could return to again and again gave her pleasure out of proportion to its characteristics. She'd flopped onto it, fully dressed, luxuriating in possession if not in comfort, the instant they'd entered their quarters.

Someone knocked on the door. Leia lifted her head and looked at Han on the other side. He stared at her, expectant.

"Your turn," she said.

"Why mine?"

"Because I said it first."

"Can't argue with that logic." Han rolled to his feet and pressed the access panel beside the door. The door slid aside, revealing a tall, awkward-looking man; the man's left arm was in a sling.

"Ah, hello," their visitor said. "I'm Tam Elgrin."

"I know who you are." Han shook his hand. "You spied around for a while, and then decided to quit. Headaches ever since."

"Something like that."

"Come on in."

Leia rose. The quarters she shared with Han were not large or well-furnished, but the two of them could make a pretense at civilization. "Can I get you something to drink, Tam?"

"No, I'm fine. I'm, uh, here to talk to you about Tarc."

"We saw him just a few minutes ago," Leia said. "He mostly talked about *you*."

Han waved him toward a chair. "So talk."

A rap at his door awakened Kyp. Still clothed—he'd settled in only to rest, and was surprised to find that he'd nodded off—the Jedi Master rose and activated the door. It slid out of the way to reveal Piggy. The Gamorrean pilot leaned against the door frame, arms crossed, a tough-guy posture.

"It's the Great One," Piggy said.

Kyp rubbed sleep out of his eyes. "What about her?"

"She wants to see you."

"Now?"

"Now."

"Where?"

"On the roof."

Kyp gave the Gamorrean a closer look. Piggy wasn't normally so taciturn. In fact, he sounded more like a bar bouncer than himself. Kyp reached out with a whisper of his control over the Force and reassured himself that he could sense the pilot, that this Piggy wasn't a Yuuzhan Vong warrior in an unusually distinctive ooglith masquer disguise. "I'm on my way up."

Kyp emerged onto the biotics facility's roof, an uneven surface of external equipment housings and rough textures. It was now dark, a glow in the west attesting to how recently the sun had set.

"Over here." That was Jaina's voice, and when Kyp turned he could see both her and Jag Fel sitting atop a condenser-unit housing. He could barely identify them by sight; they were nothing but silhouettes. There were more, smaller, silhouettes where they sat—something that looked like a basket, something that looked like a bottle.

Kyp snorted. "You're having a picnic?"

"That's right." There was amusement in Jaina's voice. "And the Goddess commands you to attend."

"You're getting strange, Goddess." Kyp sprang up to the unit housing top, landing directly into a cross-legged sitting position to match Jag's. Jaina was stretched out on her side, facing the two of them.

"It's not just a picnic." Jaina took the bottle and poured some of its contents into a glass, one of three mismatched glasses beside the basket. She handed the glass to Kyp. "We need to talk. The three of us." She poured two more glasses and handed one to Jag.

Kyp sniffed dubiously at his glass. "Paint thinner?"

"We're not that lucky," Jag said. "While we've been waiting, I've been determining its effects on local insects. One hundred percent deadly."

"Hush," Jaina said. "This is the finest example of the Borleias distiller's art. It's dereliction of duty to be drinking it when another Vong barrage might start at any minute. That means it's going to taste wonderful." She took an experimental sip.

To her credit, she did keep her reactions from her face. But through the Force Kyp could feel her physiological reaction as nerve endings in her throat protested the intrusion of the homemade brew.

Though blind to the Force, Jag had to be familiar enough with Jaina to sense what she was experiencing. His shoulders shook with silent laughter.

"Anyway," Jaina said. Her voice sounded as though she'd suddenly transformed into an elderly mechanic. "We've got a problem, Kyp. You and me and Jag."

"I wasn't aware of any problems."

"Then why do you yank yourself out of our Force connection the instant it's not absolutely vital to our current task? It's like dancing with a partner who jumps back past arm's length and brushes himself off at the end of every dance."

"That's . . . an interesting comparison." Kyp glanced at Jag, but the younger man hadn't reacted to Jaina's phrasing, and Kyp couldn't see his face. "Maybe you and I should talk about this some time. Privately."

"And maybe not. Jag's part of this situation. He was the one who suggested this talk."

Kyp felt himself grow annoyed, and became even more annoyed with himself for indulging in such a predictable reaction. "He did, huh? Direct confrontation. That is the Fel family approach, isn't it?"

Jag took a sip of the homebrew and made a noise that suggested he'd just been punched. After a moment, he said, "I come from more than one family line, Kyp. Some of them are sneakier than others."

"What does that mean?"

"That means . . . that whatever you expect this meeting to be, it probably isn't."

"A nice enigmatic reply." Kyp sipped from his glass. Whatever the fluid was, it seemed to be part alcohol, part pepper, part rotted fruit. His eyes watered. "Wait a second. You two took the antidote before I came up here, didn't you?"

Jaina snorted. "Would you mind if I cut straight to the power cable?"

"Go right ahead."

"A while back, you manipulated me. I didn't like it. On Hapes, I dragged you into some situations you didn't care for. I gave you plenty of trouble. We both lied to each other about what we intended and what we meant. Well, I thought, when you decided you wanted to join my squadron, that it meant you'd forgiven me. When I accepted, it meant I'd forgiven you. Did it mean that, or didn't it?"

"It did."

"So are we partners, or aren't we?"

"Well, we are. At least so long as Twin Suns Squadron holds out."

"No, don't do that." Jaina let some exasperation creep into her voice. "Every time we link through the Force, I can feel you preparing yourself for the day you have to cut loose and run. Believe me, I understand that. I was doing the same thing until just a few weeks back. For reasons equally as dumb. And you break the link fast so that I won't know what you're doing, not that it's done you any good. I want you to quit doing that. I want you to quit thinking about going off and being by yourself. I know your brother's dead, your family's dead, your last squadron is dead, and I'm sorry. But you don't have to leave, and you don't have to be alone."

"Uhh . . ." Kyp struggled to come up with an answer, the right answer. "I also don't want to be in the way. In your way. Between you and, you know."

Jag extended a hand. "Colonel Jagged Fel. Glad to meet you."

"Shut up, you. Jaina, it's uncomfortable."

"Yeah, I know. Jag and I are partners, too, and something more besides, and you're here, and you were sort of chasing after me for a while, and it's got to be confusing. It is to me as well. Is it going to make you leave?"

"It should."

"Then you should leave now and stop wavering."

Kyp stood. "You're right. I'm sorry I—"

"Sit down!"

Surprised at the strength in her voice, Kyp sat before he realized it. He gaped at her.

"That's better," Jaina said. "Jag, why are males so stupid?"

"Biological predisposition. Here's an example." Jag took another sip. Even in the darkness, the ripple of anguish that moved from his neck to his feet was clearly visible.

Jaina sat up, her pose a mirror of Jag's. "Kyp, it's uncomfortable because partnerships are uncomfortable. Families are uncomfortable. I know mine is. You have to put up with the discomfort because the only alternative is to lose everything.

"Once upon a time, you were kind of a kid brother to my father. I don't care about that. That relationship didn't make you my uncle. You have a relationship with me. It's not boyfriend-girlfriend. It's no longer Master-apprentice. I think we both know that neither of these is right. It's partners, whatever that means. Whatever we figure out for it to mean. If we're partners, it's something that lasts until one or the other of us is dead. And whether that pains Jag or not, he's keeping it to himself, because he's smart enough to know that he can't control my relationships for me.

"So—once again—are we partners, or do you go off to die alone?"

Kyp sighed. "I see you inherited your father's considerable powers of negotiation."

She ignored the jibe at Han's style, so very different from her famous mother's.

"That's right. So?"

"So we're partners."

"Good." She hoisted her glass. "Drink to it."

"Do we have to?"

"We have to."

Jag chuckled. "It's a drink that makes death-duels with Vong pilots pale in comparison."

TWELVE

Borleias

Commander Eldo Davip, captain of the *Lusankya*, the greatest New Republic ship engaged in the defense of Borleias, took the turbolift down to the Beltway.

The Beltway was a central corridor running the length of the Super Star Destroyer, from stern to prow. It was not a corridor for pedestrian traffic; the octagonal shaft featured a tracked hauler at the top, allowing it to be used for transportation of heavy equipment. It was wide enough that skilled pilots could have flown paired X-wings wing-to-wing along its length.

As the turbolift slowed to a halt, he pulled on a pair of darkened goggles. When the lift doors opened, the precaution proved to be an appropriate one; directly in front of him, mechanics were welding another section onto the apparatus that now filled the forward portions of the Beltway, blocking all movement forward of this point.

The outer shell of the apparatus was rolled metal meters thick. Each section of the shell was a hundred meters long, open at either end, with the prow end slightly narrower than the stern, allowing the sections to be installed in an overlapping fashion. The mechanics welded them together at the overlaps.

Inside the shell were metal cables drawn in intricate weavelike patterns through hardy metal rings on the interior surface of the shells. The pattern of the cables, their carefully monitored tensions, was not only to keep the shell straight and durable along its length; as soon as they were in place, cargo-box-sized containers were situated among them, tied off by more cables, instrument packages attached and carefully attuned.

The apparatus now stretched a third of *Lusankya*'s length, hidden away in this access shaft. None of the Vong's extraordinary visual sensors could detect its fabrication; none of their strategists could anticipate its use.

Davip sighed. Its use would mark the end of his most prestigious command. But prestige wouldn't mean a thing if the Yuuzhan Vong won, so he watched the continued manufacture of the apparatus, and wished it well.

On the planet below, on the second floor of the biotics building, Captain Yakown Reth set his dinner tray down at a table, allowing it to clatter, and sat heavily on the bench before it. He didn't bother to keep his disgruntlement from his face.

Opposite, Lieutenant Diss Ti'wyn, who flew in Reth's squadron as Blackmoon Two, smoothed down fur that had suddenly risen on his neck. A brown-and-gold-furred Bothan, Diss was unusually attractive by both Bothan and human standards, and received an enviable amount of attention in social situations. "What crawled down your flight suit and stung your butt?" he asked.

Reth snorted, amused despite himself. "We're in real trouble here on Borleias."

Ti'wyn gaped at him. "Really? I thought we were winning."

"Stop kidding. I mean, in trouble worse than being outnumbered, besieged, and doomed."

"Oh." Ti'wyn speared a cooked slice of hardy local tinfruit and popped it into his mouth. "So vent already."

"Don't talk with your mouth full. No, Diss, this is no joke." He lowered his voice so his words would not carry to the next table. "I think we're in real trouble at the command level."

"General Antilles? He has a great reputation."

"Bear with me. You know who's commanding *Lusankya*."

"Eldo Davip."

"A first-rate foulup if ever there was one."

"Granted . . . but he did do all right during the big Yuuzhan Vong push a few weeks back."

"A fluke, I'm sure. Anyway, Ninora Birt escorted a shuttle out to *Lusankya*'s repair station. She said that repairs weren't going well. Whole banks of turbolasers and ion cannon batteries were still out of commission. I didn't think *Lusankya* got that badly hammered in the last engagement. Did you?"

"Not really."

"Which points to colossal mismanagement on Commander Davip's part, which General Antilles either doesn't know about, or hasn't corrected, which doesn't speak well of his skills."

Ti'wyn shrugged, noncommittal, but he no longer looked as cheerful.

"That's just the start. You remember when the Advisory Council visited?"

"Very hush-hush. They had a meeting with Antilles and his general staff, then rushed off."

"A mechanic who's just been transferred to Blackmoon Squadron was in the hallway when they left. He says Counselor Pwoe was furious. Pwoe was saying that Antilles had refused command of Borleias, and only relented after making demands to the Council."

"What demands?"

"I don't know. What demands would *you* make?"

"Pleasure yacht, a lifetime pass to the *Errant Venture* . . ."

Reth eyed the sliced sausage swimming in spice sauce on his plate. That, as much as this talk, was going to cost him his appetite. "Stop kidding around. And then there's this Jaina Solo thing."

Ti'wyn nodded in agreement. "If we have to circle one more time just because her squadron always gets first clearance to land—"

"She and her pilots are getting special treatment in every category there is. First access to spare parts, first access to bacta, full proton torpedo loads, first repairs to starfighters and astromechs . . . Have you ever seen one of them eating here?" Reth gestured around at the rest of the mess hall, crammed with tables, ringing with noise.

"No."

"They have their own lounge, and rumor says they have their own chef off *Rebel Dream*."

"Her mother's old ship."

"Her mother's old ship. Twins Suns hasn't done anything Blackmoon Squadron hasn't, and can't do anything we can't, except show off names of important mommies and daddies."

"Keep it calm, Yak. There have got to be political reasons behind this. With politics, nothing runs right . . . but without politics, nothing runs."

Reth nodded grudging agreement. "It just keeps piling up, and I have to question Antilles's competence."

"Keep it down, will you? You're starting to sound like a mutineer in training."

Reth flashed his second-in-command a broad grin. "Nothing like that. I'm just trying to figure out whether I should put in for a transfer, try to get in with a squadron in one of the other fleet groups. I'm not sure what to do yet. If you hear anything along the lines of what I've been saying . . . well, you'll just keep your ears open, won't you?"

Ti'wyn waggled his pointed, oversized Bothan ears. "Always do."

Transport Ship *Fu'ulanh*, Coruscant Orbit

Wrapped in the concealing folds of her cloakskin, willing her shaper's headdress to remain still so as not to give away her caste to observers, the Shaper Nen Yim followed the Warmaster Tsavong Lah out onto the ganadote tongue.

Ganadotes were immobile creatures. Born as a flat, long shell about five paccs long and wide and a pace high, they were little more than a mouth, an anus, a large canal connecting them as well as opening into side stomach chambers, and a tongue.

But when grown to maturity and trained in their masters' wishes, they made magnificent entryways and viewing-boxes. Kept fed by servants bringing clip beetle shells and other nutritious waste and dropping those foods straight through their stomach valves, shaped by hormones to change their dimensions, ganadotes could be transformed into domed or spherical vestibules. The tissues that lined their intestinal tracts were beautifully iridescent, and a proper diet kept excretion to a rare event.

But it was the tongue that made the ganadote such a charming architectural feature. One trained in its use could step out onto it and, by leaning or toe pressure, cause it to extend, lower, raise, position its tip anywhere in relation to the creature's body.

And that was what Tsavong Lah did. Once Nen Yim was in place, he coaxed the ganadote tongue out over the large chamber at the heart of this living ship, over the crowd, short of the fibrous leaves that blocked off the far exit from the chamber.

Tsavong Lah threw up his hands, tossing his cloak back over his shoulders. "Priests and shapers, devotees of the Great God Yun-Yuuzhan, I salute and welcome you. Soon, you will be taken from this place to nearby Borleias, where my sire, Czulkang Lah, drives the infidels into dejection and defeat."

The listeners, perhaps thirty, castes evenly divided between shapers and priests of Yun-Yuuzhan, raised their voices in noises of celebration, appreciation.

Nen Yim could make out the faces of many, including

the shaper Ghithra Dal, whom she had accused, and Takhaff Uul, the priest who had been in Ghithra Dal's constant, if surreptitious, company these last many weeks.

"As you know," Tsavong Lah said, "you travel there to take possession of Borleias once it falls. That green, rich world, almost free of the touch of the infidel, will be your reward for service to the gods, service to the Yuuzhan Vong. Half will be the domain of the priests, half of the shapers, all united in the worship of Yun-Yuuzhan. All you need to do to claim it is raise your mighty temples, your gloriously crafted domains upon her.

"Sadly, you will fail to do this."

And there it was, the start of the warmaster's revenge, expressed in a handful of calmly expressed words.

The crowd quieted, with many of its members turning to one another, muttering questions.

"I look forward to waking each day without being assailed by the smell of sickness, the odor of the decay of my own arm. I look forward to rising each morning in the sure knowledge that I have not displeased the gods—only a few rogue priests and shapers who dared to misappropriate the god's will." Tsavong Lah's voice turned thunderous, and Nen Yim saw his broad back shake with the emotion of his words. "I look forward to knowing that those who remain behind are united in their hatred of the infidels, not in their greed for what they may obtain at the expense of others. I rejoice to think that you will soon be gone."

"No, Warmaster." That was the voice of the priest, Takhaff Uul, young for his posting, ambitious beyond his years. "There has been no such treachery. You must not think it. Only in the true service to Yun-Yuuzhan can you save your arm, save yourself from the company of the Shamed Ones."

"There are some who say that trust is a matter of faith," Tsavong Lah replied. "I say that trust is a matter of knowledge, of observation. Find one who is trustworthy, and there is trust. Find one who is not, and there is none. But I will give you a chance at life. Takhaff Uul, do you trust our gods?"

The youthful priest cried up to him, "I do, Warmaster."

"Do they trust *you*?"

"What? I don't understand."

"If they trust you, trust that your motives have been true, trust that you have thought only of their honor and not your own, I am certain they will save you. From this." He raised his radank claw arm, pointing its pincer at the enormous leaves covering the chamber's far entryway.

That was Nen Yim's cue. Beneath her robe, she stroked a tiny kin to that enormous plant, coaxing it to act. It did; it curled into a tube.

So did the ones in the distance, revealing a dark gap in the wall beyond; the gap was four times the height of a Yuuzhan Vong warrior, four times as wide.

A snuffling noise emerged from the gap, then something like a low, muted roar.

Then something emerged.

Like a Yuuzhan Vong, it had two arms, two legs. But its stance was low, crouching, animalistic. It had tremendous muscles, hard and corded enough to support its tremendous weight, for it was as tall as the gap through which it emerged. Its face was tusked, its teeth were huge, and its head swiveled as it spotted the Yuuzhan

Vong on the chamber floor. Its eyes followed these small creatures with the avidity of a hungry beast.

"This is a rancor," Tsavong Lah said. "A beast of this galaxy. You do not deserve honorable death at the hands of one of our own living weapons. When you die here, it will not be as fighters, but as food to sate the creature's appetite."

"What if we kill *it*?" That was the voice of Ghithra Dal, filled with spite.

"Then you live for a while longer," said the warmaster. "A short while."

Through the gap emerged another rancor, then a third, and a fourth. They spread out from the gap, moving along the walls of the chamber, circling their tiny prey.

Tsavong Lah leaned back, and the tongue retracted, carrying him and Nen Yim into the ganadote mouth. As the first screams began, as the first roars echoed from the chamber walls, they turned away from the feasting scene below and the warmaster led the shaper out through the back way.

"Warmaster, may I ask two questions?"

"You may." They emerged from the ganadote into a large, blood-blue corridor, and were joined by Tsavong Lah's personal guards, who marched a respectful distance ahead of and behind them.

"First, will there be no outcry from the priesthood of Yun-Yuuzhan, from the shapers?"

"An outcry? Of course there will be. A cry for blood. When word returns to us that their transport was attacked by pilots of Borleias, all its passengers slaughtered, there will be a great cry for revenge."

"Ah." Nen Yim walked along in silence for a moment, knowing that his reply had spelled her doom, too. "Should I not go with them? Or is my death to be a different one?"

"I can't kill you. You're on loan from Overlord Shimmra. Besides, I have no reason to wish you harm." They entered the stomach compartment that now housed Tsavong Lah's private transport. The eyelidlike wall on the far side was closed now, keeping the chamber's atmosphere intact. They walked to the transport's ramplike protrusion and climbed into the creature's passenger stomach. "I am pleased with you, Nen Yim. Do you plan to tell this story? To rouse hatred against me?"

"No."

"If you did, what would happen?"

She thought about that as she settled into her seat. Its fleshy surface flowed around her waist, her torso, holding her in place against the acceleration to come. "The only reason to do so would be to harm you. In which case it becomes the story of a discredited shaper against that of the warmaster. And I would die before I could present proof."

"And such a waste. Your cleverness, used in our service, more than makes up for the loss of Ghithra Dal and his conspirators. Will you use it in our service?"

"I will." She did not hesitate. Tsavong Lah said *our service*. To her, that meant the Yuuzhan Vong, not him personally, and she could swear to that with a whole heart.

"Some day soon, the seedship will return to this world and complete its transformation. I wish you to return to Lord Shimmra and study the World-Brain. I wish you to do nothing to displease the gods ... but to find that knowledge which the gods do not mind us knowing."

"I will, Warmaster."

"Then speak no more of your death. It will come when the time is appropriate. It is not appropriate now."

Coruscant

Baljos Arnjak was beginning to look like he, too, was being Vongformed. His beard and mustache were growing in; shaggy and in colors that ranged from light brown to black, his beard seemed like a riotous life-form not native to this world. The orange jumpsuit he wore when not traveling in Yuuzhan Vong armor seemed to have many more stains on it now, and some of them might have been living patches of mold or lichen. But these changes and the group's circumstances seemed to be sitting well with him; his eyes were bright, his manner animated. "Come in, come in," he said, waving the Jedi and Danni into the Lord Nyax suspended animation chamber. Bhindi was already there, perched on a stool.

"Tell me you have some information," Luke said.

Baljos beamed. "I have some information. There, that was painless, wasn't it? You can all go now."

"Don't taunt the Jedi," Bhindi said. "And don't take credit you don't deserve. *I'm* the one who dug most of the information out of the wrecked guts of those maintenance machines."

"True enough, Circuitry Girl. Not that you could have interpreted—" Baljos doubtless saw the impatience in someone's face, probably Tahiri's, for he broke off that line of talk. "We're prepared to tell you whatever you need to know about Lord Nyax. Anything Bhindi didn't find in the machine memory, we'll just make up."

Luke leaned against a wrecked computer console and crossed his arms as though to put up a defense against whatever information was to come. "So, who is he? What was he modified for?"

Baljos nodded as though that was the first pair of questions he'd expected. "He is—or used to be—a Dark Jedi. His name was Irek Ismaren."

Luke frowned, then shook his head. "No, that's not possible."

"Who's Irek Ismaren?" Tahiri asked.

Luke dug his datapad out of a belt pouch. "Like Baljos said. He was a Dark Jedi in training. A son either of the Emperor or of one Sarcev Quest by a woman named Roganda Ismaren. She was a crazy woman who modified her son with computer implants. My sister Leia ran into him on Belsavis, oh, about fifteen years ago."

He opened the datapad and began scrolling through entries. Though nowhere near as comprehensive as the database he kept in whatever hidden site might serve as the Jedi headquarters, this datapad included an abbreviated listing on every Jedi, Sith, Force-sensitive, or Force-related person or site he had ever encountered in his long searches for knowledge of the Jedi Order.

Within moments, he found the file he wanted. A face resolved into clarity on the datapad screen: aristocratic, handsome, somehow unfinished in a teenaged way, framed by curly dark hair.

It was the face of a younger Lord Nyax.

Suddenly Luke felt as pale as Lord Nyax. He showed the image to Mara.

She nodded. She noted some of the details that appeared on the screen under Irek's name. "So he should be about thirty now."

"Yes. And of normal height."

"Except," Baljos interrupted, "he spent most of the intervening years in that suspended animation chamber, so he's physically younger than his chronological age. His vital processes were slowed. He was subjected to the medical treatments I mentioned earlier, treatments that kept his bones growing long past the point they should have sealed, that gave him lots more muscle mass. As a baby, he'd had a computer apparatus implanted in his brain by his mother; it helped give him enough focus— *monomania* may be a better word for it—to learn to control the Force far out of proportion to his age. When he was here, that apparatus was augmented to make his control even greater. It apparently stimulates what's left of his brain in ways beneficial to Force control. He was equipped with lightsaber weapons, their use part of the hard coding in his brain implant—"

Luke snapped the datapad shut. "How did this happen?"

Bhindi said, "It appears that after leaving Belsavis, he and his mother came to Coruscant and hid here . . . and by 'here' I mean in this very facility. His mother carefully monitored his progress in the Force, training him so that he'd be the most powerful Dark Jedi in existence, and gave him medical treatments to make him much bigger, more imposing, more physically powerful. She also arranged to bring in the ysalamiri to keep him hidden as his presence in the Force grew stronger."

"Then something happened," Baljos said. "The notes are not exactly clear, but it seems like they found and took on a partner, another Dark Jedi, and at some point Irek and the new partner got in a dispute and dueled. The partner was killed, and Irek took a lightsaber thrust right through the skull. He died."

"Died," Luke said.

"*Technically* died," Baljos added. "Brain activity ceased. He fell down and didn't move anymore. But his mother and the attendant medical droids were able to maintain his autonomic functions and keep his body alive. Her journal, not surprisingly, gets a bit harder to understand at this point, and becomes increasingly demented over the years, but it becomes obvious that she kept his body in suspended animation and had the medical droids insert increasingly sophisticated components into the computer apparatus in his skull."

Luke grimaced. "With what purpose?"

"I think," Baljos said, "that she was trying to make him into her son again—an unlikely prospect, since most of the portions of the brain that pertained to memory and the less violent emotions were charred into carbon—and also to make him into a new leader for the Empire. She was just crazy enough to imagine he could be Emperor Irek, loving son, Dark Jedi, and unconquerable tyrant."

Luke exchanged a look with Mara. She didn't let any of her emotions reach her face, but he could feel them through the Force, a revulsion for a woman mad enough to keep her own son on the butcher's block like that for so many years. "What happened to Roganda Ismaren?" he asked.

"She was the female corpse we found here. We ran cell samples against her records in the files. There's no mistake."

Luke gave him a disbelieving look. "Irek killed her?"

"He's not Irek anymore. *Lord Nyax* killed her. He didn't recognize her. She was just another moving shape in the way when he broke out of his holding tank." Baljos shook his head. "Very nasty business. It gives even mad science a bad name."

"Does he have any weaknesses?" Mara asked.

"Oh, yes." Baljos gestured at the suspended animation unit. "He's not ripe."

"Ripe," Luke repeated.

"It appears that a groundquake caused some ceiling rubble to drop onto one or more of the ysalamiri, killing them and damaging the unit. He woke up, burst out, went on a rampage, and fled. But he wasn't due to come out for another couple of years." Baljos pointed at one of the computer consoles. "All his operational programming was *there*, plus the refabricated 'Irek' memories Roganda planned to implant in him, and they weren't transferred over. He has his instincts, he has some combat programming, and he has some deep-level motivations— such as to seek out Jedi and kill them, to seek out hot-points of the Force and control them, to conquer the universe, little things like that. But he lacks memories, tactical skills . . . even language, I think. I doubt he's even verbal."

"So we can't even talk to him." Tahiri looked downcast. "Maybe that's a weakness, but it doesn't make things easier on us. He can't be reasoned with."

"I guess that leaves me with only one more question." Luke returned the datapad to his belt pouch and prepared himself for what he expected to be more bad news. "Is there any way to save him? To befriend him, teach him about the light side?"

Baljos finally became serious. "I don't think so. He's had almost all humanity burned out of his brain. He's just a predator whose only goal is to dominate."

"Great," Luke said.

Viqi spent almost her every hour in the chamber that concealed the *Ugly Truth*. Though not technically proficient, she knew enough about machinery—and could glean more from the ship's computer memory—to have a good sense of the resources available to her here.

Ugly Truth was definitely capable of spaceflight, and her inboard diagnostics indicated that every ship's system was undamaged, operational. The ship was fully fueled, and battery power, for starting up systems and even providing her with some discretionary lights and occasional cool air, was adequate to last for weeks more.

The problem was the exit chute. It had collapsed during Coruscant's fall or subsequent bombardment. Small chunks of duracrete and ferrocrete had fallen, then metal beams had twisted and more rubble had fallen onto the beams, the whole mass crushing into an impenetrable plug.

Floors above the hidden hangar, she'd found a hole providing access into the exit chute above the plug. Here there were signs that someone had been working, digging away at the plug from above, hauling blocks of duracrete into an office chamber at that level. She supposed that the worker had been the pretty boy who'd given her the locator.

She'd even found the boy's name. In the ship's computer records was information about the family that had owned the *Ugly Truth*. Hasville and Adray Terson had been the founders of Terson Comfort Carriers, an airtaxi company; Viqi had seen the ubiquitous vehicles of their fleet, even ridden within them during her secret activities aiding the Yuuzhan Vong. The ship's records included a holo of their son, Hasray, the boy with the remote.

Another little sad story, she decided. She pondered that for a while. She couldn't *feel* the sadness of it—far from it, she was elated that the boy's sacrifice meant her salvation.

Viqi spent most of her time studying the ship's controls and diagrams, digging into the ship's stores of food, regaining her strength. Occasionally she had to venture forth—very quietly, very carefully—to work on unplugging the exit chute or to find the chamber, down the hall on this floor, she had chosen for a refresher.

This day, she emerged from the refresher and peered up and down the corridor with her customary caution. There was no sound, no sign of movement. Slowly, carefully she headed back toward the Terson family quarters.

Something wrapped around her neck from behind, jerked her off her feet. She landed on her back, choking, and stared up . . . into the features of Denua Ku. The warrior held his amphistaff in one hand; the other end of the weapon was coiled around Viqi's neck.

She gaped up at him. He was dead, she knew he was dead, he'd died back in the furniture manufacturer's. But now he stared down at her, helmet off, eyes neither angry nor solicitous. "Get up," he said.

She struggled to her feet, assuming control over her expression, her manner, her breathing. As she rose, the amphistaff's tail slid from around her. "Denua Ku," she said. "I'd thought you had died."

"I ran." The warrior's voice sounded bitter. "My duty dictated that I return to my commander and describe what I'd seen—the giant *Jeedai*. Now that my superiors are informed, I can return to confront the monstrous thing . . . and kill it, or be killed by it. Why did *you* not seek out the Yuuzhan Vong and tell them what had happened?"

She let some scorn creep into her tone. "A human, alone, wandering about the rooftops, waving down coral-skippers? Do you know what happens to them? I do. I was shot at twice." That was a lie; she'd never ventured to the rooftops. But she'd seen the skips on patrol, seen how they fired at anything that might be an inhabitant of the planet caught above-ground.

"So you came here? Why?"

"I knew the people who lived here." This lie came smoothly to her, too. "Hasville and Adray Terson, and their boy Hasray. They were wealthy. I knew their quarters would have preserved food hidden in them, and I was right. I knew that would give me time to figure out how to return to the worldship without getting myself killed. How did you find me?"

He reached under his armor at the armpit and pulled forth a creature—an insect about the size of one of Viqi's fingernails. It looked like some sort of beetle, but was the red color of arterial blood. Though its wings were folded along its back, perfectly shaped to its carapace, they vibrated, causing the little creature to buzz constantly.

"This is a nisbat," the warrior said. "When it is near any of its hatchmates, it makes this noise, increasing in volume as it gets closer."

"So?"

"So one of its hatchmates is within you."

Viqi couldn't keep her eyes from widening. "Something that size is *inside me*—"

"No. It was implanted in you when it was fresh-hatched. It cannot grow. It cannot even vibrate. But it can be felt by its fellows."

"I am . . . grateful to it. That it has allowed you to find me."

"Hmmm." Denua Ku's acknowledgment sounded neither accepting nor dubious. "Now you will be able to return to the worldship."

"I am delighted."

"After we find and kill the giant *Jeedai*."

Viqi's heart sank. She kept it from her face. "Shall I hold him down while you kill him?"

Denua Ku's lips twitched up in a smile. "Amusing. Is that as funny in Basic as it is in our tongue?"

"If our two cultures share anything, it is irony."

The warrior held up a hand. From other doorways in the corridor emerged more warriors—a party of two dozen or more, Viqi calculated.

And with them was another voxyn. This one was worse off than the previous one; it was a sickly yellow almost everywhere, and in places, its scales were flaking off completely. Its head hung listlessly, and it did not even bother to snap at the warrior nearest it.

"Ah." Viqi forced a smile. "Even better."

"Come along." Denua Ku led the way toward the nearest emergency stairwell.

Viqi followed, her smile fixed, her mind racing.

She would find a way to elude them. She would pry the nisbat from her body, wherever it was hidden. She still had her locator tucked away, and the stairwell to the *Ugly Truth* was closed, hidden; she would be able to return here. She would clear that exit chute and blast off to safety.

And if it were humanly possible, she would see Denua Ku dead first, dead for daring to force her back into his plans when her plans were so much more important.

She kept her back straight and her manner haughty. No matter whom she aided, no matter what she wore, she was of the royal lines of Kuat.

THIRTEEN

Coruscant

In a deep tunnel, a maintenance causeway sealed off from the surrounding habitat areas, a passage constantly dripping with nearly opaque seepage from the levels above, the voxyn became more alert. It raised its head and began the familiar side-to-side sweeping gestures. The Yuuzhan Vong warriors became agitated and allowed the voxyn and its handler up to the front.

"Warriors, flank it," Denua Ku ordered. "We cannot lose this one. They are too rare now."

Two warriors moved up, one on either side of the voxyn. They stayed out of reach of its claws, even when it meant sloshing through black pools of liquid on the floor, but nothing would protect them from its acid if it decided to unleash some in their direction.

Two hundred paces farther on, the voxyn stopped. It stared upward and to the left.

"Find an access," Denua Ku ordered.

Two warriors ran up the passage, and in moments found stairwells leading upward. The voxyn had to be dragged from its position, closest to the target it felt, to the stairway, but once hauled into that shaft it bounded up the stairs with an energy Viqi had not seen it display before.

Mara crept along the metal girder forty meters above the floor. The light from the lamps, dying glowrods, and torches below barely reached her; with her dark garments and skill at movement, she doubted very much that she would be seen.

The floor below was irregular, partially buckled, the result of one of the quakes that Danni said had plagued Coruscant since the Yuuzhan Vong had begun to shift its orbit. It was covered in black material, gummy and sticky, the sort of material Mara had seen on countless roofs of buildings on other worlds. Its use here meant that this surface was not intended as a work or habitation area—but now it was full of beings, a constant stream of haggard males and females of a variety of species emerging from and descending into stairs at the chamber's four corners. Wearing tatters, not interacting, barely blinking, they carried duracrete blocks and rubbish and portions of bodies, hauling these things out through a side tunnel and returning unencumbered.

Clearly they were excavating something in the chamber or chambers below that black floor, and doing so at the bidding of another. But where, and what, was that being? There was no sign of the Yuuzhan Vong, no sign of Lord Nyax.

From the end of a metal beam that bobbed occasionally under the combination of her weight and the stray breeze that moved through the chamber, Mara could look straight down at the center of the floor. It sagged, suggesting that there was a single large chamber beneath. She pulled out her comlink. "Luke," she whispered.

"I'm here."

She knew that; she could feel him, dozens of meters away, toward one of this chamber's four upper corners, at the hole Elassar had found. He was with Tahiri, Face, and Kell. Any of them could have been the one to crawl out on this metal beam, but it had been Mara's turn.

"I suspect it would be child's play to join one of the work gangs," Mara said. "I don't think they'd react if a wampa in a war helmet and a dancing skirt started working with them."

Face's voice came back: "Give me a minute, I can work up that disguise."

"How about you just keep your current outfit and go see what they're digging up?"

"Spoilsport. Give me about ten minutes to get down there."

"Will do." She stiffened. "Wait a second. Something's changing."

The line of workers stopped in place, every one of the dozens of blank-eyed Coruscant survivors turning toward a far corner of the chamber. Mara strained to see, then gave up and brought out her macrobinoculars.

In that corner, a flap of sheet metal was pulled aside by something on the other side . . . and Lord Nyax stepped through.

Mara felt a hiss try to escape her. She stilled it, an unnecessary precaution, as at this distance no living creature could have heard her. But the contrast between the malevolent Force presence she could feel from that man and his cheerful looks atop that monstrously tall body was startling.

She almost dropped the macrobinoculars. "Luke, did you feel that?"

"I did. Maybe you should get back here."

"Maybe I shouldn't." She returned her attention to the man in the distance. "But keep talking to me."

"Will do. What are you seeing?"

"Lord Nyax. He's come through the wall and he's walking toward the work crews. He's alone."

"How's his expression?"

"Happy. Childish-happy." For a moment, she could see into Lord Nyax's thoughts deeper than mere visual evidence should allow her. "He's pleased with their progress. They've got it ready to go."

"Got *what* ready?"

"What they told him about." Mara shook her head again as if trying to fling the alien thoughts from her skull by centrifugal force. "I can't seem to close myself off, Luke. I can't seem to block it."

"Me, either. Or Tahiri. I'm coming out there."

Mara looked back. In the distance behind her, she saw a dark shape emerge from a ceiling-high hole in the wall and come trotting across intact metal beams, more nimble than any acrobat.

She felt another sensation in the Force, a hunger that seemed decidedly out of character for Lord Nyax. She returned her attention to him.

The thing with Irek Ismaren's face stopped just short of the nearest work crew and was now looking toward the corner of the chamber immediately beneath Luke's entry point. There were shrieks from the stairwell there.

Figures burst up from the stairwell—armed and armored Yuuzhan Vong warriors emerged, moving fast, and the fifth one out of the stairwell was being dragged by a leashed voxyn. That was the hunger, the desperate craving of the voxyn to find and destroy all Force-users.

The voxyn's head turned as its gaze swept the room. Mara saw its attention flash across Luke, across her—she felt its awareness of her like a physical touch—and then come to rest on Lord Nyax. It lunged in his direction, its handler unable to hold it back despite the leash. A second warrior grabbed the leash, added his strength to that of the first, and they managed to drag the voxyn to a halt.

Lord Nyax smiled as the warriors, twenty of them now, spread out in a semicircle. They approached him, amphistaffs ready, some of them handling thudbugs or razorbugs. They moved through the crowd of workers, contemptuously shoving those beings aside, hurling them off their feet.

The beam Mara was on bobbed more deeply as Luke arrived. He stretched out behind her and pulled out his own macrobinoculars.

Mara felt a sudden surge of hatred—not for Luke, not for Lord Nyax, but for the Yuuzhan Vong. She knew it to be a sentiment from outside her, and that kept it from being quite as compelling as it could have been.

And in that same instant, the workers screamed in rage of their own and swarmed the Yuuzhan Vong warriors.

The warriors swung and stabbed. Mara saw workers pierced through heart and gut and brain. When those attacks were not instantly mortal, they continued running and leaping at the Yuuzhan Vong, crashing into them, bearing them to the floor by weight of numbers.

The voxyn handlers went down. The voxyn leaped free and charged Lord Nyax, its growl of rage rumbling through the chamber.

A lightsaber, a red one, ignited in Lord Nyax's hand. Then Mara took another look. This wasn't a normal lightsaber; the energy blade emerged from the back of his metallic glove. It pivoted as he flexed his right hand. Another emerged from his left glove.

The voxyn, canny and old, charged to within three meters of Lord Nyax and then arched its back. It made a noise like a bedchamber's worth of carpet being suddenly ripped in two, and a gout of dark, smoking liquid sprayed from its mouth.

A portion of flooring between the voxyn and Lord Nyax tore free, lifting into the fluid's path. The voxyn's acid splashed across it, almost instantly burning through it, but its momentum was arrested. It and the flooring fell, the sound of the chemical reaction of the acid audible even at this distance.

Fallen Yuuzhan Vong warriors were rising now, having torn themselves free of the masses of people bearing upon them. Mara saw limbs being severed from torsos by expert amphistaff blows, saw trails of blood, some of it jets of arterial blood gouting high into the air, from the frenzied but ineffective workers as they were cut down.

More red lightsaber blades sprang forth from Lord Nyax's body. Mara saw blades emerge downward from his elbows, upward from his knees.

"We have to help," Luke said.

Mara turned. Luke was wrapping the cord of his beltgrapnel, long abandoned but definitely a useful tool for the exploration of Coruscant's lower reaches, around the metal beam.

"Help who?"

"Help the Vong. Yeah, I know, I know, it's something you've never heard anyone say before." Luke rolled off the beam and fell, his descent arrested by his hand on the cord; more cord deployed from his belt as he descended. "I'm not worried about the fate of the Yuuzhan Vong," he told her. "But we desperately need *any* resources we can use against Lord Nyax."

Mara hissed in vexation. She tucked her macrobinoculars away, grabbed Luke's cord, and swung out over open space, then slid down after her husband.

In the corner of her eye, she saw the voxyn charge Lord Nyax. He dodged under the beast's leap and flexed an arm. His elbow-blade sheared through the voxyn's gut, slicing the beast cleanly in two. It landed in pieces behind him.

Then, as Mara swung around on the rope during her descent, she saw the woman.

The woman was dark-haired, attractive, standing at the top of the staircase by which the Yuuzhan Vong had arrived. Unlike the workers, she was alert, watching the fight with an expression of detached interest.

She was Viqi Shesh.

Mara felt coldness sweep over her. The woman who had helped betray Coruscant to the Yuuzhan Vong, the woman who had stolen Mara's son, Ben, was *here*, palling around with her Yuuzhan Vong masters while the world crumbled around them.

She opened herself to Luke through the Force, something she preferred not to do while cold thoughts of murder were strong in her, and let him see Viqi through her eyes. "Viqi first," she said.

"Lord Nyax first," he answered. At ten meters above the floor, he detached the cord spool from his belt and let go with his hand, dropping the remaining distance. He landed in a tuck and roll and came up in a full-speed run straight at Lord Nyax.

Mara spared one last look at Viqi, a glance that, had it become a physical manifestation of her anger, would have sliced through the woman as cleanly as an amphistaff point, and dropped. She came up in a roll and followed her husband.

Ahead, the first pair of Yuuzhan Vong warriors had reached Lord Nyax.

Viqi watched the huge pale man slaughter Yuuzhan Vong warriors.

The first two warriors stopped a dozen steps from the thing and hurled thudbugs. The pale man twitched and the lightsaber blades from one forearm and one knee rose, incinerating the living weapons.

Two more warriors raced up and, under cover of more thrown thudbugs, charged, whipping their amphistaffs around, one lashing out with the tail and the other with fangs.

The pale man stepped in close to the second warrior. The first warrior's fang attack missed by a meter. The pale man's left forearm blade lashed out at the second warrior, who blocked the attack by catching the blade in an amphistaff coil. Then the pale man's left elbow blade raked across the warrior's throat, separating it from his body. Meanwhile, the pale man's right-arm, right-elbow, right-knee blades rose, darted, swayed, and wherever they went, incandescences flared—sign of thudbugs being vaporized.

The pale man flipped the dead warrior's amphistaff toward the first warrior. The warrior contemptuously swept it out of the way, overcorrected as his own staff came back to block a lightsaber thrust—and could not block the other lightsaber blade as it simultaneously thrust into his helmet's eye socket. He fell, smoke pouring from the mask as he died.

More warriors arrived—two still threw thudbugs, four more skidded to a stop beside them and waited for a bare second to calculate their strategy.

A piece of ceiling steel whirled down like a spinning sawblade from above. It flashed across the warriors' position at knee height, and just for a fraction of a second Viqi thought that it had missed. Then those six warriors collapsed, legs severed at the knees, blood gouting from the stumps and limbs.

Seconds had passed. Eight Yuuzhan Vong warriors and their voxyn were dead. Seventeen more remained.

These warriors approached more cautiously. Directed by Denua Ku, they circled around the smiling, confident pale man who towered over them.

The whirling steel panel came around for another pass, but this time, a chunk of machinery, an air-cooling unit a meter on a side, fired off from the floor as though it were a guided missile and hurtled into the sheet's path. The sheet wrapped around it with a ferocious, almost feral shriek of metal bending, and both fell to the floor.

The pale man looked off to Viqi's left. She followed its gaze. There, advancing on the pale man, lightsabers lit, were Luke Skywalker and Mara Jade.

Viqi's eyes grew wide. What were *they* doing here?

The Yuuzhan Vong, too, seemed caught off-guard. Denua Ku had no more love of the *Jeedai* than any warrior, but he was smart; Viqi saw him wave his warriors back, waiting for the intentions of the Jedi to be revealed.

It was time to go. No matter who the victor was, Viqi would either end up dead or pressed once more into the service of the Yuuzhan Vong. She spun to sprint to the stairwell.

She tripped over an outstretched leg. It was clad in vonduun crab armor.

She looked up, confused. All the Yuuzhan Vong warriors had been ahead of her. Where had this one come from? He was the tallest she'd seen, and wore unusual black-and-silver armor. So did the shorter warrior next to him, the one with the distinctive branding marks on his face.

That one said, "What do we have here, Explosion Boy?" His voice was cultured, his Basic perfect.

The tall one said, "Dunno." He, too, spoke Basic. He reached down, seized one of Viqi's ankles, and straightened. He held her upside-down at arm's length. "Runt of the litter, I'd say."

Disoriented, Viqi could only watch as a lithe female Jedi, lightsaber blazing, ran past the three of them, paying these Yuuzhan Vong warriors no attention.

A clang over her head startled her. She looked up—down, at the floor—and saw her locator lying there.

She reached for it, but the tall warrior swung her to one side. "Grab that, would you, Poster Boy?"

"Got it." The one addressed as Poster Boy seized the device and straightened. "Ah, a military-spec vehicle locator. Uulshos makes these. Hey, it's live."

Viqi finally found her voice. "That's mine."

"Not anymore, Senator."

Luke and Mara approached Lord Nyax and his Yuuzhan Vong attackers. They kept their guards up, their senses—both physical and Force—alert.

Luke searched the face in front of him. He looked for some trace of humanity. He saw only smiling mockery, and he could feel the thing through the Force, its appreciation at having slaughtered warriors, its appreciation at the thought of slaughtering Luke and Mara.

There was no recognition in its emotion, no acknowledgement of kinship of any sort.

"I don't know if you can understand me," Luke said. "But whatever you're doing, whatever your plans are, I have to stop you."

Lord Nyax's smile grew broader. It seemed to recognize Luke's intent, even if it could not grasp his words.

Then it answered—not in words, but in images. Luke saw the power of its will, expressed through the Force, rolling over the remaining people of Coruscant like water roaring down a canyon through a burst dam. He saw them sweeping across Coruscant, killing and eating everything in their way—the Yuuzhan Vong, the disobedient, the Force-blind. He saw the workers here boarding the machine beneath their feet, crashing it through kilometers of buildings until they came to some place, a source for more power to fuel this glorious, deliriously happy destructive impulse.

In that instant, Luke joined in the plan. He longed to slaughter the outsiders, those who did not understand or join. He longed to taste their flesh.

He turned to Mara, beckoning her to join. She was facing the Yuuzhan Vong warriors, preventing them from surprising Luke with an attack, but her gaze was yanked to Luke. Her eyes widened, and he could feel her leaning toward him, leaning toward acceptance of this crucial duty.

But the sight of her brought memories. Luke saw worlds of beauty. He saw his son, composed of Luke and Mara and years to come. Around the edges of Lord Nyax's command he felt the Force, its other natures, the life from which it flowed.

He turned back toward Lord Nyax and struggled to find the words to express his thought. "I . . . stand . . . in . . . your . . . way."

It was the Jedi way. Jedi did not attack. But to position oneself in the path of a violent aggressor who would not yield achieved the same result.

All he could ever do as leader of the wartime Jedi was lead them into the path of the enemy. That was, Luke realized, perhaps his greatest limitation, and in struggling against it without understanding it, he may have hampered the Jedi effectiveness against the enemy.

But once recognized and accepted, it was also perhaps his greatest strength. Whether by accident or design, by his own will or by the permutations of the Force, he had always found his way into the path of the great enemies of all things living.

And here he was again. "I stand in your way," Luke repeated, and was pleased that he had regained control over his voice. "What you see, you will not achieve."

The expression on Lord Nyax's face turned from mocking amusement to seriousness . . . even sadness, for a brief moment, as though the thing had at last recognized some kinship and discovered that it did not bridge the gulf between the two of them.

Then it charged.

Kell finished binding Viqi's hands behind her back and looked up in time to see Lord Nyax lunge toward Luke.

Luke raised his lightsaber, caught the downward sweep of Lord Nyax's right-hand forearm weapon. He spun clockwise, narrowing his profile as the left-hand forearm blade thrust toward him, and kept his guard up in time to intercept the right-hand elbow blade. Mara leapt forward, unleashing two fast blows that the thing's left-elbow blade caught, then folded over nearly double as she leaped back from a strike from its left knee.

The Yuuzhan Vong warriors unloaded handfuls of thudbugs and razorbugs, heedless of which of the targets they might hit, but the two Jedi and Lord Nyax flicked the weapons out of the air or dodged them entirely.

Two Jedi? Three. Suddenly Tahiri was in their midst, coming up on Luke's left, blocking a follow-up blow from the elbow blade on that side.

"Bad," Kell said.

Face nodded. "Bad bad." He pulled his blaster rifle from the wrappings on his back. "But who to shoot first?"

"We're no good here." Kell gestured toward the stairwell. "Let's see what they're doing down below. If it's important, I can blow it up."

"That's our Kell."

Kell set Viqi on her feet, then hauled her up over his shoulder. Following Face, he descended the stairwell.

Denua Ku watched the pale *Jeedai*, and for a moment admiration almost drowned out the revulsion he felt at the notion of having abomination-machines like lightsabers touching one's own flesh.

The pale thing fought with a savagery and speed unlike those of any warrior he had ever seen. And it was *untrained*. With his experienced warrior's eye, he could see that its movements were instinctive, a fact revealed in the creature's failure to throw effective combinations of blows, its inability to gauge which way its enemies would leap when it attacked them.

If it had been born Yuuzhan Vong, if he'd been able to train it for a year, even half a year, he could have turned this thing into the greatest warrior who was not himself a god. As it was, he'd have to kill this thing.

Even if the *Jeedai*, too, wanted it dead, it was still an abomination. And it was the greater threat. It had to die first. He threw his last razorbug, then lunged forward into hand-to-hand range, probing at the pale thing's back with the tail-tip of his amphistaff.

The pale thing spun, sending its knee blade toward Denua Ku's guts. He blocked the sweep with his amphistaff, but the impact was tremendous; it threw him back off his feet. He rolled backward and came upright, saw one of his warriors perform a similar probing assault . . . and this warrior took a forearm blade through the throat.

Nine Yuuzhan Vong warriors down. Sixteen to go. The numbers were becoming worse.

A tremendous mechanical roar shook the chamber. It lowered slightly in volume but became steady, filling the air.

FOURTEEN

"It's a delaying tactic!" Mara shouted over the roar.

"I know!" Luke shouted back. "It's working! I'm being delayed!" He stopped a forearm-swing and was driven back a step, stopped the follow-up elbow swing and was driven back a step, jumped back to avoid the knee-strike and discovered it was only a feint; Lord Nyax's leg snapped back and caught a Yuuzhan Vong warrior in the crotch, collapsing the warrior despite its armor.

Every step took the Jedi and the warriors toward the center of the chamber. The floor vibrated beneath their feet.

"What?" Mara said.

"I didn't say anything!"

"Not you! Speak up, Face!"

Luke waved Mara back. She jumped up and backward in a somersault, taking her out of Lord Nyax's range, and took out her comlink, holding it up to her ear. Tahiri took her place, swinging her lightsaber defensively, eyes wide as she analyzed her attacker's motions and patterns.

* * *

"I said, it's a *big machine*," Face shouted. Here, at the source of the vibration, the noise was much worse.

He, Kell, and their struggling cargo were on a catwalk two levels down from the floor where the Jedi and Yuuzhan Vong fought, one level down from the side-passageways by which the Vong must have arrived. And the catwalk itself was the top level of a deep, deep chamber—a chamber that housed a single vehicle.

Had that machine been set up on any world but Coruscant, it would have been considered a skyscraper. It was hundreds of meters tall. At its base were treaded appendages that could roll like tank treads or lift and move independently like feet. All along its surface were hydraulic arms; some ended in what looked like plasma cutters, others in huge ball-like weapons, still others in manipulator hands.

At the top was a sensor station surrounded by transparisteel panels, and packed into that station were living beings. Many of the workers who had not been on the floor above at the onset of the Yuuzhan Vong attack were here, and more were shoving their way way along a catwalk extension that led to a door in that station.

Down below were more beings, tirelessly carrying hunks of debris away from the machine's base.

The whole thing roared like a fleet of antiquated Podracers. The vibration cut into Face's skin wherever the vonduun crab armor did not cover it.

"Tell her it's a construction droid," Kell shouted. "It looks completely functional."

Face shouted that information into his comlink.

"Did she hear you?"

"I don't know."

"Tell her it's moving."

Far below, the treads spun into action. The construction droid's machinery whined as the gigantic machine lurched into action . . . and then crashed into the duracrete wall before it.

Unable to hear, Mara bit off a curse. She tucked her comlink away and jumped back into the fight, deflected a pair of thudbugs, took a swipe at Lord Nyax's hand; its arm rotated and it caught the attack on its lightsaber blade.

Luke flipped over the pale thing, striking as he went; his blow was blocked.

Tahiri, in front, lunged forward . . . and stumbled, right into the path of a knee blade. Mara reached out, an effort to shove with the Force, knowing that she was too late, knowing that the knee-blade would emerge in a fraction of a second from the back of Tahiri's skull—but Tahiri whipped to the side, still in control, still in balance, even as Luke crashed feetfirst into Lord Nyax's neck, forcing its head down toward its own knee-blade.

The blade turned itself off. Lord Nyax's head passed through empty space. Luke, backflipping to his feet, offered up an expression of bafflement and frustration.

Mara sighed. It had been a feint, an effort to trick the thing into spearing itself with its own weapons. But its designers had been too thorough. There were fail-safes.

The floor rocked under their feet. Mara felt the crash from below as much as she heard it.

Lord Nyax leapt upward a half-dozen meters and then, impossibly, just hung there in space, smiling down at the Jedi and the Yuuzhan Vong.

Mara realized, a fraction of a second too late, that it had merely grabbed the same cord by which she and Luke had descended. Then the floor went out from under her.

The construction droid plowed into the wall before it, smashing steel and duracrete out, allowing blue-white sunlight to spill in. It lurched and wobbled as it continued, internal balance compensators having a hard time keeping up with the irregularity of the surface it moved across.

The catwalk under Face's feet rippled. "C'mon!" He turned back toward the stairs they'd descended, but the catwalk mounting on the corner nearest the droid's exit hole snapped and dropped, snapping the next mounting toward him and the next mounting after that. The catwalk fell all along one wall, except for the mounting behind Face and Kell, turning their footing into a steep ramp.

Face managed to get his hands on the catwalk railing. As his feet went out from under him, he held on. He looked up, could see Kell holding on above him, could see the ceiling of this chamber split and collapse as one of its supporting walls gave way under the droid's destructive exit.

Bodies began spilling through the split in the ceiling. Some were bodies of workers. Others were Yuuzhan Vong warriors.

Then there were the bodies of his Jedi friends.

As he felt his footing give way, Luke sprang, with the last bit of traction the flooring gave him, toward Mara and Tahiri. He hit them like an overly aggressive ball-player, catching one in each arm.

The patch of floor they were heading toward opened, giving him nothing to land on. With the Force, he shoved at his own back, propelling him through the rent, toward the metal wall he saw before him, the wall and the catwalk there . . .

He saw that their arc was going to miss the catwalk. They would hit the wall and plummet. But in that instant, the left end of the catwalk broke free of its moorings and dropped, bringing it beneath their ballistic arc. A moment later, they hit the swaying thing, bending it down still farther, but Mara and Tahiri grabbed its trailing end and held on with their considerable strength.

Gasping for breath, Luke looked around. He and both of the others had switched off their lightsabers midleap. "Good instincts," he said.

"Good teacher," Tahiri said. She looked up, past Luke. "Hey, Face, is that you?"

"Hold on, hold on, I'll get a line down to you."

Face tied off the cord he'd once used to safeguard his passage across an elevated walkway. He dropped the other end down the swaying catwalk toward the Jedi. In moments, Luke, Mara, and Tahiri swarmed up to join them. The construction droid was only just pulling out onto the avenue beyond the building.

"Did you see Viqi Shesh?" Mara asked.

Kell jerked a thumb up toward the stairwell behind them. "She was still at the bottom of the steps when the big boom hit. She took off."

Mara clambered up to the base of the stairs. "I'm going after her."

"Mara, no." Luke's voice did not carry a plea; his tone

conveyed simple truth. "Lord Nyax is more important. I can feel him moving up there. Moving away. We have to go after him, bring him down."

Mara sighed, shut her eyes. After a moment, she nodded.

"I lost her, I'll go after her," Kell said.

Face pressed the locator into his hand. "No. You go after *this*, Mechanic Boy. It could be our ticket out of here."

"You go after her, then."

Face gestured toward the construction droid, which leaned at an alarming angle toward the next building over as it turned rightward onto the avenue. "I'm going after that. Nyax sent it off for a purpose. We need to know what that purpose is."

Mara pounded her fist on the bottom step, then stood. "Let's go," she said.

Up on the half-collapsed floor above, Denua Ku hung, unable to climb, unable to descend.

A three-meter length of rebar emerged from his gut. It was slick with his blood. He knew that his lung had been punctured.

The pain was extraordinary. He did not mind pain, did not fear it, but it was beginning to fade in a way that suggested imminent death rather than recovery.

In the silence left by the infidel machine's departure, he heard feet padding softly across the remaining floor. He looked up. Viqi Shesh, most of the way around the chamber toward the hole by which the pale monster had entered, her hands tied behind her back, paused and looked at him.

"Tell them I died well," Denua Ku said.

"I'll tell them," she said. "I'll tell them you died whining, that you died begging for infidel medicines, anything to alleviate the pain."

Denua Ku snarled. He reached for his pouch, for his last remaining razorbugs.

Viqi laughed at him. Before he could bring out the weapons, she reached the corner and ducked through the hole there.

Lord Nyax led the three Jedi on a high-speed run through the ruins of Coruscant. He could travel faster than they could, because from time to time he'd simply leap from one building to the next one over, usually a leap too great for them to match. Yet they could always feel him in the distance, sense his movements, sense a feeling of expectation and even anxiety from him.

Once they caught up very close. The bodies of five lightly scarred Yuuzhan Vong warriors, young ones, lay in a brightly lit corridor, their wounds still smoking. In the distance, the Jedi could hear the footsteps of Lord Nyax fleeing.

"Where's he going?" Mara asked.

Luke thought about where they started this fight, where they'd been since then. "It's a big arc. Maybe part of a big circle."

"Why?" Tahiri asked. She breathed more easily than Luke or Mara, the energy and resilience of youth standing her in good stead.

"He's not fleeing," Luke said. "He could have left us behind some time ago. So he wants us to follow him. Into a trap?" He shook his head. "He would have gone straight. No, he's just leading us on a chase. A diversion."

"So where does he want us *not* to go?" Tahiri asked.

Mara turned abruptly, headed back the way they'd come. "To wherever it sent that construction droid." She pulled out her comlink. "Mara to Face. Come in, Face."

Face ducked behind a pillar between two smashed-in panels of transparisteel. He got out of sight just in time. Outside, a wingpair of coralskippers flew by at his exact altitude—the same altitude as the top level of the combat droid. "Face here. I hear you."

"Are you still with the construction droid?"

"Well, yes and no." He leaned out of the shattered viewport next to him. In the distance, he could see the coralskippers hovering outside the mound of rubble the construction droid made when it plowed into the side of a giant ziggurat of buildings. "It's ahead of me. It's digging through construction. Moving a lot faster than those things are rated to move, I'll bet. I'm cut off from it for the moment. I'm going to have to track it from floors above and hope they don't fall out from under me."

"Leave a tracking signal open. We need to find you."

"Done. Face out." He sat there for a few more moments, gasping in the warm, moist, cloying air of Coruscant, then rose again. "I hate this job."

The Jedi circled around the growing accumulation of coralskippers hovering outside the collapsed hole the construction droid had bored into the ziggurat's side. On an upper floor half a kilometer from the gathering, they met up with Face and peered at the ziggurat. "Interesting," Luke said.

"What?" said Tahiri.

"This is one of the monolithic blocks that served the Old Republic as a government center," Luke said. "A lot of it belonged to secondary bureaus, to embassies and legations from non-Republic worlds, and to businesses and organizations more or less allied with the Old Republic."

Tahiri gave him a skeptical look. "How do you know that?"

"Because, youngster, the few surviving databases and filemaps that mentioned the old Jedi Temple indicated that it was—" Luke pointed. "—somewhere there. I've been all through it, kilometers and kilometers of it. By the time I got to look at it, of course, Emperor Palpatine had long destroyed every remaining trace of the Jedi."

"Maybe not every trace," Mara said. "Why do you suppose Lord Nyax is digging there?"

"Because . . ." Luke considered. "Because he has some kind of implanted memories or instincts? Perhaps he wants to destroy any remnant of the Temple because of lingering emotions. Or maybe he knows about some portion of it that was never on the public databases."

"Either way," Mara said, "we have to find out."

Luke smiled. "One of the advantages about having been all through that region is that I know quite a few ways in and out. C'mon, let's bypass these skips."

Deep in the guts of the ziggurat, the construction droid leaned against the sloping black wall, driving its plasma cutters into the smooth surface, hammering the glossy wall with its mechanical limbs. Chunks of dense stone fell away from the impact points, but the wall yielded only very slowly.

Luke and his companions peered at the action through a crack in a duracrete wall a couple of stories up. Much of the construction that should have been beneath them had collapsed as soon as the construction droid had plowed its way to this point, meaning that the creaking and sagging of the floor beneath them heralded a further collapse that was probably imminent.

"What's beyond that wall, farmboy?"

Luke shook his head. "I don't know. I didn't know this area was here. I'm not sure there were any visible accesses into it before. Hey, we have Yuuzhan Vong coming."

Despite the danger that her extra weight might present, Mara leaned in over her husband's shoulder to look. Yuuzhan Vong warriors were scrambling over the rubble and rushing toward the construction droid.

Coruscant survivors rushed out of the construction droid's base to meet them. Unarmed, ill-fed, they still had a tremendous edge in numbers over the warriors, and Luke saw several of the Yuuzhan Vong go down under struggling masses of bodies. The stronger survivors picked up chunks of stone and brained the troops.

More Yuuzhan Vong entered. More survivors swarmed in, now coming from surrounding areas of rubble instead of just from the droid's base.

Luke looked back at the others. "He's near. He's calling to them. Calling for help."

Face pulled his helmet off, touched his forehead. He looked troubled. "I know. I can feel him. In my head. I want to go down there." He looked up into their worried expressions, offered them a wan smile. "Well, mostly I *don't*. But I can feel the draw."

"You're strong," Tahiri said. "Well fed. You have hope

still. He'd have to exert himself more to control you. But I suspect he can. I'm not sure he can't control *us*."

"Kell to Face." The voice, small and tinny, floated up from Face's helmet.

The Wraith leader pulled his helmet up beside his features. "Face here."

"I've found the source of the locator signal. We're in luck. It's a spaceworthy transport. It's our passage back to Borleias."

"What kind of condition is it in?"

"It's ready to go. Oh, it's blocked in by several tons of rubble."

"Can you handle that?"

"What's my bag full of?"

"That's what I thought."

Luke looked again at the battle raging below, a battle where his only opponent of consequence was the creature they called Lord Nyax. "Face, our mission is over. I want you to round up the others, get to that transport, and prepare to leave Coruscant."

Face grinned at him as though he were waiting for a punch line. "And what about you silly Jedi types?"

"We're going down there." Luke closed his eyes, just for a moment, as the weight of that decision pressed upon him. He was about to lead his wife and a teenager into a situation he wasn't sure *he* could handle, a situation that was likely to get them all killed. He looked at Face again. "If we die here, the other Jedi need to know about Lord Nyax. You're going to tell them."

Face thought about it, his smile disappearing. "I normally try to argue against suicide missions."

"But you know what Lord Nyax can do."

"Yes. So all I can do is wish you luck."

Face left.

Luke took a couple of deep breaths, turned to the others. "Ready?"

"Ready," Tahiri said.

Mara just nodded.

Luke ignited his lightsaber and sliced into the gap he'd been peering through, widening it.

Lord Nyax watched as his workers swarmed toward the warriors he could not sense. He did not like the fact that he could not feel them, but he did enjoy seeing his workers kill them—though it was usually at a cost of twenty or thirty workers per warrior.

But he was summoning more workers from all around. No matter how well they hid in the ruined undercity, his call reached them and forced many, most, to climb free of their hiding holes, to stumble and then walk and then race toward the scene of this conflict.

And he could feel the wall weakening. Soon it would give way completely. The woman who had told him of this wonderful machine—he thought she was up at its summit, making it move—had been right.

Then he sensed something and looked up. A bar of energy flashed, and three people fell out of a hole in the ceiling.

They drifted laterally to the top of the slope of the black wall, riding it down, using their power to slow their descent, keep their balance, increasing the friction between the clothes on their feet and the wall's surface.

Lord Nyax moved to be beneath them. He ignited his blades, all of them. He knew they'd be here, knew it from the moment they stopped chasing him. He wished they'd go away instead of tiring him.

The foremost of them, the male, slid down until he was not far above Lord Nyax's reach, then leapt free, somersaulting to land somewhere behind him. Lord Nyax reached out as the male came down; he slid a sharp-edged piece of stone toward the male's landing area, timing it so that the stone would shear through the male's legs. But the male slowed his descent and rotation, landing atop the stone instead of in front of it, and bounded off, toward Lord Nyax. Meanwhile, the women leapt clear of the stone, spinning down toward him, igniting their weapons as they came.

Lord Nyax leapt free of the center of their formation, bounding up over the head of the red-haired female. He hit the stone wall feetfirst, shoved off, and rotated to a landing many steps away from the three pests.

Then he made a thought and drove it into their heads.

It hit Luke like a razorbug fired straight through his forehead. Luke staggered under the pain. His back hit the irregular floor. He waved his lightsaber up and in front of him, a defensive form, but there was no follow-up blow for him to counter.

There was, however, a new priority. He was to switch off his lightsaber and then go attack the Yuuzhan Vong. He leapt to his feet and turned his weapon off. He could see Mara and Tahiri doing the same.

But that would mean dying—and, worse, failing.

No, it's what he had to do.

No, he couldn't do that.

He stood, frozen by the dilemma, straining against the

thought that filled his mind, the thought that was slowly driving out every other consideration.

So he did what he had to whenever he was confused. He reached out, touching Mara in the Force. He didn't have to open his mind to her; his mind was as open as it could be, held open by Lord Nyax's thought. He just had to reach for her, and she was there, locked in as much confusion and pain as he.

She had no answer for him. He reached for Tahiri and found her to be identically immobile.

He felt Lord Nyax grow impatient, then angry, and Lord Nyax expressed his anger through pain. Luke felt his fingers and toes, hands and feet, shins and forearms explode. He fell, writhing, then stared in amazement as he realized that his limbs were still attached—the pain was real, but no injury had caused it. He could feel Mara's pain, feel Tahiri's.

There was something different about Tahiri's. He looked over to where she lay.

She was rolling to her stomach, forcing her way to her feet. Off-balance, weaving as she stood, she nevertheless managed to pick up her lightsaber and ignite it. She looked at Nyax, anger blazing in her eyes. "I know something about pain you don't," she said. "Pain drowns other people. I just swim in it." She took a step toward her tormenter.

Luke could feel Nyax's anger, his moment of confusion. And though Luke couldn't move, he could act. He reached out through the Force and grabbed the stone that Nyax had tried to use against him moments earlier. He jerked it toward his enemy.

And though he was weakened by pain, by distraction, it flew those few meters and slammed into Nyax's back, driving him forward, slamming him off his feet.

Tahiri leapt forward, bringing her lightsaber down in an all-out attack. Nyax managed to get one of his arm-blades up to intercept it, then kicked out, shoving off against a pile of rubble. He slid away from Tahiri, and the slide continued well past the point that it should, carrying him clear of her . . . but he left skin and blood behind on rubble he crossed.

Luke felt Nyax's astonishment, his outrage at having been wounded, however trivially. Then Nyax drove another thought into Luke's brain: Kill Tahiri.

This time, Luke was ready for it. He'd had a moment to center his thoughts and, most important, emotions. He was ready with his memories of Tahiri, all the time's he'd been delighted as she'd made another gain in her study of the Force, all the hopes he'd had for her future and happiness. He could hold up like a shield his memory of her love for his nephew Anakin Solo. All those memories blunted Nyax's attack, shattered its speartip.

Luke reached for Mara again and found her similarly armored, but with logic, not emotion. Running through her mind was a cold calculation of allies and opponents, actions and consequences. Uppermost in it was a realization that Nyax could rule any individual, and out of individuals whole galaxies were made.

But deep beneath the analysis was a stream of emotion, an awareness of their son Ben, of what he would be if Nyax could find him and shape him.

Luke came up on shaky legs, felt Mara doing the same. And though Nyax was not letting up on the pain-energy, it affected Luke less now. He could feel Tahiri's part in that, the way she opened herself to the pain, was not daunted by it, was not shut down by it.

They faced Nyax as a single creature. The part of them that was Mara rejected the false truths Nyax tried to impose upon them. The part of them that was Luke rejected the false hatreds, the lying enmities. The part that was Tahiri made the pain part of what they were, a fuel for their strength.

Nyax looked between them, and a flicker of distress, a childlike expression of fear, crossed his features.

Then all four of them felt the wall break. Whatever was beyond it roared forth to sweep them away.

Elsewhere

Above Borleias, on a routine surveillance sweep in her X-wing, Jaina Solo was jolted out of her detachment by a surge in the Force. She could feel Luke and Mara in the surge. She knew they were in danger. And she could see Kyp's X-wing wobble as he, too, was hit by the sensation.

Thousands of light-years away from Borleias, Ganner Rhysode, Jedi Knight, kept a firm hand on the controls of his rickety transport as he closed the last few meters to dock with the space station ahead. But his arms spasmed as the Force seemed to howl at him. His transport jerked forward, hitting the docking bay at a greater velocity than he intended. As he shook his head to clear it, he heard the dockmaster over his comlink: "Idiot."

In an artificial environment dome, part of an ever-growing station hidden away in the Maw, Valin Horn,

Jedi apprentice, jerked awake so violently that he fell from his narrow couch. He sat up, trying to remember what nightmare had caused this reaction, but he couldn't. Then he heard the wailing of the infant Ben Skywalker from two compartments down, the voice of an adult trying to soothe him, the voices of other Jedi trainees as they compared details of what they'd just felt.

Coruscant

Rushing up a flight of emergency stairs, Bhindi ahead of her, Elassar behind, Danni stumbled as the sensation hit her. She crashed down atop the steps, bruising shin and ribs, and lay there gasping.

Elassar knelt beside her. "Don't move. Let me look."

"I'm not hurt." She ignored the Devaronian and heaved herself upright. She knew she had to look as rattled as she felt. "Something happened. Something just . . . got loose."

FIFTEEN

Luke swam out of a sea of—not pain, not shock, but something between exultation and complete confusion. His back was against a mound of rubble, and his wife and the girl were beside him. He couldn't remember their names, or his own.

Red fluid dripped down upon his shoulder. He craned his neck to look up and saw a body on the mound above him, that of a human man. Its right arm was missing and blood poured down the rubble below, one stream of it pooling and then dripping onto Luke.

Luke. That was it, Luke. And Mara and Tahiri. And the Yuuzhan Vong, and Nyax. Luke rose, saw his lightsaber a few meters away, and yanked it to him with a casual display of the Force. It struck his palm with far more energy than he'd intended, and he dropped it again.

Then he saw Nyax, standing beneath the hole in the black wall. The hole, one of the construction droid's wrecking claws still within it, was twenty meters up. Nyax danced on the pile of rubble beneath it. His was the uncoordinated, artless, dance of a child. It was a dance of joy.

Mara rose beside him. Luke had known she was unhurt.

"Force energy," she whispered.

This must have been a wellspring of it, he thought. The old Jedi Temple must have been built above because it was here. They were guarding it. And guarding the planet from it.

Nyax finished dancing. He turned to look at the Jedi. His expression was so full of uncomplicated happiness that it seemed impossible that he would ever try to hurt them.

Nor did he attack them now. He simply raised a hand.

Above him, a portion of the ceiling, a plug some ten meters across, shot straight up and out of sight. Debris rained down, but drifted to one side before it could hit Nyax. Tremendous crashing noises emerged from the hole above, and the walls all around them began to shake.

Tahiri joined Luke and Mara, tucking something away in her backpack. "We're in trouble," she said.

One of the advantages of running around in a lawless, ruined city several kilometers deep, Face reflected, was there was always gear to find.

Such as this airtaxi. It had been perhaps the thirtieth one he'd seen since leaving the Jedi, the fourth undamaged one he'd come across—and the first one to start up with a single press of the controls. Now he roared along the tumbled canyons of Coruscant, following a comm beacon, keeping well below rooftop altitude.

It was a necessary precaution. He saw a lot of coralskippers. All seemed to be heading toward one location . . . the same location he'd recently fled.

He reached the vicinity of the beacon, gained until the signal was its strongest. That put him directly opposite the collapsed corner of a building. He could see something shining silver there—a simple antenna, attached so recently that nothing had had time to grow on it; no dust or soot had darkened it. "Face to Kell," he said. "I see your antenna."

"Drop six stories and drift over to the next building. Come in the first big window," Kell answered. "The access to where I am is in the main chamber there."

"On my way." Face lost altitude and sideslipped. He peered in through the shattered viewport of what had once been a luxury apartment, could see the stairwell reaching from the ceiling. He gunned his thruster and crashed through the framework around the viewport, then cut power. His airtaxi dropped half a meter to the floor.

Seconds later, he squeezed in through the access hatch of the vehicle named *Ugly Truth*.

Kell was above him in the pilot's seat. He didn't turn around. "Did you feel something a couple of minutes ago?" Kell asked.

"No."

"Good. Me either, then."

Face looked up through the cockpit viewport at the jumble of rubble overhead. "Do you really have enough explosives to blast through that?"

"Approximately . . . but that's not what we're going to do."

"Ah."

"A detonation like that might damage this frail little flower of an escape ship." Kell pointed down toward his feet. "But the building wall on that side isn't a support wall. Support comes from the building's metal skeleton. So I've planted shaped charges to blow that wall out."

"And then what?"

"And then I hit the topside nose repulsors. We tilt forward, I hit the thrusters, we punch free, and we rotate for a while, everybody screaming and vomiting, until I regain control."

"Kell, sometimes I hate you."

"Yeah, but I'm still the best pilot you ever saw."

"Where are the others?"

"En route. I got a comm message to them."

"How? There are kilometers of rubble between us and them! A comm message couldn't possibly penetrate."

Exasperated, Kell finally did look down at his leader. "Do you remember something about us putting a sensor package up at rooftop, then running a direct cable down so Danni and Baljos could get a constant sensor feed?"

"Oh, that's right."

"I broadcast to that sensor package—"

"Never mind, never mind, I get you now. I'll set up for the others getting here."

The hole above Nyax's head widened. No more rubble poured down upon him. Instead, sunlight did. First it was a tiny shaft; then it broadened into a blue-white column of brilliance. He bathed in the light, held out both hands to capture it, rubbed it into his cheeks.

Luke could feel Tahiri's sense of shock; it matched his own. "Did he drive a hole all the way to the surface?" she asked.

"I think so," Luke said. He turned his attention to the beings at the summit of the construction droid. He could feel their confusion, too. Nyax, his objective accomplished, had released them. As their volition returned, their physical exertions, their outrage at the way they had been violated for so long, overwhelmed them. "I have to get up there," Luke said. "Persuade them to drive that thing out of here before the building comes down."

"No, you don't," Mara said.

He looked at her, surprised at such a merciless, unnecessarily cruel statement. But then he sensed her amusement at his mistake.

"Just tell them," she said.

Luke reached up and found minds—dozens of them, all receptive to the Force. In the wash of Force energy emerging from the crack in the wall, he found he could reach any of them, all of them.

He projected a strong demand for silence, a sense of calm, and could feel them quiet. Then he formed a picture in his head: the building collapsing, the construction droid driving in reverse to get away. He projected that image with all the strength he could muster, bolstered by the Force wellspring.

He felt them react—shock . . . and then belief. In moments he heard the metal tower's engines roar again, and could feel their intention to crash their way back out through the rubble pile behind them.

Luke thumbed his lightsaber into incandescence and marched toward the creature with Irek Ismaren's face. *Let's finish this.*

But Nyax, ignoring him, lifted straight up into the air and floated up through the hole his Force powers had made. In a moment he was out of sight.

* * *

Danni, Elassar, and Bhindi scrambled in through the access hatch.

"Take the seats forward," Face ordered. "These rear ones are for the Jedi; we don't want people climbing over each other when they board. Copilot's seat is mine. Where's Baljos?"

"He's staying," Bhindi said. "Instead of me."

Face sighed. Once it became likely that resistance cells would be of little use here, he'd told Bhindi to pack up for a return to Borleias. He hadn't anticipated Baljos being so resistant to having his studies cut short. Baljos's choice here might prove to be a scientific boon someday . . . or it might be a useless way to commit suicide.

But it *was* Baljos's choice.

Face dogged the hatch shut, then struggled up the makeshift ladder and into the copilot's seat. He strapped himself in. "Ready when you are."

"Boom," Kell said. He thumbed a hand remote.

The *Ugly Truth* rocked as the wall beneath its keel blew out into the street beyond.

Kell didn't wait to evaluate the situation, the size of the hole. He shoved his control yoke and the transport lurched forward. Face's stomach rose into his throat as the transport leaned out into the open air above the avenue, then leapt free of the building to plummet nose-down toward the ground.

The construction droid's internal turbolift opened and the Jedi stepped out into the machine's topside control chamber.

The scores of people packed into the chamber didn't notice them. Their attention was riveted on the forward viewports. Beyond them, mounds of rubble were falling away . . . and beyond hovered a cloud of coralskippers.

Even as the construction droid burst out into sunlight, the coralskippers opened fire, pouring plasma bursts into the machine's front face. Shocks from impact points dozens of stories down rocked the control chamber. Diagnostics screens lit up; alarms blared. Tatterdemalion workers who had, minutes ago, been mind-controlled slaves now shrieked, possessed again of enough intelligence to realize that their doom was at hand.

"We've got to get them out," Tahiri said. "The weapons—"

Luke shook his head. "This droid's weapons won't do much against coralskippers. We have to use other weapons."

"What weapons?"

Mara said, "Us."

Luke raised his voice, drawing on the Force to strengthen it. "Everyone out! Down the emergency stairs. Don't take the turbolift; it's *evil*." He added the mental image of the turbolift snapping open and shut like the mouth of a malevolent carnivore.

The Coruscant survivors continued shrieking, but crushed forward toward the two opposite stairwell exits, leaving the Jedi some room in the middle. The parting of the sea of flesh also gave them a clearer view of the coralskipper formation and the incoming plasma fire.

"That fountain of Force energy is what made Nyax stronger," Luke said. "It's pure power . . . and we can use it, too." To demonstrate, he raised a hand like an orchestra conductor . . . and a mound of rubble against a building a hundred meters ahead rose into the air. Luke clenched his fist and drew it toward him, and the rubble swept toward the construction droid.

The coralskippers to the rear of the formation had no chance. Chunks of duracrete, stone, and ferrocrete plowed into them from behind. Dovin basal singularities snapped into position to swallow some of the improvised missiles, but even that was not enough. Luke's missiles smashed into yorik coral, sweeping coralskippers out of the way.

Eyes wide, Tahiri mimicked Luke's gestures, but with the face of a building to their left, to the right of the coralskippers. Chunks of facing blew forth from the building, hurtling and falling among the coralskippers.

Mara continued to add her voice and her Force presence to the orders Luke had given, spurring the workers to flee more quickly, but most of her attention was on the chamber's controls, its walls and ceiling features. She found what she wanted and reached up to undo a hatch in the ceiling. Bright light spilled in from above and a metal ladder lowered. She went up topside.

Coralskippers rose from the formation in sudden flight, attempting to get away from the stream of crude projectiles, but those who rose first ran into another stream, this one moving much faster; chunks of rock and duracrete pounded into the yorik coral, eroding it like a superpowered sandblaster, destroying those vehicles.

At first Luke thought that Mara had initiated that attack, adding her strength to his and Tahiri's, but he realized after only a moment that it felt wrong. He leapt up through the hatch Mara had opened, landing beside her on the construction droid's roof. Tahiri was only a second behind him.

From here, they had a clearer view of the sky full of coralskippers and of the ziggurat behind them.

From the ziggurat emerged a column of rubble. As it rose, it parted, arcing away from its point of emergence in all directions like a water spray. But this spray was being flung kilometers in every direction, chewing through building tops and coralskippers as it landed.

And above its center, where the rubble no longer rose, floated Nyax. Giant boulders danced in and out through the rubble spray, weaving a lovely spiral through the air.

"Another Jedi academy graduate," Tahiri breathed. "He can lift really big rocks."

"Very funny," Luke said. He gauged the leap from the construction droid's roof to the nearest solid surface on the ziggurat, decided they could make it. "Let's go."

Viqi heard a noise in the distance, a roar as if some dam had finally opened its valves to let countless tons of water through. The floor rumbled under her feet.

She ignored it. She ignored the pain in her wrists, pain caused by her struggles against her bindings; those struggles had gone on until she'd found a jagged piece of metal protruding from a wall, and now she was free again.

She reached the Terson's apartment building and the floor of their chambers. She was trembling with exhaustion and dripping with sweat by the time she stumbled into the living chamber . . . and then she froze, almost all remaining hope draining from her.

The secret access stairs were down, and, of all things, an airtaxi rested in the middle of the chamber.

She took the stairs up as fast as she could and stared in anguish at the hole in the wall through which the *Ugly Truth* had left. All her work was undone. She would have to start again, searching, hiding, surviving, until she could find or repair another functional spacecraft.

Well, it was likely that the airtaxi was functional. That was a starting point. She descended to give it a look.

On the front seat was a pile of preserved food from the *Ugly Truth*, and a note:

Senator Shesh:
We thought you would probably need these more than we do. Don't eat them all in one place.

Love,
The Wraiths

Only then did Viqi sink down to the carpet. Only then did she begin to cry.

The ziggurat was a series of high, broad steps. The Jedi leapt up to the next step, ran its width, and then leapt up to the one above, again and again, until they reached the roof.

From here they could see the hole in the ziggurat roof widening. With every moment that passed, more tons of rubble poured up and out of the hole and flew out to pour onto surrounding kilometers of buildings. Some streams diverted to hose coralskippers out of the air. The lines of giant boulders still danced their merry circles around Nyax.

Luke led the others off at an angle, to where each of the boulders in turn dipped down to within meters of the ziggurat's surface. As the next one swept low, they leaped, propelling themselves farther with use of the Force, and landed atop the irregular duracrete surface.

Luke could feel it as Nyax detected them. The pale giant rotated in the air to face them, his smile changing from one of simple pleasure to one of malice. "This is going to be bad," Luke said.

Mara nodded. The wind at this altitude whipped her hair into a life of its own, making it look like a candle flame in a strong breeze. "Any ideas?"

"I have one." Tahiri knelt to improve her balance while she stared ahead. In the distance, this stream of boulders took a sharp turn, then moved to within a few meters of Nyax's position and beyond. "Just past that point. Distract him. I'll finish him."

Luke cocked an eyebrow at her. "*You'll* finish him. How?"

There was something in Tahiri's eyes that sent a chill down Luke's spine. "He could fight the Jedi just by feeling us in the Force," she said. "He couldn't feel the Yuuzhan Vong, so he had to watch. Well, I'm both." She rose and turned away from Luke and Mara, then took the long leap to the next flying boulder back in line. She raced its length, then leaped again to the third boulder down.

"What do you say we take her at her word?" Mara said.

"I'm too tired to argue."

Their boulder reached the end of its straightaway course and turned. It turned more violently than its predecessors had, but Luke and Mara could feel Nyax's intentions in the Force; they kept their feet planted and did not budge.

As their vehicle came closer to Nyax, Luke stretched forth his hand. He snatched a portion of the rubble stream from beneath them, bent its course, sent it hurtling toward Nyax.

Nyax reacted without moving, regaining control of the stream, hurling it at Luke.

Luke leaned over backward, rotating his boulder with him. The oncoming stones crashed into its side and bottom as the rotation continued.

Upside down, clinging by virtue of her enhanced Force strength, Mara ignited her lightsaber and hurled it. It twirled under the flow of boulders, almost invisible through the dense rain of duracrete; then, as it came within meters of Nyax, it twirled up and at him.

His expression changed to one of startlement. With none of his own blades active to protect him, he slipped sideways, out of the lightsaber's path, then turned to watch it as Mara directed its flight. She sent it around in a long loop, preparing it for another approach.

Mara and Luke came upright as their boulder completed its rotation, and Luke could feel Nyax's attention on him, too, waiting for his attack. Luke made it, shoving in the Force, trying to hurl Nyax off balance and onto Mara's blade. The attack was a success, but Nyax activated all his blades as he was shoved, and with contemptuous ease he swatted Mara's lightsaber away.

Power flowed through Nyax, such power as no being alive had ever felt. He could reach down into this world, reach through the false crust beneath him, through the natural stone crust beneath that, all the way to where stone turned to sluggish fluid and through to where super-heated metals ran like river water. He could crack this world in two, could force the meaningless worker-things to convey him to another, and crack that one, too.

And he was tired of these creatures. They were weaker than he, but so stubborn. Even inventive.

Nyax raised his hands. He would crack the stone they rode on and send it and them hurtling down into the ruins.

Something slammed into his back, just below the point where his internal armor plate protected him. His eyes snapped wide. He had not felt it coming. He used his power to overcome the pain.

A second thing struck him. He felt bones in his lower back shatter. Numbness flowed across his legs. He exerted greater control over himself, desperately trying to force sensation into those limbs, as he turned.

His third antagonist, the smaller female with the yellow hair, rode another boulder, lying upon it and gripping it with one hand. She looked at him with alien mercilessness in her eyes. She barely registered in his special senses—she must have closed herself off to the power, reducing his ability to detect her, his ability to anticipate her moves.

Something was wrong. He had the pain under control. He was full of the power. He should be able to make anything happen, anytime.

He did not understand, for he had not been trained in the ways and use of the Force, that the catastrophic failure of the body's functions could interfere with use of the Force. All he did understand was that his control over the boulders, over the debris flow from the ever-widening hole beneath him, was faltering.

The yellow-haired female held up a third missile. It had legs that writhed as she held it.

Nyax gaped at her. It was one of the alien creatures, one of the types flung by the warriors he could not feel. Her type was not supposed to use this. Only the flat-nosed aliens were.

It was unfair. She had cheated.

Before she could throw it, Nyax lost control. He fell, screaming, into the pit he had created.

All at once, the boulders came crashing down onto, and often through, the ziggurat roof. Luke and Mara leapt free, using their augmented power to soften their landing, and rolled up to their feet, looking among the rain of multi-ton missiles for a head of blond hair.

"There," Mara said, and sprinted. The distance of a ballplaying field away, Tahiri lay atop a small dome. But as Luke watched, as a boulder arced down toward her, the young Jedi leapt free. The boulder crashed through the dome and was gone.

"Face to Mara, Face to Mara, do you read me?"

Luke skidded to a halt and pulled out his comlink as his wife reached and embraced the younger Jedi. "Mara's a little busy right now, Face." He leapt to one side and a mass of ferrocrete the size of a Y-wing smashed into the roof beside him. "For that matter, so am I. What is it?"

"Tell me that the whole mess with the fountain of rock was you."

"It was."

"We're inbound. So are a couple of Vong capital ships. You want a lift?"

"We do."

"We'll be there in two."

The three Jedi leapt from the ziggurat roof edge to the stubby wing of the *Ugly Truth*. They squeezed in through the open hatch. Before they were buckled into their restraint couches, Kell had heeled over in a stomach-churning dive into the avenue below. Luke had a glimpse of the construction droid, thought they were going to plow right into it, and then they were level again and accelerating along the avenue.

"So," Face said, his tone conversational. "Is property damage on a massive scale normal for Jedi?"

"That's just if you're friends with them," Kell said. "Wait until you're married to one."

"We need to go back," Luke said. "Nyax isn't dead."

Face and Kell exchanged a glance. "Are we saving him or killing him?"

Luke sighed. "Just getting in his way."

Kell shook his head and gained altitude. As soon as he reached rooftop level, he looped around again, back toward the ziggurat.

Nyax lay in pain at the bottom of the pit.

He'd never known what pain was before he met those three with the power. Now there was nothing but pain.

He would find them, and he would kill them. He must do so soon because he could feel his strength ebbing. No matter how much strength he drew from what lay behind the black wall, he could feel himself failing. Soon he would sleep.

He extended himself, finding the minds of every living thing his power could detect. Where a mind was strong and complex enough to hear him, to obey, he looked through that creature's eyes.

In the first few moments, he could see only a blur of superimposed images. Then he learned to subtract some, overlap others, remap the image into a coherent one in three dimensions.

The power-wielders who had hurt him were not visible. But two chunks of coral he could not feel with his own power, big ones, were approaching him from two different directions.

His enemies had to be aboard them, hidden by whatever power they possessed to block his senses. Since they never gave up, they must be coming back after him. They had to be aboard because he would not sleep until they were dead.

He roared out his pain and sent ton after ton of rubble into the sky.

Kell lost altitude and slid to a landing on a rooftop four kilometers from the ziggurat. From here, they could see the two Vong mataloks, cruiser analogs, approaching from north and south.

Two sprays of rubble leapt from the hole in the ziggurat, each going after one of the mataloks. Nyax's aim was getting worse; in the first few seconds of the attack, neither Vong ship took a hit.

And both fired, raining plasma projectiles as numerous as raindrops into the ziggurat.

Luke jerked as he felt his flesh burn. He looked at his arm, but no blackness appeared there, no seared flesh. It was Nyax, his pain being transmitted to all close enough to feel it, and he could see that pain reflected in the faces of Mara, Tahiri, Danni, even Kell.

Then the rubble streams hit the mataloks. They poured across the vessels, some small portions of them being swallowed by voids, the majority eating away at the yorik coral as though it were sugar. The mataloks sideslipped, desperately trying to avoid the streams of destruction, but the rubble blasts tracked them, followed them, wore them down.

A constriction in Luke's chest, one he had been unaware of until now, suddenly loosened, vanished. "He's dead."

"Lord Nyax?" Face frowned back at him. "I don't think so. Look, more rubble than ever is flying out of there."

"Luke is right," Mara said. Her voice had a distant quality as she tried to interpret what she felt through the Force. "Nyax is gone. But he's imbued his surroundings with some of his hatred. Some of his last intent."

The mataloks rose above the rubble-stream, launching a new volley of plasma before the blasts tracked them, tore into them again. In the distance, more Yuuzhan Vong capital ships raced toward the disturbance.

"It's going to continue," Luke said, "as long as some part of him is there. As long as some part of him can exert his will on his surroundings, and that wellspring of the Force allows it to happen. But he's gone." He took a deep breath. "Let's go home."

"Not quite yet," Kell said. "You hear this?" He dialed

up the comm board, and suddenly everyone could hear a noise—sniffing. No, sniffling. Weeping. "This is from an open comlink Face left behind for stragglers. Back where the *Ugly Truth* was. So someone's there."

"And I bet I know who," Face said.

Viqi, leaning against the side of the airtaxi for support, finally heard the hum when its volume rose higher than the sounds of her own distress. It sounded like repulsors, and the noise floated in through the shattered viewport. She moved up to it to look.

The *Ugly Truth* drifted up into her view, hovering mere meters away.

Her heart lifted, then as swiftly sank. Through the ship's viewport by its access hatch she could see Mara Jade Skywalker staring at her. The woman's features were expressionless, but icy hatred of Viqi Shesh showed in her gem-green eyes, and that hatred froze Viqi in her place.

Can I even ask her for mercy? Viqi asked herself. *Can I stoop that low?*

The answer was simple.

Of course I can. And once I am free again, once I escape, I will make her suffer for that indignity. Viqi composed herself and began rehearsing the words she would say. Pleas for her life.

"Viqi. I knew you were lying. I knew you would return here."

Unbelieving, Viqi turned.

Denua Ku, his front a solid smear of blue-black blood, stood leaning against the doorway into the apartment. He coughed, a racking, painful sound, and blood dribbled from his mouth. His head hung low.

But it did not matter. He was still more than a match for her, and he held his amphistaff in his hands.

"I will now kill you, Viqi." He took a faltering step toward her. He was already almost within reach with his amphistaff.

Viqi could hear the sound of the *Ugly Truth*'s side hatch powering up to open. She knew it could not open in time. Cold resolve flooded her, knowledge that she could inflict hurt in her own inimitable style one last time.

"No, you won't," she said. "Yuuzhan Vong can't kill me. Noghri can't. Jedi can't. You're all beneath me. There's only one thing in the universe that can kill Viqi Shesh."

She turned and stepped out through the shattered viewport.

Luke and Mara watched her fall. Luke even felt it when she died, a faint diminishment in the Force.

"How about that," Mara said. "I get my wish."

The Yuuzhan Vong warrior who had confronted Viqi raised a handful of razorbugs to hurl at the *Ugly Truth*, then fell over on his back. His chest heaved once. Then he was still.

Shaken, Luke settled back in his seat and strapped in. "*Now* we can go."

Tahiri gave him a look that suggested he had taken leave of his senses. "Before, you said 'go home.' I thought *this* was your home. Coruscant."

"No." Luke put an arm around her shoulders, his other arm around Mara's. "I thought it was, but I was

ENEMY LINES II

wrong. No matter what color the sun is, no matter what the furniture is like, home is where my family is."

Tahiri nodded, considering that. She settled against him, face against his shoulder, and closed her eyes as if to sleep.

And for the first time since they'd made landfall on Coruscant, she smiled.

Face said, "Ready for a run to space, Explosion Boy?"

"Always ready, Poster Boy. Hold on to your awards." Kell lifted off, turned away from the ziggurat, and accelerated to full atmospheric speed.

SIXTEEN

Borleias

Luke's expedition returned to a Borleias that was changed—at least in the vicinity of the biotics building and the other areas held by New Republic forces.

On the surface, everything looked worse. Luke and Kell had to pilot the *Ugly Truth* through layered defenses—dovin basal minefields and coralskipper patrols—that surely would have led to the destruction of a vehicle controlled by lesser pilots. Outlying buildings around the biotics building had been smashed by frequent capital ship bombardments. Round-the-chrono coralskipper squadron sorties against the ships in orbit had reduced the *Lusankya* to a flying wreck, had battered the other cruisers and Star Destroyers. Blackmoon Squadron, one of the elite units quartered out of the biotics building complex, had lost three pilots only today, including its commander and second-in-command. The pilots, soldiers, and crews ran on caf and stubbornness, some barely able to stay on their feet as they came on duty.

But in his first hours home, Luke was able to peer beneath the surface.

Kyp Durron welcomed Luke back with an unam-
biguous smile and handshake; when he'd heard the tale
of Lord Nyax, he offered no criticism of Luke's handling
of the matter.

Han and Leia seemed at ease with one another, no lingering tension flavoring words they exchanged. They
told Luke that, with the likelihood very high of an all-out
push by the Yuuzhan Vong in the Pyria system, they were
postponing their next resistance run in order to give
Jaina whatever support they could.

Jaina was different, too, somehow at ease. She did not
burn any less brightly for the loss of her brothers, she did
not fight any less fiercely against the Yuuzhan Vong, but
she was in balance, no longer leaning toward the dark
side. She smiled easily and often.

His family, recently torn apart and flung in all directions, not yet reassembled, was healing.

It was the biotics building's mess hall, but was not
being used for that purpose now, and would never be
used for that purpose again. Its tables were all arrayed
with chairs only on one side so they could face the head
of the room, the seats occupied by General Wedge Antilles, Colonel Tycho Celchu, and Luke Skywalker. Now
those tables were filled with divisional heads, squadron
commanders, ship captains, spies, Jedi.

"The Starlancer project," Wedge said, "is a laser-
based superweapon roughly analogous to a Death Star
main gun, with two important differences. The first difference is that it distorts space and time to accelerate its
destructive force through hyperspace, allowing it to be
used as a first-strike weapon against enemy star systems

light-years away." Muttering from those who were not in on the Starlancer secret filled the air, but could not compete with distant detonations—the Yuuzhan Vong bombardment was now nearly continuous, the New Republic forces not numerous or rested enough to beat it back as in weeks past. Even now, squadrons of tired pilots were defending the biotics facility from that pounding, but could not defend it completely.

Wedge pointed to an area of empty air and a hologram image filled it. It was a trifling bit of sleight of hand, Tycho standing by to activate the holoprojector at the right moment, but there was, Wedge thought, a certain amount of dash to it. And he could see Iella at the back of the room, smiling at his display.

The hologram showed star-filled space. Then four irregular vehicles zoomed into view. Three were identical; they looked like Y-wing cockpits merged to the join of sixty-degree angles made of wide pipe, with a third pipe splitting the angle into two thirty-degree angles. The fourth vehicle was similar, but had three pipes radiating from a central hub at the cockpit's stern. A fourth pipe emerged from the hub at a ninety-degree angle to the plane they suggested.

In the image, the three identical vehicles separated to form the points of an imaginary triangle. The fourth took up position at the center of the formation.

"This is not to scale," Wedge continued. "It's an animation. These vehicles separate to distances of several light-seconds. Then they go through their activation sequence." In the display, light flared from the outer two pipes on each of the identical vehicles. The light beams

streaked from one vehicle to the next, joining them together as a triangle of light. Then, from each of the three
vehicles, the central pipe fired, its light hitting the central
vehicle. Finally, the fourth pipe of the central vehicle
fired. Its laser beam, brighter than all the others, leapt
forth into space . . . and disappeared.

"The Starlancer weapon uses a giant lambent crystal,
a Yuuzhan Vong–engineered living crystal, to focus this
power and perform the hyperacceleration I spoke of.
And now it's ready for its final use.

"Oh, the second point of difference between this weapon
and the Death Star main gun is this: the Starlancer beam
doesn't work. It's a fake."

The murmurs rose. Wedge saw Luke grin.

Wedge raised his voice to carry over the babble, to
quiet it. "The purpose of the Starlancer project is to dic-
tate exactly when the Yuuzhan Vong in this system begin
their all-out push against us. They 'know' that the weapon
threatens them; they have the example of Anakin Solo's
lambent-based lightsaber to compare it to, and to be offended by. They 'know' that we've appropriated their
technology, and this galls them. They 'know' that once
it's ready to fly, we can destroy their worldship in orbit
around Coruscant; we faked up a low-power demonstra-
tion of this by positioning one of our capital ships outside the Coruscant system and firing off a laser battery
attack at that worldship to coincide with the firing of our
fake weapon array. So they 'know' that as soon as we
float the fully operational version, they have to hit us
with everything they've got.

"And this, ultimately, will distract them enough to allow
us to initiate a complete evacuation of this facility . . . and

to take this final battle in this system to them in ways they haven't anticipated."

There were many words and expressions of relief after that statement. Wedge saw his officers exchanging glances. "That's right. This defense is, ultimately, not a suicide mission, despite anything you may have heard." That was something of a deception. The New Republic Advisory Council and self-appointed Chief of State Pwoe had demanded that it be precisely that, a suicide mission. But Wedge had chosen to interpret his orders a trifle differently. "The wounded and nonessential personnel have, over the last few days, been transported—very uncomfortably, I'm afraid, in the guise of cargo and other such deceptions—to our freighters and cargo vessels upstairs. Tycho?"

Tycho rose and hit a button on the datapad in his hand. "Your revised orders have just been transmitted to you. You have an hour before things get under way. I suggest that if you have anything remaining here dirtside that you want to keep, you'd better gather it up now."

"If you have any questions," Wedge said, "address them to your controllers. We have no time remaining here. Dismissed."

The officers rose and crowded to the exits. For a few moments, until almost all had departed, their voices almost did drown out the sound of distant conflict.

"How's your new squadron?" Wedge asked Luke.

"Not bad. My predecessor was a champion of discipline over talent, but the pilots I inherited are pretty determined. We'll get along fine."

Wedge called to an officer just reaching the door out. "Eldo. A moment?"

The bulky captain of *Lusankya* returned, pushing his way through the scattered chairs. His face was much harder to read than it had been weeks ago, when he'd arrived insystem, but that suited Wedge; then, the only things to read had been confusion and distress. "General?"

"I just wanted to say I'm sorry for knocking your command out from under you. I'll make sure it doesn't reflect badly on your record."

The commander gave him a wan smile. "Badly? General, I'm about to pilot the largest, most terrifying single-pilot starfighter the universe has ever seen. Live or die, I'm going to go down in history."

"That's a good way to look at it." Wedge extended his hand. "Good luck."

Luke settled into his X-wing cockpit with a noise of satisfaction. In the weeks since he'd left, Wedge had been using the snubfighter as a personal transport, and had had the vehicle maintained with the sort of monomaniacal thoroughness that another fighter pilot could appreciate. "How're you doing, Artoo?"

His astromech beeped at him, similarly cheery, happy to be back in action once more.

"Blackmoon Leader to squad," Luke said. "Blackmoon Leader is ready. Report readiness by number."

"Blackmoon Two, ready." That was Mara, in the E-wing that had belonged to the squadron's former commander. He hadn't been lost in combat; battle stress had finally reduced him to a shrieking paranoid, leaving him unable to pilot a child's recreational landspeeder, much less a weapon of war.

"Blackmoon Three, ready."

"Blackmoon Four, anxious to drive it in deep and break it off."

Luke watched as the Starlancer pilots brought their ungainly craft out of the special operations bay on repulsorlifts. The three corner vehicles looked the same as ever, but the fourth, the central unit, had a new addition: in its astromech bay, behind the cockpit, rode a faceted jewel the size of a human. It stuck out of the astromech housing by a meter and a half, glistening in the sun. It was identical to the crystal that had been shattered by a Yuuzhan Vong spy in one of the biotics building's sub-basements—and was just as fake.

Somewhere out in the jungle beyond the kill zone, Yuuzhan Vong observers would be seeing this, reaching in alarm for their villip communicators, speaking in rapid, agitated language to their commanders.

One after another, the elite squadrons, those that had been stationed out of the biotics complex all these weeks to reinforce the notion that this was the most critical point of Borleias's defense, announced readiness and lined up: Gavin Darklighter's Rogue Squadron. Jaina Solo's Twin Suns. Saba Sebatyne's Wild Knights. Luke's Blackmoons. Wes Janson's Taanab Yellow Aces. Shawnkyr Nuruodo's Vanguard Squadron. The *Millennium Falcon*. Less than two kilometers away, squadrons off *Lusankya* dueled with coralskipper squadrons and capital ships moving in on the facility, but the elites wouldn't be reinforcing them, wouldn't be confronting the planet-level attackers; they'd be lying to the enemy instead.

At General Antilles's command, the Rogues, Twin Suns, and Blackmoons lifted off. The Starlancer pipefighters lifted off in their wake. Then the other elites rose. It was a convoy of starfighters, blastboats, and one light freighter, and in some ways it was among the deadliest armadas the New Republic had ever launched.

On the holocam screen, Wedge watched the squadrons of the last Starlancer sortie take off. "Alert *Lusankya*," he told Tycho. "As soon as the pursuit is on, he's to initiate Operation Emperor's Spear."

"Done," Tycho said.

"This," Czulkang Lah informed Harrar, "is it. Their all-out attack to destroy my son."

"How will it play out?" the priest asked.

"All their best pilots protect the lambent vehicles. They expect us to send overwhelming hordes of coralskippers against that fleet. Once our fighters are poised to attack, they will initiate whatever means they have to confuse our yammosks, to destroy communication among our forces." Czulkang Lah offered up a nearly lipless smile. "But it will not happen so. Moments after our forces engage, mobile dovin basal mines will enter the area and begin stripping the enemy shields. All the fighters assigned to that engagement have been carefully drilled in individual pilot initiative. A disruption of yammosk control will not inconvenience them in the least. Their most famous fighters will be overwhelmed and destroyed. The menace the crystal represents will be ended. And with the ground-based fighters weakened by exhaustion and loss, the ground facility will fall within an hour."

Harrar nodded. The old warmaster's confidence was welcome in these uncertain times. "All these individual-initiative fighters . . . they know not to harm Jaina Solo?"

"They do."

"The gods smile upon you, Czulkang Lah."

"May it be so. Now, I must turn my attention to the battle to come."

Harrar bowed and withdrew. He gave no sign of it, but he was most pleased. At last, the Yuuzhan Vong goals in the Pyria system were within their grasp.

Danni Quee switched over the Wild Knights' blast-boat comm board to unit frequency. "This is Wild One. Gravitics suggest a large formation of coralskippers moving our way. It looks like a minimum of one hundred skips. Estimated time of interception, ten minutes."

"Wild One, Ace-One. That's enough for the Yellow Aces, but what are the rest of you going to do?"

"Ace-One, Rogue Leader. Pipe down."

"Correction, sensors are bumping those numbers up. One hundred and fifty minimum."

"Ah, that's getting better."

"Now?" Tycho asked.

Wedge considered, still focused on the sensor display correlating all the data from the various squadrons. He nodded.

"*Lusankya,* commence Operation Emperor's Spear." Tycho listened to the response, then lowered the ear-piece. "*Lusankya*'s away."

"Start evacuation of this facility."

Tycho returned to his comlink. "Commence Piranha-Beetle. Repeat, commence Piranha-Beetle."

"Get on up to *Mon Mothma*, Tycho. If at any time you

lose contact with me, whether it's while I'm in transit or for any other reason, you take command of the operation."

"Done."

"And make sure my shuttle is standing by. I don't want to come trotting out of this building to find only a note of apology waiting for me."

Tycho grinned and extended his hand. "May the Force be with you, Wedge."

Wedge shook it. "If it was, how would I ever know?"

Kasdakh Bhul said, "*Lusankya* is leaving orbit. We have reports that fighters are leaving her belly and escorting her."

Czulkang Lah frowned. "Did you not tell me earlier that all her fighters were at ground level, defending the infidel base?"

"Yes, Czulkang Lah."

"Well?"

"It was our Peace Brigade advisers who told us this, based on their listening to the talk between their fighters and their triangle ships."

"So there was lying in that talk."

"That is my opinion."

"Have those advisers stand by on one of our ships. Kill one of them for this mistake. Every time a new mistake of this sort costs us lives, kill another."

"It shall be done." Kasdakh Bhul returned to studying the blaze bug niche and listening to the villips on the wall. He then turned back to the commander. "The red triangle ship is now breaking from orbit."

"Good. That will be easy prey; she carries few weapons." Czulkang Lah gestured to get the attention of his fleet commander. "Dispatch two mataloks to eliminate that atrocity."

"It shall be done."

Lusankya turned with a slow awkwardness that no Star Destroyer commander would have tolerated from a chief pilot. Her maneuver was too great, in fact, and once her gradual port-side turn was completed, her nose drifted a few degrees back to starboard before the mammoth vessel was correctly lined up.

Then her thrusters engaged and she began a ponderous acceleration straight toward the Domain Hul worldship.

"Confirmed count, two hundred and ten coralskippers," Danni said. "A couple of those gravitic anomalies in their wake. Time to interception, three minutes."

Luke said, "All squadrons, all squadrons, reverse course. Head back toward our pursuit and initiate Stage Two on a one-minute countdown." He put his X-wing into a tight loop. "Beginning countdown . . ." His finger hovered over the transmit button. "Now."

The two Yuuzhan Vong cruiser analogs approached the *Errant Venture* from opposite angles.

The *Errant Venture*, built as an Imperial Star Destroyer, captured by smuggler Booster Terrik, and converted into his own private gambling parlor and mobile hotel, was, unlike other ships of her class, painted a screaming red from bow to stern. The color was alleviated only by lingering signs of battle damage and running lights. Recently the home of the Jedi children, she was known to be an easy mark; the Yuuzhan Vong had not bothered with her much because she posed them no threat, spent much of her recent time running missions out of the Pyria system, and was in general a far less significant target than the biotics base or the other New Republic capital ships.

But now her time had come, and as the mataloks closed on her, the pitifully few defensive batteries she had opened up, peppering the enemy vessels with insignificant spikes of pain.

The Yuuzhan Vong commanders returned fire, but paced their plasma cannons, waiting for a distance that would allow them to unleash true pain on the offensive red triangle. Then, in the moment before they reached the optimum distance, *Errant Venture*'s other weapons opened up. As the Imperial Star Destroyer rotated to bring each matalok within sight of the greatest possible number of weapons, thirty turbolaser batteries fired at each target, turning the hull of each cruiser analog into a superheated, explosive ruin.

In a matter of seconds, the two mataloks were gone, an expanding cloud of gas and rubble the only sign they had ever been there. Their commanders would never know the deception performed against them—how, as *Lusankya* suffered more and more battle damage, many of her undamaged turbolasers and ion cannons were transferred to the other capital ships in the fleet, making *Lusankya* a little-armed shell of a Destroyer, keeping the others at full destructive power.

Errant Venture continued on her course until the gravity well of Borleias no longer gripped her with any significant strength; then the Imperial Star Destroyer leapt to hyperspace.

Charat Kraal, commanding one of the squadrons racing toward the pipefighters and their heretical crystal, breathed a sigh of satisfaction. All they had to do was keep the enemy fighters in this region of space long enough for the support mines to reach this area, and the mines assigned to Jaina Solo's X-wing would grab her, bring her into Charat Kraal's grasp.

Her starfighter was among the cloud of oncoming craft. The specially engineered auxiliary dovin basal on his coralskipper could sense that craft's specific gravitic signature, and it communicated its excitement to Charat Kraal as a continuous buzz through his cognition hood.

The oncoming starfighters had divided into squadron units and were mere moments from reaching maximum firing distance. Charat Kraal selected a target within Jaina's squadron, the craft with the claw-shaped extensions.

Then all the oncoming craft vanished.

Charat Kraal blinked, then focused his attention on his second dovin basal. The question he asked it was wordless, but understood: *Where is the vehicle?*

But the dovin basal didn't know.

The four vehicles that the infidels called pipefighters were still ahead in the distance, however. Shaken and confused, Charat Kraal oriented toward them and kept up the pursuit, as did the others of his mighty coral-skipper force.

Soon, they pulled within firing range of the flying blasphemies. Charat Kraal's contempt grew as the foremost coralskippers of his formation began firing. The pipe-fighters did not bother to maneuver. Perhaps their pilots were too inexperienced, too frightened.

Charat Kraal willed that thought away. It made no sense. Even the most inexperienced pilot could try to maneuver out of the line of fire, and these didn't. One by one, the four vehicles detonated under the plasma cannons of their pursuers, the crystal-bearing vehicle last.

The thought came hard to Charat Kraal: *Were they even occupied by the living? Or could they have been abominations controlled by other abominations?*

Kasdakh Bhul looked inconvenienced at having to bring incomprehensible news to Czulkang Lah. "The coralskippers pursuing the lambent fighters report that all the infidels' protective fighters have disappeared."

"Disappeared. Fled?"

"No, it seemed to be an orderly jump into darkspace. And there is more."

"Tell me."

"The mataloks sent to destroy the red triangle ship are gone, as is the red triangle ship."

"All destroyed? It put up an impressive battle for something so ill equipped."

"Unknown. The matalok commanders did not report their target putting up a fierce struggle."

Czulkang Lah scowled, but turned his anger away from Kasdakh Bhul. The warrior did not have much intelligence to offer, but it did require courage to deliver unhappy news to a senior officer.

And this was unhappy news. Mysteries were piling up.

He didn't like mysteries. They meant that he had not correctly interpreted every variable.

And that was one way to lose an engagement.

Once free of Borleias's gravity well, *Lusankya* fired off her hyperdrive, a microjump that left her escort screen of starfighters behind. The jump took her halfway across the solar system before a dovin basal mine dragged her back into realspace.

This wasn't an unexpected turn of events. Her crew knew it would happen, though not precisely where. In terms of stellar distances, she was not far now from the Domain Hul worldship commanded by Czulkang Lah, but it was not likely that she would be able to make another jump to get closer; the space between this point and that was doubtless thick with dovin basal mines.

Her crew immediately transmitted a signal on the fleet frequency. It said, in effect, *I'm here.*

Though she'd been built to carry a crew of more than a quarter million, not including ground troops, things had changed. There were no weapon batteries to operate. Life-support systems were shut down over most of the ship. Communications were restricted to a few comm channels. Shields and a few other critical systems were largely governed now by droids taken apart and then reassembled straight into system relay points. No one monitored fuel expenditure, thruster heat conditions, stores, supplies.

She now carried a crew of one.

A minute later, the squadrons that had just abandoned the pipefighters appeared in her wake, yanked out of hyperspace by the same dovin basal mine. They turned, moving up and around *Lusankya*, a protective screen.

And coralskipper squadrons began moving against them.

The *Millennium Falcon* was not among the vehicles protecting *Lusankya*. Instead, the transport dropped out of hyperspace at the edge of one of the thickest of the dovin basal minefields, the one on the primary arrival vector from Coruscant space.

"I don't read any coralskippers," Leia said.

"Good! Anyone for sabacc?"

Leia gave him a look.

"You know I'm kidding. Ready the grav decoys."

Leia flipped the series of switches on the weapons board before her. It had been a single concussion missile power-up sequence switch, but it had, in the last few days, been temporarily replaced. "Five live," she said.

"Fire one."

She returned the first switch to its down position. The *Falcon* rattled slightly as a missile launched from the concussion missile tube.

Leia watched it on the sensor board. It roared into the middle of the minefield, then slowly turned toward the distant engagement zone. It moved far more slowly than a missile should.

On the board, the wire-frame images indicating points in space where gravity was distorted remained constant . . . except in one area. The wire frame wrinkled there, and the distortion moved, at first slowly and then with increasing speed, in the missile's wake.

She smiled. "It's taking the bait."

The bait was an instrument package that used the Jaina

Solo-developed technique of gravitic signature simulation. The missile she'd fired carried with it the exact gravitic signature of the *Millennium Falcon*, as did the other four missiles the *Falcon* held ready.

"Fire two."

"You really like sounding military, don't you?"

Han grinned. "Only when I'm *giving* orders."

"Second missile is away."

SEVENTEEN

Wedge watched on the monitors as *Lusankya*'s starfighters screamed back down into the atmosphere, then began escorting the last personnel transports up. With the transports was a small, private yacht, a converted blastboat that carried Wolam Tser, Tam Elgrin, and a boy named Tarc. Wedge wished them success in staying away from the Yuuzhan Vong—now, and forever.

Iella stood by the door, waiting. Other than Wedge, she was the last person in the biotics building's operations center. "You can't do much more here, Wedge. Time to go."

"Not quite yet. As long as there's a chance their Peace Brigade friends are trying to crack our comm traffic, them knowing that I'm still here could still cause them to wonder why." He gave her a conciliatory look. "I'll be along. I have a shuttle standing by."

"Come on."

"You go. Now. Don't force me to make an order of it."

Married long enough to know where duty absolutely defined Wedge's actions, Iella gave an exasperated shake of her head. She came over for one last kiss. "Don't get hurt."

"You, either."

"I *want* you to be able to retire again."

"You, too."

"I love you."

He kissed her a second time. "I love you, too. And I plan to prove it over and over again." He smiled against the sick feeling that suddenly roiled within him, the fear that there would be no over and over again, that this was the last time she would see him. "Now go."

She went.

He returned to the sensor board and forced the conversation, the sensation out of his mind. Whether it was a valid premonition or just ordinary fear, he had a job to do.

He watched as the biotics complex's starfighter defenses continued to crumble, as Yuuzhan Vong air and ground forces continued their approach.

Charat Kraal led his squadron around toward Domain Hul. His villip had just told him that *Lusankya* was coming . . . and that Jaina Solo's squadron was among those escorting her.

He was confused. He didn't like being confused. No Yuuzhan Vong warrior ever endured being confused.

The only appropriate response was to kill something.

The elite squadrons guarding *Lusankya* fought with tremendous skill. Czulkang Lah made sure that the patterns flown by the blaze bugs, showing the development of that conflict, would be seared into the memory of the worldship's brain. He knew he would enjoy watching it again and again.

Coralskipper squadrons entering that combat zone emerged depleted, tattered . . . when they emerged at all.

Reports of his sensor advisers indicated that the coralskipper assaults were taking their toll. New Republic pilots were falling. And *Lusankya* was being taken to pieces. Despite the fact that an unusual amount of power was being directed into her shields, the ship's weapons batteries were silent, and great chunks of metal were said to be tearing free of the superstructure under the constant pounding from coralskippers and capital ships that ventured close enough to strike.

Wedge charged out of the operations center. The biotics building shook with the pounding it received from distant plasma cannons, impacts so loud that he couldn't hear his own boots on the duracrete floor. Chunks of the ceiling rained down; he threw his arms over his head for protection, catching a blow on his right wrist from descending debris.

He made it up the staircase to the ground level without seeing any other personnel. That gave him a grim satisfaction. No one had managed to outstubborn him, to defy his orders in order to make sure that Wedge had company on his escape. It was a little comforting, but the thought that he might be the last member of the New Republic standing on Borleias was oddly unsettling.

Through the transparisteel in the doors at the end of the main hall he could see distant flashes, narrow red streaks heading one way at the speed of light, more wobbly orange-red streaks headed the other, clear evidence that Wedge's last forces were still fighting their delaying action. Then he slammed through the doors, emerging onto the kill zone, and could see that the engagement was continuing at every degree of the compass.

The kill zone itself was full of craters and destroyed vehicles. Everything that had been fit to fly was up in space now; the vehicles too wrecked to lift off had been destroyed by Wedge's engineers, standard operating procedure, though the Yuuzhan Vong were not in the habit of studying captured technology. Some of them had been additionally hit by distant plasma cannon fire aimed at the biotics building. There were no functional vehicles to be seen.

No functional vehicles. Where was his shuttle?

Then he recognized it, a heap of burning metal whose shape suggested it had once been a *Lambda*-class shuttle.

Wedge grimaced. A pilot had died waiting for him. It was another tally mark for the list—the list he'd once hoped he'd retired; the one he carried in his heart.

He shoved the thought to one side. He'd join that list in a minute if he didn't act. Punctuating his thought, a plasma cannon projectile hit the biotics building far over his head, plowing through ferrocrete and transparisteel, sending sharp, lethal chunks down toward him.

Wedge sprinted away from the building's face. There was no purpose in going into the main docking bay, except perhaps to hide; it was open, and he could see from here that nothing more useful than a small cargo lifter was left within it.

The special operations docking bay was almost intact, though, and still closed. Wedge hoped they hadn't boobytrapped it. He reached the main door, tapped his authorization code into the keypad, and then flinched as he heard the biotics building take a hit from something big.

The force of the explosion, though weakened by distance, pushed him into the door. He spun to look and watched as the building folded over like a fighter punched once too often in the midsection; the top portion at the center tumbled down onto the kill zone where he'd been standing just seconds before.

The docking bay door ground open. He backed in and spun, eyes trying to pierce the darkness of the interior even as the overhead lights began to flicker on.

The special operations crew had left behind a landspeeder that looked as though it had been slow-roasted for the eating pleasure of some alien giant. Nearby was a half-finished pipefighter, one they'd been assembling in case any of the others failed during their bogus tests. And then Wedge's heart soared—off to the right, near the still-opening door, where the lights were last to come to full brightness, was an X-wing. There was no astromech waiting beside it or tucked in place behind the cockpit, but otherwise it looked intact, its cockpit raised as if in greeting.

The vehicle's surface was scratched and burned everywhere, but there were a dozen shiny patches in place on the hull, not yet painted to match the snubfighter's color scheme, and the canopy was gleaming, unmarred, obviously brand-new.

Wedge raced to it and climbed up into the cockpit, adrenaline letting him move like a man half his age. He'd commenced the emergency power-start procedure before gravity had quite settled him into the pilot's couch, and brought up the vehicle's assignment and diagnostics before lowering the canopy and buckling in.

The text board on his control panel swam into letters before it was even at full brightness:

INCOM T65-J "X-WING" IDENTIFIER NUMBER 103430
CURRENT PILOT: FLIGHT OFFICER KORIL BEKAM
CURRENT DESIGNATION: BLACKMOON 11
CURRENT ASTROMECH: R2-Z13 "PLUG"

"Too bad you're not along for the ride, Plug." Without an astromech, Wedge would be able to perform only the most basic insystem navigation; he wouldn't be able to plot any interstellar routes. But if he could get up to his forces in this vehicle, accept a broadcast nav course or land aboard one of the capital ships, he'd be fine.

He triggered a command on his datapad, sending an authorization code to the X-wing.

CODE NOT RECOGNIZED, AUTHORIZATION FAILED.

The diagnostics board was now up. Power, shield, weapon, and thruster systems seemed to be fine, but the board showed unrepaired damage to the snubfighter's computer and communications systems. Wedge swore. The time pressures that had forced the mechanics to abandon this vehicle before it was quite repaired might have doomed him. That point was accentuated by a new sound—the *whumf* of some large craft making an awkward landing near the special ops docking bay. No, it was *adjacent* to the docking bay—Wedge saw the back wall of the building, hardy sheet metal, bow in from the displaced air.

Wedge scrolled down in his datapad to personnel

records, called up the details of Flight Officer Koril Bekam, and transmitted *his* authorization code.

AUTHORIZATION ACCEPTED. Power-up of the remainder of vehicle systems commenced.

The docking bay door was now fully open, spilling sunlight across Wedge and the X-wing. Wedge saw a detachment of Yuuzhan Vong warriors, twenty or more of them, pass by the bay, headed toward the biotics building.

The data board indicated that two engines were up, three, four, then thrusters and repulsors reported ready. Lasers came online, and the bar indicating shield readiness struggled to become a solid green.

A Yuuzhan Vong warrior skidded around the corner of the special ops docking bay and halted, facing the X-wing, his posture suggesting surprise. A moment later, nine or ten more raced up behind him and turned toward Wedge.

Wedge gave them a smile—humorless, feral. He flicked his lasers over to stutterfire and sprayed the crowd of enemy warriors, saw some of them dive back the way they'd come, saw others caught in the beams.

Even set on stutterfire, where each beam was fired at the lowest useful intensity available to an X-wing weapon, the lasers were meant for vehicles, not individuals. Striking the Yuuzhan Vong, the beams superheated flesh past the point of cooking, past the point of boiling, straight to the state of gas or even plasma. Warriors hit by the beams simply exploded, torsos reduced to nothingness, limbs hurled in all directions.

Wedge grimaced, then fired up his repulsors and thrusters. In a smooth motion, his X-wing lifted, sideslipped out from under the docking bay roof, and turned the direction opposite that from which the warriors had come. He kicked his thrusters over to full and raced at maximum acceleration away from the docking bay and crumbling biotics building. Over his shoulder, he could see the Yuuzhan Vong troop carrier, an egg-shaped thing, towering over the docking bay, squadron after squadron of warriors emerging from it at a dead run. The troop carrier opened up on his X-wing, sending glowing plasma balls after him, but Wedge twitched the vehicle to port and the flood of burning material fell into the jungle beneath him.

There wouldn't be time for a checklist, even an abbreviated one. He had to get up into space and rejoin his forces. He switched his X-wing comm unit over to command frequency. "Blackmoon Eleven to *Mon Mothma*, Blackmoon Eleven to *Mon Mothma*, come in."

The unit came alive with comm traffic. Wedge recognized the voice of Tycho, directing starfighter squadrons, of Jaina issuing commands to the Twin Suns, of many other officers under his command. But no one responded.

He put on a little altitude, preparatory to making the run to space. "Blackmoon Eleven to anyone. Please respond."

Nothing.

He growled. He'd have to rely on his own sensors and instincts to choose the best course offworld, and could easily blunder into squadrons of incoming coralskippers. Well, those were the breaks. He could either complain or prepare. He pulled back on his yoke—and then flashed past a small Corellian freighter, a scarred sky-blue YT-2400. He knew the ship, which was far newer than the similar *Millennium Falcon*, but still a rickety thing held together by wire and meanness.

In the glimpse he had of it before leaving it behind, he thought that it looked mostly intact, despite smoke pouring out of one of the engine housings, and believed he'd seen people outside it, moving. He began to loop around.

"Blackmoon Eleven, this is *Ammuud Swooper*. Come in, please."

Wedge frowned. How did they know his designation? Then it made sense. He couldn't broadcast voice, but his transponder must still be working, must still be sending out this X-wing's identifier code for friend-or-foe sensor recognition. "*Ammuud Swooper,* you have Blackmoon Eleven. Go."

"Blackmoon Eleven, come in. This is *Ammuud Swooper*. Please reply."

Wedge passed over the downed freighter again, this time at reduced velocity. He could see men and women atop the freighter, illuminated by the sparks and glow of welding torches.

At this range—he pulled his comlink out of his breast pocket and thumbed it on. "*Ammuud Swooper,* this is Blackmoon Eleven. Are you receiving me now?"

"Barely, but we have you. We were downed by plasma cannon fire but we've almost got a patch ready on our engines. We can lift in a couple of minutes . . . but the unit that shot us down is pretty close, north-northwest. Can you hold them back for us?"

"I'll give you your two minutes. Maybe more. My comm board is shot, so if I don't respond to further communications, don't take it personally. Blackmoon Eleven out."

"Thanks, Eleven. *Ammuud Swooper* out."

Wedge reduced his speed still further, then looped

around to pass over the freighter on a north-northwest course. In seconds he saw the enemy unit *Ammuud Swooper* had spoken of, approaching through a patch of thick grasses surrounded by jungle; there were a dozen Yuuzhan Vong infantry, two dozen reptoid slave-warriors, one coralskipper, and what appeared to be an unwounded rakamat, this one tall and lean rather than mountainous, and with only half the armament of a full-sized version, but still plenty against a lightly armed freighter.

Or an X-wing, for that matter.

Even as he calculated their numbers, Wedge switched over to stutterfire and sprayed lasers across their position. Warriors and reptoids went down and grass ignited in front of the rakamat as he fired. Then he flashed over their position, plasma fire from the rakamat following, and saw on his sensor board as the coralskipper rose in pursuit. He put all discretionary vehicle power into his rear shields for a moment, heard thumps over his audio as his sensors informed him that plasma ejecta had hit the shields and been stopped.

It had taken six X-wings and a hidden cache of explosives to kill the last rakamat they'd fought against. This one might be only half as powerful as the last, but Wedge was a third as powerful as the previous force. The odds were bad.

On the other hand, Han Solo had made a generation of people think that Corellians ignored the odds, no matter how long, and Wedge was as Corellian as Solo was.

Then the idea hit him, and Wedge managed another humorless grin.

The coralskipper hot on his tail, Wedge looped around until he was approaching the rakamat and its covering troops from a cross-angle to its path. He fired again, spraying lasers indiscriminately into the grasses to the left of the rakamat, scattering the Yuuzhan Vong warriors and reptoids there. From here, he could see the rakamat's legs as it moved stolidly toward the freighter, could time them in their steady, docile motions.

Plasma rained toward him from the rakamat, from the coralskipper behind. Wedge sideslipped and continued to fire into the grasses, setting them ablaze, kicking up gouts of dirt and steam. Now his vision was useless, but his sensors still showed the huge mass of the rakamat, distorted by the heat from the fire.

Wedge dropped to grasstop level, heard scrapes and thumps as his lower hull was grazed by foliage—perhaps even by irregularities in the terrain. Ahead, he could see the very top of the rakamat, as its plasma cannons elevated, preparing to catch his underside as he popped up over them.

He flipped an overhead switch and his S-foils closed from the X-shaped firing position to cruise position. And as he entered the zone where the grasses were blazing, he twitched his yoke down, then up.

He had the barest flash of rakamat legs to his left and right, a looming shadow over him, and then he was rising.

For a bare moment, no plasma came streaking after him. In going under the rakamat, in emerging low from the wrong side, he'd thrown the creature into confusion. He switched his S-foils back into firing position as he climbed.

In that moment, the pursuing coralskipper roared through the fire and saw the rakamat immediately before it. The pilot must have panicked. Over his shoulder, Wedge saw the bow of the coralskipper wobble as the pilot was torn between following Wedge under or bouncing over, and that moment of hesitation doomed him. The skip's bow rose and, at several hundred kilometers per hour, the skip plowed into the flank of the rakamat.

There was no flash of light, no noise of the impact—Wedge was racing away too fast for the sound to catch him. There was only the grisly image of the coralskipper tearing through the creature, emerging in a different, narrower shape, the rakamat being flung in two pieces away from the point of impact, the remains of the coralskipper arching up in a ballistic course and then gradually down toward the ground.

Wedge looped around to mop up. There was unaccustomed tension in his arm, and he realized that he was gripping the yoke too hard.

"I'm not going to say it," he told himself. "I'm not."

I'm getting too old for this.

Lusankya was visible to the naked eye now, a tiny needle pointed straight for Domain Hul.

Czulkang Lah squinted up at it, irritable, his diminished eyesight insufficient to provide him with any details of what he was seeing. He gestured at an aide, who correctly interpreted the nonspecific motion and stroked the enormous circular lens in the center of the command chamber's ceiling. It distorted, stretching details at its periphery into blurriness, magnifying the enemy ship's image until it dominated the scene.

The ship had already sustained tremendous damage. The deckplating everywhere was torn, rough, like a road that had once been smooth and then had been traveled over by herds of rakamats with spike weapons on their feet. Flame jetted out from its hull in dozens of places. Its guns were mostly silent; Czulkang Lah saw only two batteries that were still active, and they seemed to be firing at random. They posed little threat to his coralskippers.

But there were still squadrons of enemy starfighters out there, mostly concentrated at *Lusankya*'s stern, maintaining a savage defense over that area of the ship.

Kasdakh Bhul moved to stand beside him. "Our pilots report that the *Lusankya* abomination is almost destroyed. Lack of responsiveness indicates that most of her crew must be dead and most of her weapons eliminated. She will not be able to send her lasers and bolts against us."

Czulkang Lah carefully positioned his feet so that the blow would not cause him to lose his balance; that would be unseemly. Then he swung his arm. His vonduun crab armor correctly interpreted his haste and snapped his arm forward. His armored forearm cracked across the back of Kasdakh Bhul's helmet, sending his second-in-command staggering forward.

Kasdakh Bhul regained his balance and spun. Czulkang Lah could see the younger officer's features graduate from an expression of anger to one of surprise.

"You see, but you do not understand," Czulkang Lah said. "They never intended to use their weapons upon us."

"Oh." The younger officer's voice became unreasonably reasonable, a type of mockery useful in that it could be persuasively denied afterward. "So this was simply an infidel sacrifice? An apology? They are saying, *We are sorry for being bad; here, have our greatest weapon?*"

Czulkang Lah offered him a smile nearly devoid of teeth. "You persist in being an idiot. I am proud to say I did not train you; you would have been my most repellent failure. Did you not notice? They never protected their weapons. They only protected their engines. What does that tell you?"

The younger officer scowled. "That they wanted the thing to get here quickly?"

"That their engines *are* their weapons. Are you sure you are not an ooglith masquer with nothing actually inside?"

Kasdakh Bhul ignored the undisguised insult. "Then their intention—is to ram us?"

"Wisdom. At last. So, even an ooglith masquer can learn a little when submerged in knowledge."

"Then we must make sure the abomination is incapable of reaching us. Of maneuvering adequately to ram us."

"Very good. Issue the orders, Ooglith Masquer."

Three coralskippers, all that remained of the latest wave, turned and sped away.

Doubtless they'd regroup with reinforcements in a minute and return. Luke checked his sensor and status boards. He was now two pilots down, and the remainder of his units were battered; he had some plasma scoring on his starboard top S-wing and engine. "Blackmoon Leader to squadron," he said. "We have a moment. Anyone with stripped shields, now's the time to commence a power restart." He goosed his thruster to come up behind and below *Lusankya*'s port-side thruster banks; he kept well to port of them. This position gave him a good view of the Yuuzhan Vong worldship ahead. "Anything I should know?"

"We have Blackmoon Eleven back on the status board." That was the voice of Lieutenant Ninora Birt, Blackmoon Ten, the squad's new communications specialist. A freelance smuggler, she'd loaned her expertise and her freighter, *Record Time,* to the cause of this operation. Her freighter had been half destroyed during the taking of Borleias, and the job had been completed above Coruscant weeks later; now, with a new military officer's commission, she was still fighting the good fight.

Luke glanced at his status board. It did indeed indicate that Blackmoon Eleven was active. Distance and direction suggested that the X-wing was on Borleias.

"No way." That was Blackmoon Five. "Koril's in bacta somewhere. I saw the medics haul him off."

"Doesn't matter," Luke said. "Concentrate on what's at hand."

"Blackmoon Leader, this is Twin Suns Leader."

"Go, Goddess."

"Sharr is detecting skips regrouping in a bunch of different units. All at a uniform distance away from *Lusankya.*"

"We'll set up for a new wave, then. Thanks, Exalted One."

Finally Jaina could see the incoming squadrons on her sensors. There were a lot of them, eight groupings at least, and the three squadrons at *Lusankya*'s stern were losing strength. "Time for a Goddess chase, don't you think, Sharr?"

"Ooh, your words thrill me, Great One."

"Don't be so thrilled that you screw up."

"Ooh, your supportiveness thrills me—"

"Get back to business, Sharr."

"Right." Sharr was silent for a long moment, during which the units of coralskippers got closer, moving in from all directions. Then: "Nearest dovin basal minefield is ahead and to port. The Goddess should aim for that. Piggy, when do the incoming units get close enough to recognize us by sight?"

"Forty seconds, but if the Goddess goes off straight toward that minefield, she'll pass close enough for them to see her."

"Ooh, right. Adjusting course . . . Twin Suns Leader, prepare yourself for the chase. Three, two, one . . . chase."

A missile roared away from Twin Suns Ten, streaking off to port at nearly a ninety-degree angle to their current course, aiming toward the largest gap between any of the inbound squadrons. Jaina activated her gravitic signature and transponder switches. Abruptly her designation on the sensor board went to Twin Suns Nine, while the outbound missile, just as instantaneously, became Twin Suns One.

There was a momentary wobble in the movements of skip squadrons to port. Then four of the squads in that direction changed course, converging on the missile.

"Well done, Sharr," Jaina said. When she'd switched to the Twin Suns Nine identity, her comm system should have activated a program to alter her vocal characteristics, making her sound like an older woman, one with a deeper voice.

"Thanks, Nine. And nice to have Leader gone. She's so bossy."

Kyp cut into the conversation: "Heads up. We still have incoming contacts to starboard. Prepare to repel boarders. Break by shield trios on my command . . . three, two, one, break."

While Beelyath held position within the Twin Suns Ten-Eleven-Twelve shield trio, Sharr kept his attention on his special sensor and comm boards. The distant missile code-named Goddess, and now, courtesy of Cilghal's biotechnical magic, characterized by the precise gravitic signature of Jaina's X-wing, had onboard computers and logic programs that allowed it to execute its mission on its own, but Sharr could still feed it priority updates.

He switched to a wire-frame view of local space as the Goddess missile and the coralskippers pursuing it entered the dovin basal minefield. The green wire frame superimposed on the scene showed the spatial distortions caused by the mines and their gravitic influence on their surroundings.

Sharr kept the missile's speed down to that of an X-wing's standard cruise rate, allowing the pursuing skips to gain on it. So far, they were still far enough in its wake that the pilots could not see it with their naked eyes, could not realize that it wasn't the true Jaina Solo.

The Yuuzhan Vong pursuers were good. They were gaining faster than he expected on the missile. With his sensors, superior to the missile's, Sharr drew a course revision on his screen, sending the missile on a path that would take it past mine after mine, while giving more and more pursuers the chance to approach it. He executed and sent the course revision, then lost sight of his sensor board as Beelyath sent the B-wing into a veering turn that crushed Sharr into his restraints and caused his vision to blur, all despite the starfighter's inertial compensators.

"Comfortable?" Beelyath croaked.

"Huh?" Sharr grunted. "Sorry, I was sleeping."

EIGHTEEN

Though he could not see the distant X-wing, Charat Kraal's cognition hood created a glow in in the distance, a glow he knew actually existed only in his mind, showing the enemy vehicle's position.

And his opponent was good, as he knew Jaina Solo to be, but this day she was flying with more skillful reckless abandon than he had ever before seen, leading the coralskippers deep into the dovin basal minefield, doubtless hoping to elude them by passing through such a difficult and dangerous area at high speed.

For a moment, doubt flickered in Charat Kraal's mind. Why would she have left the relative safety of numbers, of her personal squadron, to lead the Yuuzhan Vong here by herself? There seemed to be only one possible answer: so she could attempt to kill them all without any of her fellow pilots to share the glory.

Was she that overconfident? Was she that mad?

Could her confidence be warranted?

The pilot to Charat Kraal's port side opened fire with his plasma cannon, sending a stream of red glows off toward the distant target.

Charat Kraal cursed to himself. Of all the traits of the

infidels' starfighters, the one he truly envied was the ability they gave their pilots to talk to one another, voice to voice. The yammosk war coordinator kept this flight of pursuers coordinated and pointed in the right direction, but could not prevent a pilot with a rogue streak from firing on an enemy they were supposed to capture alive.

Charat Kraal dropped back a few lengths and slid in behind the errant pilot. From this close distance, he could see that the yorik coral of the coralskipper ahead was marked with the symbols of Domain Hul. Making no effort to disguise his action, he carefully aimed at that coralskipper's stern and fired a single plasma cannon shot straight at it. As he expected, a void from the other coralskipper appeared in the path of the plasma projectile and swallowed it.

That pilot ignored the warning. He continued firing at the distant Jaina Solo and now sideslipped to starboard, distancing himself from Charat Kraal, indicating in no uncertain terms his intent to continue following his own warrior spirit, even if it meant disobeying direct orders.

Charat Kraal growled to himself and followed. He fired again, this time a continuous stream of plasma, intending to kill rather than to warn. The Hul pilot banked away more sharply, his voids intercepting the incoming plasma, and then rolled into a maneuver designed to swing him around behind Charat Kraal.

Finally, Charat Kraal grinned. In a moment, he would have another kill, this one a disobedient pilot from another domain, and would have reinforced his reputation for order and ruthlessness in his own unit.

The other coralskippers of the unit continued on their original course, closing on Jaina Solo.

Czulkang Lah made a noise of displeasure. The pattern of blaze bugs in the darkened sensor niche told the whole story of Charat Kraal's pursuit. He did not blame Charat Kraal for this momentary diversion, but was not happy at the lack of discipline shown by the other pilot. It would be best when that warrior was dead, best if he died painfully and ignobly enough to discourage other warriors from similar acts of self-glorifying disobedience.

"What is wrong?" Harrar asked. "This is the Jaina Solo pursuit?"

"It is." Czulkang Lah pointed into the mass of blaze bugs, though he doubted that the priest, unused to the complexity of battlefield images, would be able to interpret what he saw. "The pursuers are not acting in concert. It appears that one wishes to kill Jaina Solo. If we are lucky, this notion will not spread to the others."

"We cannot have that. We must capture her. Must extract from her the truth about her trickery, the truth that she has nothing to do with our gods." Harrar turned to another of the command chamber's officers. "Have my ship alerted and readied. I will enter the minefield and join the pursuit."

At Czulkang Lah's reinforcing nod, the officer did as instructed.

Then something changed in the blaze bug image, and for a moment Czulkang Lah thought that perhaps he, too, was misinterpreting what he was seeing. Two of the coralskippers closest to Jaina Solo, though too far away for her infidel lasers to have hit them, had disappeared, simply winked out. Even with his enfeebled eyes, Czul-kang Lah could see the blaze bugs that had represented them, now darkened, flying to the darkened back of the display niche, ready to reenter as a new contact when needed.

What had happened?

Sharr Latt was getting the hang of it now, the method of calculating the gravitic pull of a dovin basal mine on one of the Goddess missile's passes, then coming near it again and using its own gravitic attraction to whip the missile around and slingshot it in a new direction.

The missile, mostly solid-state, not disadvantaged by the physical limitations of a living pilot, could survive much tighter turns and more strenuous g-forces than the pursuing coralskippers. On the last pass the missile made past one specific mine, the two closest pursuers had followed the missile's path exactly, had been caught by the mine's gravity, had been torn to pieces by their own daring.

Plasma projectiles flashed past the bubble viewport of the B-wing's crew compartment. Fascinated with his deadly toy, Sharr ignored them, relying on Beelyath to keep him alive.

The squadrons protecting *Lusankya* broke toward different incoming squadrons. Jaina, still masquerading as Twin Suns Nine, kept her silence as Kyp Durron scattered her shield trios in the path of incoming coralskippers.

As the distant skips came within maximum laser-effective range, she reached for Kyp in the Force, found him there, found him waiting for a better shot. She reached for Jag as well, detected him, could even faintly feel the intensity of his focus, his state of alert relaxation. But she could not interact with him as she could with Kyp, could not afford to be distracted, so she withdrew from that contact.

Then Kyp was firing and her hand was automatically squeezing her lasers' trigger, firing a quad-linked blast at one incoming skip. Both her shot and Kyp's were intercepted by voids, but Jag's, a fraction of a second later, plowed into the enemy starfighter's nose, destroying the dovin basal there, depriving the craft of its capabilities of flight and defense. Kyp and Jaina each poured another salvo of laser energy into the craft; it burst, exploding as the lasers superheated internal moisture to the state of gas, and vented atmosphere into space.

"One Flight, Twin Suns Five." That was Piggy. "Suggest you come to zero-one-zero ecliptic, hold that course for ten seconds, take targets of opportunity."

"Twin Suns Two, copy." Kyp led Jag and Jaina around in the indicated direction. Ahead, Jaina could see where Four Flight—Beelyath and Tilath—had gotten on the tails of two skips and were chasing them directly across One Flight's path. Jaina gauged Beelyath's and Tilath's firing patterns, timed them, felt Kyp doing the same . . . and, as the enemy skips crossed before them, as Beelyath and Tilath sent stutterfire laser against the sterns of the skips one last time, Kyp, Jaina, and Jag fired from the skips' port quarter, their quad-linked lasers hitting yorik coral instead of voids. Both skips detonated, sending a cloud of gases and yorik coral chunks hurtling along their course.

But now the wingmate of the first skip they'd hit was behind them, closing, firing. Jaina didn't listen to the good-shooting congratulations coming across the comm board; she followed Kyp as he made a tight loop up and to starboard, trying to elude their pursuit.

Jag looped tighter, forcing the pursuer to divide his attention between his clawcraft and the two X-wings, and managed to come around behind the coralskipper even as it managed to maintain its position behind the X-wings. He poured laserfire into its stern and top hull, but all of it was dragged into the skip's defensive voids.

Jaina felt a sort of mental shrug from Kyp. "Break," she said, aloud and through the Force but not over the comm frequencies, and she broke to port as Kyp broke to starboard.

She gritted her teeth against the g-forces her tight turn exerted on her, but got oriented around toward that skip— just in time to see an X-wing flash over and past it at a right angle to its course, in time to see plasma projectiles tracking that X-wing strike the coralskipper instead. They chewed through its hull and the skip suddenly turned away, no longer anxious to fight.

Piggy's distinctive, mechanical laugh sounded over the comm board.

Jaina grinned. "Nice fleeing, Piggy."

Wedge's X-wing reached low Borleias orbit as the *Ammuud Swooper* lumbered along behind. He tried to remind himself that the Corellian freighter "lumbered" only in comparison with a starfighter, of course; the freighter was nearly as fast and nimble as the *Millennium Falcon*.

He dropped back to give his personal comlink a better chance to reach the ship. "Blackmoon Eleven to *Swooper*, do you have an exit path?"

"We do, Eleven. Can you receive it?"

"I've been patching my comlink and datapad into what's left of the computer on this battered baby. Just transmit me the directional and I'll escort you out."

"Will do, Eleven. Many thanks."

Wedge waited until the numbers appeared on his datapad screen, then reoriented to *Ammuud Swooper*'s outbound course. He could only estimate, based on what he remembered of Borleias's current position in orbit around the star Pyria, but he believed that the course would take *Ammuud Swooper* in the general direction of the Deep Core worlds. Doubtless the freighter would only take a short hyperspace jump, a few light-years, and then correct to take them toward the rendezvous point.

The starfighter's sensor board beeped with a new contact. Wedge took in the new information and bit back a curse. A squadron of coralskippers was headed their way, and would intercept Wedge and the freighter long before they were clear of Borleias's mass shadow.

Charat Kraal poured plasma cannon fire into his opponent, saw some of it flitting around the edges of his target's void and chewing into its hull.

As he'd suspected, the only kind of pilot foolish enough to disobey orders like that, to seek personal glory at the expense of duty, was a green pilot, one fresh from teaching. He might have gloriously fast reflexes, but he didn't have the experience or will to defeat someone like Charat Kraal.

His target waggled side to side, signaling that he was quitting an exercise, the only way he had to communicate that he was surrendering. He brought his voids around from his stern to his bow, symbolically baring his stomach, further sign that he was giving up this fight.

Charat Kraal fired again, pouring damage into his target's stern, and, as he gained altitude relative to the other coralskipper, into its canopy. He saw the canopy crack and then explode outward from the atmospheric pressure within, saw one of his plasma projectiles hit and burn entirely through the torso of the pilot. That coralskipper continued in straight-line flight, a flight that might never end.

"Disobedience is death," Charat Kraal said aloud, as though the spirit of his enemy might hear him. "Unless you win. And you cannot win by surrendering." He looped back around toward the portion of the minefield where his pilots and Jaina Solo were.

And he frowned. The cognition hood showed him the locations of all those fighters, but there were four fewer coralskipper glows than there should have been, even counting the pilot he'd just killed.

Jaina Solo was whittling down the numbers of her pursuers. Charat Kraal shook his head and accelerated toward the action.

Luke's X-wing blasted through a cloud of flame and vapor spilling out of a dying blastboat analog. He tensed against the impacts that would come if there was solid matter in the cloud, but emerged on the far side without hitting anything. He fired the instant he was free of the cloud, his quad-linked lasers barely missing Mara's on-coming E-wing and ripping into the nose of the coral-skipper chasing her. His shot missed the dovin basal housing at the bow but tore into the yorik coral beneath it before a void moved into place to intercept the rest of the damage.

The coralskipper, its pilot doubtless spooked by Luke's magical arrival from within a cloud of flames, banked away from Mara, breaking off pursuit. Luke looped around to roar up in his wife's wake. "Oh, *there* you are."

Her voice, across the comm board, sounded amused. "Afraid I was running out on you?"

"You know what a jealous, possessive man I am."

"Starfighter Command to Blackmoon Squadron, Yellow Aces." The voice was Tycho's. "We're seeing increased defense at the worldship. Break off stern defense and move up to escort. We also need our spotter in place."

"Blackmoon Leader copies." Luke checked his sensor and comm boards. The Blackmoons were in pretty bad shape, down to about half strength, though most of his losses were from damage to and withdrawal of starfighters rather than their destruction. He also read that the mysterious Blackmoon Eleven was off Borleias and engaged with what looked like an entire squad of coralskippers.

He couldn't let that be his problem right now. "I'm your spotter," he said. "Two, assume control of the squadron."

Mara said, "Negative on that. I'm your wing."

He sighed, but knew better than to waste time by arguing. "Correction, Blackmoon Ten, take command."

"Ten copies."

"Leader's away." Luke kicked in his thrusters and

roared straight toward the Yuuzhan Vong worldship, away from his reinforcements, away from everyone but Mara.

Charat Kraal sped along in Jaina Solo's wake, leaving his other pilots behind through sheer piloting skill. Kilometer by kilometer he gained on her and knew, at last, that he was a better pilot than this infidel.

All he had to do was get in range, disable her abomination-craft, and wait for a capture ship to assist him.

The tiny gleam he could only see in his cognition hood, the one that indicated Jaina Solo's position, grew to a size indicating that he should be able to make out some details of the X-wing. But he could not; he could only see thruster emission from one engine. Yet it could not be moving so fast with three-quarters of its power gone.

His coralskipper's gravitic sensors created the illusion that space itself was rippling in the distance ahead of Jaina Solo, the visual image of a dovin basal mine. She seemed to be aimed almost directly at it.

Charat Kraal smiled. Her intention was clear—take a close pass by the mine, using its gravitational attraction to sling her around and accelerate her beyond Charat Kraal's ability to overtake.

But it would not work that way. The mine would detect her specific graviational signature, recognize her as a most-wanted target, and reach out to strip her shields, perhaps annihilating her engines in the process.

He had her. He had won.

Her vehicle whipped around the dovin basal mine and came straight back at him. The turn was so abrupt that no living thing could have survived it, so unexpected that Charat Kraal sat stunned for a long, deadly moment.

His surprise communicated itself to the coralskipper, which waited for instructions—dodge? Defend with voids? Open fire?

And when Charat Kraal finally saw his target, made it out for what it was—a missile, unarmed, faster than any starfighter or coralskipper when it chose to be—he was only two-tenths of a second from impact.

Harrar's pilot turned to the priest. "Jaina Solo is destroyed. It appears that Charat Kraal rammed her."

Harrar shook his head. "You must be mistaken."

"I think not. I witnessed the two images merge. There was energy released. Both images are gone." The pilot pulled his cognition hood back on . . . and then stiffened.

"Well?"

"You . . . were correct. Jaina Solo is not where I thought she was. Not in the minefield at all. She is in the vicinity of the worldship."

"And Charat Kraal?"

"Still dead."

Eldo Davip sat alone at the control console of *Lusankya*, sweat dripping from his face despite the efforts of the chamber's cooling system to keep him comfortable.

He wasn't on the Super Star Destroyer's bridge. That chamber, once brilliantly clean and huge enough for snubfighters to land in, was destroyed; he'd seen the holocam image of a dying coralskipper corkscrewing its way into the front viewports, crashing through, annihilating everything there.

But no one had been there, no officers, no droids. It had been left lit as bait, though no ship's controls operated there.

All ship's controls were routed here, to an auxiliary bridge deep in the vessel's stern, a place where the command crew could operate if the stern were gone or the vessel somehow captured. Even this small chamber seemed empty and strange now; Davip was the only person left. Everywhere else, computer gear was patched into the ship's controls.

Every few moments, another shudder racked *Lusankya* and the lights momentarily dimmed. Red showed on the screens of every diagnostics terminal, indicating that the systems they monitored were destroyed or nonfunctional. The only exceptions were the systems Davip's own terminal controlled: main thrusters, gravitic sensors, localized life support, localized power.

He spared a glance for the door at the back of the chamber. Newly installed, it was a crude plate of armor that would lift out of the way—once—and give him access to the starfighter that lay beyond. The starfighter was already pointed along the shaft that led to *Lusankya*'s stern. It was a way out for him . . . assuming that the damage the Star Destroyer was taking didn't collapse the shaft, didn't ruin the starfighter. If it did, he was dead.

Well, dead or alive, he was going to finish this fight with a bang. He returned his attention to the sensors, to the large signal that indicated the Yuuzhan Vong worldship ahead.

* * *

Wedge accelerated away from the *Ammuud Swooper* and toward the oncoming squadron of coralskippers. His sensors showed two eager skip pilots moving out in front of the others, the better to engage him first. He expected *Ammuud Swooper* to turn tail, dive back into the atmosphere, and try to find a safer exit vector, but the freighter came stolidly on in his wake. The reason why was soon evident: coralskippers from the vicinity of the biotics building site were now climbing after them.

There was nowhere to run.

In moments, the lead skips came into visual range. They separated and began launching plasma his way—all but daring him to fly between them, to try to persuade them to fire on one another by accident.

Wedge smiled mirthlessly. A novice pilot might try that very thing, but would find his shields stripped by a deft use of the coralskippers' voids. Without shields, his X-wing would be easy pickings for the skips. Instead, he veered to starboard, passing on the outward side of the skip in that direction, firing stuttering lasers at that craft until his weapons could no longer depress to hit it. He saw his shields flare as a bit of plasma hit them and was deflected, but his diagnostics didn't indicate a direct hit.

Then he was past the two lead coralskippers. They turned to follow. The oncoming ten also vectored as if to head him off, but they weren't making the kind of speed the lead coralskippers were.

Ammuud Swooper maintained her original course, and none of the coralskippers remained directly in her path. Wedge frowned at the sensor board. Why?

He increased the angle of his starboard turn. The two

coralskippers continued to accelerate in his wake. The other ten turned so that their course paralleled his, pacing him instead of intercepting him.

That was it. At least one of the lead skips had to be the squadron commander. He wanted a duel. His pilots wanted to watch. They figured the commander could finish Wedge off, then they could catch up to *Ammuud Swooper* before the freighter could get free of Borleias's mass shadow.

Well, it wasn't going to work that way.

Wedge veered toward the pacing coralskippers, maneuvering so unexpectedly that the skips on his tail took an extra moment to turn after him. The maneuver was harsh enough to cause Wedge's sight to gray out just a little—he could see his vision contract, as though he were flying into a tunnel, but he shook his head as he straightened out his course and his vision returned to normal. He began firing into the midst of the ten skips, and, as he'd hoped, there was no immediate return fire: the squadron leader had doubtless instructed his pilots not to interfere, that Wedge was his alone to kill.

Wedge sprayed his stutterfire over the flank of one skip, then, as he gauged the speed with which its void intercepted the laser, switched to quad link for a harder punch. His shot, beautifully placed, dropped between the defensive voids and hulled the skip. It detonated into the small, grisly cloud characteristic of a dying coralskipper. Wedge roared past the cloud, missing it by mere meters, hearing the *ping* of small chunks of yorik coral striking his shields.

As soon as he was past, he looped around, opposite the direction the skips were heading. He was rewarded by the sight of the skips slowing, turning back toward him as he circled. The lead skips punched through the same hole in the formation he'd just been through and turned after him, gaining ground.

In a moment—tunnel vision returning as he performed a turn too hard for his body to quite withstand—he was lined up on the formation again. The nine remaining witness skips had done an impressive about-face and were now reaching the cloud of gases and coral chunks that had once been one of their own number.

Wedge armed and fired a proton torpedo, then switched back to stutterfire lasers and began spattering red beams among those targets. Their voids came up and effortlessly caught the energy.

Then his torpedo hit. It didn't reach any of the functional targets, but hit the largest remaining chunk of the destroyed coralskipper, deep in the midst of the formation of skips as they passed around it.

It detonated in a bright flash, its energy hurled outward in all directions simultaneously, slamming into every coralskipper within its explosive diameter. The skips' voids could intercept only a fraction of the released energy.

Wedge looped up and around the expanding gas cloud, pouring on speed to gain a little ground on his pursuers while he waited for the sensor board to clear.

When it did, the numbers were like a lifeday present. Six of the ten coralskippers in that formation were gone or smashed into smaller pieces. Two more were on ballistic courses toward Borleias's atmosphere. The last two were turning to join up with the squadron leader and his wingmate, but even they seemed to be moving sluggishly.

Impossible odds had just been turned into one-third impossible. And in the distance, *Ammuud Swooper* continued plodding her way toward her hyperspace launch point.

Czulkang Lah evaluated the data and variables. He did not like the conclusions he was reaching. There was altogether too much attention being paid to the Domain Hul worldship, too many missing infidel resources, too much unexplained behavior from the gigantic triangle ship now mere minutes from reaching him.

"Prepare to disengage," he commanded. "Select a Rimward withdrawal course and execute it on my order."

He could feel the eyes of his officers on him. Some would be concealing anger at what they interpreted as an act of cowardice. Some, knowing how bad his eyes were, wouldn't bother to conceal it.

He understood their anger. He felt it himself. But he knew, too, that he did not serve the Yuuzhan Vong cause by needlessly sacrificing a resource as great as a healthy worldship, not when he could withdraw now and assault again later with victory more likely. So he ignored them, ignored their stares.

One of his officers said, "Subsurface dovin basal clusters are being maneuvered into the correct position."

Then Kasdakh Bhul stood beside him once more. He stared up through the command chamber's viewing lens. "There is something wrong with the oncoming triangle ship."

"I should hope so, considering the damage that has been inflicted upon her."

"I mean, she is not what I expected. I have been forced to learn something of the infidel vessels, and this one is not dying the way she should. Her skeleton is wrong."

Czulkang Lah squinted up through the viewing lens, but all he could make out of the approaching vessel were her outline and the flashes of light, exchanges between starfighters and coralskippers, all around her.

He moved to the blaze bug niche, reached into it until he pointed straight at the glowing creatures representing the triangle ship, then irritably waved toward himself. Blaze bugs from the back of the niche swarmed to the center, joined with the image of the triangle ship, and caused it to grow in apparent size and detail. Czulkang Lah kept waving until the triangle ship dominated the niche, surrounded by blaze bugs engaged in dogfights.

The triangle ship had suffered tremendous damage. The topside extension where her commanders were said to remain was almost gone. No sputters of light leapt from her flanks or belly—all her weapons were dead. And her nose was destroyed, the front one-quarter of the vessel worn away by the constant attacks by coralskippers and Yuuzhan Vong capital ships.

But something protruded from the vessel's bow, like an enormous needle, reaching from where the ruin began to where the vessel's original prow would have been.

"That is what I mean," Kasdakh Bhul said. "It is like a stinger. Their vessels don't have stingers, just compartments."

Czulkang Lah felt something like dread creep through his chest. "Are we ready to withdraw?" he asked, his voice curiously calm.

"Not yet," one of his officers answered.

* * *

Individual coralskippers, separated from squadrons or the last survivors of their squadrons, broke out of the worldship's orbit and moved to intercept Luke and Mara. The two Jedi did not slow to engage. They juked and jinked to avoid plasma cannon fire, they responded with laser-fire, and they roared past, heading relentlessly on toward the worldship while their enemies turned after them.

Then they were just above the worldship, on a diving course toward its surface. They vectored to enter orbit and whipped around the worldship's equator, heading toward its far side, the side faced away from the star Pyria. They crossed the terminator and were suddenly plunged into darkness.

In moments, sensors showed an intact squadron ahead of them, an equal number of miscellaneous skips arriving over the horizon from behind, and enough empty space around the two Jedi to give them a few seconds of breathing space.

"This would be as good a time as any, Luke," Mara said.

"No argument here." Luke switched on the apparatus they'd wired into his comm unit, and the comm units of several of the prestige pilots of *Lusankya*'s guardian squadrons, just prior to the launch of this mission. "Broadcasting location," he said. "I'm going to stay on the straight and narrow as long as I can stand to."

There was a touch of laughter to Mara's voice: "You know, *I've* said that in the past."

"Very funny."

Luke's forward shield flared into incandescence as something hit it—not a plasma ball, for he would have seen that coming, but something that had not been illuminated until it hit. Probably a grutchin. He tightened, clenching his jaw as though hardening his body could harden his X-wing against incoming fire. He was a sitting duck until his task was done.

Mara moved up before him, drifting back and forth, making herself the main target of the oncoming skips but never moving so far that her shields did not offer protection to Luke.

Luke could feel her reaching for him in the Force. It wasn't a gesture seeking reassurance, not really; he could feel her confidence, her focus on her task.

It took him a moment to understand. She wanted to be there, with him, in case something happened, in case one or the other of them suddenly winked out of existence. It was suddenly hard for him to swallow.

Then his sensor board yowled as something huge materialized in space behind him, no more than two hundred meters in his wake.

It was *Mon Mothma*, dropping out of hyperspace. The great Interdictor immediately began drifting to Luke's port, away from the worldship's surface; she had to have been on a slightly different course before entering hyperspace.

A moment later, a cloud erupted from *Mon Mothma*'s underside—her complement of starfighters, squadron after squadron streaking away from the launching bays, some to guard the Destroyer, some to head off incoming coralskippers from ahead and behind.

The crude gravitic sensor that was part of the X-wing's new instrument package lit up. *Mon Mothma* had activated her gravity-well generators. If the plan was going according to schedule, she'd be activating her yammosk jamming, too.

"Last act, Mara."

"Let's catch our breath before we join the other players, farmboy."

"Let's do that."

NINETEEN

The worldship's navigation crew did not have to be told to maneuver away from the Interdictor. But once they did set a new course, a noise akin to dismay wafted from their area.

Czulkang Lah merely looked at Kasdakh Bhul. The warrior moved to the navigators, spoke briefly with them, and returned.

In pained tones, he said, "There is confusion. Five dovin basal mines have just chased five *Millennium Falcon*s into our immediate space. Their attempts to seize the infidel ships are interfering with the worldship's dovin basals."

"Five *Millennium Falcon*s."

"Yes."

"And even one is enough to cause us grief."

A few kilometers away, another New Republic ship winked into existence—*Errant Venture*. It immediately opened up with all guns, directing damage against the worldship's surface, against the nearest Yuuzhan Vong capital ships.

"I've breathed," Luke said.

"Let's get 'em."

With four coralskippers closing on his tail, Wedge hurtled away from *Ammuud Swooper*'s course. The freighter was less than a minute from being able to enter hyperspace. A minute . . . surely Wedge could hold the skips here that long. Even at the cost of his life.

Czulkang Lah watched as his fleet became uncoordinated. Suddenly coralskippers swarmed like awkward trainees. Villips everted as the commanders of his capital ships stopped receiving gravitic orders. The spike at the nose of *Lusankya* was now visible through the viewing lens above; more of the ship had eroded, revealing even more spike. The gravitic interdiction of one of the triangle ships in orbit above the worldship was keeping his dovin basals from maneuvering Domain Hul out of *Lusankya*'s path.

He ignored his commanders. "Activate my son's villip," he told Kasdakh Bhul.

A moment later, the villip installed in the most prominent niche everted and took on the features of Tsavong Lah. "What news, my father?" the warmaster asked. "Has Borleias fallen?"

"Borleias has fallen," said Czulkang Lah, his voice weary.

"And have you slain all the infidels? Or do some of their forces remain to flee?"

"Some forces remain."

"But still, a great victory."

"No, son. Limited facts can point at victory when in fact there is only defeat to taste."

The villip frowned. "Defeat? You have achieved the conditions of victory. You have once more brought glory to Domain Lah."

"In a minute I will be dead. Too many clever minds, however heretical they may be, have undone me."

"But—"

"Be quiet, my son, and know that my last words were reserved for you. Fare well, and may the gods smile upon you, as they once did upon me." Czulkang Lah reached up to stroke the villip. It inverted, carrying Tsavong Lah's expression of bafflement with it.

Kasdakh Bhul stepped before him. "We are on the verge of victory, old one. Pull one last strategy out of your mind. Give us that last success."

Czulkang Lah stared into the face of a warrior too stupid even to know regret. The old warmaster held his silence. He'd promised that his words to Tsavong Lah would be his last. He would not diminish their value by breaking that promise.

One of his officers, his voice quaking in fear or anger—or both—asked, "Shall I give the order to abandon Domain Hul?"

Czulkang Lah nodded.

Suddenly space was swarming with New Republic reinforcements. Gavin let off his thruster and watched, bemused, as four TIE Interceptors off *Mon Mothma* strafed the coralskipper duo he and Nevil had been dueling, shredding them by virtue of fresh pilots and fresh lasers.

"Rogue Squadron, regroup on me," Gavin said. "Let's

let the latecomers escort *Lusankya* in. Blackmoons, how are you doing?"

"Rogue Leader, this is Blackmoon Ten. We're, ah, not doing too well. Four actives remain, not counting Blackmoon One and Two, who are detached."

"Recommend you sit back and watch for a minute, then."

"Can't do it, Rogue Leader. One of our own appears to be in a furball back at Borleias. We're going back after him."

"We'll come with you."

Wedge finished his loop and headed back toward his four pursuers. They were firing long before he was aligned, but two of them, the survivors of Wedge's proton torpedo attack, were not firing accurately; their undersides were charred, and Wedge suspected that those two coralskippers were damaged. Injured, and in pain.

Not that two healthy ones couldn't kill him. Wedge sideslipped, rotated to change his profile, juked and jinked to keep incoming plasma and grutchin fire off him.

As he approached the coralskipper formation, he drifted to port and squeezed off some stutterfire laser at the healthy skip on that side. He fired for only a fraction of a second, letting the short series of beams drift forward from the target's cockpit, watching as the skip's voids moved with the streams of coherent light and swallowed them; then he switched the weapon over to quad-linked fire, flicked his targeting reticle back toward the cockpit, and fired, all in one quick motion.

The voids continued forward for a brief, deadly fraction of a second. Wedge's lasers slammed in behind them, punching through the pilot's canopy, punching through the pilot.

Wedge's X-wing shook as plasma, not completely deflected by his shields, seared through his starboard lower S-foil. His diagnostics lit up with their report. Structural damage, but no interruption of engine power. The S-foil might collapse if flown into atmosphere, especially in firing position, but should hold up to all but the most rigorous of maneuvers in space.

The last healthy coralskipper and its two injured wingmates were on his tail, pouring plasma after him; he heard impact after impact as the superheated projectiles hit his rear shields, watched the alarming drop of his shield power.

His sensor board beeped, alerting him to an object in his path, on collision course, less than a second away. He began to twitch the X-wing yoke, to sideslip him around the obstacle, but instead switched weapons controls back to proton torpedo and fired on it. Only then did he shove the yoke down.

He saw the brilliant flash of the torpedo detonating above him, felt his X-wing rock as the shock wave from the explosion hammered him, but he switched back to lasers and hauled back on the yoke even as he was being battered. He was through the detonation zone in an instant—and there, meters above him, was the last healthy skip, its pilot still recovering from the unexpected detonation. Wedge fired and saw his lasers tear into the skip's underbelly.

There was another explosion, this one far less severe, as the skip vented gases through the crater Wedge's lasers punched in the yorik coral. The skip suddenly ceased maneuvering.

A shrill alarm had been wailing in Wedge's ear since the explosion. Finally he could spare an instant's attention to his diagnostics board.

He cursed. His shields were down. Whether they had failed from the proton torpedo explosion or been stripped as a last act of the coralskipper's voids, he did not know, but he suspected the latter; it would explain why his last shot against the skip's underbelly was not blocked.

Without shields, he was nearly as good as dead. He spared a glance for the two injured skips. They would be closing on him now, predators coming after injured prey.

Instead, they were moving away at high speed.

Wedge laughed. Seeing the last intact skip of the squadron destroyed had caused their nerve to fail; they probably hadn't even detected that he had lost his shields. He wondered what they thought he was—another supposed godly manifestation, like Jaina?

Then he stopped laughing. His sensors showed the coralskipper squadron from planetside had left the atmosphere and was racing up in the wake of *Ammuud Swooper*. They might intercept her before she reached a point from which she could launch into hyperspace.

Unless he maneuvered himself in the way. Unless he persuaded a second squadron to duel with him.

But if he did that, his X-wing shieldless and damaged, he would die. He would die alone, and he would die anonymous, flying another pilot's X-wing with no record left behind of his having been here. Iella and his children would never know what had become of him.

He swung around on an intercept course and hit his thrusters.

Turning his back on the *Ammuud Swooper*, leaving her to be destroyed by the Yuuzhan Vong when she was so close to escape, would not allow him to live. It would just give him time to tidy up his affairs before guilt—the crushing weight of responsibility abandoned—caused him to find some other way to die.

Coming in at an oblique angle to the new coralskippers' course, Wedge fired at maximum possible distance. On his sensor board, he saw no indication that his laserfire had done any damage.

But after a moment the squadron of skips vectored, angling toward him.

He could have cheered. They, too, wanted a challenging kill rather than some defenseless freighter. Had their decision not guaranteed his death, he *would* have cheered.

Wedge kept up his fire, jerking his X-wing back and forth in a bone-jarring evasive pattern, seeing plasma fire streak above, to port, to starboard. His sustained lasers fired straight down the voids of the foremost skip, only occasionally drifting far and fast enough to one side to hit yorik coral.

He felt a tremendous impact and the starfield was suddenly rotating outside his canopy. The X-wing no longer responded to his control of the yoke. Systems failure alarms shrilled in his ears, and he knew he was dead.

Eldo Davip locked down the auxiliary bridge controls, then slapped the button for the new door at the chamber's rear. It slid open instantly, undamaged, revealing the Y-wing beyond.

A Y-wing. He shook his head as he ran to the cockpit and clambered within. The starfighter was as old as he was, if not older; he suspected it was one of the assembly of "spare parts" vehicles that had been used to fabricate the pipefighters. As he closed the canopy, the door into the auxiliary bridge snapped shut and another bulkhead slid open, meters ahead of him, allowing him a view of space flanked by the emissions of *Lusankya*'s powerful thrusters.

He started up the starfighter's engines but couldn't yet launch. A jury-rigged screen and set of controls went live, and once again Davip could see through *Lusankya*'s remaining forward holocams, could see instrument readouts.

The dying Super Star Destroyer was drifting to starboard. This probably wasn't navigational failure. Instead, some dovin basal on the surface of the worldship had to be exerting its gravitational power against *Lusankya*, trying to turn the vessel aside.

It might work, too. No dovin basal was going to be able to entirely deflect the millions of tons of *Lusankya*, to counteract the tremendous kinetic energy built up during the ship's constant acceleration toward the worldship. But a dovin basal might be able to turn her protruding spearhead aside, to reduce the penetration of impact.

Davip wouldn't have that. He resumed direct control of *Lusankya* and increased thrust output from her starboard engines, redlining them, bringing the spearpoint back in line.

He'd just stay here and make sure everything went according to plan.

* * *

Czulkang Lah watched as the sharp prow of *Lusankya* grew in the sky, approaching with a meticulous precision that he could, with a growing sense of detachment, appreciate.

Up close, the crudeness of the protruding spike became evident. He could see scarlike welds suggesting that the thing had been assembled in sections within the triangle ship. Still, its simplicity, and the fact that it had succeeded in serving its intended purpose, was admirable.

It entered the worldship's atmosphere and, a moment later, struck the viewing lens immediately above.

And Czulkang Lah was gone.

The prow of *Lusankya* hit the worldship.

Eight kilometers up, before the shock of that impact had even been transmitted along *Lusankya*'s body, Eldo Davip fired his thrusters and shot out of the vessel's stern.

He passed between two of the vessel's thrusters and saw his diagnostics light up as they anticipated possible life-support failure, but then the yellows faded to a safe green.

But still he was feeling vibration. Had he sustained damage that the diagnostics didn't detect?

It took him a moment to realize that the vibration wasn't from his Y-wing. It was from him.

As he set a course to take him to a formation of allied starfighters, he tried to stop shaking.

But he couldn't.

Coming around the far side of the worldship, Luke and Mara saw *Lusankya* dive into the worldship's surface. It seemed to Luke that a ripple spread out from the point of impact, either a shock wave or an animal contraction of pain.

The Super Star Destroyer, her kinetic energy scarcely slowed by the impact, continued to plow into the worldship. Hundred-meter-long remnants of the ship's superstructure sheared off from the solid core, but that core plunged inexorably deeper into the worldship.

In moments, as the orbit of the two Jedi brought them closer to the impact zone, *Lusankya*'s core was swallowed by the worldship, her superstructure scraped off and left behind, mountain-high, on the worldship's surface.

Then the surface of the worldship shuddered. Luke knew what that meant. Eight or more kilometers below the surface, the spearpoint of the core had exploded. Then the next hundred-meter section behind it would detonate, then the one behind that, a chain of destruction reaching all the way back to what had once been *Lusankya*'s stern.

As they passed over the Super Star Destroyer's wreckage, the mountain of scrap leapt skyward, propelled by a volcanolike eruption from beneath the surface as the last of *Lusankya*'s core sections detonated. The flash from the explosion was brilliant and the force of the explosion jetted into the sky, looking for one brief moment like a red-orange lightsaber blade kilometers in length.

The surface of the worldship heaved. Great jagged cracks flowing with a red-black substance Luke did not care to contemplate spread out from *Lusankya*'s impact point as the worldship began to die.

* * *

His ship protected by the remains of Charat Kraal's special operations group, Harrar watched the crash and detonation. He could feel blood drain from his face, could feel the strength of his legs begin to fail. He sat heavily in the captain's seat, wordless.

"The infidels appear to be grouping again," his pilot said. "Shall we join these coralskippers in a counterattack?"

"What's the point?" Harrar whispered. "Take us back to Coruscant. Take us back where we can look on victory instead of disaster."

On his next spin, Wedge saw the squadron of skips turn back toward him. He aimed and fired after them, a final, defiant gesture, but his weapon failed to discharge.

On his next spin, he could see the incoming skips but, beyond them, witnessed the brilliant flash of light that heralded *Lusankya*'s demise. "I'm not exactly going to miss you," he said.

The incoming coralskippers opened fire. At this range, only one of the plasma projectiles hit; Wedge felt it crash into and through the X-wing's stern, and suddenly he was spinning even faster, watching the stars rotate by at bewildering speed.

Then things became more complicated. Unable to quite resolve the picture outside his canopy into a comprehensible one, growing dizzier by the minute, Wedge thought he saw red lasers flashing among the orange-red plasma balls. He was certain he saw one coralskipper detonate, then two.

There were E-wings and X-wings near him, the latter painted in the standard New Republic colors, and his comlink crackled to life—a woman's voice, fading in and out: "Blackmoon Ten . . . Eleven. Are . . . with us?"

He activated his jury-rigged comm board. "Blackmoon Ten, this is Blackmoon Eleven. That's a copy. Still here, but about to throw up."

"Hold on . . . shuttle. It'll be here . . . minutes."

Then there was a new voice, stronger because the broadcasting X-wing hovered only fifty meters away. Wedge recognized the voice as Gavin Darklighter's. "Blackmoon Eleven, what did you think you were doing going after an entire squadron?"

"My job."

"That's 'My job, *sir*.' "

Wedge grinned. "My job, *sir*."

"Son, if you develop piloting skills in proportion to your nerve, someday they'll call you the greatest pilot of all time."

Gavin, baffled, stared down at his comm board. "Blackmoon Eleven? Are you still there?"

But Blackmoon Eleven didn't respond—at least, not with words. The only thing emerging from Gavin's comm board was laughter. Laughter that was somehow familiar.

The New Republic forces staged mop-up and withdrawal operations. Starfighter squadrons collected themselves, escorted rescue shuttles, defended their capital ships from the uncoordinated attacks of the Yuuzhan Vong.

But it would not be long before a new yammosk was brought into the system, not long before more Yuuzhan Vong reinforcements made the system untenable. One after another, the divisions of Borleias's defenders launched into hyperspace to travel to their first rendezvous point.

The world they left behind was, for now, Yuuzhan Vong property. The stand here had served its intended purpose. The Advisory Council and its supporters had enjoyed months in which to plot their next moves—defenses, surrenders, tricks. But the Advisory Council might never know what else had been done during those months: what plans had been made, what foundations had been laid for a resistance that would not depend on them.

EPILOGUE

Tsavong Lah sat alone on his seat in his command chamber. He could not speak.

The gods *must* love him. They had restored his arm to him. They had allowed him to root out treachery that had threatened to topple him. They had given him Borleias, whose defenders had, at last, fled.

The gods must *hate* him. They had taken his father from him. Not only his father, but the fabled warmaster, Czulkang Lah, whose methods of teaching, whose strategic innovations, though introduced decades before the war on this galaxy was launched, had made these conquests possible. The Yuuzhan Vong would be struck like a coufee in the guts by news of Czulkang Lah's death and the utter destruction of Domain Hul.

Which was it? Had he earned the hatred or the affection of the gods?

He sat back, hollow with the loss he had just experienced, uncertain within a universe that had just grown darker and stranger.